RAVEN OF THE SEA

AN O'BRIEN TALE

STACEY REYNOLDS

STACEY REYNOLDS

AUTHOR'S WORKS

Raven of the Sea: An O'Brien Tale
A Lantern in the Dark: An O'Brien Tale
Shadow Guardian: An O'Brien Tale
Fio: An O'Brien Novella
River Angels: An O'Brien Tale
The Wishing Bridge: An O'Brien Tale
The Irish Midwife: An O'Brien Tale
Dark Irish: An O'Brien Novella
Burning Embers: An O'Brien Tale

His Wild Irish Rose: De Clare Legacy
The Last Sip of Wine: A Novel of Tuscany

Published July 1, 2016
by Stacey Reynolds

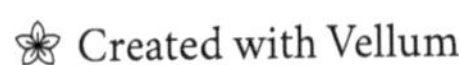

This book is dedicated to my family, but especially to my husband Bob. He is both a brave and honorable warrior and wonderful partner and father. To my sister, also a writer and published author, who has been my lifelong friend and has always watched my six. Lastly, to the enduring spirit of the military child. Military children are the most well-rounded, resilient, cultured, ass-kicking sector of the childhood population. It is in that spirit that I dedicate this to my five military kids Alexandra, Robert, Clara, Brigid, and George. You grew up in the duffle bag, and I admire you more than you'll ever know. That said, you may not be ready to read this until you have your own children.

CHAPTER 1

MAY 2012, SOMEWHERE OVER THE ATLANTIC

"Attention passengers aboard Aer Lingus Flight 1350. We are due to arrive on schedule to Dublin Airport in 2 hours and 43 minutes. We will now dim the cabin lights. If you require anything, please use your call button located on the arm of your seat. Thank you for flying Aer Lingus."

Branna O'Mara was used to traveling alone. She was used to being alone, period. Orphan status aside, her particular brand of employment didn't require hordes of people other than the occasional phone call to a plumber, roofer, or HVAC tradesman. She was done with school for now, and she found herself in that particularly awkward phase in life where her peers were either studying for finals or picking out china patterns. She was almost twenty-four and had a foot in neither camp.

Solitude was the new normal. Dating had always been sporadic for her, and in the last year non-existent. Without the social network of college, she had to make an effort to meet people, and it seemed barely worth the effort given her genuine lack of interest. Besides, her life was busy, full. Dating someone, who would eventually cease to be around, just seemed like wasted energy.

So, she worked. Her parents left her with a comfortable livelihood.

Her education was in business and real estate even though she hadn't finished her degree. She'd quit school a year before she was finished, when her mother had gotten really sick.

That was fine, though. She was her own boss, and she was good at her job. She owned property in coastal North Carolina, Boston, San Diego, San Clemente, Yorktown, and most recently in Tampa, Florida. Some were paid off and others carried low mortgages, she was in the black on all fronts, which was not bad for her early twenties.

The Tampa residence had been her first independent property purchase 14 months ago. She'd made the move on a fixer upper, lived on Cuban take-out and energy bars, and done a lot of the work herself. The rest of the properties were given to her. Her mother had transferred it all to her on her eighteenth birthday. She'd thought that her mother had wanted to teach her the business, but the real motive would reveal itself five years later.

She'd been an orphan for exactly nine months, and she paid no inheritance tax on the properties since she owned them all outright. It seemed convenient that her mother had been given this foresight, considering she wasn't diagnosed until Branna was 22, but it ended up saving her from having to liquidate the estate in order to pay half to the government in inheritance taxes. In this instance, Caesar had not received his pound of flesh. God, on the other hand, had taken everything worth taking.

Now she owned a thriving real estate business. She had them all full of steady, dependable renters. She did very well with it. Well enough to support herself and do some philanthropic work. She was the head cheese at the Major Brian O'Mara Memorial Foundation. The only cheese, actually. Employees cost money, and she could run it herself with good volunteers.

She helped wounded veterans with the extra costs of outfitting their homes to fit their disabilities. She knew a lot of tradesman who were ex-military or supported the troops. Everything from wheel chair ramps to special bathrooms alterations, she did what she could with the funds left over from her living expenses coupled with a knack for fundraising.

Now, she'd made the tricky decision to take this adventure to the next level. She was going international. The red tape was insane, but she was doing it.

Her father, Brian, had inherited that first Boston property and one other home on the passing of his mother. Branna's mother, Meghan, had inherited one in historic Alexandria, Virginia, which was also where her parents had met. The others were acquired at almost every duty station they had ever lived.

Branna's father had been a Major in the Marine Corps, an infantry officer. He was first generation American, Boston Irish to the core. He moved around from age 19 until the day he died, but he never abandoned the Red Sox or the accent. A unique combination of Boston salt and Irish cream.

God, she missed him. He was bigger than everything. But that was the nature of war. Only the strongest and bravest and noblest of men were offered up as sacrifice. She'd lost her dad in the second Battle of Fallujah, and it had killed her mother right along side him. Not right away. It was a slow, suffering, suffocating death. She bore the decline in lonely silence, a lady until the end. Having a daughter was not enough to make her live. Like an amputee, her mother had lost a huge piece of herself on a dusty street in Iraq, and had never gotten over it. As if Branna needed another reason for the current anti-dating trend, this is what she'd learned. She was better off on her own. True love gutted you in the end.

* * *

Dublin Airport

As Branna headed for the car rental kiosk, she was thrumming with excitement. Finally, she was here. All of the careful planning, the arrangements, and the research had paid off. She was soon to be the owner of her own little piece of Ireland.

Her dad had told her about it so many times, almost like reading her a bedtime story. They'd planned to go there for a graduation present, but he was killed when she was in the eleventh grade. Finally, she was going to that fairytale place her father had loved so dearly. He'd visited Clare with his parents when he was young. He loved telling her all about the beautiful coastal towns and green, rolling moors.

The cottage was modest. It wasn't much to look at from the pictures. She had found this little gem after receiving some random spam from an Irish real estate site. She called up a family friend who was stationed in England to see if anyone in his command was taking a trip to Ireland. He hopped on the next flight and checked it out himself.

The price had been outrageous when it first went on the market, delusions of grandeur and all that. The price had dropped dramatically, as she knew it would. There was a particular excitement to this purchase. This was the first one she was buying for herself. Not as an investment, but as a private residence. Ever since she'd seen the listing, she'd started planning to go ex-pat. Knowing that the price would drop, waiting and getting her affairs in order.

She had a sizable survivor benefit from her parents. It was to be her nest egg. A gypsy her entire life, it was time to pick a home. Smack in the middle of nowhere, Ireland was just the fresh start she needed. She knew no one, expected nothing, and would enjoy a change of scenery. She'd given up on true happiness, but perhaps this move would bring the clean slate she longed for.

Fisher Street, Doolin, Ireland

"What the bloody hell do you mean another buyer?" Michael looked like a kettle that was about to boil over. Sean O'Brien had given his son many things. Great height, blue eyes, a sharp wit. That temper, however, was Mullen to the bone. The O'Brien's had a fair bit of temper themselves, himself included, but Sorcha Mullen had crushed him to dust on first meeting. Mullen tempers were the thing of legends and honestly, that is half the reason he'd fallen for her. There wasn't anything more beautiful than his wife with her blood up. Her sons, on the other hand, looked downright dangerous.

"Easy lad, let Jack explain. I am sure this is all a misunderstanding." Jack McCain was the town realtor. Not a particularly successful one, but he was local and honest, and the O'Brien's were nothing if not loyal.

"You see, it is quite a funny story, really," McCain said as he tugged at his collar. Father and son raised an unamused eyebrow. Michael folded his arms over his broad chest. McCain cleared his throat. "Well, apparently the owner had listed the property locally with me, but it was also on various internet sites. It is common enough. It generates more exposure, even international interest if the property is interesting enough. I never thought anything of it, you see. The property is so modest, and in a bit of disrepair. It never occurred to me that there would be any other offers once the price dropped. No one around here has looked twice at it except young Michael, here. So there was a small oversight." He took a breath before continuing.

Michael hissed out a "Bleeding Christ!"

Sean broke the tension with a simple demand, "Out with it Jack. What's happened?"

With the slow dread of a man bound for the gallows, Jack told them. "Apparently there has been a cash offer from an American businessman, O'Mara something or other."

Michael immediately flew into a rush of Gaelic expletives and then switched to English after he'd vented his spleen. "A bloody American? An American for Christ sake! What in the hell would some Yank want with my house? And I say *my house* because you assured me this was a done deal! Gentleman's handshake, earnest money! How could you let this happen, Jack?"

With every word Michael shouted, Jack McCain flinched like a whipped puppy. "Lad, I am so very sorry. I cannot tell you how terrible I feel. I gave you the information about the price drop as soon as I legally could, and we started everything rolling right after the holiday. I just had no idea this American had drawn up an offer that very same weekend."

"Apparently they'd sent someone to check the place out, while I was on holiday a few months ago. The sly bugger actually got the tour from Ned instead of someone from my office. The man never made an offer."

Jack rubbed his neck, nervously. "This American must have been watching for a price drop as well, although I'm not sure how they caught wind of it so early. The offers came in within hours of each other. We have another person in the office that handles Internet offers. I wasn't told for days. They accepted the offer that Friday evening before yours, which was the middle of the night here in Ireland. It was a cash deal so it was done by Saturday except for the money coming through."

"Ned Kelly was at his son's home when the American and our Internet liaison tracked him down with the offer that weekend. The daughter, Diane, who has Power of Attorney in her father's absence, signed your offer here on Tuesday morning."

"Now it is a matter of sorting out who has the rightful first dibs. This is the type of stuff you see in some posh part of London or some Paris flat, maybe Dublin. We are a small operation; we often do verbal agreements to start. I just never expected a bidding war. How the hell he even came across the listing is beyond me. Michael, I am so sorry."

By this time Michael had his hand clapped over his face rubbing it with a fury. "So, let me see if I have this sorted. I play the shameful arse kisser with Ned Kelly for two bloody years, while that crackpot has it priced like Buckingham Palace, and you let some greedy American who has watched *The Quiet Man* too many times rip the rug out from under me? No! I don't accept it!" He slashed his hand across the air.

"This is a local cottage, not some posh, holiday, self-catering shite! Surely you can tempt this Yank with one of the furnished, newer places on the market. This would never pass muster for a holiday renter. Make this go away, Jack. I have more right to this place than some outsider looking to ride the tourist euro!"

Sean had been silent, feeling his son was old enough to handle his own affairs, but he finally spoke. "We will get a solicitor if we have to, Jack. Michael is from a local family. He's a public servant. That must mean something."

Jack put his hands out, palms down. "Just relax. I will do what I can. Aye, Sean, it does mean something. Didn't Michael pull my own grandson out of the water last October? I owe you, lad. I need to meet with Ned and see if I can persuade him in your direction. Diane is beside herself at the mix-up. Ned is Ned. He never gets spun up about anything. I will do all that I can to set this right. I have been digging into the specifics of both offers to see if there are any details that would cause your offer to trump the other. I won't stop until I have done all that I can. I promise you."

Michael looked at Jack and a stab of conscience hit him. "Look, Jack. I am sorry I lost my temper. I just can't believe this. I really thought this was done. I actually paid rent to Diane to move in early before the closing. I just started cleaning it up. Jesus, how can this be happening?"

Sean put a hand on his shoulder, speaking softly and confidently. "Son, we will fix this. If we can't, we will find you another place. You know we love having you home in the meantime."

Michael looked at his da, the biggest man in the world, and actually believed him. Sean O'Brien took his big, strong son in his arms and hugged him.

Michael said, "Da, I know you and Ma would let me move back in, but hear this. I will squat in that bloody cottage until that Yank with the fat wallet drags me out dead."

Gus O'Connor's Pub, Fisher Street, Doolin, Ireland

Branna pulled into the little pub at 9:30 AM with a sigh of relief. She was here. She'd made it in one piece even with the narrow roads, the quirky stick shift, and non-stop rain. It didn't help that she'd spent the entire drive rubbernecking at all of the wonderful sites and green rolling hills and roadside ruins that she desperately wanted to stop and see. She would have to re-drive it when she got settled. It was stunning, even in the foul weather.

The people she'd met during her refueling and bathroom breaks had been unbelievably pleasant and helpful. All of the American style jokes about crabby, fighting Irish must be the direct result of alcoholic steel workers in the American north and too many re-reads of Angela's Ashes. The people she'd met seemed happy and lighthearted. Hope spread in her chest at the thought of making a home here.

She was hungry and needed coffee. She scanned the small town. Doolin wasn't a huge tourist draw, but it was known for good music and pubs. Pubs had more than beer, right? It was also strategically placed for trips to the cliffs and to the Aran Islands. She walked into the door of Gus O'Connors, with its black trim and sparkling window panes, and was enveloped in the warmth of well worn tables, smells from the kitchen, and beautiful hardwood. There were some well worn but lovingly polished tables to sit and eat or enjoy a quiet pint. But the pride of the place was a beautiful golden oak bar that displayed sparkling bottles of whiskey and beer taps as long as Branna's forearm. The only customer was a solitary man sitting at the bar who apparently took no notice of her entrance as he seemed to be engrossed in paperwork he had spread in front of him on the bar. There was an empty stage area and an old piano, and mirrors, signs, and local art scattering the walls. It looked as though it had seen decades of use, but it was clean and inviting. She stopped at the doorway, not wanting to track water into the interior.

Michael was sitting at the end of the pub, going over the session list with a cup of tea, when he heard the front door open. Most tourists took breakfast at their guesthouses, but it wasn't uncommon to get an early bird or even a zealous day drinker at 9:30. Gus O'Connors was a hotspot, if any place in Doolin could be considered a hotspot. What came through the door didn't look like a day drinker. It was a small young woman. She was stomping her feet at the door and fiddling with her umbrella. She was dressed smartly, conservatively for someone her age. She was a looker, too, if you liked young and uptight. Her dark hair was pulled back in a tight bun, but he really couldn't get a good look at her face. Pub lighting could hide a multitude of sins.

"Can I help you, love?" the voice startled Michael out of his appraisal. It was Jenny, the morning server.

"Yes, ma'am. Thank you, I would love a small bite to eat and some coffee if that isn't too much trouble. I have a meeting this morning."

Hmm, American. He couldn't place the accent other than that. She was obviously on holiday. Her meeting was undoubtedly at the Tourist Office.

Jenny led Branna to a small table and gave her the breakfast choices. After an explanation of the full Irish, her mouth dropped slightly. "Is that all for one person?"

Jenny giggled, "Yes, dear. It's good to start the day off with a full belly. Perhaps something smaller?"

"I'm sure it is lovely, but do you have toast and coffee? I've been traveling since yesterday and I'm still a bit off. I just need something light." Branna said.

"Well then, how about some of my homemade bread and marmalade?" Jenny replied.

"Oh, my that sounds perfect," Branna replied. "I'll have that."

Jenny walked over to the coffee pot and asked, "How do you take your coffee, dear? We've just got cream from the dairy this morning." She told her that black was fine. Jenny was a soft, pretty, woman that looked to be about thirty, and she gave Branna an admonishing look. "My, my girl. You need more to start your day, a wee thing like you. I'll put some local butter with your bread at least." Jenny gave a definitive nod, as if the matter was settled.

This made Branna laugh. "Well, if you insist. If I am going to live here, I better start eating like a local, I suppose."

Michael stiffened in his seat. Jenny asked, "Live here? You mean you aren't on holiday?" This caused little alarms to go off in Michael's head.

"No, I'm not on holiday. I've just purchased a small home on the outskirts of town. I am meeting with Jack McCain. I need to 'close the deal' so to speak. I just couldn't wait any longer, so I came in person!" Jenny's mouth dropped open and her eyes darted to Michael. He did a quick sideways gesture with his head, to silence her, then he addressed the woman.

"I couldn't help overhearing your news. Have you settled in the new town homes as you come into town?" That's when he got a proper look at her. She had eyes like the sea. Clear and dark and very blue. Skin like pale cream. Christ, she was lovely. It took him a second to realize what she was saying.

"No, actually it's a fixer upper on Burren Way? It's a lovely little cottage. It just needs a little work."

Bloody hell. "Um, yes, I know the place. If you don't mind me asking, what is your name?" he asked.

She stood up and strode over to him. "Forgive my manners, I'm Branna O'Mara." She stuck out her small hand, and it reminded him of a young boy, in mimic of his father. That idea quickly vanished when she made contact. A shot of electricity went through him at the contact, up his arm to his chest and a distinct tingle a bit further south. Her eyes shot to his, and he knew she'd felt it, too. *Jesus wept. This is not happening.*

Surely this little whelp from America was not the big, bad Yank with the fat wallet? *She must be a daughter,* he thought. She seemed young to be a wife, so maybe she was one of those gold digger types.

"So, is it your da who's bought the cottage? Are ye here with your family?" he asked. Something flickered in the girl's face, then the look was gone.

She kicked up her chin like a defiant puppy. "No, I am here alone. I purchased the cottage. I must be getting back to my breakfast. My meeting is in 15 minutes. It was nice to meet you, Mister?"

"Michael" he replied. "Michael O'Brien".

She brightened. "Oh! Like the tower?" she asked.

"Aye, the very same," he replied cooly. "My people have been here for generations."

Branna quickly finished her bread and coffee. That nice server was right about the butter. Perfect. Speaking of perfection, that broad shouldered man candy at the bar was a stunner. She rarely took notice of men, and when she did, it was a passing admiration. She could tell, even while he was sitting, that he was big. Broad swimmer shoulders that tapered to a trim waist, pale blue eyes with a ring of green in the center. He had sandy brown hair, cut military style, and pale, smooth skin with a light dusting of freckles under his eyes.

When he turned around and spoke to her, she'd felt a little jump in her tummy. That accent. Good God. A sweet, smooth Irish baritone. Rolled r's and long vowels, and a musical, magical property that was unique to these people. She wondered, fleetingly, what he sounded like when he sang.

Her father used to make her giggle gleefully when he put on his fake accent. There was nothing fake about this guy, though. She had to remind herself about her anti-dating policy and focus on his questions. That handshake. She'd never felt anything like it. Like jumper cables zapping her up the arm and right to her belly. *Bad idea, sister. Let me count the ways,* she thought to herself.

His mood seemed to shift quickly when she'd talked about buying the old cottage. It was subtle, but he'd instantly cooled toward her. Maybe he didn't like Americans. What a boring but fashionable trend. Whatever. Michael O'Brien was not a puzzle she had time for, and she didn't want to be late. She changed her cell to a global pre-paid and given Ned the new number, but she hadn't heard from anyone in several days. She didn't like being out of contact, so she'd sent e-mails, telling them she was coming.

Mr. Kelly had been so sweet to call her personally and accept her offer. He assured her that she could move in immediately, even before closing. He told her that the realtor was extremely busy, and that he would be her point of contact from now on. He'd insisted she call him Ned. Ned Kelly, how adorably Irish. She was fairly certain that this Ned was not a notorious, Australian outlaw. She couldn't wait to meet him.

He sent her notes checking in every day or so, and sent her more pictures of her new home. She had her long term visa processing, she had her luggage, she had a small amount of household goods on the way. She just needed some face time with both of them, and she couldn't wait to finish the closing and get the keys to her new house. The money was sitting in an escrow account waiting for the papers to be signed. She was paying cash, so this was going to be smooth sailing. If all went well today, she'd be sleeping in the cottage tonight.

Michael heard her leave. Surprise and anger had left him completely, feckin speechless. Jenny spoke with caution. "Seems a bit young to be an American business tycoon. Do you think she has kin here? The name is Irish enough." Brannaugh O'Mara was certainly an Irish name. Christ, Jack had assumed it was a man. Michael had prepared to tear into the aforementioned greedy-Yank-with-the-fat-wallet when Jack told him that the O'Mara bloke was on his way. The email had been missed at first, having gone in general office email, so she'd come with little warning.

He'd been prepared to throttle the thieving bastard if it came to that. What he wasn't prepared for was Branna O'Mara, with her big blue eyes and hope in her smiling face. How in the hell was he going to handle this? He rubbed his face vigorously with both hands. He looked into Jenny's knowing face.

"Guess you can't wrestle her for it, eh? Well, I know you haven't had any dealings with the ladies in a while, but you need to handle this delicately."

He didn't miss the jibe about the females. Everyone knew he had given off women since his annulment from Fiona. "I'll do no such thing. She wants to play with the big boys, make her grand business schemes, she can pay the price. She'll get that bloody cottage over my dead body."

Jenny shook her head, "What women lack in size they make up for in cunning. It's simple survival," she said, giving him a sideways glance. "She's quite a beauty. Brains, money, and looks. You are in trouble old friend."

Michael returned the shrug, "I hadn't noticed." Christ, he hadn't even believed that when he said it.

Jenny snorted, "Sell that one to the tourists," walking in back to the kitchen.

CHAPTER 2

Branna walked down the main street of the beautiful little village in a dream state. Old buildings with shops and pubs, and the opposite side went gradually up hill, with a stream running along the roadside. It was scattered with sheep. Sheep, for God's sake. They had markings on them like someone had spray painted them, probably similar to branding cattle. The buildings were bright colors and traditional looking, with shingle or thatched roofs and painted stone and mortar. The roads were winding and surrounded by lush greenery and wild flowers. Heaven.

She'd lived a lot of places. She'd known many types of neighborhoods, varying climates. They'd even spent a small amount of time in the desert when her father had recruited in Arizona. She did one tour in Japan, been born there actually, even though she only remembered glimpses of it. This move didn't scare her due to the change; it scared her due to the finality.

She was making this move as a long-term solution to her problem. *Where do you go when you have never had a permanent home and your last family member dies? What happens when you are the last man standing?*

People used the term "starting from scratch" pretty liberally, but this was it. This was scratch. As she took in the details of this little village, she decided that all things considered, scratch was pretty fantastic.

Branna walked into the realtor's office and the door chimed. A pretty young woman was behind the desk. She had a sign on the front that said, *Doolin Travel Services*. Branna backed up and looked at the door, then looked back at her. "I'm sorry, I thought this was the office of Jack McCain, the realtor?"

She answered, "Oh yes, you've come to the right place. Mr. McCain lets me run my travel agency out of the same office. I answer the phones and run the front desk for the realtors. Is he expecting you, Miss?"

She answered, "Yes, he is. My name is Branna O'Mara. I've just arrived from America on the red-eye."

She handed the woman her card. The young woman's name tag said *Miriam O'Shea*. She looked from the card to Branna's face, raising her eyebrows in surprise. "Oh, yes. He mentioned you were on your way. He hasn't been able to reach you, but we found your flight details in the general email yesterday. Let me just ring him."

Branna was getting a very strange vibe off this young woman. Hopefully the paperwork was ready. She really wanted to go see the place and get her keys. Miriam phoned the back office and she heard murmuring, but couldn't make out what was said. Miriam gave her a sideways glance and spoke into the phone. "Yes, Mr. McCain, there's a Miss O'Mara waiting to see you. No, you heard me correctly. Miss O'Mara." She hung up and smiled weakly. "He will be here shortly. Can I bring you some tea?"

Something was definitely up. She politely declined the tea. Just as she was looking down the hall to see if Mr. McCain was emerging, the front door chimed again. She turned to see an elderly man and what appeared to be his middle aged daughter. There was no mistaking the family resemblance. They had the same rosy cheeks and smiling brown eyes. The old man looked straight out of central casting, wearing a wool driving cap and tweed vest, despite the warm weather.

Behind her, she heard someone approaching. “Come in Ned, Diane, I was just coming to fetch Miss O’Mara.” Jack McCain, the realtor. Had to be. He’d put a weird emphasis on the “Miss” when he talked.

The woman said, “Miss O’Mara not Mister, aye, Da told me on the way over that we had our wires crossed on that one.”

Branna was looking back and forth now, completely puzzled. “Oh my, dear. You must think us rude, altogether.” Diane Kelly put out her hand to Branna and introduced herself. “You have already spoken to Da on the phone, I believe.”

Ned Kelly in the flesh. Branna wanted to throw her arms around him, but she had apparently shocked the crap out of everyone else already by not being a man.

In a grand gesture, Ned took his hat off and bowed to her. “And you must be dear Branna. It’s a pleasure to meet you lass, and you are even lovelier than I’d imagined.” Branna blushed, putting her hand forward to shake. He planted a chaste kiss on it.

“Da, you sneaky old charmer. You’ve been holding out on us,” said Diane. “We were all under the impression that we were meeting with a Brian O’Mara.”

Branna flinched inwardly at the name. “Oh, my. I didn’t think. My father originally owned the business. His name was Brian. I took ownership six years ago. I just sign my paperwork B. O’Mara. It made the transition easier.” Branna saw understanding in Diane’s eyes when she spoke of her father in the past tense. She recoiled from the pity she saw.

She knew she didn’t strike a commanding figure. She looked young for her age. Even when people were being nice, they didn’t initially take her seriously when doing business. Another reason she used the B. instead of her full name. She stood up a little straighter. “I am so glad to meet you all.”

Mr. McCain was not a tall man, but he was stout with a belly that hung a little over his belt. That aside, he was dressed professionally, well groomed, and greeted her with a warm smile. He seemed nervous, however. When he returned her greeting, his eyes were direct, but he pulled at his collar and he was flushed. "Perhaps we would all be more comfortable in my office?" The secretary gave her a nervous wave that seemed to wish her luck, like she was going off to be interrogated.

Diane Kelly, Ned's daughter, was whispering to her father. She couldn't hear the particulars, but he seemed to be reassuring her. "There, there, love. Everything will get sorted." *Sorted?* She did not like the sounds of that. As they entered Jack McCain's office, he motioned to the chairs for them to sit. He seemed nervous. Branna said, "Excuse me, Mr. McCain."

He interrupted before she could finish. "Please dear, call me Jack. We are quite informal here in Doolin."

She nodded gratefully, "Ok, thank you, Jack. It's just, my presence here seems to have put everyone a bit on edge. I would think a house sale in this economy would be a joyous exchange, but you all seem like you are walking the last mile on death row. Please, put me out of my misery and tell me what the problem is."

Jack gave her an appraising look, surprised at her candor. He sighed and motioned again to the chair. "Please, Miss O'Mara, or Branna. Do you mind if I call you Branna?" She gave a short nod and he continued. "We seem to have had a slight mix up with the offers." He continued, but the last thing she heard was *offers* as in the plural use of the word.

"Excuse me, Jack. I think I misunderstood you. It sounded like you said offers, as in more than one?"

He looked at her sheepishly, "Well, that's just it, you see. The mix up has to do with the other bidder for the property." So, he told her. The entire bloody mess was spilled out as Diane shook her head, face pink with the stress. More tugging on the collar from Jack, sweet Ned patting his daughter's hand with an easy smile.

When he'd finished his tale of woe with the name of the other bidder, aka the scoundrel that was ruining her life, she almost jumped out of her seat. "I'm sorry. Did you say Michael O'Brien? Tall, sandy brown hair, local family?"

Jack looked at her in surprise. "Oh! So you've met?"

She sighed and pinched the bridge of her nose. "Yes, only briefly at Gus O'Connor's. I had breakfast there. He never mentioned anything."

She was starting to put pieces together. The surprise on the waitress's face, the cool attitude adjustment she had sensed when they'd talked about her buying a cottage. *That freaking snake!* She thought of Michael O'Brien with his smoking hot body and his *I'm so local* shitty-guy remark. He was trying to steal her cottage. *Oh, hell no.*

"Excuse me, Jack. Maybe you don't understand. I spoke with Mr. Kelly over the phone after the transaction. As a matter of fact, we've been in touch regularly. Not only did I immediately wire the earnest money and sign the paperwork, I have since set the balance aside in an escrow account. An account that your Internet team set up, I might add. This house is paid for in full. I wired the monies within hours. I just left my life in America. I was told I could move in today. I have a long term residency package processing. I have moved to Ireland and left my home all based on the purchase of this cottage! You can't do this!"

The more she talked the more upset she became. Her voice started to go up both in pitch and volume. " What is this? Some kind of shake down? You think you are going to weasel more money out of me now that I am here? You were obviously expecting a man. Now that you see some young woman you think you can push me around?"

As soon as she said it, Diane gasped and McCain looked genuinely startled. He flinched at every word she spat, but her final comment seemed to genuinely surprise him. "Oh no, my dear. We would never pull such shady dealings. This truly is an uncanny and unfortunate mix up. I hate to think you would feel the least bit deceived. We run an honest business. I assure you, we would have called you sooner, but your phone was not working. We didn't have your new contact info and you came so quickly. Had we known you were coming, we would have told you to stay put until we..."

At this point Branna broke back in. "Stay put? Stay put!" She was fully yelling now. She paused to breathe and collect herself. *Breathe, don't get hysterical. You are a businesswoman.* In a calm and chilling voice she spoke again. "Mr. McCain..." His face sank slightly at the return to the formal, or maybe that she just looked homicidal. "The fact remains that I am here now. I have signed paperwork giving me every expectation that I will be sleeping on Burren Way tonight. I have no intensions of turning around and retreating. This is your mistake. You said yourself that my offer technically came in first and I met your asking price. Ned, here, has kindly invited me to move in as soon as I like. Mr. O'Brien's situation is unfortunate, but it is not my problem. I am going nowhere and I want my closing documents and I want my keys...if you please." She noticed Diane raised her brows and gave a begrudging grin.

Branna turned to Ned Kelly and said, "Mr. Kelly, I so enjoyed speaking with you on the phone and through our emails. I think we both came to the understanding that I was a perfect fit for your home. You genuinely seemed happy to sell it to me. Has anything changed?"

The sweet old man actually blushed, "Why no, my dear. You are a sweet young lady. I love the idea of you staying on with us in our small village. I would be most happy to accommodate you."

Branna started to smile, but then he continued, "However, Michael is such a nice lad. This is all so unfortunate. To be sure, I am quite put out by the unfortunate turn this all has taken. He being a local boy and all, I have known him since he was a small babe running about in his nappy. I am afraid I cannot simply dismiss his claim; given the genuine interest he has shown in the cottage. My daughter was perfectly with in her rights as my Power of Attorney to accept his offer. He has been inquiring about the place for some time. I guess I didn't know how serious he was until I learned that he'd started the buying process."

As he continued Branna shut her eyes to fight back the tears. *I will not weep like a little girl in front of these people. I will not be weak.* Shaking her head back and forth, she opened her eyes to see a look of contrition on all of their faces. She straightened her back, bucked up her chin. "I understand your concern for this local man, Mr. O'Brien, but as you have said, my offer was accepted first. We have spoken for weeks off and on. You said nothing."

Ned shook his head. "You'll forgive an old man for his waning memory. I am afraid I got a bit confused when I spoke with my daughter. I didn't fully grasp how far they'd gotten with Michael's offer." Diane gave her father a strange look, but kept her own counsel.

Jack interrupted, "Well, that is where the lines are a bit blurry. See the offer was put in through our Internet sales team on Saturday evening. It was a long holiday weekend and I was not available until Tuesday morning. I am the listing agent. Although they can accept the offer in my absence, the time change made it the wee hours here in Ireland. I took Michael's offer and earnest money bright and early Tuesday morning. Your international wire didn't clear until Tuesday afternoon, since you didn't expedite the wire. Yes, technically your offer was first, but your wire didn't clear until after Michael's funds were given."

At this point he noticed that she was rubbing her face, just as Michael had done, trying to control her temper. "I wasn't told that there was another offer lurking out there or I would have expedited it. I would have been in constant contact as well. This is completely unprofessional!"

He had the good sense to look sheepish, "It's all quite unusual. In my 18 years in real estate I have never had such an occurrence. So, you see, it is important that we protect both of your rights in this. We need to study this a bit, get some more expert opinions on this, and make a decision that is most fair for everyone concerned. You both met the asking price to the penny."

At this point she had wrapped her arms tight around herself. She looked at Ned. "We spoke afterwards. I didn't talk to Jack, but I talked to you. You said nothing." Her eyes started misting and she cleared her throat, fighting the response.

Ned noticed her self-protective position and placed his hand on her shoulder. "Listen, lass. I thought your offer came in first, I really didn't understand how complicated this was going to get, or how serious Michael was. I think Jack was using a business email of yours and I accidentally deleted your personal email. My technical skills are a bit primitive," he said as he blushed. A pang of guilt hit her. He was an old man. "You changed your phone and have been traveling, we couldn't reach you, to tell you to wait."

She noticed he didn't make eye contact when he said that last bit about the email. She wondered if he was hiding something, but then pushed the thought away. "I know this might seem a bit much to take in right now. I am quite sorry for the whole misunderstanding, but hear me now. This will all be grand when it is done. You are not alone, love. I've already arranged a night at our finest local guesthouse. Bridhe makes the finest breakfast you've ever tasted. Tomorrow we will all meet at the cottage and sort through this together. Young Michael will be there as well."

She bristled at his name and received another pat on the shoulder. "No, lass. Don't be angry with Michael. This is all just a strange twist of the fates. I can imagine he is just as put out about the whole affair as you are. Just try to have a rest today, go see our lovely cliffs, have a pint of cider. The rain has stopped, so you can get yourself a bit of fresh air after your travels and trust me to do right by you, aye?"

Branna looked in his kind eyes, and then at Jack McCain and ceded for the moment. She trusted Ned. She felt like she knew him. There was an instant kinship formed and as she looked at the motherly concern in his daughter's eyes, she softened. She understood in her heart that these were good people. Jack McCain seemed honest enough, but she sensed he had already allied with the local team.

She stood, her back straight, and stuck out her hand. Ned again kissed it and gave it a little pat. "It was nice to finally meet you all. I will do as you say. I haven't slept or eaten much, and I need a hot shower. If you could point me toward the guesthouse? I will call you this evening for the specifics on tomorrow morning."

"Ah, yes. You had breakfast at Gus's. The Killilagh House is just down the road, my dear. Just a good stretch of the legs. Tisn't far at all. Can I take you there, myself?" Branna assured them she could find it. She needed to get away from everyone.

As she departed and began to walk to her car, the gravity of her situation hit her. She was homeless, essentially. This simple transaction was going to shit, and she was homeless. How the hell does someone who owns six houses end up homeless?

She considered that smug Mr. O'Brien with his cute little freckles and cool tone and decided she was furious that he'd not said something to her at their first meeting. She had been completely blindsided. He'd lied by omission, and the more she thought on it, the more ticked off she became. Her steps became purposeful as she headed toward Gus O'Connor's Pub. She wasn't going to stew on this all night without first taking a chunk out of him.

She stepped into the pub and saw the same pretty waitress behind the bar. There were a lot of people there for lunch, but she didn't see him. She approached the bar. "Excuse me, Miss?"

"Hello, again. I'm Jenny, dear, how can I help you?" She maintained as non-aggressive of a tone as she could muster, "Is Mr. O'Brien still around?" Jenny's face told Branna that she knew exactly what was coming. "I promise not to hurt him, I just need a word. Please. Now, if he is here." Jenny exhaled hugely and pointed to a back area that was marked "Staff Only" and under the sign written on paper read *Rehearsals, No entry.* Branna very quietly pushed through the door before the sounds from the bar could carry. *The element of surprise, never lose it.*

She walked down a short hall where she heard voices. She peered around the corner as she heard what sounded like a familiar voice. "Jaysus, Robby! Can't you put the music sheets in order before you pass them out? These are totally cocked up!" As she peered around the doorway, keeping out of sight, she saw that it was indeed Michael O'Brien.

"Well, how about you make your own copies, ye lazy fooker!" a few chuckles followed by a deeper commanding voice. "Lads, language! We've got a lady here."

At first she thought they had seen her, but there was indeed a female and two other men with them. They were all arranging music. They had stands and instruments strewn around their feet. Interesting. She noticed that Michael had changed clothes. He had some sort of navy blue utility pants on and a plain white undershirt, but what she noticed were the military styled combat boots. She saw his shirt draped on the back of his chair. It had some sort of insignia on the sleeve and a nametape. *Holy shit, is he a cop?* Then she noticed the oversized bright orange duffle. IRCG,Garda Cósta na hÉireann and some sort of crest. Under it in English were the words Rescue Swimmer. *Jesus, a local super hero.*

This was starting to look a little more like she was on the losing side. She heard him speak again. "We need to hurry this up. I have duty at four and then I have to meet that bloody American at my cottage tomorrow morning." *Excuse me? That would be my cue, buddy.*

Branna straightened her back, lifted her chin and strolled into their rehearsal. "Oh really? What if that bloody American wants to talk about her cottage now?" Everyone was startled and then with morbid curiosity, actually looked a little pleased to be witnesses to the big event. Word of this mess had obviously made it's rounds to the locals.

"Well, well. If it isn't the wee Yankee tycoon, come to grace us with her presence." He set his music down on the stand, and pulled up his chair to take a seat. If it was possible to sit like a cocky jerk, he was doing it. He spread both arms out across the backs of the neighboring chairs and did a wide cross of his legs.

Branna was fuming. "As a matter of fact she is. I've come to tell you, oh mighty King O'Brien, that it is my house. Mine. Paid in full. Whatever local back door deal you are trying to pull is not going to happen. I am not going anywhere. Got it, pretty boy?" She heard a little mumbling, and some signs of amusement from the peanut gallery.

She shot them a look that would melt the flesh off their bones, and they all looked at their feet, all except the older man. The man that had told them to watch their language was openly meeting her eye. He wasn't rude or aggressive. He had his arms folded across his chest and was wearing what she could only describe as a look of pleased fascination on his face. He had the identical blue eyes as Michael except no ring of green. He had the same hair, though peppered with silver, and the same physical size and presence. *So this is the dad.* She wondered, not for the first time, what it would have been like to know her own father as an adult, to have him at her side. She shook herself and re-engaged her target.

He was standing again and sputtering indignantly, completely offended by her comment about back door, shady deals. He wasn't aggressive, but he was visibly as upset as she. "Now you listen to me, Miss O'Mara. I have been dealing with Ned Kelly for almost two years negotiating the purchase of my cottage. You don't even look old enough to be in this pub!"

She noticed that his accent got thicker the more worked up he got. "So, you can just engage those wee little feet with your little pink toes and get back in that rental car. Head toward Dublin and buy the first ticket back to your mummy and daddy, because you are not getting my house!"

She flinched at his words. He had no way of knowing her situation, but his words were like a knife in her heart. She had no one to return to, and didn't that sorry fact just stoke her up for a fight.

She stalked toward him with a finger pointed and poked him square in the chest. "You listen to me, Mr. O'Brien." she spat, throwing his own words back at him. "I will not be heading for Dublin. I won't be heading anywhere but Burren Way. I may not look like much next to your big, badass self, but you would be wise not to underestimate me. If you think for one minute that I am going to slink back to America with my tail between my legs, then you don't know anything about O'Mara women. I will Eat.Your.Lunch." She poked him in the chest three times with those last three words, staring up at him like a blood thirsty, little scrapper. He stared down at her speechless.

He finally betrayed himself with one side of his mouth turning up, suppressing a grin. "You've got a little steel under that polish, don't you duchess?"

She swiftly turned and began walking out. "You bet your ass I do," she shot over her shoulder. Then she stopped abruptly, looked at his music stand, and used two fingers to knock his carefully arranged sheet music all over the floor. One of the other band members barked out a laugh. She nodded at his father, "Good day, Mr. O'Brien." and walked out of the room like a boss.

She heard the various comments as she walked down the hall toward the main pub. "Are you sure she's not a Mullen?"

"Well, you are a verra pretty boy, mighty King O'Brien!" with choruses of laughter.

She heard him reply, "Shut your gob, the lot of ye!" She allowed herself a small grin and she passed through the pub. She heard Jenny mumbling something about missing all the fun, as Branna left the pub.

Sean O'Brien was an intelligent, honest man. He'd worked for twenty-five years with the Garda, the Irish police. He'd met his Northern wife while she was spending the weekend in Dublin. She was a student, and he was on duty. They'd run into each other, literally, in a teashop. Sorcha was a handful. Gorgeous, passionate, and short tempered. She was the most loyal of allies and the fiercest of enemies when you crossed her.

Sorcha was a true mate and a loving mother, but being a Catholic in Northern Ireland in the 60's and 70's had a tendency to forge a strong personality. At 5 ft. 2 in. and barely 8 stone, she had gone head to head with him, times uncounted, over the years. She was completely undaunted. She met him nose to nose, or nose to chest in any case, and she looked spectacular doing it.

As he looked at his son picking up his sheet music scattered across the floor, it wasn't the mother and son comparison that struck him. He thought back to the dark haired young woman that had stared up at his impressively large son and poked him in the chest. Three times. While growling. It was quite something to watch, when you weren't on the receiving end. She was sharp, too. She had obviously been watching and listening before she entered, and she immediately picked up on the resemblance between them.

It was a shame, this mess about the house. It really was. For under different circumstances, this O'Mara girl may have been just what the doctor ordered for the fat headed son of his. She was a lovely young lady. Dressed conservatively and small of stature, but there was nothing small about Branna O'Mara.

Doesn't the good Lord throw some interesting things our way, he marveled. He found himself rather looking forward to tomorrow morning. Michael had asked him to come along, and although his son didn't really need him, he was surely not going to miss it. He looked over at Michael's sister, who was grinning with unhidden delight as she watched her brother pick up the scattered papers. Brigid was another handful, just like her mother. She looked up at her dad and wiggled her eyebrows at him. Sean burst into laughter and gave her a nod. Very interesting things, indeed.

As Michael rearranged his music, he did a playback in his head of the confrontation that had just occurred. He remembered Jenny's advice about handling things delicately. In hindsight, he probably should have listened to her. He had misread that little American at breakfast. She seemed unthreatening, even vulnerable. He thought a bit of cocky body language and dismissive dialogue mixed with a little male assertiveness might scare her right back to the airport. Man, had he been wrong. He thought about those big blue eyes looking up at him. He was almost a foot taller than her and easily had a hundred pounds on her, but he knew that she would rather die than cower to him. Like a warrior facing off and relishing the challenge, confrontation didn't make her cower, it called her to battle.

This was getting messier by the hour. He pushed away further thoughts about her perfect, fair skin and the witch mark at her temple. Definitely wasn't going to think about her mouth. No makeup, but a distracting ruby blush at her lips and cheeks as she flushed with anger. Nope, not thinking about the lips, or the spot in his chest that still tingled where she'd poked him. That little hellcat was going to make trouble. He really needed to rethink his strategy, but later. Playing always helped him clear his head.

"Show's over boys, and you," he pointed at his sister, "Brigid, you can wipe that satisfied grin off your face. We need to practice and we only have a couple of hours. Your bowing sucked on that last set."

She smiled sweetly, "Yes, brother dear. Oh, and you missed a sheet under your chair, love. There's a good lad." The men chuckled as he picked it up.

* * *

BRANNA DROVE straight to the Killilagh House from the pub. Better to retreat quickly after her sneak attack. She re-played the scene in her mind and decided that although she had come out on top in the argument, this was going to be tough. This wasn't some businessman or investor she was going up against.

She thought about that duffle. He was a Coast Guard rescue swimmer. Not military, but para-military and definitely tough guy material. You had to be strong, brave, and have no fear of your own watery death to do that job. In the USCG, they were the elite swimmers with matching balls of steel.

The rocky Irish Sea, the Atlantic Ocean, and the jagged cliffs of Coastal Clare were not the gigs for novice weekend warriors. They knew advanced first aid and life saving tactics, even the volunteers. They went into that water no matter how cold it was, were actually trained in cold weather and cold-water missions. He was big, too. He had the long, lean muscles of a swimmer and the height and build of a warrior. She'd seen the type. The Marines generally had two types. Big and strong or lean and fast, from what she had seen. She'd wager he was a mix of both.

He'd never acted aggressively toward her, even though she had provoked him by poking him in the chest. Which told her that he wasn't a brute. The problem was this; people were most dangerous on their own turf, especially if they thought they were defending their home. Her daddy taught her that. He honestly felt like the wronged party, which was a shame.

She couldn't let that sway her, though. He was local. He had family, friends, and a support system. She, on the other hand, had herself. Without that cottage she was homeless. It was just the price range that made this doable, and she already had several plans in action. She had a small amount of furniture and belongings being shipped. She had paid fees, filed paperwork for her long term visa, and put renters in all of her homes. This was a done deal. She'd acted quickly, having anticipated the move and shot into action as soon as the offer went through. She wasn't turning back. She wasn't going to rent some overpriced flat in a tourist area and slowly dwindle her funds. That Boy Scout was going to have to find another house. Period. She needed this to work.

CHAPTER 3

Branna walked up to the Killilagh House, and as she went in the front entrance, she was met by a thirty-something woman and two young boys exiting where she had entered. "Boys! Use your manners!" the woman admonished.

As they ran for the garden they yelled back, "Yes, mother. Hello Miss! Welcome to the Killilagh House!" and giggled with mirth as they shoved one another and tried to trip each other in the grass.

They had local accents and were adorable. She loved kids, and had always found that watching little boys was similar to watching little puppies wrestling, nipping and rolling around together. The woman, obviously their mother, introduced herself. "My name is Liz, and you must be the Miss O'Mara everyone's been buzzing about."

Branna blushed a little. "Please, call me Branna. Yes, I can imagine I've made quite a spectacle around here. I do appreciate you putting me up tonight."

Liz waived her hand. "Oh dear, not at all. It's a fine mess Jack has made. He's a good sort, as good as any. He's just a little behind the times. His small town livelihood hasn't caught up with the speed of the Internet. Ned made sure to tell me what a dear girl you were, and that we were to welcome you like family. So, breakfast starts at seven and goes till 9:30." As she continued, Branna listened to the musical quality of her voice. She was very kind, and she immediately made Branna feel at home.

"So then, you didn't come all they way from America with just that little satchel, I'd expect. Shall we go get your bags, then?"

Branna nodded and they went out to the car park area. Branna took her rucksack and one of the smaller suitcases, which she handed to Liz. "I'm only staying one night, so this should be sufficient."

She hoisted her camouflage rucksack on her back, a small bed roll hanging off the bottom. She stopped, momentarily, untethered the bed roll, and left it in the trunk. The innkeeper looked at it, and did a once over on her. "Were you in the military, dear? Or was it a sweetheart of yours?"

Branna answered, "No, my father was. This was his backpack."

The woman brightened and asked,"Ah, he's retired then?"

Branna paused and measured her response. This was going to come up. She was young and here alone. People were going to start asking about her family. God, she hated pity, but she wasn't going to lie. "Um, no. He was killed in combat, in Iraq several years ago. I just keep this bag for...well, I just keep it because it was his favorite."

She shrugged and started to walk toward the house. She thought the woman was behind her, but she looked back and Liz had taken a pause, frozen in place and looking at her intensely. Branna straightened her spine, adjusted the pack, and met the woman's eyes. Liz exhaled, getting the message, and started rolling the other bag to catch up to her.

As they walked back through the guesthouse, Branna took it all in. There was well-worn furniture in a common room, a wood burner, pamphlets, comforting and tasteful. Not the sterile furnishings of the latest hotel chain. There was a little sign sat on the mantle giving the WiFi password. Off to the left was the breakfast area and she eyed the coffee pot and an assortment of teas. She liked Irish tea. Black and strong, it was almost as good as coffee if you need a kick in the pants, and she did. Liz followed her gaze. "Yes, it's about tea time. You must be bone weary from the traveling. We'll take you to your room and let you freshen up. I'll put the kettle on and see if I can't round up a little bit to nibble on."

"Thank you, Ma'am. I don't need much. I know you don't serve anything but breakfast. I'd be happy to pay."

Liz swatted that thought away. "No, dear. Ned made sure to tell me to take care of you, and you look like you need a little time off your feet. Don't you think on it a minute. Just go now, and get settled. I'll come knocking when it's ready."

Branna used her key to get into her room. It was small, but she had a double bed and a little en suite bathroom with a shower. The room was well used, the bed linen soft and worn with several washings. It was spotless, however, and very cozy. She eyed the bed and briefly considered crashing. She knew that if she went down now, she would be crashed for hours. Moving around like she did, she understood jet lag. Better to gut it out the first day and wait for nighttime to sleep. The sooner she got on the local sleep schedule, the better she would adjust.

She went in the bathroom and washed her face. She also brushed, flossed, and took her hair out of the tight bun. It was starting to give her a headache since she had been awake for a day and a half with the hairdo snuggly in place. As she released her long, thick, black hair and fingered her scalp, she moaned. So nice to get those pins and tie out. She stepped into a trickling, tepid shower and cleaned off the travel bugs. She put fresh clothes on, took her towel off her head, and brushed out her long tresses. She braided it loosely, not wanting the tight feeling again. She was stiff from the traveling. Branna liked long hair, but she liked to look neat. It was almost to her hips and could get a little wild if she didn't keep it restrained.

Her daddy used to quote Paul's Letter to the Corinthians. "A woman's hair is her glory." That must have stuck on some level because she had always had long hair. She was sporting a little luggage under the eyes from lack of sleep, but the soap and water routine sparked her up a little. She changed to a pair of khakis and a knit, collared top. It was plain but clean and not too bad on the wrinkles. She put on some comfortable shoes and headed out.

As soon as she got some caffeine and a snack, she could start exploring. She needed to hit a grocery store as well. She needed to buy coffee and some sort of energy bars, her go-to meal. Cooking for one was a big nuisance when she could just pop a protein bar in her mouth and keep working. No dishes, either. She knew how to cook, very well in fact, but nothing said lonely loser like sitting alone at your dining room table.

It was time for tea. Hopefully it wasn't some big tower of sandwiches and scones like in the Jane Austen movies. She needed some fresh air and she really wanted to do a drive by of the cliffs and scout out her cottage. The thought of King O'Brien calling it his cottage chapped her ass. He should be at work if she'd heard correctly, so she wouldn't run into him again unless she toppled off the cliffs into the sea. A quick flash of him giving her mouth-to-mouth stormed her mind. *Stand down, girlie. No dating. Definitely no dating that thieving swine, no matter how good he looks.*

* * *

MICHAEL LOOKED out over the open sea from the deck of the small ship. Things had been calm today, but they were headed to a call of a fishing boat dead in the water. As they approached the boat, he recognized it. It was called *The Sea Mistress* which was undoubtedly named after some fight with the wife over spending more time on it than on her. Jamie Sullivan was the owner's son, and he appeared to have her out without his da at the helm. He was about twenty-two years old and learning the trade. He had a few men with him. He looked up as they approached and Michael almost pitied him. Almost. Boating 101, check your fuel.

He didn't have to worry about whether to rat the kid out to his father. The crew would be more than happy to pass on this blunder, the poor bastard. His father was lucky the kid stuck around to learn the fishing trade. It was bloody hard work, rubbish schedules, and not a steady paycheck. Most lads his age were headed straight out of Doolin to the city for steady work or to university. It was a small operation. They traveled around the islands and down to Dingle. His da was certainly going to give him some shit over this one, though.

Once they'd aided young Jamie on his way, they headed out toward the islands. With the humming of the engine and the steady rocking over the swells, Michael's mind began to wander. The deep, clear blue water reminded him of a certain set of clear, deep blue eyes. Brannaugh O'Mara. Brannaugh was Gaelic for raven. She'd changed the spelling, probably an American thing. No one could butcher Gaelic better than their neighbors to the West. O'Mara meant "of the sea". With those stormy blue eyes and silky black hair, he couldn't think of a better name. *Christ,* he thought. *What a feckin mess this is.*

He cursed to himself. It wasn't his fault that she'd jumped the gun and moved here before the closing. She should have known not to rush to Ireland before the deal was done. What kind of eejit hops on a plane before she had confirmed everything? *A twenty-three year old, inexperienced, impulsive, overly enthusiastic woman-child, that's who.*

He was only five or six years older than her, but he knew that was a big age gap with regard to life experience. She was probably one of those sheltered, privileged American girls with the perfect house, perfect life, and perfect dog. She'd probably not seen much of the world outside of the protective arms of her parents. He actually felt a little bad for her. She had some pluck, though. She was probably used to getting her way.

Fiona had been that way. She wasn't the hellcat this Branna had turned out to be, but she had her ways. If she didn't get what she wanted, she made you pay, or she got it from someone else. Why in the hell he was comparing his ex-wife to Branna O'Mara was a mystery, and he was stopping. Now. He had to push his pity aside and be ruthless. He had waited for this house for almost two years.

Fiona had wanted to rent a new flat, liked a little more polish. She thought he was nuts to inquire about the old place. "I am not living in that little hovel. I'd rather rent than move into that antique and spend years trying to clean it up. Plus it's overpriced, and you know it. Forget it, Michael!" she had said. The marriage had fallen to pieces slowly but surely, starting pretty soon after the wedding.

Once the annulment had gone through, creeping up on their third anniversary, he quit traveling back and forth between their flat and his cousin Tadgh's place. His cousin was the one that had finally told him about Fiona's extra-curricular sex life. She'd made the mistake of not sticking to a random fuck with a tourist or some of the more discreet men in the area. She'd tried to screw his own cousin, and Tadgh had not only turned her down, he had finally told Michael what half the town already knew.

Michael supposed he had always suspected. He'd ignored the gossip about what she was up to while he was out to sea. She went out a lot, but he figured she was lonely and she always made him feel guilty about his job, the time he spent with his family, even his music. She played and sang a bit too, but she only liked it if she was the star attraction.

Yep, doomed to fail for several reasons. Once he was out of that mess, he'd started to get serious about the cottage. He wanted a place of his own. As humiliating as it was to live with his parents for a year in his late twenties, he'd done it. He saved a lot of money and worked on negotiating with Ned and Jack. Now it was all going to shit, and Branna O'Mara was nothing but an obstacle. He could not afford to get distracted.

* * *

BRANNA WAS on the winding road to the famous Cliffs of Moher, and she was brimming with excitement. She'd seen pictures on the internet, and they'd actually shot a couple of movie scenes there, but from everything she had heard and read, it was nothing compared to the real thing. She caught glimpses of it from the road and followed the signs toward the official visitor center and parking. School was back in session, so the crowd was not overwhelming at all. It was misting rain, again.

She'd never minded the rain. She loved the rain. Thunderstorms and lightning had always excited her. She had a strong memory of being a small girl and running out the back door into a storm. Her parents weren't those uptight, helicopter parents. They had strapped her on their backs even as an infant and taken her along on their adventures. Elephants in Thailand, boogie boarding on the beaches of the Carolinas, horseback riding in Arizona.

The problem in this particular instance had not been the pouring rain or the mud all over her pajamas. It was the clapping thunder and lightning strikes way too close to home, and a tornado watch for the county, earlier that evening. Her mother had come tearing out after her in the rain, screaming, *Get your butt back here right now, little girl!* She had finally caught her, giggling and splashing, and then marched her back to the porch on her hip.

Her daddy was shaking with laughter and holding a towel for each of them. Her mother, coming down from the adrenaline rush, began laughing as well. She was pretty small, probably three or four years old. That's all she remembered, but the feeling of freedom and joy mingled with the happy laughter of her parents is a memory that clung to her. It was a comfort to her, especially on a rainy day.

As she followed the walkway up to the viewing point she could hear the sea crashing against the cliffs. As it all came into view, it took her breath away. So vast and dramatic. The green land plunging to the grey and brown and black of the rocky cliffside. It went on way farther than she had imagined. It was probably impossible to get the entirety of it into one photo. Down below there was a rock arch jutting out of the sea as the water went wild around it. There were caves, too.

My God, is there any place more beautiful? As she stood there taking it all in and breathing the sea air, she heard some tourists approaching. They were Americans as well, she could tell by the accent. They did the regular oohs and aahs. The older boy with them said, "Mom, what does that sign mean? It says, *Do you need to talk?* I don't get it. Why do they have a phone number? What does that have to do with the Cliffs?" The mother seemed puzzled by it as well. Branna had seen it too.

She turned to them and they asked her if she knew what the sign meant. She explained, "It's for people who are depressed. It's a suicide hotline."

The puzzled looks gave way to understanding. Then they looked down. All the way down. "Damn, what a way to go," said the father, who had been silent up until this point.

She had to agree. Suicide was selfish and weak. She wondered briefly if Michael had ever been called to fish a body from the depths below. Then she walked back to her car and drove toward town. She was hungry and tired. She would have to wait until tomorrow to see the cottage. The enormity of her situation was resurfacing, weighing on her heart and mind.

Branna went back to her guesthouse to check her email and find a nice place for dinner. She didn't have a kitchen in her room or even a fridge, so she needed to find a little spot to get a meal without drawing too much attention to herself. If she picked something touristy, it would be crowded, but she would blend. Gus O'Connors was out since she wasn't sure who would still be around. McDermott's seemed a good choice, since she was hoping for some live music and to add some craic to her day.

She put a brush through her hair again since the windy cliffs had tousled her braid. She put it back in her tight bun, grabbed a light sweater and headed over on foot. She could hear the stream and the sheep as she walked alone and it was a peaceful feeling to have nowhere pressing to be. McDermotts was starting to fill up by seven. She grabbed a small table near what looked like a performing area, since the bar stools were all taken.

A handsome man, nicely built, came up to her table and handed her a menu. He was wearing a Kill Your TV t-shirt and faded jeans. He had light hair, almost blonde, that was all one length, and almost to his shoulders. He had it tucked behind his ears. She guessed him to be in his mid-twenties, and he looked like a cross between a garage band hipster and a pretty boy Calvin Klein model. His name tag said Tadgh.

She looked at it and must have made a face, because he said, "It's pronounced Tige, like tiger without the –er. It's the Gaelic form of Timothy. American, eh?"

She stifled a giggle. "Am I that obvious?"

He answered with a broad, easy smile. "No, not at first sight. You've no camera or travel book and you look like a local, but I know all of the locals and you don't have the Gaelic, so…" He shrugged one shoulder.

Branna blushed and his smile got bigger. "How does someone look like a local?" she asked.

He explained, "Well, don't wear an Aran fisherman's sweater unless you're out fishing. Don't wear trainers with your khakis." He looked off with one eye cocked up, as if in deep thought. "Don't have an umbrella that reads 'I HEART DUBLIN.'" Then he leaned in just a little, "And it helps to have eyes like the sea and skin like cream."

He smiled at that, looking at her with unhidden appreciation. "The moms will scoop you up and drag you off to the nearest priest, marry you off to one of their sons." Moms came out like mams and she giggled.

Branna liked this Tadgh fellow. He was easy going and charming. "Well, it just so happens that as of this morning, I am a local. So, if I don't want to be rushed off to the nearest priest, I better go put my sneakers on." Tadgh looked puzzled, and then realization shown in his eyes. Oh shit, this was it. She'd just chased away her first potential friend.

He cocked his head and gave her a wry grin. "Well, well, well."

She cut him off. "No, no, no! Don't even start! I don't need to hear about what a greedy, cottage stealing Yank I am!"

He burst out laughing and shook his head. "Don't worry your pretty head about it, girl. I love my cousin, but there is no way I am taking sides on this one. Not after the lashing you gave him today."

Branna's face fell. "Your cousin?" she moaned. His eyes were hazel, but he had the look of his cousin in every other way. He was as disgustingly handsome as Michael.

"So, what did he tell you?" She asked, even though she was afraid to hear it.

"Oh, he didn't tell me anything. He's on duty. His sister, on the other hand, had a front row seat. You're already a legend around here." He was grinning so widely, she wanted to smack him.

She handed him back the menu and said, "I'll have the soup of the day." Then she put her head in her hands. She could hear him chuckling on the way to the kitchen.

Branna was really fighting the urge to cry. She was good at putting on a strong face, but inside she was ready to lose it. What had seemed like such a promising fresh start, just 12 hours ago, was turning into a nightmare.

She didn't need friends, family, or anyone. She really was okay on her own. It would have been nice, though, to have some friends. She would've at least preferred to be on amicable terms with the locals.

Now everyone was going to hate her, even if she got the cottage. As she started the self pity roll, a bowl of soup slid in front of her along with a basket of bread, and a small glass with something amber in it. Tadgh sat down in front of her and folded his arms on the table. He looked a little less humored this time. "You looked like a one man pity party, so I thought you could use some company."

"Are you going to tell me to go back to America too?" she said. He looked abashed. "God no, woman. Single girls, who aren't kin, are a rare commodity around here. You will never escape now." She gave him a half grin.

"Actually, I came to apologize," he said more seriously. Branna cocked her head at him. "This must not be humorous at all from your end of things. Michael's, either." She tensed a little, and he said with an understanding look, "Yes, he can be a force to be reckoned with. Dreadful tempers, the lot of them. He's not a bully, though, Branna. You mustn't judge him too harshly. He's had..." He paused, choosing his words. "He's had challenges up until now. He's a good sort. The best, actually."

Branna rubbed her face. "You aren't making me feel better. So, you think I should just give up?"

He shook his head. "That's not what I'm saying at all. You moved here for a reason, yes? You wanted this to be your new home. You're not some holiday weekender. It's a grand and brave thing, moving abroad and leaving your home and family. If you chose Doolin, then you should see it through. It's easy for everyone to jest and gossip." He swept his hand across the room. "Other than the regular tourist tomfoolery and the local drama, we don't get shook up around here very often. No one knows you yet." He shrugged, "It's easy to have laugh at your expense and Michael's, but it isn't very funny is it?"

Branna shook her head. "No, it really isn't."

Tadgh nodded to himself as if coming to some unspoken conclusion. "I think you might be good for this place. I know you think you have nothing but enemies to look forward to now, but I won't be one of them. Do I wish you'd choose another house? I have to admit, I do. Just end this nasty business, before it gets any gas, and find another place. I've got a nice condo right next to me you might like. Thin walls." At this, he wiggled his eyebrows at her.

She laughed and her shoulders relaxed a little. "No offense Tadgh, but I don't want a condo. This is what I do." She pressed her hand to her chest as she spoke. "I take run down, neglected properties and give them new life again. I make them wanted again. This place is perfect. It's me." He thought that was an odd comparison, but decided not to pry.

Tadgh stiffened as one of the other employees yelled. "Tadgh, get off your arse. We've got a full house!"

He gave Branna an apologetic glance. "One of my many jobs." He motioned to the amber liquid. "Drink up, woman. You look like you need it." Branna looked at the glass of whiskey and shook her head. "I don't drink much, and I am already tired enough."

He shrugged, picked up the glass and said, "Slainte." Branna clinked her clean soup spoon to his glass and he took a sip. He sighed with pleasure, and she noticed again how handsome he was. She didn't feel a spark, but she never really did. He was certainly a looker, though.

"Yes, jet lag is a nasty business. I'll let you slide tonight, but if you are going to blend in as a proper Irish lass, Branna O'Mara, you'll need to share the occasional pint or drink o'whiskey with your neighbors."

Again the man from behind the bar bellowed, "Tadgh!" Tadgh turned to the man and yelled back. "Shut your gob, you old woman. I'm coming!"

Just as he left the table some activity started at the performing area. She hadn't noticed the men setting up, but she did now. *Oh, shit.* The elder Mr. O'Brien had a guitar. The other man, Robby, if she remembered right, was holding a bodhrán and the pretty woman and another man from the rehearsal room were also setting up microphones and stands.

She scanned the room, and there was no sign of Michael O'Brien. *Shit, shit, shit.* She was positive she had heard him say he was working tonight. Maybe she could sneak out. She went for her wallet, ready to abandon her soup, when someone spoke. "Dia duit, Miss O'Mara".

She looked up into the dusty blue eyes of Michael's father and jumped a little. "Sorry, dear. I didn't mean to startle you. We were never properly introduced earlier today. My name is Sean, and as you've guessed, I'm Michael's da."

She was speechless. He was smiling warmly at her and she wasn't quite sure what to do with that. She was expecting hostility. The fact that, despite his age, he was extremely handsome was not helping her flummoxed state. She spoke cautiously and quickly moved to babbling, "I'm pleased to meet you, sir. Truly. I am sorry about the scene I made at your rehearsal. I just, well, I was pretty upset after my meeting and I wanted to, um…"

He leaned forward and said, "Take a piece o' hide out of my son? Yes, I gathered as much."

She winced, " Well, yes. I suppose that's exactly what I wanted to do. I swear I'm not a terrible person. This is all such a mess."

Sean put his hands out, palms down. "No dear, you don't need to explain. I understand your predicament. I honestly do. It doesn't mean I don't side with my son on this, but no, dear, don't apologize. Neither of you are to blame for this situation. It is so improbable as to seem impossible, but here we are. Don't run off, though, Branna. 'Tis a small town and we all need to try and be civil until everything is sorted. You just enjoy your soup and enjoy your first night with us. Get a good night's rest and I'll see you tomorrow, yes?"

Branna exhaled and found herself lowering her hackles a bit. She nodded and smiled. "Thank you, Mr. O'Brien. I think I'll do that. Thank you for, well, just being kind, even though I took a hunk out of your son today." She gave a self-deprecating smile.

"Not at all dear," he replied.

"Oh, Mr. O'Brien?" Sean turned to her. "Speaking of your son, will he be performing with you tonight? I just…I don't want to make any trouble and if it really would be better for me to go, I can just duck out now."

At this, Sean interrupted her. "No, he's on duty all night. Don't worry. You've got a small reprieve." He gave a slight chuckle and walked away.

As he rejoined the other musicians, Branna's eyes were drawn to a tall, pretty woman with shoulder length, fiery, red hair. She had icy green eyes. She was staring unapologetically at Branna. She had a bitchy air about her and then got a not-so-sweet grin across her face. She turned and walked off and the moment was over. Branna was relieved. She really didn't need any more confrontations today. She should have taken the whiskey, was her last thought before the music started.

* * *

As Branna walked home to the guesthouse, she thought dreamily about the beautiful music she'd heard. The books had been right. These were true musicians. The woman, who she knew now to be Brigid, Michael's sister, had a lovely voice. Smooth and clear and true. The traditional music they'd performed varied from funny to tragic to bawdy. Sometimes the room would be silent and serious and other times it was roaring with laughter or people singing along. At one point, Sean had called for Tadgh to come up and play "Michael's part". He took Sean's guitar and the older gentleman took the vocals. Sweet Irish cream meets deep, smokey whiskey. His voice was as stunning as his daughter's. Tadgh played wonderfully, they all did. He even chimed in for a little back up vocals. It had been a wonderful evening.

She remembered the times her father would sing to her. He loved celtic music. He didn't speak fluent Gaelic, nowhere near it, but he knew the songs by heart. He'd sing to her on the beach house deck, them swinging together in their hammocks. He'd sing along to faster, funny songs and grab her mother from the kitchen and swing her around. When she couldn't sleep, he'd sing soft and soothing songs to her to lull her back to sleep.

This music was as much a part of her as if she grown up on these rocky shores. She'd even remembered their old piano and learning to play it. She had shut this part of her memory off for years, too painful to bear. Now, in the dreamy aftermath of the music session at McDermott's, she let those happy memories wash over her without any pain. The absence of her crushing, ever present grief was temporarily a short, welcomed respite. She would sleep well tonight.

* * *

Michael was bone weary by the end of his shift. He usually liked tea, but this was a double shot with extra sugar kind of morning. Normally his male ego refrained from fufu coffee bars, but he needed the caffeine. Today was the big show down. Luckily he was on the ship last night. As a rescue swimmer and active duty Coast Guard, his heli station was in Shannon. A sixty kilometer drive one way was less desirable than the local station, which was dilapidated and mostly volunteer. It was a busy station. They deserved and needed a better facility. One had been in the works for a while, but government red tape insured that everything was harder, longer, and more expensive than it needed to be. For now they got by with an old building that flooded, had shit parking, and was way too small. Still, it was close. Close was good after a 12 hour shift.

As he left the county route and followed Burren Way, Kelly's cottage came into view. There was a small box truck in the drive and Ned's VW. Also, there was a tan BMW that he recognized as Jack

McCain's car. His father had texted him that he was riding with McCain. *Hmm, no hellcat... yet.* Good. He wanted to get Ned alone. He parked behind the truck and realized it was actually a moving truck. A small one, but the logo was on the side. What in the hell? Had that Yank actually showed up with furniture, ready to move into the cottage?

His blood pressure was already starting to rise. Then he noticed another little car headed toward him on the road. It turned into the drive, a rental car with the American woman driving it. She got out of the car, grabbed her handbag, and locked it. As she approached, she looked curiously at the truck. She noticed him and bristled visibly like a little porcupine. "Is this your truck? Moving somewhere are we?" She had her hands on her hips and she was looking up at him with her brow crinkled. "No, tisn't, so don't get your knickers in a bunch. I can assume, then, that it isn't yours either?"

He motioned toward the door with his head. "Let's get this over with. You'll want to be getting that plane ticket as soon as you can." She marched in front of him with a stomp in her step. He heard her mumbling something that sounded like "arrogant jackass." He was ashamed to admit to himself that he was actually goading her a bit. That temper of hers amused him. Yes, as prickly as a little porcupine. Jack and Michael's father, Sean, greeted them at the front door. "Please, both of you come in. Ned and Diane are already here, and I am sure you both had a rough night."

Michael was listening to Jack, but then he looked over at Branna. She wasn't looking at either of them. She was looking at the outside of the cottage. He'd forgotten that she had seen only pictures, and only had a second hand account of the place. Her hair was bound tightly at the back of her neck in a bun. Her face was tipped up, and she was smiling.

She was an uptight person, he noticed. At least around him, her body language was defensive and guarded. Now, however, she looked more like a happy child staring up at the Christmas tree. She had love in her eyes, and the object of her affection was his cottage. She was so pretty, she looked so happy, and he realized then that this was as important to her as it was to him. *Hold on dumb ass. That is your cottage she is getting all moody over. Don't get sentimental. Put her on her way.*

As Jack McCain began talking, Branna tuned him out. She was here. After the cliffs, she had felt a little off kilter, so she had decided not to try and find the place. She'd let that Boy Scout distract her when she'd pulled up, and she was just now getting a good look at the place. *Baby Jesus in a manger.* The place was perfect.

It was a long, stone and mortar, one story cottage. The thatch had long been replaced by slate. That was good. Slate could last a century if you were lucky. It had a stone chimney and was painted that classic white wash so common to this area. Old windows, but none seemed to be broken or damaged. A flat rock walkway, leading up to a dark gray/blue door. It was simple, but it looked sound.

The paint was peeling in several areas on the house and the trim. A shed attached to a rickety carport was set back from the house. The shrubs around the house were in need of a trimming and there were even unruly rose bushes. She actually felt a tightening in her throat and stinging in her eyes. It needed some love, but it was perfect.

Without addressing any of the men, she opened the front door. She vaguely noticed two people standing in the main room, but she couldn't break herself away from the spell of this house. To the right was a living room area. It had a big, rough, stone fireplace with a simple oak mantle. It was blackened from decades of use. It was clean and unlit, but she suddenly envisioned glowing peat burning and radiating heat through the cottage. The floor was flagstone as well. Worn and in good shape, solid beneath her feet.

To the left of the hearth was one bedroom. Empty except for a fireplace, it had a bathroom just outside the door. It included subway tile, a claw foot tub, and a simple sink and toilet. She noticed the toilet had the chain and tank up high. It was old, but she assumed it worked or she would have heard differently by now. She walked back out and into the common area. The kitchen was small and galley style. It had been updated a little, it was sufficiently plumbed and wired, but it was very simple. Small fridge, small cooker, and a butcher block in the middle that looked older than Ned. It was smooth and dipped slightly in the center, like it had seen a lot of use. She ran her fingers over the smooth, cool wood.

It was the end of August, but it was comfortable in the house. The ocean breezes in this coastal town helped to keep it cool year around. The windows were open and the old, yellowed drapery blew around with the cross breeze. The stone exterior made the cottage cooler in the summer and insulated in the winter.

She continued her appraisal of the kitchen. It had simple wood cabinetry. There was a rug next to the main kitchen area that looked like it might be a spot for a kitchen table. There was no furniture in the place, save the appliances. Branna noticed a nook between the kitchen and another bedroom door. It was a perfect little nook with a window seat and a worn flat cushion. She walked dreamily through this modest abode and had never felt such a pull from a place. After all the moving she'd done, all of the places she'd lived, she finally found one place that called to her "you are home."

As Ned Kelly watched the little dark haired lass tour his cottage, he felt a warm glow in his heart. She ran her hands over each windowsill, along the cabinetry and counter space. She lovingly stroked the old doors and hardware. He'd known she would love the place just from speaking with her and getting to know her during their two phone calls. She had an old soul and an air of sadness to her. As he watched her take in every detail of his humble cottage, he knew he had made the right decision when he'd talked with Diane last night.

His daughter thought he was mad, but he was sharp as ever. Young Michael was a good lad, the best. He loved this community passionately and the people here. He was a good family man and a brave servant. He loved this cottage as much as she. Yes, his solution had come to him slowly but surely ever since he'd learned of the conflicting offers. He hadn't been sure until he laid eyes on the girl, and heard about the big tussle at Gus's place. He simply couldn't bring himself to be unfair to either, and he would not rush his decision. The fates were at work here, and they needed breathing room.

Michael stood next to his father and watched Branna walking through the cottage, and he found that he couldn't take his eyes off her. Her longing eyes and gentle caresses seemed so private, like he was glimpsing something she wouldn't want him to see. He looked around then, seeing it anew through her eyes. It was a simple, modest place, but there was something so elemental and inviting about it.

His mates would never take this place on. They wanted new flats, condos, or to be right near town, close to the pub scene. This was off the path a bit, quiet and unremarkable and admittedly a bit dated. Small too, considering a family had lived here. It had few modern conveniences aside from decent plumbing. Everything was functional. The kitchen was very simple, not ancient but not modern.

It suited him, except for the heating. There were hearths in the main room and one bedroom and a hot stove in the other bedroom. It was warm enough, but it had cold spots, and the fireplaces didn't help with freezing pipes. All in all though, he loved this old cottage. Watching her, he warred between intimate pleasure and territorial jealousy. What in God's name was going to come of all this?

As Branna entered the second bedroom on the other side of the house, she noticed that the wood burner had recently been used and there were a couple of bags and a bed roll in front of it. She came out of the room and looked at everyone as if waking from a dream. "Has someone been staying here?"

Diane answered before Michael could. "Yes, dear, forgive me for not mentioning it yesterday. There was so much being said, it slipped my mind. Michael was given permission to sleep here and start work on the place before the closing. By me, you see. We agreed on it before we realized you were on your way. He's paid rent, mind you, and just moved in two days ago. Two months rent to bridge the time."

Branna looked at Michael and he had his arms crossed over his chest. That smug look on his face caused the blood to rush to her face and thump in her ears. "Excuse me, Diane. I appreciate how unusual this situation has been and how in all of the confusion, you thought it appropriate to let him move in early. The fact is that I am here, now. I was told, also, that I could move in right away. I have my bags in the car. Mr. O'Brien," she waved a hand in his direction, "is just going to have to get a refund and find accommodations elsewhere. Mr. Kelly had foregone any rent, but I assure you, if money is the issue, I can pay whatever you'd previously requested." At this Michael threw his hands up in the air.

"Not bloody likely. Mr. O'Brien is going nowhere! You've got some bollocks coming in here and laying down the law like some self-appointed princess!" As they both began taking shots at each other and talking heatedly over one another, Ned Kelly took his cue and stepped in the middle of the room between them.

In his calm and paternal manner he put his hands out in a motion to quiet the room. "That's enough," was all he said. Both Branna and Michael fell silent.

Sean had remained quiet as he watched this scene unfold. All the players were here, and he a mere spectator. What a pile of ballsch this was. Jack and Ned had made a mess of things for these two young people. He knew how much this cottage meant to his son. Fiona had put him through the ringer these last few years. He'd never disliked the girl, but she was troubled. He'd known the marriage was a bad idea.

Now, in the aftermath of that failure, his son was battered and bitter. All he wanted was to live simply, do his job, play music, and fix up this old house. He needed some peace and independence. Sean and Sorcha loved having him at home, but they knew he wasn't happy. He was a man. He needed his own space. He wanted this for him, he really did.

However, as he watched that dark haired young woman tour the cottage, he saw that she too needed this. He didn't know her story, but there were wounds there. Wounds and yearning that went bone deep, maybe deeper than Michael's. She had left everything, which was such an odd thing. She didn't backpack across Europe in an effort to find herself, like so many young people did. She'd paid cash money to go ex-pat. He didn't know why she'd left America, but now that she was here he felt terrible for her. Her draw to this place was just as strong as Michael's and one of them was headed for some serious heartbreak. What in devil was Ned going to do?

Ned cleared his throat and looked at everyone in the room. His daughter stood beside him, now, and spoke softly. "Are you sure about this, Da?" He just smiled and nodded. "Thank you all for agreeing to meet me here this morning. I know this has been very stressful on everyone, and honestly, I have thought of little else since we discovered this mix up. Now, I have a proposal for you that I have carefully laid out. Diane will give you each a copy when I've finished explaining."

By this time, Michael was looking from Jack to his da in confusion. Branna's eyes never left Ned's face, but he noticed she looked worried. She wouldn't look at him, but she obviously didn't know what was coming either.

"Now, I know you've both got your heart set on the purchase of this cottage. The problem is that I can't very well split it in two." He watched as each person showed their distress in different ways. Michael was rubbing his neck and face and Branna had her arms wrapped protectively around herself. "So here is my proposal. In three months time I will sell this place to one of you. Until then, you are both to live here."

Jack's mouth dropped. Branna's eyes shot up to his and Michael just cursed in Gaelic. "Ned, you must be joking?" This came from Sean O'Brien. Ned calmly looked at him and replied, "I assure you, I am quite serious." At this point Branna broke in, "Mr. Kelly, Ned, I have to agree with Mr. O'Brien. You can't be serious?"

"I assure you dear, I am. Now hear me out. Let me explain my expectations. If by the end, you can't agree to my terms, you will be given a refund of everything you've paid out and you can walk away." Branna gave him a look that said, *Not bloody likely.* He continued, "Ninety days from today, I will sell this cottage for the agreed asking price to either you, Branna, or you, Michael. I will take these months to observe the two of you, talk with you, and become acquainted with your plans for this home you desire. You both will be given three months to get to know this house and surrounding area, and all that goes in to taking care of this old place. At any point if you decide this house, this town, or this arrangement is not what you want, you can walk away. You will relinquish any rights to argue for this house in the future, however."

He took a breath, smiled sweetly, and continued. "I am on the city council. I have spoken with the civil magistrate. He agrees that we need to keep this out of court, and that I, as the owner, should have final say in who takes ownership. I am not prepared to toss either of you out at this point. It wouldn't be fair to either of you for me to make a hasty decision. I need this time and so do you. That said, if either of you attempt to start civil litigation regarding this, I will deny both your offers and take it off the market."

He noticed that everyone involved was looking at him as if he were mad. "I assure you, I am quite sane. I know this must seem a bit out there."

At this point Diane broke in, adding her two cents. "I told my father, and I will tell you all as well. I think that this idea is indeed quite mad and improper. What will everyone think, these two shacking up together in our family house? And you, Da, are the same man who forbade me to live with a man when I was younger. Would you ruin the reputation of this young woman with your harebrained plan?"

Ned scoffed at this. "You know as well as I that you were young and foolish, and your companion at the time was a plonker."

Diane blushed. "Well, am I wrong?" he asked.

She gave a capitulating sigh. "Ok, Da. You were right about the plonker, but that is beside the point. This is a lot to ask of them. It will start tongues wagging around the village something fierce!"

Ned answered her concern with an indulgent smile. "Don't worry on that account, although we all know that the tongues are already wagging." Then he looked at Sean and Jack. "We have a bit of standing around here. If we show solidarity, it will help with the local gossip. Besides, we all know half the young people in the county are shacking up together before or instead of marrying. Honestly, it may raise a few eyebrows initially, but people won't think twice on it in a few weeks."

Branna was stunned. Of all the scenarios she pictured, this was not even a consideration. "Ned, I want you to know that I appreciate the lengths you are willing to go in the pursuit of fairness, but this is completely unacceptable. I don't even know this man. He could be a deranged pervert for all I know! I moved here for some peace and solitude, not to be pulled into this craziness. I can't just move in with him!"

Michael started in next, "Pervert? How dare you say something like that, as if I am not even in the room! I have lived here most of my life! I am not going to let some snot nosed little Yank come in here and start..."

At this point Sean let out a loud whistle and yelled "Quiet, the both of you!" They both looked at him, shocked, and both shut up instantly. Unlike Ned, he had the "Don't mess with big daddy" vibe going with a very commanding presence.

"First of all, I have to take umbrage at your comments regarding my son, Miss O'Mara." He addressed Branna in this and she shrank mentally from him. "He's a fine, upstanding member of this community and a good Catholic boy. You've nothing to fear from him on that front. Now, I think this will go a lot smoother if we quit interrupting Ned and let him finish. Go ahead, man." He nodded at Ned as if this was all that needed to be said.

Ned continued, "Thank you, Sean. As for you, Branna darlin', I don't want you to fear at all for your safety. Young Michael here is a good sort. I would never have even considered this if I thought you would be placed in any jeopardy or Michael was the sort to compromise you in any way. Now, that said, you've both got a good share of temper. You need to accept this situation is a long-term commitment. Three months is a long time to argue, so best get that out of your system, quickly."

"With regard to the house, Jack will retain your earnest money. Branna, your balance will be removed from escrow and returned to you so that you have access to your funds. Michael, your rent money will be returned to you."

As Michael began to argue, Ned stopped him with a hand up. "No, son. I'll not take a dime of rent from either of you. We made this awful mess for you and I will not profit from it. You will each be responsible for your part of the power bill. If you need a phone or internet you will have to sort that out between you. As for furniture, I have a bed, a wardrobe, and dresser for Branna, a table and four chairs, and some fresh linen and kitchen items. Michael, I am assuming you have your own bed and such, so I didn't bother. Branna, you will take the bedroom with the fireplace and use the bathroom with the large tub." At this, he winked at her. "Michael, you will keep the other bedroom with the wood burner and en suite shower. There's plenty of turf and wood in the out building to keep all three rooms warm for the next three months."

At this point Branna was shaking her head back and forth and Michael was pacing back and forth, running his fingers through his short hair. Ned continued talking. "I know this will take some getting used to, but it is three months of your life. If the cottage means that much to you, then you will indulge this old man and agree to my wishes. If neither one of you is willing to back down, then these are my terms. If someone wants to bow out now, I will take no offense. Better now, and save us all the trouble. Jack or someone else is waiting to help you find another place."

Branna stiffened and looked at Michael. His gaze was challenging. "Surely, you aren't going to agree to this?" Michael said.

She looked at him intensely, brows furrowed. He thought she was going to cave. She could see it in his eyes. Well, he didn't know who he was dealing with, if he thought that. "I'm not going anywhere. If these are the terms, then so be it. Feel free to back out if you can't take it, O'Brien."

Michael gave her a wry grin. "Not on your life, darlin'. Count me in, Ned. She won't last a week."

Ned clapped his hands together, "Well now. Diane, would you please give each of them a copy of the agreement?" Diane passed out a copy to Jack, Branna, and Michael then she spoke. "Branna lass, we've got no Internet here. You must need to get in touch with your kin."

Branna stood silent a moment, and seemed to measure her response. Then she did a mental shake and answered. "No, Ma'am, but thank you. I checked my e-mail at the guesthouse, and well..." Branna lifted her chin and stood up straighter. "I have no family. Both my parents are dead. It's just me."

You could've heard a pin drop in the room when Branna dropped that bomb. Diane was visibly shaken, and had her hand over her mouth. "I'm so sorry, dear. I had no idea. Surely you have siblings or extended family?"

Branna answered as lightly as she could manage. "No, I don't. My family tree was pretty sparse. My parents were only children. No grandparents left. Like I said, it's just me." She swiftly changed the subject. "Ned, I am assuming that truck is full of furniture, and my car has my bags in the trunk. We should get that unloaded before it rains." She stood there for a moment as they all digested what she'd said.

Michael's eyes shot to his father when Branna had admitted to being an orphan. His da's face reflected his own. *Jesus, no family at all.* He wanted to kick his own arse, thinking back to that nasty comment he'd made in the pub. *Head toward Dublin and buy the first plane ticket back to your mummy and daddy.* She'd been visibly taken back by the careless comment, and he'd patted himself on the back. It never occurred to him that someone as young as she would have lost both parents. No brothers or sisters, either. God damn.

He stared at her now, willing her to look at him. She wouldn't meet his gaze. She was yammering on about where to put the furniture. *Look at me,* he thought. He felt his father put his hand on his shoulder. "You didn't know, son. She knows you didn't know."

The air shot out of his lungs in a rush. "Jesus, Da."

Sean just shook his head, "I know, son. I know."

CHAPTER 4

Branna hustled around the house busily putting things away. She'd insisted on carrying in her own luggage. She needed a show of independence right now. Sean and Michael were bringing in her furniture, putting the bed together and setting up the dinette set that Ned had provided. She was going through boxes with Diane that contained a small amount of dishes, flatware, a teakettle, and some basic cookery. She was desperately trying to not look at anyone. She could feel the pity rolling off everyone and it was about to do her in. Saying it out loud, that she had no one, was a rough thing for her to admit to herself, let alone a room full of strangers. She didn't want their pity and she didn't want to look weak, especially in front of Michael.

"We didn't know. I mean, I didn't know. My father might have, but he's never one for over disclosure." Diane was speaking gently to her as they worked.

Branna's face was kind. "Of course you didn't. How could you? No one did. It's just," she paused to find the words, "how things turned out for me. I'm ok, Diane, really."

"If you don't mind me asking, dear, how did it happen? You're so young to have lost both." Branna took a deep breath. "No, I don't mind. My father was a Marine, an Infantry Officer. He was killed in combat during the second Battle of Fallujah. He was in the worst of the fighting. It was several years ago, when I was in high school. My mother died nine months ago from breast cancer. They just didn't catch it early enough."

She noticed the men milling around, adjusting furniture. When she'd explained about her father, Michael froze in place, bent over one of the chairs. Now he was looking her way, standing still. She refused to look at him. She was ready to crack and she was not going to let him see her vulnerability. His father broke the tension.

"Well then, the truck's unloaded. I've texted Aidan and Patrick and they are getting Michael's furniture out of the garage." He said to Branna, "Two of my other sons."

She nodded, "Three boys and a girl, quite a handful."

Sean corrected, "Five boys, actually. Seany is still in school and Liam's off at University."

"Oh, my. Your daughter must be one tough cookie!" she joked.

"You have no idea. Just like her mother," Sean said with a smile. She found it interesting that he could be so commanding one minute, and like a sweet papa bear the next. She found that she liked Sean O'Brien, and hoped she could make a tentative peace with him. He actually had the same bearing as her own father. "Now then, Michael and I will go in Ned's truck and bring his furnishings back. It shouldn't take long, eh, Michael?" Michael had been quiet through the chatter, but she could feel him. She was keenly aware of him as he moved through the house.

"Yes, everything has been ready for weeks. It should only take a few minutes with the four of us working. Diane, thank you for all of this," he motioned around the house. "It's an odd scheme your da has come up with, but we'll try to make the best of it for now."

Branna looked at him, finally. His eyes were intense, too intense. She looked away before she spoke. "Yes, we will. We agreed to this and I suppose it's time to call a truce, at least for now." She gave Michael a brief nod and started working again. He was behind her, staring at her again. *Just go get in your car and give me some recovery time. God, just go!*

Sean cleared his throat and said, "Diane, let me walk you out to the car. I think Jack and Ned are waiting outside."

They both walked out, but she could feel Michael behind her. "Branna, I wanted to tell you that..."

She spoke over him. "It's supposed to rain later today, so you better go get your stuff. I have some items coming. It's not much, but I would appreciate it if you left some room for me. It's just three pieces of furniture and some personal items."

She was talking fast, afraid to let him speak. She could hear the remorse in his voice. She couldn't take it right now. She was on even footing when she was fighting with him, but if he was kind to her, she was going to break down.

"You had no way of knowing. I didn't take it personally," she finally said. "I'm the same person I was before you knew. It doesn't change anything. I'm fine. Just go. Everything is fine."

He was still standing there. She could feel him. "Look at me, Branna." This was the first conversation that he'd used only her first name. His voice was deep and gentle.

She exhaled, then chucked up her chin and turned. He was closer now and he was looking her in the eyes. *Jesus, did he have to be so handsome?* "I've got to go, but I'll be back. We need to talk about all of this. This situation, it's more than a little peculiar. I personally think Ned Kelly's gone round the bend, but if there's to be a tentative peace between us, we need to talk. I'm afraid we got off on rather a bad foot." Branna couldn't speak with him this close to her, so she just nodded. "Well, then, I'll be back in an hour or so and we can figure out where to put everything."

"That sounds perfect. I need to go to the grocery store. I don't have any food. I need a few things. You don't happen to have a coffee pot in that garage do you?" He didn't. Fiona had taken a lot of their household stuff. "Well, I can pick up a small coffee pot until mine gets here." She wiped her hands on her pants, nervous under his gaze. "Okay then. I'll finish up with this and be on my way as well. Are there any community boards around here or a local paper? I can't keep driving that rental. It's too expensive. I need to find a cheap, reliable car. I sold mine. It was too expensive to ship, and the steering wheel was on the wrong side, obviously."

She looked at him, all vulnerability gone. She was all business. Michael had watched her through the last two hours and realized that she wasn't uptight so much as controlled. She would give flickers of emotion but she clamped down tight on them, afraid to show any weakness. He'd already learned her body language to some extent. She had this way of straightening her spine, maybe to appear taller since she was a little wisp of a thing. She dressed very conservatively, maybe so that people would take her seriously. That's probably why she bound her hair up all the time as well. He'd thought her to be about twenty years old, but Ned said she was twenty-three. The only time she showed emotion was when she was pissed off. She shot that chin up and made eye contact, then. She was a fighter in her own way.

He remembered her question. *Jesus, no car and no food.* He hadn't let himself think of her as anything but a pain in his ass. She really was starting over. If he needed something, anything, he had dozens of people he could call. She had no one. Car rentals in these touristy areas were a dear price. It would be thousands of euro a month to keep that little car. When he'd heard that she'd paid cash for the house, he'd assumed that money wasn't an issue. He'd assumed, stupidly, that she had rich parents who were indulging their spoiled daughter.

He answered, "Yeah, I guess you will need something to drive. You will see a board at the grocer. I'll grab the local paper at my da's house. I'll call my cousin, Tadgh, as well, and ask my brothers. They might have heard of something."

She said, "Thank you. You have no reason to help me. If it will put you out at all, I can look on my own."

He answered, "It's no bother. You can't very well walk everywhere."

Just then Sean poked his head back in the house. "Your brothers have rehearsal at three." Branna loved listening to Sean's accent. It didn't hurt that these O'Brien men were so pleasing to the eye. She wondered briefly if all the O'Brien men were as good looking as these two.

They certainly didn't grow them like this in the states. She might have to get her friend Anna over here for a visit. Anna was renting and managing her North Carolina beach property. They'd been friends as children. Anna didn't exactly have a no-dating policy, but she had often remarked how she just couldn't find "that spark".

Military brats had it rough. Being around all that testosterone and Alpha males made normal men suffer in comparison. When a daughter's dad got up in rank, and she got older, the young, tasty Marines running around were off limits. This, however, was primo hunting ground. For Anna, not her. Nope, not interested whatsoever in sampling the local cuisine. Not at all.

She was startled out of her train of thought by a hand waving in front of her face. It was Michael's. "Branna O'Mara, are you in there?" She snapped to attention. "I'm heading off. I'll see you later unless I run into you at the grocer. I'll need supplies as well."

"Thank you, Mr. O'Brien, for helping today, for bringing in my furniture and everything. This has been an odd day. I know we are on opposing sides, but I appreciate your kindness."

"Call me Sean, dear. Odd is an understatement, but it wouldn't be very Christian of me to leave you to struggle on your own. Michael here has reason to be put out, but this is not your doing. It will all sort itself out in good time."

As Branna finished unloading the kitchen items and linens that Diane and Ned had lent her, she thought of her mother. How many times had they moved? Not a few boxes and a few pieces of furniture but a truck load of household goods. It always took her mother weeks to get unpacked. Half the time her father was whisked away on some training mission or sent off on a deployment soon after they'd relocated. Her mother had told her that it only took a few good fights for her dad to see reason.

They had begun downsizing all of their things when her mother was pregnant. The piles of dog-eared paperbacks, mismatched furniture from their younger years, chipped dishes, extra tables, old electronics, vinyl records and cassette tapes that were obsolete. It all went in a garage sale or to the dump. They used the money to buy her crib. After that they kept it manageable.

Branna had been practical about what she had kept. She'd used most the furniture from their house at the beach house. She left most of it and only chose a few items that she didn't want getting used and abused by renters. She had packed up the photo albums, some keepsakes from their travels, her grandmother's china and stemware, her favorite books, and her business files and supplies. She'd traveled with her medical records, her laptop, and her date book.

She brought two full suitcases and a garment bag and donated her lesser-worn clothing to a women's shelter. She could run almost everything involving the business off the laptop for now, but she needed to get the Internet set up. Her parents had taught her to hang on to quality, not quantity. That was going to help her in this small place, now that she had a temporary roommate.

Good Lord, what would her parents think of this? How had she gotten herself in this deep? This seemed like a sensible plan last month. Why in the hell hadn't she waited to jump on that plane? *Talk about a rookie move, O'Mara.* Her father would have never made such a stupid mistake. She should have stayed put until the deal was done. She'd gotten over excited, not kept her emotions in check, and she had impulsively set the wheels in motion. It never occurred to her that this mess was waiting for her. What was she going to do if she lost this place? She may have to settle for that little condo Tadgh was talking about. She might indeed have to go back to America with her tail between her legs.

She thought briefly about the handsome O'Brien cousin. *You should see it through. I think you could be good for this place.* She wasn't really attracted to Tadgh, not like she should be. He was a hottie for sure, but she didn't feel that initial whammy. She thought back to the one time Michael had touched her, before she knew who he was. That handshake was certainly a whammy. She shut down that train of thought quickly. She did know who he was now, and whammy or not, she needed to keep that apple up on the tree.

It turned out there was no grocer in Doolin. There was a Super-

Valu about fifteen minutes drive on the way to Ennis. She got a bag full of energy bars, coffee, and some basic staples, a little bit of dried fruit, apples, raw carrots, coffee and some ramen. She also picked up a cheap coffee pot. She eyed the meats, vegetables, and other real food, but kept walking. Cooking for one was a pain, and she had a lot of work to do.

The house needed some TLC as soon as possible, and she didn't need much to keep her going. She considered bottled water, but Ned had assured her the water from the well was "the finest sweet water she'd e're taste in her life". She also splurged on a little bottle of heather and rose bath salts. She was thinking about that big claw foot tub in her bathroom. *You are going to be having your little soak with a man in the next room.* That thought was more that a little unnerving.

She'd never had a roommate other than the three-week interim she had bunked in with Anna in North Carolina. She had certainly never lived with a man or done much else with a man for that matter. She had dated a little in high school and college, but nothing serious. She'd commuted from home, so the indiscretions and dorm room hook-ups had never been a phase for her. Then her mom had gotten sick, sicker, she corrected herself. So, her life by 23 had been pretty void of the roommate/boyfriend rotations of other young women her age.

This was going to be awkward not just for those reasons but because of the person himself. A full foot taller than her, masculine, and a job as a super-hero. This was the big league, and she had to carefully control her response. She didn't want to let her guard down in any way. She'd learned pretty quickly in her business that people underestimated young women. They also tried to take advantage of them. She'd learned that in Tampa with shady contractors.

She paid for her groceries, loaded them, and drove for home, mentally reminding herself to drop her records off to her new local doctor. She was very healthy, but she had some minor issues from time to time that required a visit. She hated going to the doctor but she hated hospitals even more. She'd found a local practice with a small office to see to her basic medical needs. Dr. Troy in North

Carolina had referred her to Dr. Mary Flynn and filled her in on Branna's history and her unique parameters for medical care, and Dr. Flynn had agreed.

So, all was well. She just needed to drop off her paperwork and get the introductions out of the way. She could do that tomorrow, however. Now she needed to get home and start working.

As she drove back to the cottage, she noticed a sign that read "Irish Linen". She stopped there briefly and spoke with the owner of the shop. She was a very sweet woman and very helpful. She seemed to genuinely enjoy helping her with her selections. She bought a lovely little squared tablecloth and some simple linen curtains trimmed with embroidery, perfect for the windows in the main rooms. The curtains were old and yellowed and needed replaced. She also bought some heather scented linen water for the curtains and her bed linen. She bought two soft, goose down pillows and made herself stop shopping. She was on a budget, after all.

As Branna pulled into her drive, she noticed two things. The truck was there and the front door was propped open with a kitchen chair. As she exited her car with her five bags of booty, she saw one man backing out of the truck with a sofa in hand. He wasn't Michael, but the coloring and general look were the same. He looked older and had the same military style haircut. Blue eyes were like Sean's. Strongly built, just as tall, but a little leaner through the face, his boyish features all gone. He looked up at her and grinned. He was drop dead gorgeous.

"Dia duit, Miss."

She smiled shyly. "Hello, Sir." The other end of the couch was surfacing at this point and a smiling younger man was tunneling out of the truck. He also resembled his brother, but his hair was a little longer and had slightly more auburn tones. He had a mischievous look about him and he was also a looker. That was some potent DNA.

"Oh, Sir is it?" The older spoke shortly in Gaelic to him. She didn't speak the language, but telling a little brother to shut his hole was clear in any language.

"You must be Michael's brothers?" They were grunting with the lifting. "Yes, you can call me Aidan. This fat headed lout is Patrick." Branna acknowledged them with a nod. "Well, then can I help you in any way?" she said as she watched them struggle. "No lass, just inch past us with your parcels. We'll handle this."

As she stepped into the house, she heard some rumblings from the other bedroom. Michael poked his head out, but said nothing. Another head popped into view and she was met with a cheery grin. "Well, hello there, Branna!" She was relieved to see a friendly face. "Hi, Tadgh, what brings you here?"

Michael surfaced behind him as Tadgh walked out to greet her. He gave them both a calculating look. "You two know each other?"

Tadgh laughed, "Oh, to be sure. Old friends, right?" he winked at her and she giggled. She noticed that Michael's brows were scrunched into a scowl. Maybe he thought everyone should ostracize her. "Relax, cousin. She came into McDermott's last night. Be careful of this one. Never trust someone that passes up free whiskey." The other two were carrying in the sofa and Patrick said, "Amen to that, brother. Blasphemy." Michael turned his back as if he was getting bored with the conversation. "Over trusting her won't be an issue. Don't worry on that account."

His words stung, even though she shouldn't care. She hid her reaction and walked to the kitchen. She set her bags down and walked toward her room. "I need to change out of these clothes. Thanks for your help, Tadgh, Patrick, Aidan." Then she waltzed past the men and closed her door.

She heard Tadgh say, "Do you have to be such a dickhead?" She covered her mouth, stifling a laugh.

Michael was ultra aware of Branna as she worked around the house. She had changed into some sort of track pants that were loose and rolled at the waist. She had on a little t-shirt that said Dropkick Murphy's and had a skeleton playing bagpipes. There should have been nothing extraordinary about this get up. She wasn't showing much skin, except a sliver of tummy when she lifted her arms. She still had her hair bound up at the base of her neck.

He noticed, as she worked, that long strands worked loose around her face and little baby curls around her neck as she began to perspire. He'd thought her a scrawny little thing in those tailored clothes she wore. He'd been wrong. Now he could see a very nubile set of curves were hidden under all of that starch. Round, shapely ass, smooth skin, and high, round breasts. He was trying like hell not to ogle her. He was sneaking quick glances when she was unaware. His brothers were doing a fare bit of ogling as well. Good thing she didn't have any Gaelic.

Branna was really trying to concentrate on her work. She'd unpacked her clothes, her groceries, and hung the curtains. Now she was wiping the sills and sweeping the front room. At first she could hear them putting the bed together, then moving furniture around the house. They were all speaking in Gaelic and she couldn't understand a word. It was starting to piss her off.

They knew she couldn't understand them. They could be planning to throw her body off the cliff or plotting their next move to get her out of this house. They could be having a frigging spelling bee and she wouldn't know the difference! Tadgh had left a little while ago. It wasn't just that she worried about what they were saying. They were deliberately excluding her and even though she shouldn't care, it chaffed.

As they came walking through the living room rattling on and chuckling to one another, she finally snapped. "That's it! I've had enough!" They stopped and looked at her, shocked at her tone. "This is my home too, buster." She was addressing Michael now, pointing a finger at him. "You don't have to like me, respect me, or trust me, but from now on you will speak English when you are here in my home with me."

She pointed at each of them as she spoke. "You jackasses know I can't understand you! You could be planning my death for all I know! It's rude! At least give me a few weeks to learn some Gaelic insults before you go chattering away in my presence. English, got it?"

At this point she was staring up at these three big men and each was wearing a different expression. Patrick looked a little scared and slightly amused. Aidan had his arms crossed loosely over his chest, with a grin and grudging respect plain on his face. Michael started to argue with her, but then someone started the slow clap…right behind Branna.

She spun around, surprised to find a small, middle aged, very beautiful woman in the open doorway. Behind her was Sean O'Brien. She had auburn hair and green eyes. It was obvious where Brigid and Patrick had gotten their coloring. *So this is the mother.* She walked into the cottage and spoke with a beautiful Irish lilt. "God bless all here." She had the sweetest smile Branna had ever seen.

In a flash, her face changed. "Now, you three!" She didn't point at them. She didn't have to point. They were practically standing at attention. "What kinda manners did I teach you to be rambling along without a second thought for the lass's feelings? And her just arrived here alone, with no kin or friends to aid her! This is a dreadful spot she's in, forced to live with a man she's ne'er met before. A man who then brings two more men over, and she can't understand a bloody thing you're saying!"

She got calm again. Branna wasn't sure which was scarier, angry or calm, but she liked this woman's style.

She turned to Branna with the sweet smile back in place. She offered her hand and introduced herself, "My name is Sorcha O'Brien, dear. These three wee mongrels are my sons. They'll be apologizing now, and will speak English when you are at home." She looked at the three men who topped their mother by at least a foot. They grumbled their different apologies. Well, two of them did.

"I'm sorry, Michael, love. I didn't catch that?" Branna looked at Michael and actually pitied him. His ears were red but his arms were crossed and his chin was up, a stance of defiance. His mother narrowed her eyes, hands on her hips.

He sighed, "All right, all right. English around the Yank." Branna wanted to smack him, maybe kick him in the face. Although, she'd need a stool, since the smug bastard was twice her size.

On an exhale Sorcha said, "Well now. How are you settling in here in our small town?" Branna was amazed how this small woman was able to command these four large men. Her husband stood grinning behind her. That said something. He didn't try to intervene when she was opening a can of whoop ass on their sons. Smart man.

Branna answered her a bit more weakly than she'd intended. "I am doing okay, Ma'am. Thank you for asking."

Mrs. O'Brien gave her a doubtful look. "Call me Sorcha, dear. I can imagine this has been a trying two days for you. I've heard all about what's happened, and I wanted to stop by and welcome you properly."

Branna smiled at the lovely woman. She was petite, with the softness of a woman that had carried six children. Not plump, but soft and beautiful, in a motherly sort of way. Branna noticed that her husband rarely took his eyes off her.

She continued, "Now, as for these three. Let's see. I missed most of it, I suspect, but Patrick was inquiring how old you were and whether you had a boyfriend back in the states. Though, I can't imagine why since he is getting married in a couple of weeks. Aidan was commenting on whether it was too late to get a third offer in with Jack, and move in with you, too. Then Michael said..." At this point both the brothers were rubbing their red faces and Michael cut her off. "Ma! Please."

Another sugary smile. "Well, lad. If ye won't say it in front of her in English, then don't go saying it in front of her in Irish. Get the picture?" The three said in unison, "Yes, Ma." As red as the men were, it couldn't hold a candle to Branna's face. She could feel it burning with embarrassment. They weren't plotting her death. They were checking her out! She wondered, in a flicker of curiosity, what Michael had said. He was quick to cut his mother off, before she repeated it.

"Thank you Ma'am, I mean Sorcha. I appreciate the gesture. I hope we can get through this whole ordeal without too much collateral damage to anyone. I really just wanted to come here and make a fresh start. I swear, I had no idea about any of this. I didn't mean to cause so much trouble."

She meant it. As the weariness of the last two days settled in, and her jet lag nagged at her, she really just wanted to crawl into her borrowed bed and cry. Sorcha put her arm around Branna and said,

"Not at all, dear. Let's stop all this and have a cup of tea. You look like you've been working a bit today, and the time change is probably catching up with you. If you're feeling up to it, stop by Gus O'Connors tonight and hear us play."

Branna marveled, "Do all of the O'Brien's play an instrument? Do you all sing?"

Sorcha laughed, and it was sweet and musical, "Of course dear, you're in Ireland now. Best learn to sing along."

After taking a few minutes to start the kettle and make everyone tea, she turned to each of her sons and kissed them on the head. They had to bend down to her, but they obviously knew the drill. Sean finally spoke, "Don't be late to rehearsal boys," and then offered his arm to his wife as they left.

CHAPTER 5

As his brothers left the cottage, Michael's palms started to sweat. Christ, he'd been so hell bent on getting this cottage. What the hell had he agreed too? Alone for three months on daily, intimate terms with a woman he didn't even know? He was trying to figure out how to start a conversation when she spoke. "You have a very big family." He nodded, glad for the distraction. "Yes, I suppose it would seem big. You've still not formally met my sister. I have two more brothers as well." She nodded. "You're lucky." That's all she said.

"Branna, listen. I do owe you an apology and not just for earlier with my brothers. I guess I never really took a minute to think about your end of things. Showing up here like you did, walking into this bloody awful screw up. You're no better off than I am, are you?"

She shook her head and sighed. "Well, I'm afraid I didn't take it very well. I know I kind of tore into you at the pub."

At this he laughed, "Kind of?"

She smiled and shrugged one shoulder. "My dad said it was my Irish temper."

He nodded thoughtfully, "Aye, I suppose I can't argue with that. I am sorry about your parents, too. It's a terrible thing, to lose them both so young."

She stiffened a bit. It was barely noticeable, but he saw it. He thought it best to change the subject. He clapped his hands together. "Anyway, I haven't had much luck with Tadgh or my brothers on a decent car for you. I did send a message to Liam at Trinity. He might know someone at the university looking to unload a car. Haven't heard back yet, but you never know."

Branna was glad he hadn't pried further about her family. "Thank you for that. I can keep the rental for five more days before I have to re-up. Hopefully I'll find something soon." Michael put out his hand in offering, "Will it be peace between us for now?" She gave it a firm shake, "Yes, for now." She felt that same thrill go through her at the contact. She tried for a quick release, but he held on to her. She looked at him and there was speculation in his intense gaze. *Do you feel it, too?* She felt a tightness in her lower belly.

Michael let her go and backed away just a bit. God, she felt achy. She wondered if she was coming down with something. She shook herself and readdressed him. "Will you be singing tonight? With your family, I mean?" she asked. He shook his head, "God, no. I'm knackered. I worked the night shift last night."

She'd forgotten, "Oh, yes. You must be. Knackered...tired or exhausted." She'd spoken her translation out loud.

He laughed, "Sorry about that. I agreed not to speak Gaelic around you. Slang, on the other hand, well I'm afraid that's here to stay." He was smiling, and there was no sarcasm or bitterness in what he said. It occurred to her that he could be quite charming, when he wasn't on the defense.

Suddenly, she felt a little guilty. "About that, Michael. I may have overreacted a little. I didn't mean to get you in hot water with your mom." She laughed a little at that. "I don't expect you to give up your native tongue just because some pushy Yank came on the scene. It's quite beautiful, really. I wish I knew it. I was just feeling..." she paused with a small smile. "A bit knackered myself. Tell your brothers, too."

Michael smiled widely, "See, you're catching on already." He rubbed his top lip nervously, "Listen, you had a right to be put out. I'd never have admitted that in a temper, mind you, but you were right.

We were deliberately alienating you and it was a shitty thing to do. I can't promise I won't slip into the Irish on occasion, but we'll try to give you time to catch up."

"I guess we are both going to have to check our temper. This is going to be an interesting three months." She said this with a wry grin.

He raised his eyebrows. "You think you'll last that long, do you?" He leaned in when he said it, a playful look in his eye.

She poked him in the chest, playfully this time. "You bet your ass I will, big guy."

He said, "Christ, you are going to be trouble."

* * *

As Michael took out the leftover stew his mother had sent with him, he could hear her in the bath. She was in that big tub. The house was small and he could hear the light splashes and whirling water. He could smell her bath water for God's sake. Roses and heather, he'd seen it when she'd unpacked her groceries. He could just picture her in there all pink and steamy, cleaning her body. All that long hair was probably swirling around the tub like something out of a mermaid tale. He heated the stew on the stove and stirred slowly as he set down some mental no-no's for himself. The number one rule was that the new housemate was look, don't touch. He probably shouldn't even look, unless he absolutely had to. As he thought about those big, stormy blue eyes, he knew he was in deep, deep shit.

Branna slipped into blissful peace as she let the scented water cradle her whole body. Traveling always made her feel achy and grungy. She'd briefly considered waiting until Michael was gone, but decided no. She was going to live with him for 90 days. She was not about to start bathing based on his work schedule. She could hear him milling around in the kitchen.

It was actually a curious feeling, being in the bath with him in the next room. She closed her eyes and saw his face, those intense blue, green eyes. She wickedly let her mind travel to his flat stomach and long, lean limbs. He always wore jeans but the ass in those jeans was tight and powerful. She wondered what kind of woman managed to catch Michael O'Brien's eye.

She was embarrassed to admit that she wondered what he thought about her. What would he think of her as she was now? She felt a tightening in her lower belly and tingling in her nipples. They were just at the water's edge and the mix of warm water and cool air made them tightened. She felt an ache in her hips and arched her back a bit. She realized, to her shock, that she was getting aroused. The marked lack of genuine arousal throughout her entire teen and adult life was why it was so shocking. Even during the fumbling good night kisses and embraces of her few dating experiences, she'd never felt that raw sexual stirring that her friends talked about.

Her friends often joked about what a prude she was. Little did they know. She'd never even touched herself, let alone let a man get that far. Man, she really was a prude. Nothing wrong with a little harmless fantasizing, though. The thought of Michael kneeling by the tub, and letting his hand slip under the bath water, was not helping bring her down out off the rafters.

The sane part of her brain was instantly horrified. She shot up out of the water and opened her eyes. What was she doing? *Holy shit, O'Mara! Your first night here and you start getting hot and bothered with him in the next room?* The room was chilly with the window cracked, and her bathwater splashed onto the floor. That cool breeze was enough to snap her back to reality. She was breathing hard and could feel the flush of her skin as much from the hot water as from her arousal. As she dried off, the rub of the towel on her flesh was making her feel worse, not better. What the hell was wrong with her?

She was shaking her head with her denials. *No, no. You do not want him. This is stress and fatigue and some sort of hormonal craziness that has nothing to do with your new roomie. Maybe it's jet lag,* she thought. *Does jet lag make you horny?* Regardless, she was not going to cozy up to the man that had just admitted he would never trust her. That arrogant jackass didn't deserve to be her fantasy man.

Branna sat one the edge of the tub and dried her hair, trying to recover from the storm she had brewing. She rationalized that she was, after all, a grown woman. She'd been put in this strange situation and although she had the no-dating policy, she still had the same base urges as any twenty-three year old female. She was a victim of some natural, unfortunate chemistry. It had nothing to do with Michael O'Brien and more to do with complete physical deprivation.

She had no parents, no siblings, no close friends, no lovers. She rarely had physical contact with anyone save the occasional handshake. This was all just new for her. She had been on her own for nine months and she was experiencing sensory overload, nothing more.

When her hair was finished, she braided it and rolled the braid up at her neck and bound it. She put on a pair of linen trousers and a blue button down shirt. She was ready to face what lie beyond that bedroom door. She was in control.

Michael couldn't believe how long the hair dryer went on shrilling from the bath. How much hair did that woman have? To his disappointment, she surfaced from her bathroom fully dressed with her dark hair neatly pinned. *Do you ever let all that hair down?*

The thought of all that long, silky hair tickling his body, or spread out wildly over the pillow was niggling at him. He envisioned long black tresses spilling down a pale, smooth, bare back and hips as they arched and curled. That thought went straight to his groin. He stared down, as if to command obedience. *Down boy. This is day 1 of 90 days. Not a good start.*

He watched her peripherally as she came into the kitchen. She was dressed in those crisp tailored clothes again, but something was different. His problem south of the border was not subsiding as she bent down with her ass toward him to grab something from the fridge. He was standing at the counter finishing up his stew and the kitchen was small. He looked away before she busted him checking out her ass. He moved over to rinse his bowl as she came up with some carrots.

The look on her face stopped him in his tracks. Gone was the steely ice princess. She was flushed, her eyes were a little dazed, and her pink mouth looked more pronounced. She looked at him and quickly away, like she was hiding something. Her breathing was a little erratic. Didn't that just crank up Mr. Happy?

God, she smelled good, too. Not just like the heather and rose bath water, but something womanly and all together appealing. She had a heat rolling off of her. *Christ, get away from her before you do something stupid.*

He washed the dish and quickly backed away. "I'm headed to bed. I need to catch up before my next shift."

She seemed to come out of the daze and said, "I just need to eat something, and I am headed to hear some music."

Michael looked down at what she was holding, an energy bar and a raw carrot. "Is that your dinner? How the hell do you live off that?"

She looked at it and shrugged. "It is perfectly nutritious." "Aye, if you're a rabbit." She rolled her eyes and began rinsing her carrot.

Michael paused before he went into his room. "Look, this is going to be awkward for a while. It's bound to be. We both just put our life on hold for three months. I just think…well, I'll play nice if you do."

She turned, and whatever daze had come over her earlier was nowhere to be seen. Her eyes were sparking. "Just don't worry about you over-trusting me, right?"

Michael sighed and put his hands on his hips, trying to reel in his temper. He was trying to keep things civil, but this woman was a pistol. "Listen, you don't understand," he started.

Branna gave a swipe of the hand. "I don't want to hear it Michael. You think you are some kind of victim here? Get the nails out of your hands, buddy." Her voice was starting to get louder. "You didn't put your life on hold. You'll go to work, see your friends, you'll have Sunday roast at your mom's house, just the same as you always have. You just ended up with an unexpected roommate. From where I am standing, you are making out like a bandit in this deal. Whereas, I could be tossed out on my ass at anytime. With the trend I've got going, I am probably screwed. So, spare me the sob story. You don't have to like me, but do not question my integrity. If you can't take me at face value, that is your damage."

She paused and noticed that Michael was still staring at the ground with his hands on his hips. She was prepared for his heated rebuttal, but he was quiet. He finally looked up and calmly said, "Are you finished?"

OK, not what she was expecting. She shifted her weight from foot to foot, "Yes, I suppose I am for now."

He folded his arms over his chest and raised his eyebrows. "Feel better?"

She thought on it for a second and let out a large exhale, "As a matter of fact, I do."

He nodded approvingly, "Good. You've got a fair bit of temper, haven't you?" Not waiting for an answer, he continued. "Well, I'm afraid you'll be in good company. It is nice to hear you use my given name as opposed to mighty King O'Brien, pretty boy, and…what was that other one? Oh yes, arrogant jackass." He smiled, "Although, I do like the sound of 'my Lord' or maybe 'my liege'. Yes, that would do nicely."

He was grinning at the mere thought of it when he got beaned in the back of the head with a carrot. Branna started giggling and his eyes went to her face. She was beautiful when she laughed. "Don't hold your breath, big guy," she jibed. He picked up the carrot and threw it back at her. "Take your rabbit food, ye little hellcat."

Michael was going to have to remember to listen to Jenny more often. She had warned him to handle this delicately. His first instinct had been to fire back at Branna, but he had decided to let her vent. She was probably as tired as he was, if not more so, given the time change. She was angry and scared. The fact that she was spectacular when she was angry was cranking him up even more. His long shirt was hiding one hell of a hard on.

If he let loose, he might just close in on her and take her in his arms and let her feel what she was doing to him. Once she knew how he was responding to her, he would certainly lose the moral high ground and she wouldn't feel safe. He had to quell the feelings she was stirring.

Now that he was alone in bed, he was able to rethink the entire episode and realize that he had acted correctly. As soon as she had vented her spleen a little, she seemed to calm down. She'd even been a little playful, throwing that carrot at him, and that laugh. Jesus, she lit up the room when she laughed. It was sweet and mischievous.

He really needed to detach himself from this situation. It was only the first night and he was already letting her get in his head. She was also affecting a less intelligent organ that had a tendency to get most men in trouble. As if to make his point, his partner in crime was still hard as a rock. Jesus, this was the first night. How in the hell was he going to do this for three months?

* * *

BRANNA HAD ENJOYED the drive to town. It was only a few minutes but she needed to roll the windows down, feel the cool air, and be alone to clear her head. She didn't know why she had been spoiling for a fight with Michael. He'd actually made an attempt at an olive branch. Truth was that fatigue coupled with sexual frustration had made her edgy, and she had taken it out on him. Maybe she was hoping he would fire back, insult her, and give her a reason to stay pissed at him.

He hadn't reacted that way at all. He had given her a little space, and let her get it out of her system. Whether it was a strategy or just the fact that he was also tired, she was glad it hadn't escalated. Three months of this was going to be torture if she didn't find something to do. She needed to work. First thing on the list tomorrow, get the internet up and running at the cottage.

Gus O'Connors was hopping tonight. Branna managed to find a seat at the bar only because some tourist with a chivalrous streak had given up his seat. He wasn't hitting on her in exchange. As a matter of fact, she was getting a reading off him that was "no girl's allowed" and he seemed pretty close with his traveling companion. She bought them a drink and started chatting with them. Alex and James were their names. They were taking a flexible thirty-day holiday around Ireland and Italy. Alex was gorgeously Mediterranean and James was preppy, pretty-boy British. Yep, definitely not interested in her. Well, that made things easier, actually.

As she nursed her club soda, and they drank their Hendricks and tonics, British pretty boy James spoke. "So, let's hear it darling." Branna looked at him questioningly. He looked at Alex, "Oh, a challenge. Spill it, sister. Your story, your tale of woe. Don't leave anything out." Alex rolled his eyes, "Don't start James. You're being nosey."

James gave a distinctly British *humph*. "You know better than to doubt me, I can see it plain as day. Her body language, dressing like she is 40 years old instead of like the hot twenty-something she is. Displaced purposely. Ooh," he turned to Branna, "is it a stalker? Did you flee from love gone sour? Changed your name, dyed your hair?"

Branna burst out laughing, "Is he always like this?" Alex smiled, "Actually no. Most people bore him. He is actually very perceptive." James nodded, "See, you shouldn't doubt me. So what is the stalker's name?" Branna laughed and shook her head, "Sorry to disappoint. There is no stalker."

"Oh, no. A much sadder tale from what I hear." The voice came from behind them. The tone was saccharin sweet with an underlying bitchiness. Branna turned to see the pretty red head from the night before, with the same steely green stare and menacing grin. "The way I heard it, she's run from America to start fresh in our little town. Little Orphan Annie is it?" Branna stood up to face her. The woman was several inches taller than her.

"Excuse me, I am not sure we've met? Since you think you know all about me, then I am sure you know my name. I didn't catch yours?" There was no mistaking the bridled aggression in Branna's tone. James whispered, "See, this is why I stay away from women, too scary." Alex shushed him.

Fiona stepped inward and motioned the bartender. "Whiskey, neat." Jenny, the barmaid looked at her with distaste, but she got her a drink. "My name is Fiona, and you, little Annie, just happen to be shacking up with my husband." A whistle came from behind Branna. "Didn't I tell you?" James said to Alex. Alex shushed him again.

It finally soaked in what the woman had said. "You're Michael O'Brien's wife?" As if on cue, she heard the baritone voice behind Fiona. "Ex-wife, thank you. You can go now, Fiona."

Fiona turned that acid grin on him then back to her. "Ah yes, St. Michael divorced me when I didn't live up to his high standards."

"Annulled, not divorced," he bit out. "Oh yes, you are right." Her tone was mocking. "Let's not anger the church in all of this, my mistake. Well, little Branna. It seems your dance card is quite full this evening. Two tourists and two O'Briens. Tráthnóna maith, Tadgh." She nodded over Branna's shoulder and Branna turned to see that Tadgh had indeed joined the party.

He was looking back and forth between her and Michael, ready to intervene if he needed too. She could take care of herself, however. She needed that to be heard loud and clear.

She turned back to Fiona. "Well, as much as I have enjoyed the local soap opera, you can leave me out of it next time. Oh, and Fiona?" she leaned in close. "Call me Little Orphan Annie one more time and you will be looking up at me from the floor. Do we understand each other, darlin?" She rolled her r's, just like the natives.

Fiona seemed a bit rattled, then quickly recovered. "Feisty, aren't you, wee one? Michael always did like the feisty ones. Be careful though, he bores easily." With that she strode away. As she left, she ran her arm over Tadgh's bicep and he maneuvered away from her touch.

She turned back to the three men. Alex grabbed James from his stool and muttered something about needing to go have a smoke outside, offering the other seat to Michael. Branna took Alex's hand. "It was nice meeting you. Where are you staying?" She was delighted to hear that they were staying at the Killilagh House. "Here, take my card. If you boys want to meet up again I could sure use the company." Alex took the card and kissed her on both cheeks. James did the same and whispered in her ear, "You bet your ass, darling. I want a full report." She whispered back, "Very long story and very G rated." He gave Michael a once over, then Tadgh. He exited with another little humph and a look that said, *Yeah, right.*

Michael was watching the exchange with a stern expression. Who the hell were these guys and why was she so chummy with them? The last thing he needed was her bringing a man back to the cottage. God, he hadn't even considered that. What if she started seeing someone? She also seemed pretty cozy with his cousin.

As if on cue, Tadgh spoke up. "What brings you here, cousin? Can't sleep?" Branna added, "You really should sleep. You shouldn't go on duty sleep deprived." Michael bristled, wondering if they were trying to get rid of him. "You two hens can quit pecking at me. I have the next two nights off unless there's an emergency."

Jenny approached. "A pint of Creans, thank you Jen." He looked at Branna's drink. He picked it up, sniffed it. "Soda water? Christ, that won't do." Behind her Tadgh said, "This one owes me a drink, don't you lass?" Branna said, "I guess I do, don't I? Jenny, get this boy a whiskey, please." Tadgh put his head back and laughed, "Oh no you don't. You know exactly what I mean. You're supposed to let me buy you a drink."

He turned to Jenny. "Make that two and put them on my tab." Branna shook her head, "I don't think I am ready to go that local. Jenny, what do you suggest?"

Jenny smiled warmly at her, "Smart move, girl. You've gotta keep your wits with these O'Brien boys. How about a pint of Bulmers? It's a hard cider."

Branna smiled back at her. She liked Jenny. "Cider sounds wonderful." As she looked at Michael, she was startled to see that he was giving Tadgh the stink eye. *What? Am I supposed to be on the shit list for three months?*

"So, why are you out tonight? Did you come to hear your family play?" He took his drink and lifted it to them both.

"Slainte." They clinked glasses. "Yes, for a bit. I couldn't sleep. I also wanted to let you know I got a text from my brother up at Trinity. He has a German friend that is headed home. He is looking to sell his car quickly. Liam said it's in good shape. It's an older Volkswagen Passat. He is willing to hold it for two days, but then he has to sell it elsewhere. The price seems pretty fair."

Branna perked up. "Oh my, that sounds perfect. I'm afraid I don't know much about cars. I can head out in the morning. Hmm, I guess I can take my rental, drop it off in Dublin instead of Ennis, take a cab to the college. I guess we need to go to the title bureau. Is that what you do here?"

Branna was starting to talk fast, mostly to herself, running through her options. All of the sudden her train of thought was lost with a hand on her arm. "Relax, Branna. I can take you tomorrow. You can't just drop your rental off, and assume this is going to work out. Leave it here, I will take you and we can spend the day up there sorting it all out."

She gave a sigh of relief. "Thank you," but then the wheels started turning again, "I don't want to put you out, Tadgh. You don't to want spend your whole day off…"

He cut her off, "Yes, indeed. Spending the entire day with a beautiful woman, instead of lying around my flat doing the wash. Now that is a hard decision."

Branna looked at him, chewing her bottom lip. Tadgh asked, "You're not used to asking for help, are you?" She shook her head. He cocked his head, grinning. "It's no bother."

During this exchange, Branna could feel Michael beside her. His silence was palpable. She turned to him and he had a grim sort of look on his face that she couldn't read. She put her hand on his forearm. He was solid and warm. The touch didn't lose that electricity she felt whenever they made contact, but she fought to keep her bearing.

"You don't know how much I appreciate this. I know we got off on the wrong foot. You didn't have to help me." She looked directly into his eyes. "Some people would tell you not to lift a finger to help me get settled. It was more than I expected and I'm grateful. Even if this car doesn't work out, I'm grateful."

He said nothing. Her hand on his arm was firing off nerve endings and he was momentarily struck stupid. Her genuine gratitude and those blue eyes. Tadgh was right. She was independent and she wasn't comfortable asking for help, but when she got it, she was gracious. The fact that she might be frolicking around Dublin all day with his cousin shouldn't bother him. Really.

She set off something primitive and territorial in him that needed to be stifled. He shouldn't care that she was sitting with two men when he walked in. Her growing friendship with Tadgh should not get under his skin. He should shut the fuck up right now, but he wasn't going to. Nope, because he was an idiot. "Tadgh, I actually need to make a trip up to Dublin. I haven't seen Liam in a while. I'll take her. I have the day off as well."

Tadgh started to argue, but when he looked at his cousin, bells started going off. He'd seen that look before. O'Brien men were alpha to the core. He knew, being an O'Brien himself. It had killed him to tell Michael about Fiona, but he'd had to do it. Michael didn't blame him but the fact that his wife had turned her affections in Tadgh's direction was a wound in and of itself, a deeper betrayal than some random affair.

O'Brien men didn't share. He wasn't sure that Michael realized how territorial he was acting over Branna, but it was there. Michael was looking at him, and he knew if he argued, a rift would start between them. He looked at this wild-eyed beauty and actually considered throwing down the gauntlet. He looked back at Michael, "Aye, well then. I'll let you handle it. If it is ok with Branna, that is. Probably best, since you know more about cars than I do."

Branna's heart was pounding. She noticed that her hand was still on his arm, a heat thrumming between them. She closed her eyes a second, getting overwhelmed by his closeness. She jerked her hand away and looked at him. He watched her hand as it retreated. Then he took a sip from his pint and looked at her over the rim.

"I guess it's settled then, if you're sure it's not too much trouble. You need your sleep. You were up all night and all day," she said.

"I'll do. I'll head home after the first session."

Michael and Tadgh went to the back where the musicians were getting ready and Branna grabbed a table near the performing nook and waved Alex and James over to join her. They sat with their gin drinks, smelling of expensive cologne and cigarette smoke. "So, any blood drawn with the red haired witch or did she stay gone?" Branna blushed. "No, she left. It's really nothing. Hard to explain actually." James gave her an impatient look, "We're on vacation for a month. Spill it, Branna. Why are you shacking up with someone you obviously don't know, but should definitely be shagging, and why was queen twat face calling you little Orphan Annie? Bravo, by the way. You stood your ground with her quite nicely. If you kick her ass, I want ring seats."

Branna sighed. She really didn't like drama, but since it was her story, it really wasn't gossiping. She gave them the abridged version of everything. The death of her parents, her lack of family, the move, the real estate debacle. When she finished, both the men were dumbstruck. Alex looked at James. James mocked in his best female American accent, "It's really nothing," then looked back at her. "For fuck sake girl, you are like three Oprah episodes all rolling at once."

She put her face in her hands and groaned, "Don't remind me." Then she straightened up, kicked her chin up and looked at them both. "Look, things didn't turn out the way I thought they would. I am twenty-three, alone, and surviving. I'm fine. No one needs to feel bad, do a fundraiser, or plan an Oprah interview. A lot of people have it worse than I do."

Alex's face softened. He took her chin in his hand and said, "You are very brave. Smart and brave and beautiful. I think you are correct. You are doing fine. James, he is very un-British. He has a flare for the dramatic." It was James's turn to talk. "He's right, you know. Given all that's happened, I'd put my money on you. You're quite the little ass kicker, aren't you?" Branna smiled at this. She put her arms around both of these new unlikely pals. "Thanks, boys."

In the back, Tadgh and Michael were helping everyone move their gear, get the music in order and doing what O'Brien's do. Arguing. Brigid was at the top of the heap, "Michael, come on. You don't want your poor, pregnant sister driving all the way to Dublin alone do you? I need to buy stuff for the baby. They don't have anything around here and you know I hate shopping in Shannon."

He was getting annoyed. Mostly at himself, because she was starting to wear him down. He had a hard time telling her no. Just then Patrick piped in. "Don't let her fool you for a second, Michael. Finn offered to take her next week. She just wants to pry into that little American's head for a few hours."

Brigid was the picture of innocence. "I'll do no such thing. You won't even know I'm there." She smiled beatifically.

Next, Aidan chimed in. "Christ, Michael, do you remember when ma was pregnant with young Seany? Piss stops every half hour. Don't do it, man. You'll not get to Dublin until nightfall." At this everyone started laughing, including Brigid.

"Nice try, lass," was all Sorcha would say.

Michael headed back into the pub thanking the good Lord for lots of brothers and only one sister. Women were master manipulators. He loved Brigid more than himself. Knew her as well as his own soul. Twins were like that. He just didn't need the extra stress of his nosey peahen of a sister tagging along. As he went into the main pub area, he caught sight of Branna with the two gentlemen from earlier. A surge of jealousy went through him.

What was wrong with him? She was nothing to him. If she wanted to flirt about with half the county, what was it to him? He looked around for somewhere to settle when he heard a whistle and his name. It was the darker of the two men waving him over. Not sitting with them would be rude, so he gritted his teeth and smiled. He sat across from Branna between the two men as the musicians began to warm up. Brigid and his mother were on vocals and fiddle. His da and Tadgh were on guitar with Patrick on piano. Aidan was filling in for Robby on the bodhran, though he usually played guitar. It was nice to see his brother up there. He didn't get to visit from the North very often. Between deployments and his regular duties, family had to come second. It was probably why at thirty-one years old, his brother had never married.

Branna asked, "Are they all O'Briens?" He went through the list explaining the others filling in due to Robby having the flu and Jenny tending bar. "It must be wonderful to come from such a big, musical family." She said it lightly, but he saw a hint of sadness in her face that may not have been noticeable had he not known her situation. Before they could say anymore, the show started. They started off with a few well known tourist favorites. "Whiskey in the Jar" had everyone singing along.

Branna was mesmerized as she watched this big family play so effortlessly together. The music was full of emotion and these musicians knew their trade. Sean quieted the crowd and spoke. "Many of you locals know that it's not very often we get the two eldest O'Brien brothers on the same stage. Michael with the Coast Guard and our eldest, Aidan up in the North."

Several of the patrons let out a whoop and whistled. "We are blessed tonight to have Aidan home from Afghanistan, and God be praised, he is safe and whole." Branna's eyes shot to Aidan and then she turned to look at Michael. His eyes were burning with emotion as he looked at his older brother. Pride, relief, and a touch of sadness. She'd felt every emotion that she saw in his face. He looked at her for a brief, intense moment and then back to the stage. The crowd was going wild. Sean continued, "Michael, lad. Come join your brother on stage for a song."

As Michael walked up, Sean handed him a guitar and whispered something to him. Patrick stayed at the piano. Aidan took Tadgh's guitar and Brigid took one of the mics, leaving her violin on the chair. The crowd was ecstatic, especially the locals, to see the siblings together again. *This is what it was like to live in a small town your whole life,* Branna thought. The ties to the community were deep. They celebrated, they mourned, and they worshipped together. One girl yelled from the audience "Are they both single, then?" Everyone laughed and the two brothers blushed, tuning their guitars. It was Sorcha's time to talk to the crowd, "Oh, aye love. They're single, to be sure. I'll be interviewing after the last set." This was followed by more laughter.

Branna loved how they interacted and teased with the audience. Then everything got quiet. Aidan and Michael looked at each other, a silent communication going on between musicians, and started to play. Patrick came in on the piano. She knew this song. Mary Black had done a version of it. She loved it.

It was about lost childhood, youngsters put to work in the coal mines, but also a coming of age song. The time to set aside the books and make your way in the world. It was a deeply moving song. For the first time, she got a good look at Brigid standing up. Her clothes weren't as loose, and she noticed that she put her palm protectively over her abdomen. She was expecting. When Brigid started to sing she was magnificent, but when Michael blended in with that smooth, deep baritone, it was all she could do to not burst into tears.

School days over, come on then John
Time to be getting your pit boots on
On with your sack and your moleskin trousers
Time you were on your way
Time you were learning the pitman's job
And earning a pitman's pay.

The song continued as they put the audience under their spell. She watched with an ache in her chest as Michael's mouth moved, his fingers stroked, and his voice coiled around her in a dreamy state of pleasure and pain.

Come on then Dai, it's nearly light
Time you were off to the anthracite
The morning mist is on the valley
It's time you were on your way
Time you were learning the miner's job
And earning a miner's pay

She couldn't take her eyes off of them. Michael and Brigid blended their voices together so beautifully. It was as if they were one person. Aidan bent silently over his instrument, so in tune with the others. His guitar glided effortlessly, as it accompanied Michael's beautiful playing. She watched his long, strong fingers over the strings. Patrick was at the old piano, playing it by memory, head tilted up and eyes closed. He never missed a note as his equally long fingers stroked the keys. She had often wondered what it would have been like to have a sibling.

She felt James's hand on her shoulder. "Oh, darling. You are in trouble." She closed her eyes and let the song fill her. She instinctively moved her fingers on the table, in time with Patrick, as if she were playing. God, she missed playing with her dad. The song ended and the silence remained for a split second. Then the pub went berserk. Michael, Aidan, Brigid, and Patrick all stood and took a short bow.

Then they went to each other and huddled, their heads together in silent benediction.

Sorcha looked on with unshed tears filling her eyes, as Sean kissed the crown of her head. Branna could feel the tears start rolling down her cheeks and she couldn't take it, she really couldn't. She excused herself quickly, kissed her two new buddies on the cheek, and fled the pub.

It was raining again as she hurried to her car. She was fine. Everything was fine. She had a long day tomorrow. Time to head back. As she pulled out, she saw the silhouette of a man in the pub entrance. It was Michael. She gunned it and headed toward the water, toward Burren Way. She was feeling weak and weepy and there was no way she had the strength to put on the tough guy act right now.

CHAPTER 6

She pulled into the little cottage driveway and got out of her car. She breathed deeply of the rainy sea air. She went inside and everything was as she had left it. This was home. It was still hard for that to register. *But for how long.* She changed into a t-shirt and boxers and pulled her hair out of the pinned up bun. Her tears had ceased as soon as she'd started driving. She just needed out of that room, away from that big, loving family.

She loosely braided her hair as she looked out the window. She loved rain and it had picked up since she left the pub. A thought struck her and she acted on it before her logic took over. She grabbed some flip flops and sprinted out the front door into the yard and adjacent field. She giggled loudly as she sloshed through the rainy grass. This is what she needed. She spread her arms and let the rain drench her whole body. She let it tickle her tongue, peck her eyelids and then she put her arms down and walked. Not so far that she couldn't see the house, but enough to lose herself in the dark, wet night. Her flip-flops were squishing in the turf and everything smelled clean and new. She walked until she felt better, washed clean and ready to face life again.

She turned around when she started losing sight of the house and road. As she came closer to home, she crossed into the house's small garden. She smiled up at the night sky and ran her fingers through her hair. She was still alone; Michael's SUV wasn't there. She put her arms out and slowly twirled, losing herself in the dizzying pleasure. She was completely soaked and she felt so alive and free. It was enough for now. She had regained some balance through this unlikely baptism.

As Michael watched the strange girl through the window, he was completely fixated. She obviously hadn't seen him get dropped off, too lost in her solitude. She spread her arms and let the rain consume her. Just a small t-shirt and some thin shorts, he could see every wet contour. You could have transplanted her back a thousand years, a black-haired, pagan beauty dancing wild and uninhibited under the stormy sky. She was stunning.

As Branna walked into the cottage, she let out a yelp, startled to see Michael standing by the window. "I didn't see your car," she said breathlessly. He walked toward her like a big cat. He was holding a towel. He carefully wrapped it around her shoulders. He was careful not to touch her more than needed, but it made her heart pound. She wiped her face with the edge and simply said, "Thank you."

"My brother asked to borrow my truck tomorrow. I figured we could take your car to Dublin." She nodded dumbly. He'd been watching her. He didn't attempt to hide it. It was a little unnerving. What would he think of her childish display? He spoke softly. "You left in a hurry. Didn't you like the music?" She looked at her feet when she answered. "No, that's not it at all. It was beautiful. The way you all blend together, it was very moving."

She paused and then looked up at him. "I'm glad for you, Michael. I'm glad he's home and safe. I really am." She was talking about Aidan of course and her voice was at the breaking point. He didn't have the heart to push her. She wanted her pride and it was a hard thing to talk about for obvious reasons. "You're lucky," she said.

He smiled sadly and answered, "Yes, I suppose I am." Then he took a strand of her long wet hair in his fingers. "You're soaked to the bone, girl." His smile held a little bit of chiding.

She just looked at him, dazed at the intimacy. "I like the rain."

Michael was closer to her than was wise. She smelled like fresh rain and shampoo and earthy female and he was way, way too close to her. Her stray lock of hair was thick in his fingers. He wondered what the rain tasted like on her skin, in that little curve where her shoulder met her neck or in the curvy swell of her lower belly. He was assaulted with images. His mouth moving all over her, him kneeling down as he explored her rain soaked body. He knew his lust must be showing in his face. Her breathing was erratic and he looked at her mouth. Her gorgeous, little mouth. Then he noticed the shivering and snapped to attention.

"You're shivering." He tightened the towel, his desire extinguished as he noticed her chilled condition. He told her to sit on the couch.

"I'm fine." He just gave her an impatient look, so she obeyed. Not part of her nature, but she was actually a little chilled. She heard him put the kettle on. Then he walked over and started up a fire in the main hearth. After it started going, he went into her room and started one there as well. "It gets cool after sunset, even in late summer. You have to listen to your body." *Oh, I'm listening. It isn't asking for a towel.* She was tingling and her heart was racing.

She sat in silence, watching him work. She should be paying attention to the way he lit the peat so she could do it herself, but her eyes kept getting stuck on his biceps and traveling over that strong back as he worked. She heard the kettle start screaming and decided to be useful instead of meat gazing on her roommate. She jumped up right as he popped out of the bedroom and ran smack into his chest.

He caught her at the small of her back, then he hissed. She looked down and she was standing on his toe. Just as she went to lift her head again, she popped him in the chin. She backed out of his embrace and covered her mouth. "Sorry! Did I hurt you? Oh God, I am clumsy aren't I?"

He rubbed his chin and looked at her with a grin. "You are dangerous, I'll give you that." She noticed his eyes flare as he looked at her below the neck. She had shed the towel in the tussle and her t-shirt and shorts were clinging to her and really transparent. "I'll just go put some dry clothes on!" and she shuffled to her room, leaving drip marks across the floor.

Michael tended to the herbal tea, trying to collect himself. It was late and they had a long day ahead tomorrow. The thought of spending the day in the car with Branna O'Mara left him with mixed feelings. They had not even spent one night here together, and he already found it hard to stay pissed at her.

He wanted this cottage. Now that it was warm and filled with furniture and he could hear the rain on the roof, it really felt like a home. He should not be helping her. She was an obstacle, but every time he was near her, watching her, he felt a pull that had nothing to do with the cottage.

On cue, she walked out of the bedroom. She had oversized men's flannel pajamas on. Instead of the neat, tight little bun at her neck, she had a loose bun on top of her head with little wisps sticking out that were still damp from the rain. He wondered, with a stab of jealousy, who's well worn pajamas she was wearing. She had a tank top under it, since the front dipped down so low. The sleeves and legs were folded over numerous times.

"Is this ready?" she asked, referring to the teapot. Michael nodded and she poured both of them a cup. She handed one to Michael and he plopped a cube of sugar and a splash of milk. She added a little milk to hers as well. They stood on either side of the counter and sipped in silence.

She broke the quiet, "Thank you for the fire in my room. I guess I need to learn how to work with turf."

He shrugged, " There's not much difference, really. Just watch me next time."

She looked around the cottage and sighed. "It's hard to believe such a large family lived in here," she said.

He nodded, "Yes, we're spoiled, I suppose. Everyone is used to grand houses with four water closets. Things were simpler. Children worked, played outside, and slept four to a bed."

Branna set her tea down and looked at him, "You have a big family. Do the O'Brien's live in a castle or did you have to share a room?"

He laughed at this. "It's hardly a castle, but big enough. Brigid was the only one that got her own room, being the only girl. She made a grand show of it too. Big signs saying *no boys allowed."*

Branna giggled because his accent got thicker as he told the story. "And did you obey the sign?"

He shook his head, "God, no. We might have left her alone if she hadn't been such a braggart about it. Aidan picked the lock. We defaced her posters with mustaches and crossed eyes. Another time we glued her perfume bottle lids on, hung her teddy bear from a light fixture with a suicide note. All in good fun."

Branna was laughing at this point. "Well, then. I consider myself warned. I'll hide my teddy bear when I leave!" He grinned over his tea.

"So, that's quite a get-up for bedtime. Steal them when you left an old lover, did you?" She could feel his gaze.

"How do you know the lover didn't leave me and forget the pajamas?"

He looked at her intensely. "Not possible."

She suddenly got very warm. She briefly considered messing with him, but she told the truth. She plucked at the sleeve where they were starting to wear. "Nah, nothing so interesting. They were my dad's. He didn't really wear them that often," she blushed. "They were his slumber party pajamas."

Michael cocked his head for her to elaborate. "That's what we called it when I got to sleep with my parents. You know, every once in a while, or at hotels, that sort of thing. Apparently pops slept in the buff, normally. He couldn't very well be bare-assed with me in the bed, so these were his slumber party pajamas. It sounds stupid, I know. I just...well, I just kept them. I couldn't keep everything, but I kept these." She shrugged and took another sip of tea.

Michael felt guilty in the wake of her story. He had assumed they were some old boyfriend's. She was young, but old enough to have had a few lovers come and go. Honestly, he had such a big family that it wasn't natural to put himself in her shoes. He remembered looking down from the stage, watching her fingers beat out the tunes on the table. He reached across and took her fingers gently. "Is he the one who taught you to play?"

She was surprised, both by the contact and the question, "How did you know?"

"You're a musician. You watch hands, not people. You watch the hands on the instruments. You tap along with your fingers on the table, I saw you while we played." He had dropped her hand by now and she pulled it away.

"I used to play. Daddy taught me some and I also had lessons. I played for years. I stopped when..."

"When your da died?" he asked, gently.

She answered, "No, about five months later. It was my first recital since his death. My mom tried to keep everything normal; I kept going to school, taking lessons. Anyway." She swiped her hand across the air. "My recital came, I played, everyone clapped. Then came time for the parents to give their child a bouquet."

She sipped her tea and he suspected she needed the moment to rein in her feelings. "One at a time the moms and dads would come up, hug their kid, and hand over the flowers. My turn was coming up and I looked out at the audience to see my mother. She was stone faced, gripping my bouquet, and her hands were white. She usually walked up with my dad. He usually carried the flowers. She just sat there terrified, like this was the big reminder that she was on her own with the kid. No back up, no partner. So, she did it. She got through the ceremony with robotic precision, we went home, and she went straight to the bathroom and threw up. She said it was the cookies at the recital. I knew it wasn't. So, yeah. That was when I quit performing. I had to give my piano to a friend when I came here. I couldn't afford to bring it and, well, I haven't seriously played in years."

Michael stood there, cup in hand, not sure what to say. He noticed that she, too, acted with robotic precision. The more tense the situation, the more she clamped down on her emotions. She seemed to only cut loose when she was angry. He heard her sigh.

"Don't pity me Michael. I'm fine. You asked, I answered. It isn't a big deal."

He finally spoke, "You say that a lot."

"Say what?" She said defensively.

He answered softly, "That your fine. Everything is fine." She finished her tea in one gulp and said, "That's because it is. I am."

She rinsed her cup, set it in the strainer, and said good night. "I have one errand to run in the morning on the way out of town. We should get an early start." She stopped at her doorway, holding the knob. "Sleep well, Michael. Your music really was beautiful. Your voice, it..." She couldn't find the words, or couldn't say them. So, she just shrugged her shoulders, "Anyway, I'll see you in the morning."

As he finished his tea and rinsed out the dishes and kettle, he could hear her milling around in her bathroom. She was getting ready for bed. This was getting so complicated. It was starting to feel like some big cosmic joke. He'd been married before, but he hadn't had a female in the house that wasn't kin for a while. Fiona was nothing like this woman. Branna was courteous. She cleaned up after herself, thanked him for little things, she didn't go nuts if there was a few minutes of silence. She also seemed oblivious to how beautiful she was. Fiona used her beauty like a weapon. He shouldn't compare the two, but he kept doing it.

He flashed back to her standing in the rain, arms out stretched, the pale column of her neck exposed as she took the falling rain on her face. All he could think about was that rain-slicked body, so uninhibited. She was so controlled, tight knit, all business every time they had met. It seems it was a learned behavior. She'd lost a lot, and this defense mechanism is probably what kept her upright. The wild child lifting her face to the rain, she was the real Branna. He couldn't get that woman out of his mind as he lay in bed, waiting for sleep to claim him.

He hadn't been with a woman in almost a year. He'd had a couple of random hook ups after the annulment had gone through. One was a co-worker, after too much drink. It was mutually enjoyable, no strings sex. She had transferred since then, but even before so, it had been a one time thing and more than a little awkward in the harsh light of day. The second was a German tourist who, although a zealous bedmate, had been an empty, anonymous hook-up. Both times he had been with someone, it had left him feeling empty and slightly regretful. He had plenty of friends who operated like that for years. Sex for the sake of sex. It just wasn't in him. He needed more than a temporary release.

He hadn't felt the self-imposed celibacy to be all that difficult. He really hadn't felt that spark of mutual attraction until now. He knew it was mutual to a degree. He doubted she was cursed with the same unending arousal that was currently plaguing him. He did sense she was stifling a hint of attraction toward him, however. It was completely inconvenient of course, considering she was so near but so unavailable. The contrary little hellcat had come into his life at precisely the wrong time and for the worst of reasons. He fell asleep determined to keep his distance, and figure out how to come out on top in the war for his cottage.

Branna lay in bed, staring at the ceiling. What a strange feeling, knowing that there was a man, a stranger in fact, that was sleeping in the same house. She had been shocked two fold when she came in to find him there. For one, she thought her little jaunt out into the rain was her own private, guilty pleasure. Secondly, she was so used to solitude that it would have shocked her regardless. Having another human around, as she settled in for the night, was going to take some getting used to.

She hadn't meant for her life to take such a lonely direction, it just worked out that way. Now it was normal for her. Walking in the front door with a giant male looking back at her was something she never expected. The fact that said male was primo eye candy was beyond inconvenient. How does a woman with a no dating policy end up living with a smoking hot, Irish Coastie in the blink of an eye?

It briefly occurred to her that she was dreaming. Maybe she would wake up on the airplane headed to Dublin, and she'd find out this was a figment of her overtaxed imagination. No such luck. She had thought that many times during her life, *maybe I will wake up from this awful nightmare and dad will be here. Maybe mom will be alive.* She was done fooling herself. Life had handed her yet one more shit sandwich, and now she had to eat it. Although, life could be worse. She hadn't lost yet.

She was living in Ireland rent-free for at least the next three months, and Ned was awfully fond of her. She would not go down without a fight. And if a certain set of dusty blue eyes crept into her thoughts, she would quell the distraction. Feelings could be suppressed. She did it every day.

She thought she'd glimpsed a little heat in his eyes when he'd stood so close to her. He definitely noticed her see-through, rain soaked attire. She could feel her cheeks flush with embarrassment. The more she thought about it, though, the more she realized that he was simply baffled at what she had been doing. He probably thought she was some nutty, eccentric American.

From the looks of his ex-wife, he liked them leggy and edgy looking, not runty, brunette, and reeking of inexperience. Not that she cared in the least. She knew what she looked like. She wasn't unattractive, but she wasn't remarkable. She had her brains, her determination, and her dad's fighting nature. She was doing ok on her own. The fact that her roomie revved her engine was a distraction she could manage.

* * *

BRANNA WOKE TO A STRANGE FEELING. She'd slept heavily and it took her a minute to realize where she was. She came slowly awake to sun shining through small windows. The rain had stopped. It was stuffy in her room. Late August was warm in Ireland, at least during the daytime. She struggled to get the archaic window hardware to work, and managed to pry open the window to catch a nice breeze. She opened her bedroom door and peeked out. She needed to start coffee before she tackled any part of this day. She didn't hear Michael, so she figured the coast was clear. She shed her pajama top, leaving herself in a tank top.

She was warm from the stuffy room and the big quilts that Diane had lent her. She tiptoed out to the kitchen and immediately opened some windows and propped open the front door, then she started the coffee. She stood, staring at the pot, willing it to go faster so she could have a cup. She missed her pod coffee maker, the perfect invention for a single caffeine addict. She stretched and rolled her neck to get the kinks out and hoped the coffee vapors would start waking her up.

Michael came to stand in the front doorway just in time to see Branna stretch like a little cat. She was petite, but as she arched her back she let out a high-pitched little squeak, he could see the finely toned arms and shoulders. He remembered her shapely little legs from the night before. Under all those starched, matronly outfits, Branna O'Mara had a heavenly little body. It was soft and curvy and shapely. She was obviously fit, but womanly where it mattered.

She arched and he could see a hint of flesh at her belly and she had round, high breasts that were perfectly proportioned to the rest of her. She pulled out the crazy bun on top of her head and his heart nearly stopped. Long, silky, waves of hair that stretched to the small of her back. In the sunlight that was coming through the window, he could see that it wasn't truly black. It was very brown to the point of appearing black, with sparks of copper and gold, so subtle as to be missed when she kept it bound. To his disappointment, she was merely rearranging it and swept it back up into another tight knot.

"I thought I was going to have to scold Ned about the mice, but I guess that little squeak came from you." She jumped with another little squeak, which was perfectly adorable. He wondered what other little noises she could make, before reminding himself just why he had taken an early morning run. He was a young, virile man who was well familiar with the morning erection. This morning, however, he was not able to talk his partner in crime into behaving.

Not particularly fond of cold showers, he opted for a run. Sunny with a cool breeze, there was plenty of fresh air to clear his head. Coming through the door to a lovely, little, squeaking feline was going to put him right back in the red zone. This moody little hellcat was staring at him, brow crinkled, with her hands on her hips.

Branna's heart was racing for two reasons. Number one, Michael had surprised her by not being in his bedroom. He appeared behind her and scared the crap out of her. Number two, he was sweaty and shirtless. He had on navy blue running shorts with the Irish Coast Guard emblem on the thigh. Part of her had harbored a hope that he had some sort of physical flaw. What she had seen thus far was impressive. Now with short socks, running shoes, and silky shorts, there wasn't much left to check out that wouldn't require an R rating. He was beautifully made, broad, long and muscular. He wasn't overly muscular or ripped in that scary way that some athletes can be. His skin was smooth and it rippled beautifully over all of his muscles, but he looked healthy.

A do-gooder, beautiful voice, handsome face, and now confirmation that his body was re-God-damn-diculous, she was trying hard not to ogle him, and the only default switch she had was aggression. Time to flip the bitch switch.

"You shouldn't sneak up on people! You scared the crap out of me!"

Michael was taken back a little by her hostility. Not upset. Nope, that would have been too easy. His brief surprise turned into a laugh. "Prickly, prickly. More like an angry kitty than a mouse. Did you sleep poorly, then?"

Branna smoothed her hair down nervously and said, "No, I slept fine. I'm just not particularly civil before my first shot of caffeine."

"Okay, I'll remember that bit of advice," he said. He was still grinning and she wanted to smack that mocking little smile off his pretty face.

"Do you run every morning?" she asked. He walked into his room and grabbed a towel as he answered. "No, I'm afraid I'm not that disciplined. The small station in town doesn't have a gym, like the one in Shannon. I have to squeeze a run in a couple of times a week."

"So, a rescue swimmer? That's a pretty tough job, hardcore training. You must be fast in the water," she said. She tried to hide some of the awe in her voice. He was cocky enough.

"Yes, well the training was pretty intense. I was convinced after a while that the only way they were going to promote me was if I actually drowned."

She nodded, "Yes, my dad used to talk about the US Coast Guard.

He said the hardcore guys were the rescue swimmers. Balls of steel, I think was his description."

Michael was grinning."Well, that's quite a compliment coming from an infantry Marine. They are pretty much the measure for steel bollocks. Aidan has worked with them before. He's had nothing but good things to say."

She nodded. "Yes, they do make an impression."

She poured a cup of coffee, sniffed, sipped, and sighed. Michael laughed, "Better?" She just wiggled her eyebrows and took another sip. "It doesn't work that fast, you know. It's all in your head, woman," he teased.

She just swayed her little hips over to the pot and patted the top. She spoke in a perfect Irish accent. "Don't listen to him darlin, you know mother loves you."

Michael barked out a laugh and shook his head. "That was fine, lass. Might make a local out of you yet. We'll just have to start scouting out another house for you."

With a devilish grin, she turned and sashayed off to her room. Still in a thick brogue, "Not on yer feckin life, lad," and closed the door. She could hear him laughing through the door.

Branna came out of her room dressed per usual. Lightweight khakis, sensible shoes, button up blouse. "Do you own a pair of jeans? I thought all Americans lived in jeans." Michael commented.

She bristled a little. "What? This is perfectly comfortable. Besides, this is business. I need a car, and if I show up looking like a teeny bopper, he is going to try and screw me."

Michael raised his eyebrows, "Yes, well he is about your age, so you might be right."

She blushed, "That's not what I meant. I mean swindle, try to get more money, or sell me a lemon."

He looked at her appraisingly, "So, you think by dressing conservatively, he'll take you more seriously?" He shrugged, "Interesting theory. Never really thought about it."

She gave him a patronizing look, "Well, that's because you don't have to. You're big and male. You don't come from a position of weakness. Not that I am weak, but being small, young and female doesn't exactly inspire fear or respect. It's just how the world works."

He talked as he started rummaging through the fridge. He pulled out an arsenal of ingredients. He started the kettle and worked with efficiency making a mammoth breakfast. Branna watched as he put some butter in a hot skillet, cracked two eggs and salted them. He put two slices of bread in the oven to toast. He sliced some cheese and nibbled on it while he worked. She was shocked to see a man work so well in the kitchen.

"That is quite a spread. Do you cook a lot?"

He looked at what he was making. "Most of the time. When I'm on a long shift at the big station we take turns cooking."

Branna nodded, "Oh, like firemen."

"Exactly," he said. "You don't know how to cook?" He eyed the dried apricots she was munching on and scrunched up his nose.

"Of course I can cook. I'm a good cook, actually. I used to cook with my mother. This is just easier. Cooking for one is kind of pointless when this gives me what I need."

He turned his eggs gently, "Yes, but this is tasty. I can throw a couple more eggs on, it's no trouble."

She smiled, "Well, I've never had a man offer to cook for me, so that is tempting. I'm fine, though. This will do. I need to make a phone call before we go."

Branna called the local Internet provider and scheduled installation for tomorrow. This no Internet thing had to stop. She needed to be able to use her laptop, not just her phone. The international cell phone plan wasn't working out, so she put down a reminder to check into a local carrier. She grabbed her medical records out of her brief case and the keys to her rental. She had all of the bank info to wire money for the car if it was a done deal. She came out to find Michael freshly showered, wearing an NUI-Galway t-shirt and a faded pair of jeans.

"I need to make a quick stop before we head out of town. Do you know where Dr. Flynn's office is?"

Michael answered her with a strange look," Yes, she's the local family doctor. Are you sick? Do we need to postpone?"

Branna answered, "No, not at all. I just need to drop off my records and introduce myself. My stateside doctor set me up with her. I'll be quick."

As they walked to the car Michael walked to the driver's side and noticed that she did too. "Your name isn't on my rental contract. I need to drive," she said.

He gave her a chiding look. " God, woman. Don't you ever break any rules? You don't know where you're going. It'll be easier if I drive. You can see the countryside, tap on that little phone, make your deals." She was biting her bottom lip, nervously. "Don't be such a control freak. Give me the keys," he said.

"I'm not a control freak," she mumbled, and handed him the keys.

Michael and Branna pulled into a small office building off the main road. The sign said Dr. Mary Flynn, MD-Family Practice. Michael noticed that his sister's car was parked in the lot. "I'll come in too, that's Brigid's car. I just want to make sure that she's here for a check up, and nothing is wrong."

As they entered the office, there were two people seated and a child running around whining about there being no toys. Brigid was at the reception desk. Michael stealthily approached. Branna wondered what he was doing. The nurse was speaking, "You'll need to empty your bladder so we can get a good, clear look."

Michael popped up and scared the crap out of his sister. "Caught you red handed you little sneak!"

Brigid squealed and then hit him with the clipboard she was holding. "Don't sneak up on people! Christ, you'll put me into labor!" Branna suppressed a giggle.

"So, does Finn know you're here doing an ultrasound? I thought you two had decided it would be a surprise?"

Brigid scoffed, "He decided. I agreed to no such thing."

Michael smiled wickedly, "Oh, so you won't mind if I ring him and tell him what you're doing?" She smacked him again, "Don't you dare!"

He smiled gently at his sister. "All right then, but you better tell me afterward." He took her small head in his palm and kissed her cheek. Then he patted her tummy. "You're both fine?"

"Yes, deartháir, both fat and happy. Don't you worry about us." She stroked his face as she spoke.

Branna stood quietly, waiting for the receptionist. She felt a strange longing in her chest as she watched them. Michael turned and spoke to her, "Branna, you've not met my sister officially. This is Brigid."

Brigid's hair was auburn like her mother's, but her face looked exactly like Michael's. "Hello, Brigid. I'm glad to finally meet you. I'm afraid you didn't see me on my best day when I first came to town."

Brigid laughed, "Not at all, you seemed to be doing fine to me. So how are you settling? Is he behaving himself?"

Branna laughed, "Hardly. Total trouble maker."

Michael feigned offense. "Well, it takes one to know one, aye?"

Brigid looked between them. "Well, Branna. I know my twin better than any other living soul. If he gets too fatheaded, you ring me. He has a few chinks in his armor."

Branna was startled. Brigid looked from her to Michael. "You didn't know? Michael didn't tell you we were twins?"

Branna shook her head. Brigid said, "Yes, well he isn't one for over-disclosure. Now, I am assuming you didn't just come to spy on me. Why are you here?"

Michael answered, "She just needs to drop off her papers."

The receptionist brightened, "Oh, Ms. O'Mara? We've been waiting for your arrival. I can take those and get you set up with an initial visit. Does this week work for you?" Branna was pleased, "Oh, that would be great. Thank you for getting me in so quickly."

As Brigid kissed her brother goodbye, Branna started toward the exit, not wanting to intrude. Brigid whispered to her brother, "Getting along better, I see."

Michael put up his hand, "Don't go getting that mind working overtime. She needs a ride to Dublin to check out a car. I wanted to go see Liam, it worked out for both of us."

Brigid thought on that for a moment, "Yes, a car. I suppose she can't keep the hired car. Christ, she really did start over didn't she? The poor thing." Then she pointed at her brother with a stern look, "Don't you go making trouble for her. I heard all about her parents. Jesus, can you imagine? She's got no one left. I hope you get the cottage if that's what you really want, but go easy on the girl."

He answered her with a bit of an offended tone, "I'm taking her up to Dublin, aren't I? I'm not a demon, Brigid."

She laughed. "Demon no, but you've got a Mullen's temper and you are stubborn as on ox." He just gave her a look that said *Pot calling the kettle black?*

Branna took a seat in the car just as Michael came out. He dug through his sister's back seat and came to the driver's side with a little bag. He sat and she immediately smelled something heavenly. "Did you just steal food from your pregnant sister?"

He smiled devilishly. "Steal is such an ugly word. Besides, they're still hot." He sniffed the bag. "Ma bakes early Monday morning. It's no big deal. She'll give Brigid my share."

Branna just eyed him and gave a *hmph*. Her eyes lit up when she saw what he pulled out. Fresh, warm scones. Those apricots barely held her over. "You are a spoiled momma's boy," she said.

He took a bite and just moaned dramatically and started pulling on to the road. "Help yourself."

She just looked ahead, "It's ok, I'm…"

He finished her sentence, "Fine. Yes, I know. So you keep telling me. Just eat. Your little dried up figs aren't going to hold you until lunch."

She acquiesced, grabbing a warm scone. "They were apricots," she mumbled. She took a bite and a little moan came out of her.

He turned to her, "Good?" Michael was driving while she ate her scone. He polished off two more. He said, "You know, when a man makes you both squeak and moan before lunch time, you should thank him." She was taking a sip of coffee when he said it, and she suddenly choked and spit the mouthful all over the dash. She was covering her mouth, shaking with laughter. She started dabbing the coffee with a tissue from her purse.

She took a deep breath, collecting herself and turned to him. He had his eyes on the road, but was wearing a very satisfied smile. "Thank you for the scone, Michael."

He looked away from the road, to her, and his eyes were bright. He had the look of a little boy who was being naughty and liking it. "You're welcome. I was starting to think you didn't know how to laugh."

She shrugged, "Don't sound so surprised. Now, since you are at the wheel and I have a good signal, do you mind if I do a little work? If it bothers you I can wait."

"No, go ahead," he assured her. He was secretly relieved that they would have a distraction, not needing to talk the whole way.

Branna took the time during the ride to do some business. Her phone didn't get reception the whole time, but she managed to get some calls made and some e-mails sent. "Ok, so out of the candidates which has the greatest need?"

Michael couldn't hear the other person, so the conversation was one sided. "Ok, out of those three, who is getting help from other non-profits? Really, all three? Hmmm, it sounds like they are covered. I honestly don't know if I will be able to keep this going without the fundraising. This money may be it. I have to make sure it makes a difference. I guess I will just hold on to the funds. I don't need to make a move until the end of the year. The right case will come along. I just don't think these are it. Ok, thanks for all of your hard work, Brandy. Please tell Gia I said thank you, too."

As she hung up, she felt a little awkward. Michael was looking at her, "So, was that your banker? Shifting your millions around?"

She knew he was joking but she explained, "Hardly. That was one of my volunteers. I run a small non-profit charity for wounded Marines. I started it a couple of years ago. We are down to a finite amount of money, and I'm not there to fundraise anymore. I want to make this last bit count. I just haven't quite figured out who to give it to."

He nodded, "So it's not your millions, it's millions in donations?" She laughed, "Not quite. Some of it is from fundraising, some from my rental incomes."

"So, what does this charity do for these wounded men?" He seemed genuinely interested, so she continued. "Well, my first case was a Marine who was a double amputee. One loss was below the knee and one below the elbow. The arms are rough. The prosthetics nowadays are excellent, but your fingers and hands are so crucial to daily life. The VA takes care of a lot, but the government can be slow. I helped the family alter the house a bit to make things easier. We've done everything from adapting the TV remote to changing the shower. Another man was a big bike enthusiast. He lost a significant amount of hearing, in an IED explosion, and his right foot. He wanted the independence of riding again. We got him a modified touring bike."

Michael was appraising her, listening intently. "You keep saying we? It's you, though. You are getting these things for them, right?"

She blushed, "No, not really. I mean, yes. I put up funds. I also fundraise in the different communities, but I have volunteers. I don't have enough revenue to hire people, but I do get help. There are a lot of good people out there, you just have to ask."

"So, are you stopping?" he asked. Branna sighed, "Yes, I'm afraid I have to. We did a lot of good in small ways. I just can't keep it up now that I am not there. It's ok. It was something I needed to do, but I am ok with moving on. There are a lot of veteran charities in the US. My little bit won't matter."

"You're wrong about that. It mattered to those men. Men who wanted to take a shower without asking for help, or wanted to ride a bike, again. What you did mattered to them. You should be proud. I know if something happened like that to my brother, it would be quite something to have the Branna O'Mara's of the world lining up to help him."

Branna blushed under his praise. "Well, thank you. I hope so. Now, I have to make another call if I can keep my signal." As she tapped on her phone, Michael wondered why someone who did such nice things was hesitant to take praise for it. Then he thought about himself, Aidan, and his da. They were all public servants in some way. He remembered a time or two having a grateful parent or spouse embrace him and praise him for a rescue he'd done. It embarrassed him. He was doing his duty. So, in a way he understood. As he was thinking on this, Branna started talking on her phone.

"Yes, hello Ned this is Branna. Oh, I did. I slept very well my first night. Oh, I think he did, too. We are headed to Dublin to look at a car. Yes, well the reason I was calling was about the cottage." This perked Michael's ears up. "Right, well you cleaned it up very well and I am using all of the items you let me borrow. My stuff should be here this week. Oh, thank you Ned. I was wondering, though. Would you mind if I painted a little while the warm weather is still here?" She paused to let Ned talk. "Oh, no I can get the paint and supplies. I have painted at my other properties. The house is one story, so it shouldn't be too difficult. I just thought since I have this time, I could get working on it." She said her goodbyes and ended the call.

As she hung up the phone, Branna was smiling. He'd been so kind to her and he seemed overjoyed that she wanted to clean up the exterior paint. As she looked up, Michael was staring ahead. His jaw was tight, his knuckles were white and stiff on the steering wheel. "Is there something wrong?" She was taken back at the look he gave her. He was visibly pissed. "Good Lord, what have I done now? What's with the evil eye?"

His mouth twisted, "As if you don't know."

She sighed, "No, I really don't. You are obviously in a snit about me calling Ned. What exactly is your problem?"

He gritted his teeth, "I don't get in snits."

She motioned to the mirror. "Take a look, Michael. Total snit. Now, how the heck did you go from calm and cooperative to fighting mad?"

Michael was fuming. She was playing the innocent, but he knew exactly what she was up to. Three years with Fiona had taught him a lot about how cunning women can be. "Did it ever occur to you to consult me before making any changes to the cottage? You don't own it, and as far as I'm concerned, you never will."

Her jaw dropped. "Who's making changes?" She started stuttering. Now she was getting upset. "Would you scream foul play if I cleaned, weeded the flower beds, washed the windows? Painting is maintenance. The outside is peeling like crazy. It should be done before the season changes. Maybe the fact that you don't own a home is why you don't understand."

This pissed him off even more. "Don't give me that shite, little girl. You think I don't understand what's involved in owning a home, but I do. I'm a grown man, for God's sake!"

Now it was her turn to get pissed, "First off, don't call me 'little girl'. It's demeaning, just as you meant it to be. Secondly, just because both your balls have dropped, it doesn't mean you know how to care for a home! If the paint gets too old, it is bad for the exterior. The paint isn't just decoration, it's protection. It is long overdue, and it looks like hell from the road."

He cut her off, "Oh for feck sake. I'm in the Coast Guard! You think I've never painted a ship before? You think I don't understand the concept? We just paint because we want our boats to look pretty? Who is being demeaning now? I'm not an eejit!"

His voice was loud and his accent was so thick she had to concentrate to understand him. "You and I both know that you are manipulating that old man. Unlike you, I have a job. I would have gotten around to the painting, but I just so happen to be spending my day off driving your conniving ass to Dublin!"

Branna flinched as if he'd struck her. She quickly looked out the window so that she could collect herself. She was close to tears, and she would not cry in front of this prick.

They were almost to Dublin. If she hadn't needed him to drive the other car back, she would've pushed him out the door while they were still moving. "I'm sorry I inconvenienced you. It won't happen again," she said calmly. "As for the paint, it's happening. Since you are positive that I will be kicked out on my conniving ass in three months, you can rest easy knowing that you got a free paint job."

At this she pulled headphones out of her purse, put them in her ears, and plugged into her phone. Michael let out a big sigh. "Bleeding Christ, Branna. Branna!" She didn't answer him. He slammed the steering wheel with this palm. She didn't even jerk. She had completely shut down.

As he pulled into the car park, near Trinity College, Jenny's initial advice rang in his head again. He'd handled that as indelicately as he could have, short of pulling over and tossing her out of the car. *How can she get under my skin so easily?*

The truth was, she was right. He hated admitting that, but nothing she had said about the house was incorrect. It should be painted before the season turned. If she was really being sneaky, she wouldn't have made the phone call in front of him. She'd just pissed him off with her condescending comments about him not knowing how to take care of a house.

He had to admit that it irked him that she'd taken the initiative. She was certainly showing Ned that she was serious about owning the place. He had all kinds of ideas; he'd just let her get the jump on him. He hadn't anticipated the little hellcat being so ambitious. The house aside, he had acted like a prick. He'd yelled at her, tried to intimidate her with snide comments and body language. Now she was leaned against the window sleeping, looking like an angel, and he was awake and feeling like shit for how he'd treated her.

Michael texted Liam and sat in the idle car. He noticed she was stirring and wrinkling her brow. He thought she was waking up, but she looked uncomfortable. She started twitching and making little mewling noises. He was starting to think she was dreaming, not waking. He could see her breathing was speeding up, her hands fisted. He leaned over and gave her a gentle nudge, "Branna, we're here."

She shot upright and her eyes popped open. She jerked away, back against the window. "Branna, it's me." He was trying to speak calmly, because she looked completely freaked out and confused. He reached carefully over and pulled her earphones out. She was becoming aware, remembering where she was and who she was with. He could see the quick transformation. She began to slow her breathing. "Are you all right? I think you were having a nightmare."

She shook herself once to wake up completely, and then lifted her chin. "It was nothing." She smoothed her hair back. "I don't even remember what I was dreaming about. I'm fine."

How he hated that bloody sentence. She was still pissed at him, and there was no way she wanted to look weak in front of him, but she didn't look fine. She was also lying her ass off about not remembering what she'd dreamt about, but he decided not to push her on it.

Before he could say anything else, she spoke. "Is that your brother and his friend?" He looked at the direction she'd indicated, and it was indeed Jehns and Liam. They both got out of the car, and for the next hour she didn't even look at him.

CHAPTER 7

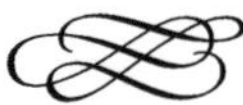

To Michael's surprise, Branna handled everything herself. She asked the right questions, test-drove the car, talked figures. Liam's friend told her how he had handled it all, being a foreign citizen, all the logistics of transferring the title and getting licensed. She took notes, paid attention, and even managed to get him to lower the price. She was impressive to watch in action. Like a businesswoman, she maneuvered the deal, giving a little but ultimately getting everything she wanted. She was leaving with Jehns to take care of the transfer of title and money wire. He didn't particularly like how the guy was checking her out, but Liam seemed to trust him. He sat there like a piece of useless luggage. Before she left, she approached him.

"We've come to an agreement. You can leave whenever you want. I'm sorry you had to waste your day, but I'd appreciate the help getting my rental back to Doolin." She barely looked at him. He knew that she resented needing him. Right about now she was wishing she'd let Tadgh bring her. He could see it on her face, and it needled him for some reason.

Tadgh would have taken her to the college, showed her the Long Room and the old texts. He would have been funny and taken her to lunch. He'd probably be in her knickers by nightfall. Women loved Tadgh. Instead she'd been stuck with him, the divorcee with a temper problem.

"I'll stay until you're finished. I can catch up with Liam for a while. I'm not in a hurry and you can follow me back," he said. She still wouldn't look at him. *Look at me,* he thought. She didn't.

"Suit yourself. I'll try to be brief." She turned to Liam and smiled weakly. Unlike with Michael, she met Liam's eyes. "Thank you, Liam. The car is perfect and you have no idea how much I appreciate your help. I hope I can come back and tour your beautiful college. There's a lot to see around here. I just need to come back another day." What she meant was that she needed to come back without his prick brother. Michael knew it, and so did she.

Liam answered her, being his normal carefree, charming self. "Not at all, Branna. Glad it worked out for both of you. Jehns is a good sort. He'd not sell it to you if he didn't think it was a good car. Let me know when you come back to Dublin. This crabby bastard doesn't know how to show a girl a good time. I'd love to show you around town."

Branna's smile was warm and sincere. Michael was fighting the urge to put an elbow to his brother's nose, which was insane and inappropriate on a lot of levels. Christ, she was closer to Liam's age than his, and Liam liked more experienced women. Aaaaand he was going to stop thinking in that bloody direction right now.

Branna was trying to keep it together. She was trying so hard that her joints were starting to hurt. She was tense and miserable and really felt like heading to Temple Bar to get drunk. Not that she drank, but she sure as hell felt like it right now. That awful fight in the car came out of nowhere, and then she'd had that awful dream. Her dad was drowning. She was watching as Michael tried to pull him out of the water. He kept slipping out of Michael's hands and he finally went under. Michael looked up at her and said, *Sorry lass, your three months is up.*

It was one of those awful dreams that a shrink would have a field day analyzing. She was ready to jump out of her skin. She didn't want him to wait for her. She wanted to be alone. She half considered just leaving from the bank and texting him.

What an awful day. She didn't even get to see the college or walk by the River Liffey. *This wasn't a date or a sight seeing trip. You can come back. This was business.*

As Liam spoke with her, she could feel Michael looking at her. She needed to exit. "I may just do that Liam. Thank you. I don't want to leave Jehns waiting, so I'll be off." She turned and briskly walked to the car.

Liam whistled appreciatively. "She is a looker, isn't she? I can't believe your luck, you prat." Michael looked at him, incredulous. "What the hell do you mean, luck? This is a bloody nightmare!"

Liam nodded. "Yes, you seem to bring out the worst in each other. Tadgh was practically drooling on the phone when he was talking about her. Just because she thinks you're a shit, doesn't mean she's all bad."

Michael swiped his head back and forth, "For God's sake, who's side are you two on? She's trying to steal my house!"

Liam looked at him like he was an idiot. "Let me get this straight. You get to live rent free for three months in a cozy little cottage with that," he pointed in the direction they had gone, "smart, gorgeous, young chippee and you're bitching like someone's put you out? You've got your eyes on the wrong prize, brother."

Michael stood there clenching his jaw, arms folded over his chest as his brother rattled on. "Do you think she likes younger men? Your loss is my gain. She's open season. Christ, did you hear her make that deal? She was brilliant." Michael was getting irritated, but if Liam noticed, he ignored it. "Tadgh said she has a sweet little ass under all those starchy clothes. Think she's free for dinner?"

Michael snapped. "For the love of Christ, would you shut your gob!"

Liam didn't seem surprised at his outburst. As a matter of fact, he seemed satisfied with himself. He'd been trying to get under his brother's skin. "I knew it! You're not as immune to her as you're pretending to be. Jesus, Michael. When you said you were driving her up here instead of Tadgh, I figured you two were getting on. What the hell happened?"

Michael rubbed his face and let out a tired sigh. "I'm sorry for snapping at you, Liam. We got into an argument on the way here, something about the house. I may have overreacted a little." Liam gave him a doubting look. "Ok, a lot. Christ, she just shut down on me. She wouldn't look at me, put her headphones on and shut down the rest of the way here. I wasn't totally in the wrong, you know!" He knew he sounded defensive.

Liam said, "Well, you've got more experience in these matters than I do. What would Da do? After Ma lambasted him, o'course."

Michael knew what he'd do. He'd apologize. Even if he was right, he would apologize.

Liam continued, "Right. Da was ever skilled at avoiding war in the cabin. Your problem is that you're too much like our dear mother and that crazy twin of yours. The difference is that you're a foot taller and about 9 stone heavier, and you probably came off like a bully."

Michael just nodded. Liam was right. Liam nudged him, "Time to kiss a little ass, brother."

Branna finished up all of her business in about 90 minutes and drove back to Trinity to drop off the young German at his student flat. After thwarting his efforts to get her to stay and party with them tonight, he texted Liam and told him they were done. Right after, she received a text from Michael. Two words: *Don't leave.*

Damn it. She didn't want to see him right now. She was excited about her new car and she knew that if she saw him, she would get upset all over again.

She texted him from the front of the building. *You don't have to babysit me. Keep the car for the day and leave when you like.* Her phone immediately started ringing. She considered not picking up, but that seemed immature and bitchy considering he had blown a whole day up here, and had found this car for her.

She answered, "Michael, you really don't need to..."

He cut her off. "Branna, stay in front of the building. Do not leave."

She disliked his commanding tone. Before she could argue, he came out the door and was getting in the passenger seat.

She looked straight ahead. "The car is still in the garage. Just pull around," he said. She did and brought him alongside her rental car. She put the hazards on and they both got out of the car. She left the engine on and her door ajar, wanting to make this short and sweet. He started fumbling with the keys and said, "Let's get a late lunch. Do you want to eat before we leave the city, or stop on the way back?"

She answered, still refusing to look at him, "I can eat a protein bar. I just want to get back."

Silence. "Branna, look at me." Chin lifted, she turned to him. "Let's just go get a bite to eat, I know you're upset with me," he said.

She stiffened. "I am not upset. I'm tired, Michael. I wanted this day to go differently, and now I just want it to be over."

He ran his fingers through his short hair, "Branna, pouting at me is not going to help the situation."

She glared at him, "Is that what you think this is? Pouting? God, you are so arrogant!" She stood up straighter and put her hand out, "Give me the keys, I need something out of the trunk."

He noticed her eyes were welling up and this conversation was not going how he'd planned. He handed them to her and she snatched them away before he realized his mistake. She jumped in the new car, locked the door, and eased down the window a couple of inches. He was cursing as she threw the keys out the window. They clinked to the pavement, then she sped down the road without a word.

Michael sat in the rental car trying to slow down his breathing. His crucial error was belittling her feelings with the pouting crack. Rookie move considering he had already been through one divorce. *Annulment,* he amended. She was hurt and she needed her pride in tact. He had done nothing but make the situation worse.

Now he was sitting alone in her rental car. He looked down and cursed again. There was her stupid protein bar, her coffee thermos, and her phone charger was sticking out of the outlet. If she ran out of battery, she wouldn't know how to get home. He slammed his palm on the steering wheel until it was throbbing.

As Branna drove through the city, she finally let the tears come. God, she was such a sap. At least she hadn't broken down in front of him. His fat ego would've loved that. He would probably think she was trying to manipulate him with big crocodile tears. She slammed her palm on the steering wheel. She took a deep breath and wiped her face.

It was done. The one big thing she needed to get done was finding and purchasing a reliable car. She was grateful for his part in it all. She just couldn't figure out why she was letting him get to her like he was. Maybe she had underestimated him. With all that hero aura and do-gooder vibe he had going, maybe she had missed the simple fact that he was trying to drive her out of town. *To hell with you, Michael O'Brien.*

Her phone started ringing. It was him, and she was not going to answer it. She heard a couple of texts come through too, but she was driving so she couldn't look. It was 15 minutes later that she had her "oh shit" moment. Her phone was making another noise. Low battery, and of course her charger was in the other car. She pulled over at the next gas station, praying to God that they sold maps.

Michael was speeding, hoping to catch up to her. She wasn't picking up her phone. He decided that calling her repeatedly was just going to help run her battery down, so he sent a brief text while he was stopped at a light. She hadn't acknowledged him. He took the most direct route and kept looking for her little red car. By the time he reached Fisher St. in Doolin two hours later he was a wreck. She wasn't there.

Branna finally read the texts that had come in. One from Michael telling her to pull over, that he had her charger. The second was from Tadgh asking how the car buying was going. She was conserving her battery, so she powered down the phone. She would use the map to get home.

The route wasn't that hard and the road signs were in English and Gaelic. She bought a cup of coffee and a granola bar. She peed, washed her face, and took note of how much cleaner the public toilets were in Ireland. Her father had taught her how to use a map when she was taking driver's education classes. He told her she had no business leaving their neighborhood in a car if she couldn't read a map or change a tire. *Thanks daddy,* she thought. *You were right.*

She took her time getting home. The gas station attendant had given her an alternate route that was just as easy, but a prettier drive. She stopped at some old ruins in an empty field. No sign or anything, but it was obviously hundreds of years old. The sun was low in the sky and the lighting was perfect through the old stone structure. She stared at it then shut her eyes. *Take a picture with your mind. Then you can always go back to it.* Her mother told her that when she was little, and it worked.

When Michael realized that Branna had not made it back before him, he called again. He ran his hands over his face. It had gone straight to voice mail which undoubtedly meant her cell was dead. *Damn it woman, why didn't you just follow me?*

He broke down and called Tadgh as much as it chaffed. Maybe she had contacted him? Tadgh went ballistic of course. "For God's sake Michael, can't you control that bloody temper for one day? Why the hell didn't you let me take her, if you were going to step on your cock?"

He kept going, bitching at Michael for being such an insufferable dickhead to such a nice girl. "I hear you Tadgh, OK? Just call me if you hear from her." He was arguing with him, telling him not to come over, when she pulled in the driveway. "Mother Mary, she's here. She's just driven up." Then he hung up on him. He went out on the porch and watched her get out of the car.

CHAPTER 8

Branna thought that Michael looked like a dad who was waiting for a teenager who had busted curfew. She breezed right by him through the front door and he followed her in. She didn't talk, but put her keys down on the counter and went in her room to plug her phone into the wall. "You didn't answer your phone," he said evenly. She looked at him dispassionately. "It had a low battery. I turned it off."

He shook his head. "You shouldn't have stormed off like that, Branna."

She exhaled, "I know, Michael. I was just…" She searched for the words. "I was at my limit. Didn't you ever just reach your limit and have to make a quick exit?"

The corners of his mouth turned up a little, "Yes, I suppose I have."

She continued, "Did you stop to weigh the pros and cons, or did you just bug out?"

He smiled a little wider, "Point made. How did you find your way home?"

She gave him a tired look. "I used a map, Michael. You're in the Coast Guard. You are familiar with how they work, right?"

He looked surprised. "What, do you really grade my intelligence that low that you didn't think I could read a simple road map? " She swatted her hand. "Nope, don't answer that. I just want to go to bed and read my smutty novel. I give in."

He started toward her as she turned toward her room. "Branna, wait. I want to say something." She stopped, but she didn't look at him. "Branna, please."

She turned and faced him. "I wanted to apologize. I overreacted in the car, about the call to Ned. I could have handled it better. I could have handled everything better." He'd shocked her, he could tell. "What? You think I am such an arrogant jackass that I can't figure out how to apologize?" She shrugged as if he'd hit the mark. Then she rubbed her temples. She was tired. Beautiful, but worn out and stressed. A pang of guilt hit him in the chest.

"Look Michael, I thought about this on the way home. I thought about it a lot. The place I went wrong was before we ever got in that car. I should have had Tadgh take me. I know you were trying to make some sort of charitable gesture by taking me but it was a bad idea. This whole thing," she waved her arms around to include the house. "this situation we are in. We can be civil, but we obviously can't be friends. You don't trust me, you don't like me, and you need to stop being so damned magnanimous and quit trying to take one for the team."

Michael started briskly shaking his head. She put a hand up before he started talking. "Let me finish. You're trying to be nice, while simultaneously resenting my presence and wondering if I am going to sneak over to Ned's house and offer up sexual favors for the deal to go my way."

Michael's eyebrows shot up at that. Then he put his hand under his chin, "Huh, do you think that would work for me? I hadn't thought of it , but…" He looked for a grin from her…nothing. He was in deeper shit that he realized. "Come on, that was a little funny."

She gave him a sad smile, and that was so much worse than no smile. "It's ok, Michael. I understand where you're coming from. If Ned sells you this house in three months, I'll be out of your hair for good. We just need to keep our distance until then. I think you would be happier that way. I want you to know that I appreciate what you did for me, today. Consider the paint job a payback for the favor and we'll leave it at that. If I want to do any other work, I will run it by you first, deal?"

Michael should be happy. She was making perfect sense and it was going his way. *Then why do you feel like you just kicked a puppy to death.* "Branna," he paused, "Jesus, you're actually being very fair handed about this. I just don't want you to feel like I don't like you. If the situation were different."

She stopped him, "Well, it's not different." He nodded, conceding the point.

"About the painting, you were right. It needs to be done. I can't let you do that alone, and I insist you let me kick in half on the materials." She was getting ready to argue. "No, I'm not going to leave you to do all that work alone. We share the house for now, we'll share the work. If you get the house in three months, you can pay me back. If I get the house, I'll reimburse you. That is the only solution that is fair and the only one I'll agree to." She pinched her bottom lip between her finger and thumb and finally gave a curt nod. "Then it's a deal." He put his hand out to shake on it.

Branna was cursing inwardly. Her dignity was intact, but she put her hand out to him like she was putting it in a lion's mouth. He palmed her hand with his big, warm one. She felt that same electricity slide through her body. He never took his eyes off her face, but she heard a sharp intake of breath and his eyes flared a little. She heard her phone ring and walked away.

Michael heard her answer. "Hello Tadgh. No, I'm just fine. No, really it's okay. I am headed to bed." Michael's hands fisted at his sides. He continued to torture himself by eavesdropping. "I'd love to meet you for breakfast. Yeah, honestly I could use a friendly face." At this, he turned and went to his room. He didn't want to hear anymore.

Michael was having trouble staying asleep. He had called a truce with Branna, but that didn't seem to sit well with him. He played back her words, *You don't trust me, you don't like me. I'll be out of your hair for good.* The problem was that he didn't feel that way. Mistrust aside, he actually did like her. She was smart and funny. From everything he knew in this short time, she was actually a very good person. The charity work she did was no small thing. Considering all that she had lost, she seemed to try and see the good in life.

She had a temper to match his own, but he was used to dealing with Fiona. She always had to be ten times madder than the person she was fighting with. She said awful things when she was angry. He was always able to keep the moral high ground with her. When Branna had turned away from him to collect herself and put those headphones on, it was the worst sort of guilt. Then she'd had a nightmare when she'd drifted off to sleep. The way she looked when she woke up. It was such a contrast to the young woman who'd spit her coffee out, laughing at his teasing. He thought about her turning up her sweet face to the rain.

He had trouble maneuvering the complexities of her personality. She seemed so young at times. Then she would switch to the smart, commanding presence she had when she was doing business. She was complicated, but in no way unappealing. Under different circumstances, he may have joined his foolish little brother and cousin as one of her admirers.

As he lay there looking for some sort of divine guidance for this mess, he heard something. At first he thought it was an animal outside or a child, but there were no houses around them. He was sure he'd heard it. It was raining again, and it occurred to him that perhaps it was a stray kitten outside. He got up and walked into the main room of the cottage. He listened, starting to think he'd imagined it when he heard it again. It was coming from Branna's room and he recognized the distressful sound from in the car today.

He walked quietly to her door. He could hear her struggling in her sleep. "No, Daddy! No, please! Daddy!" He put his head on the door and sighed, this girl was going to rip his heart out. He opened the door to see her curled up, covers off, shivering. She didn't have any pants on, but she was wearing a big cotton t-shirt. Her hands were white fists.

He spoke to her, "Branna dear, wake up." He talked gently, but loud enough to hopefully break through her slumber. He could tell the moment when she woke. Her whole body did a single jerk and her eyes popped open. She lay frozen in the fetal position, only moving her eyes. She looked at him in the moon light, recognition taking hold.

She sat up quickly, hanging her feet over the bed. She had her fists planted on either side of her thighs and she was looking at the floor, attempting to slow her breathing. "Do you need something, Michael?" She was trying to sound calm. She had her hands clenched so they wouldn't shake, but her shoulders and legs showed a small tremor.

"It sounded like another nightmare. I just came to check on you," he said calmly.

She shook her head to shake the jitters, then stood up. She noticed she was not wearing pants and pulled down her t-shirt. She walked over to the dresser and grabbed her dad's pajama pants. Then she turned to him. "I'm not sure what you heard, Michael, but I'm ok. You can go back to bed. I'm sorry I woke you." She was pulling the top out of the same drawer. She put it on without buttoning it and wrapped it tightly, like a hug.

She was trying to play it cool, but he was overwhelmed with the desire to go wrap his arms around her. His brother Aidan had nightmares, ever since the deployments started. He didn't like to talk afterward, acted similarly. She wasn't some war-hardened soldier, though. He began walking toward her with his hand out. She snapped to attention and walked by him into the living room. He both admired and hated her independent streak. She went to the sink and got a cup of water. Then she looked out the window. "It's raining again," she said.

After a small silence, she spoke, "I'm going to get some fresh air. I'm ok. You can go back to bed. You need your sleep. You shouldn't work tired." Michael stood there like an idiot. She'd made it clear that they should keep their distance. She didn't want or need his help. She walked out the front door and said, "Good night."

He could see her out the window now, putting her fingers in the streams that ran off the roof. She seemed content with that for a while, but then she stepped out into the rain and lifted her face. Not in pleasure, like before, but it seemed she was trying to wash something away. He walked over to the linen cabinet and took out a clean towel. He left it on the kitchen chair closest to the door and went back to his bedroom. He listened silently for her return, willing himself to stay put. Every part of his mind and body rebelled against passivity. He wasn't used to feeling helpless. He was used to fixing things. He heard the door creak open and the sound of light steps retreating to the other room. When the cottage was again silent, he relaxed and surrendered to sleep.

* * *

THE NEXT MORNING both the occupants of the Kelly cottage were dragging. Branna was pouring a cup of coffee when Michael came out of his room. She stopped, cup frozen halfway to her lips when he appeared in his uniform. She looked him slowly up and down, appreciating his neat military bearing. Matched with his good looks and incredible body, he was intoxicating.

Michael could tell that Branna liked what she saw. She was a little too groggy to guard her expression. The thought that she was sweeping her gaze appreciatively down his body made him start to stiffen in his finely pressed uniform pants. She turned away with her cup and took a sip of her coffee, but he knew she wasn't unaffected by him. And didn't that just make him want to toss the rulebook out the window.

"What do you have planned today?" he asked.

She shrugged. "The internet guy doesn't come until two, so I am having breakfast with Tadgh. He wants to show me around town."

I'll just bet he does, Michael thought. "Well, you're lucky to get the time. The man has more jobs than I can count."

Branna nodded, "He mentioned something about that. Where else does he work besides McDermott's?"

He cocked his head, thinking. "Let's see, last time I checked he was also working the ferry to the islands, delivering medication for the pharmacy in Ennis, and groundskeeping at Holy Rosary. Though, I'm not sure he gets paid for the last."

Branna said, "Wow, that is a list. Well, we all have to earn don't we? That's why I need the internet. I need to check on my tenants, make sure the rents were paid, and check the bookings for the beach rental."

Michael was surprised. "I never thought being a landlord was work, but I guess it is."

Branna continued, "I am not complaining. I could be on my feet all day waiting tables. There's always something, though. New leases, maintenance, landscapers, advertising. My new Tampa renters have just asked me to pay for a gardener. They are great and all, but I was clear that the landscaping was an undertaking and that it didn't come with the rent. Just little fires to put out. Like I said, I'm not complaining." She topped off her coffee while she talked.

Michael was surprised. He had known she owned several properties, but he'd assumed she used property managers and just sat on her ass with the profits. He should have known better. She didn't seem the sort to let other people handle things for her.

Michael looked at his dive watch. "Damn, I've got to go. I have to go all the way to Shannon today. I'm in the air."

Branna didn't like the sounds of that. "So when you work from here, you go out on the boat, but the helicopters are at the bigger station? Why do you switch?"

He answered, "Our Coast Guard isn't as well manned as yours. It is mostly volunteer staff. There are very few full time staff. We've not got the funding. I'm in Shannon if we think trouble is brewing. It's going to be rough farther out. Wind, big waves, maybe a storm headed this way. They need to be able to drop me right at the extraction point, not risk another boat in the mix." Michael noticed she tensed when he talked about work, so he changed the subject. He swore he saw concern in her face.

"Listen, before I go, I called my friend Ian. He's a painter. He also gets supplies for people who do DIY. He's going to drop off what we need today. Don't worry about being here, he'll leave it in the car park and I'll settle up with him later. My da will bring a ladder by as well.

He'll put it in the same place. Don't worry about the high stuff. If you want to start, just scrape and do the low areas that you can reach."

Branna folded her arms over her chest. "You know, I can paint. I've done painting on a few of my properties."

Michael sighed impatiently. "I have to leave, just do the low areas. Stay off the ladder if you're alone, ye hear?" She found it a little amusing that whenever he started getting irritated his accent got thicker.

She curtsied. "Yes, my Lord."

He grabbed his duffle, and swung it over his shoulder, then put on his hat. As he left, he mumbled, "Smart ass."

* * *

BRANNA WAS WALKING through the front door of Gus O'Connor's Pub when Tadgh waved her over. Jenny greeted her warmly. Jenny put a cup of black coffee in front of her as she took a seat. "Are you ready to try the full Irish this morning?"

Branna shook her head, "Sorry Jenny, too much for me. How about some more bread and jam?"

Jenny nodded, then Tadgh ordered. "I'll have some fried kippers, eggs, and chips. Oh, and bring the girl some rashers, for God's sake."

Jenny smiled. Branna asked, "The bread was fine. What is a rasher?" Tadgh rubbed his hands together. "It's similar to your American bacon. So, how was it yesterday? I saw you pull up in the car. It looks good on you."

Branna decided to ignore the question and keep it about the car. "Yes, I have to drop my rental off at some point today or tomorrow so I don't get charged any more. What did you do all day, more work?" He gave her a sideway glance. "Nice diversion. Yes, I was on the ferry. Now, enough stalling. Tell me what in the hell happened to send you storming out of the city on your own."

Branna rubbed a finger between her brows. This was touchy. Tadgh and Michael were family. As if he'd read her mind, he assured her, "I told you I'm not taking sides with you two stubborn goats. You had him worried, Branna. We were both worried. He'd never admit that, but he was creeping up on frantic by the time he called me."

Branna shook her head. "I think you grossly overestimate his concern. If I got sucked into a fairy ring in my new car, he'd be dancing all the way to Ned's house. It was nothing. We argued about something stupid. He got angry and I hit the eject button."

Tadgh ran his fingers through his shoulder length hair. "Yes, well blood will tell. He's got it from both sides. I'm not much better when you get my blood up."

She smiled and shrugged one shoulder. "O'Mara tempers are pretty legendary too, but he definitely won yesterday."

Tadgh put his hands on the table, "Branna, you know he's not a bad man. He'd never hurt you or anything like that." She put her coffee cup down, "I know that Tadgh, but there are a lot of ways to inflict damage. I just don't really feel like re-hashing things." She cheered up, "Tell me where you're going to take me today."

"Fair enough, love. Now, we've got several options. You can take a trip over to Aran. We could go to the Burren and have a walk, go to the perfumery, visit the caves. Better to wait on the caves, though. Tourist season is almost over. They're better to tour without a bunch of sweaty tourist flashing pictures. Any of that interest you? There's a kayak shop as well, but today's not the day for that. It's too rough."

Branna's heart lightened at the though of kayaking these beautiful coves and shores. "I think kayaking and caves are definitely on the list for later this season. Maybe the perfumery and gardens? I have to be at the house by two o'clock. The internet guy is coming."

Tadgh swiped his hand dismissively. "Can't your roommate handle that? I was planning on kidnapping you all day!"

Branna laughed, but she started to get the feeling that Tadgh was interested in more than a trip to the perfumery. "No, sorry. I need it up and running and he's working out of Shannon today. Besides, I'm not in the position to be asking for favors right now."

Tadgh's face fell. "Yes, well you won't see him for a while then. He's on a twenty-four hour shift. The Burren it is."

He paused awkwardly, "Branna, I hope you know you can talk to me. If you need a friend, that is. I know you must be feeling a bit isolated right now, but you don't have to deal with it all on your own. I don't want you to think I'm just trying to get in your knickers," he smiled bashfully. "Not that I wouldn't jump at the chance, mind you. I am not getting that vibe from you, though. I don't expect anything from you. I just thought you could use a friend. I know I could, and I like you. I love Michael like a brother, but it doesn't have to interfere with us being friends. Did that make sense?"

Branna's face lit up. "Oh, Tadgh, I would love that, too. And as far as my knickers…" she blushed, "It isn't you. You're sweet and you're quite the hottie. If I was in the market for some knicker shedding, you'd be on the short list."

At this, Tadgh barked out a laugh. "You say the sweetest things."

She just shrugged. "I just don't. Date, I mean. I don't at all. I just feel like I am better off on my own. I've seen what love does to people. It's powerful stuff. I don't want any part of it."

Tadgh chuckled silently. "Christ, woman, you act like you have control of it. I've got bad news for you, Branna dear. It's coming for you. You are too beautiful, too smart and kind to escape it. You're the type of girl someone loves forever. Jesus, listen to me. Maybe I do want in your knickers," he smiled.

Branna started giggling and smacked him. "You're wrong, Tadgh. Thanks, but I know what I am and what I'm not. I'm ok with it. I am also of the firm belief that you can control your feelings. You can rein them in and not let them dictate your actions. I do it every day."

Tadgh gave her a sad look, "Grief isn't love, Branna, and your view of yourself is so off the mark I scarcely know where to start. One of these days you're going to trust me enough to get to the bottom of this." He took her hand across the table, "Until then you can at least know that you've got one local friend."

* * *

THE BURREN WAS AMAZING. Branna walked the natural areas with Tadgh and they talked like old friends. He showed her the

Poulnabrone Dolmen, a portal tomb. To stand next to something so ancient was deeply stirring. These were the remnants of her own ancestry.

Later they toured the Perfumery where she sniffed and sampled. She loved everything, but she was on a budget. The car purchase aside, this move had stretched her monthly allotment. Her favorite perfume was the Summer Harvest, but she settled for a bar of geranium soap, which was about a quarter the price. As they walked to the car, she kept sniffing herself. "That place was really interesting, thanks for bringing me. And I don't just mean the shop. Everything about it was wonderful, including the company. It was a really good day."

Tadgh beamed under her praise. "Never let it be said that Tadgh O'Brien is bad company. We better get you back, though. It's getting late. I can come back around after the internet business is done, if you like. You'll need someone to follow you to Ennis to drop that car off."

Branna was rubbing her wrist under her nose. "Yes, thanks for reminding me! You don't need to work one of your jobs?"

He answered, "No, I cleared the day. Doesn't happen that often, but occasionally I get a free day."

Branna brightened, "Hey, I have an idea! We can go drop the car off, and then I'll cook for you!"

Tadgh moaned, "Good God, you cook? Competently? Tell me again why I'm not trying to get in your knickers?"

Branna just laughed, "Because I am mentally damaged and have a *do not enter* sign on all of my panties?" Tadgh burst into laughter and so did she.

He finally wiped tears from his eyes, "You know, it's no laughing matter. It's a tragedy is what it is."

Branna just looked out the window. "Story of my life, my friend."

"Mo cara." Tadgh replied gently.

She scrunched her brow, "Mo what?"

"Mo cara, It's gaelic. It means my friend."

Branna put her hand on his arm and squeezed. "Mo cara."

Branna roamed the aisles of the grocery and the wheels were turning in her head. She had seen a rosemary bush on the South side of the cottage. She picked up a tray of local lamb chops, baby potatoes, butter, olive oil, watercress, a lemon, garlic, mint, some sea salt and pepper. Tadgh had been so nice to her. He was so open and genuine. She was happy to have a friend, and she wanted to do something nice for him in return.

She made him stay in the car while she shopped, so that dinner could be a surprise. She also grabbed some local beer and cider. Dessert was going to be a crumble with seasonal fruit and double cream to top it off. She paid and left, loading it all into the trunk.

Tadgh was grinning, "So secretive. Did I mention, I'm a vegan?" Branna's jaw dropped, then she remembered him wolfing down the rashers and kippers this morning.

She smacked him, "You're a shameless liar, Tadgh." He replied with a self-satisfied grin. "Just seeing if you were paying attention."

The dinner was fabulous. She'd decided to use the lemon, mint, and garlic on the lamb and saved the rosemary for the potatoes. She also shaved lemon zest and some finely mashed mint into the cream for the crumble. She ate one chop, Tadgh ate two. She was offering him the last one when he pushed his dessert plate away.

"Good Lord, Branna. I'm ready to burst. You eat it. You don't eat enough. Although, you did better than that hamster food you ate at the Burren."

She lifted her chin. "They are protein bars. What is it with you O'Brien men and my diet? I get exactly what I need from my hamster food. Do you really think I would bother cooking like this if it was just me?"

He looked baffled. "If I could cook like this I would stuff myself daily. I would lose sleep so I could eat more. Women are nuts."

She pointed at him in response,"Touché, mo cara, touché."

Tadgh gave her a golf clap, "Now you're getting it."

CHAPTER 9

Branna had a solid six hours of sleep thanks to the pint of cider from dinner. She'd wrapped up the leftovers, done the dishes with Tadgh's assistance, and said goodnight. She was so relieved that he had kept to his word and not tried to make it a romantic interlude. She got up at 5:30 to start prepping for painting. She needed to scrape the old paint off today.

She was working hard when Michael pulled in the driveway at 11AM. She was hot and flushed with exertion. As Michael approached, he said, "You've started, I see. I stopped at my parents for breakfast before I came home. I didn't think, I'm sorry." He looked down the front of the house. "Jesus, you got really far, you did the whole front and this side?"

She stopped and fanned her t-shirt. "Both sides, actually. It's ok, I got an early start. It's nice you got to have breakfast with your parents."

A pang of sadness hit Michael. She'd probably give anything to be able to sit down and have breakfast with her parents one more time. She was so damned strong. Michael looked at her beautiful face, and sadness was replaced with alarm. " Christ, Branna, your face is as red as an apple. Didn't you use sunscreen?"

She put her hands on her hips, "Of course I did, I even re-applied."

He looked down at her feet where a half empty coffee cup rested, then back at her face. It was not as sweaty as it should be. He touched her forehead. Branna looked at him like he was crazy. "Jesus wept, how much water have you had today?" She looked baffled. He continued, "You know water, the clear liquid that comes out of the spout?"

She started to catch his meaning. "Umm, I had four cups of coffee." Then she looked down and amended, "I mean three and a half cups."

He gave her an impatient look. "Besides what you pressed through coffee beans?"

She smiled weakly, "Does brushing my teeth count?"

He sighed. His tone was gruff. "Come inside."

She crinkled her brow. "I don't take orders."

His face twisted with the effort of remaining civil. "You're dehydrated Branna. You need to sit down, have a couple glasses of water and rest. How many hours have you been out here?"

She counted in her head. "About five, total. Any other questions?"

"Yes, are you daft?"

She rolled her eyes. "That's debatable, but I like to think not." He just stared at her. She finally surrendered. She dropped her scraper and followed him in, grabbing her coffee on the way.

"I saw that, and don't you take another sip!" Michael said without turning around.

When they walked in he pointed to the kitchen chair. "Sit." He stopped when she didn't. "Sit, please." She sat. "What have you eaten today?"

She thought about it. "Hmm, some dried apples for breakfast and a spoon full of peanut butter for a snack."

He just stared in the fridge. "Branna, did you know we'd had a burglary?" She looked at him puzzled.

"Excuse me?" she asked irritably.

"Yes, some fiend has broken into the cottage. They didn't steal anything but they left a lamb chop, some potatoes, and some sort of pie," he replied with a straight face.

"Very funny. Those are left overs from the dinner I cooked for

Tadgh last night." She must have heat stroke. She could have sworn she saw him tense and grip the refrigerator door tightly.

"That was nice of you," he said slowly. "Did you two spend the whole day together?"

She felt like she was on shaky ground for some reason. Was he getting territorial over Tadgh? "No, what's the problem? Just because you can't stand me, Tadgh isn't allowed to be my friend?"

He shook his head. "I never, ever said I didn't like you Branna. You said it. And no, it's fine. He's a good man." He took out the leftovers and the ice tray and kept talking. He motioned to the food. "Try to help me understand why you would eat a spoon of peanut butter when you had this spread sitting in the fridge? Do you get off on self denial?"

Branna stood up and he pointed back to the seat. She growled. She actually growled at him. That was not adorable. Really. Not at all.

"Testy, testy wee one. Don't get your knickers in a bunch."

She gritted her teeth. "For your information I was saving that for you." He looked at her and his expression softened. She waved her hand dismissively. "It's no big deal. I just though you'd be tired and hungry after such a long shift. I wanted you to have something ready before you went to bed."

Michael set a glass of water down in front of her and pointed at it. "Drink, all of it you little hellcat." She stuck her tongue out behind his back. "I saw that."

"What, do you have trick mirrors installed or something?" He turned and slowly stalked back to her. He leaned in speaking softly to her with one hand on the back of her chair and one on the table. "I have eyes in the back of my head, lass. You've got spirit, I'll give you that." He grew serious. "You need to take better care of yourself. You need to treat yourself the same or better than Tadgh or me or those wounded men you help. Now, I know you're a reasonable woman. So, I am going to heat up that food and you are going to eat it, sitting down, with two glasses of water."

"But I left it for you." Her face was so sincere and uncalculating that it moved him immeasurably.

Had Fiona ever in three years showed him this sort of thoughtfulness? How is it that this peculiar, young woman who had decreed that they would not be friends treated him better that his own wife? He tucked a loose strand of hair behind her ear. "Drink up, Branna. I'll split it with you." He noticed that when he touched her, she closed her eyes. Then she caught herself, but he felt it. The same overwhelming electricity that he'd felt before. Touching her was like a lightning strike.

He heated the food up in the oven and put it on two plates. Branna insisted he take the lamb chop. She had warm crumble with the leftover cream and a small amount of potatoes. "Christ, woman. If I'd known you could cook like this I'd have been nicer to you." He took his first bite of the warm crumble with the double cream. He moaned with pleasure.

"You know, if a woman makes you moan with pleasure before noon, you should thank her," she said.

He laughed that she'd thrown his words back at him. "Oh, I'll be thanking you. This is gorgeous all together. I've changed my mind. Can we be friends?"

She got up with her dirty plate and breezed by him. "Nope, never." Her tone was teasing.

Michael eyed the third glass of water he'd given her. The contrary wench hadn't had a sip more than the two glasses she'd agreed to. He got up and palmed the glass. He very casually walked into the kitchen behind her. "Branna, dear, you didn't have the rest of your water."

Just as she started her retort, he dumped the entire glass of ice water on her head. She was frozen and gasping with her hands splayed out.

Michael said sweetly, "There's a good lass." He knew right when she was going to move. He laughed and ran out the front door. She chased him for a little while and stopped. He stopped about five feet from her and taunted. "Oh, the little Yank is out of breath. You need longer legs, hen."

She stopped and stood at attention. She relaxed her face. He didn't buy it for a minute, but he played along. "Well, I guess I deserved that.

You're right, too. I could never catch you on foot." As she talked she paced.

Branna was going to get him. She had an ice cube in her panties and one in her cleavage. This bastard was going to pay. She knew she'd left the hose on. She had washed the bird poop off the scrapers. She lunged for the hose and fired. He saw her lunge but he was too far away. She opened fire and said, "Dance, white boy!" It was so sweet. Full blast as he instinctively tried to block the stream with his hands.

Suddenly, he stopped and ran straight for her. He grabbed her in a bear hug and they both tumbled to the ground, the hose lost in the struggle. He flipped mid-air so he wouldn't land on her. Then, because he was twice her size, he maneuvered her around, on to her back. She was giggling, wiggling and screaming like a little piglet. He pinned her arms above her head and trapped her legs with one of his.

"Apologize," he crooned.

She spoke through her laughter. "Not happening, you started it!"

He shook his head "Tsk tsk tsk. I was merely helping some daft little harpy cool her body temperature, administering first aid. I deserve an accommodation. You assaulted me and you've made a mess of my uniform. Come on Branna, admit you were wrong." His face was diabolical. "No? Well then, I'll have to take punitive measures."

She actually looked a little worried but she quickly stifled it. She raised her head up to within an inch of his nose. "Do.Your.-Worst.Buddy."

Michael threw his head back and laughed. "When you say uncle it is going to be so sweet."

In the midst of the shit-talking, a third voice broke in. "I've sat in on a few union negotiations, but this real estate negotiating uses quite a different technique."

Both Branna and Michael froze. They looked at each other with a mutual, unspoken "oh, shit". Michael looked up and shot off the ground. He remembered his victim on the ground and gave her a hand up.

"Aye, hello Da. You've brought the ladder." He looked sideways at Branna. She was stock straight with her hands clasped behind her. She was a mess. Her bun was lopsided, her clothes disheveled, and she had a little dirt on her face. Michael stifled the urge to laugh. She looked like she'd been sent to the school master's office for fighting.

"Hello Mr. O'Brien. We were just...um."

A higher feminine voice appeared from behind him. "Aye, you were negotiating. We heard. Branna, dear. You're going to need a bit of training from his sister if you want to come out on top next time."

"Ma, please!"

She smiled and walked over to her son. "What? The girls need to stick together." She winked at Branna. "You O'Brien men are quite the bullies when you get your mind set."

Now Sean was laughing and shaking his head. "Don't you believe a word of it, lass. Her clansmen are the worst bullies this side of the Irish Sea. Cunning too."

"That's enough out of you two. Now, Branna why don't you and I go have a cup of tea while the men unload the truck." She gently hooked her arm in Branna's and walked toward the house. Michael whispered, "Run!" And his mother said, "I heard that."

Branna was nervous as she walked into the house with Michael's mother. As they walked toward the kitchen, Sorcha noticed the water and ice cubes splattered on the floor. "Oh dear, I'm so sorry. Wait and I'll mop that up. I don't want you to slip. We were just, um..."

"Branna, dear I have five sons. I know what the starts of a water fight look like more than anyone. Who drew first blood?" She was giving Branna a sideways grin.

Branna relaxed a little. "Michael did."

She nodded, "Aye, I figured as much. He is a child of the water. Any particular provocation?"

Branna started to deny it, but she knew this woman was smart. "Actually, I was being rather a pill. He brought me in out of the sun. Said I was pushing heat stroke. I think he was exaggerating, but he force fed me and made me drink some water. I'm afraid that quite often our good intentions seem to end up with one of us or both getting angry. In this instance he decided I needed that third glass of water." She giggled as she said it.

Sorcha was listening quietly as Branna talked, while first mopping and then starting the kettle. She was secretly captivated by this beautiful, young woman. She was a tough cookie it seemed, but something about her sad eyes provoked a motherly instinct.

"Well, Michael does have a fair share of first aid training, love. If he was worried, it wasn't over nothing."

Branna sighed and shrugged one shoulder, "Yes, I guess deep down I knew that. I didn't mean to push it. I just get set to a task and don't really pay attention."

Sorcha understood, "Aye, women are like that aren't they? Always putting their comfort last, always trying to do so much. Well, most women. I've met a few that always put themselves first. My son was married to one." Sorcha had wanted to probe to see how much Branna knew about Michael's ex-wife. She was waiting for a discreet way to introduce the subject, and she'd just found it.

"Yes, I met her. She wasn't very nice."

Sorcha said something unintelligible under her breath in Gaelic. "She was a good enough child when she was younger, but she changed. It started before the marriage, but Michael didn't see it. She hurt him, that's all I will say on it. He's been a little hesitant to…" she searched for words.

"Get back on the horse?" Branna offered.

Sorcha smiled, "Yes, exactly."

Something occurred to Branna. "Was her last name Mullen by any chance?"

Sorcha looked scandalized. "Heavens, no. Why would you ask?"

"It was just something I heard someone say that first day," she was blushing now. "When I stormed into Michael's rehearsal, they asked him if he was sure I wasn't a Mullen."

Sorcha laughed, slapping the counter. Branna was sliding a cup of tea toward her and arranging milk and a sugar bowl. She stopped, wondering what was so funny. "Maybe I don't want to know? Is it that bad?"

Sorcha's eyes gleamed with mischief. Branna was struck by how much she looked like her son just then. Then she caught on. "It's you. You're a Mullen." Not a question, but Sorcha answered anyway.

"Guilty as charged. We're sort of known for a fierce streak. Not cruel, mind you, but fiery and passionate. Sometimes it comes out as love, sometimes rage. We fight for what's ours and you don't want to cross us."

Branna thought about it. "So, it's a compliment?"

Sorcha laughed again. She had such a beautiful face, no trace of pain. Branna found her soothing in a strange way. "Well, I like to think so. I suppose that depends on who you're asking. My Sean might not think so some days. Mullens are strong minded, especially the women. Sean said I should have come with a warning label."

Branna stood up a little straighter, took a sip of her tea. "I think I like it. I like being compared to you. You certainly seem to handle your men rather well."

Sorcha set her tea down on the saucer. "O'Brien men give as good as they get, it's true. They have a long history in this county. They're well respected. There are old tales about them. O'Brien men love deeply, passionately. They say that they only have one true mate, and the road to finding her is never easy. Once they love her, they love her only, forever. If he loses his mate, it does him in. O'Brien men are fiercely protective and they don't share. They've a bit of a possessive streak. It's not in a toxic way. They just give their loyalty completely, and they expect it in return. They don't like other men sniffing around their women."

As Sorcha spoke, Branna was nervously stirring her tea. Talk of love did that to her. Her parents had loved each other like that. She remembered the way they looked at each other, their reunions after a deployment, and the way her mother had slowly shut down after his death. She looked at Sorcha and gave her a sad smile.

"My parents were like that. I remember being younger and thinking that I wanted what they had."

She wasn't completely making eye contact but Sorcha had a way of tilting her face, willing you to look up. "And now? What do think now, Branna?"

Branna smoothed her loose strands of hair down. "Now I see the price. I see what it costs, a love like that. When my father died, it was the beginning of her death. She never recovered. At the end she couldn't wait to die. She wanted the pain to be over. Not just the cancer, but the pain of losing my dad. I may as well have lost both parents on that street in Fallujah. If that's what love does to you, I'll take a pass."

Sorcha's heart was breaking. She knew that this girl was proud, she didn't want to be pitied any more than Sorcha would have. "You're assuming you have control of it, lass. The heart is a powerful thing."

Branna chuffed. "Tadgh said the same thing."

Sorcha sharpened up. "Tadgh? My nephew? Have you been seeing a lot of him then?"

Branna hastened to correct her. "Oh, no. It's nothing like that. We're friends. He's really my only friend."

Sorcha reached over the counter and squeezed her hand. "You've got more than you think, Branna. No one here is your enemy."

"Thank you, Sorcha. That is a relief to hear, regardless of how this all turns out. The only two people that seem to hate me are your son and his ex-wife."

Sorcha brushed that away with her hand, "Don't pay any attention to that witch."

Branna choked a little on her tea as Sorcha continued. "As for my son, from what I just saw, he not only doesn't hate you, he seems rather fond of you. I know he has a strange way of showing it. He probably wouldn't even admit it, but I know my son. You're a good girl, he knows that in his heart. That fat head gets in the way is all."

Branna knew she shouldn't ask, but she was an idiot, so she did. "You said that O'Brien men only have one true mate. Is that why he is so mistrustful, because he lost Fiona?"

Sorcha dismissed this with another wave. "No, dear. Fiona wasn't the one. We all knew it. She was needy, attentive in her own way, a little wild. Michael thought it was love, thought that her moodiness was exciting. It's different when you have to live with it. She's a selfish, vain woman. Nothing was ever enough. She couldn't understand the hours Michael kept or his sense of duty. No, she wasn't his mate. He knows that now. I think the whole affair just soiled him on the idea."

Branna should not be as happy about that little reveal as she was. Why should she care if Michael had met his true mate, if there even was such a thing? He was nothing to her. As if on cue, the men walked in, joined by a third. He was older than Sean, old enough to be his father. She wondered, given the resemblance, if they were related.

"Ah, hello David. Did you get everything unloaded?" The older man walked over and kissed her on the cheek.

"Hello Sorcha, how has my son been treating my favorite daughter in law?" She smiled, "Like a queen as usual. Branna, this is Michael's grandda, David." Branna shook his hand and suddenly felt very shy, being surrounded my so many of Michael's relatives.

David was a big, handsome man. White hair, but the same broad frame and height, and the same dusty blue eyes as his son. He smiled broadly. "I've heard a lot about you, lass. It's a pleasure." Branna cringed to think what he had actually heard, but decided to ignore that elephant in the room and just smile back at him. He said, "I need to borrow your boys sometime next week, Sorcha. We have some things to move before the wedding. I'll be calling Tadgh as well."

Branna was wondering what was afoot when Michael finally spoke to her. "You met my brother Patrick. It's him who's getting married, next weekend in fact. Poor sod."

Sean nudged him, "Careful, son. That sour attitude will curdle the cream."

Michael put his hands up. "You're right, da. She's a lovely girl. I'm sure it'll be grand. Grandda is right, we have a lot to do. You've got my schedule now. I'll help any way I can."

As everyone said their goodbyes, Branna watched the family. The men all hugged each other and Sorcha. What would it be like to have four generations, all living in the same town? Brigid had one daughter and had another on the way.

Branna had moved around a lot, and her grandparents died when she was young. They were a fading memory of presents and birthday cards and weeklong visits once a year.

Sorcha leaned in and wrapped her arms around Branna. Branna was stiff at first. It had been so long since someone had really hugged her. The only hug she could remember in the last year was her friend Anna when she left for Ireland. This was different though. There was something so motherly and warm about it, and Branna let herself thaw a little, returning the embrace.

Sorcha released her and brushed her stray hairs on one side. "Thank you for the tea, Branna. It's nice to get a little girl talk now and then."

Branna smiled at her, "Thank you, Sorcha. I hadn't realized I needed some girl time, but I did."

Michael was alone in the cottage with Branna again. As thoughts of his parents faded, his final thought on the matter was that nothing could deflate an erection like your parents walking on the scene. As he looked at Branna, hair tousled from being pinned beneath him, he remembered her writhing and giggling under him, and that defiant look in her eye. He hadn't known her long, but he was increasingly aware that he couldn't make himself hate her.

Quite the opposite, he had to admit that despite his efforts, he was seriously attracted to her. And there was the rub. He had been utterly faithful to Fiona, despite her behavior. Since his divorce, no woman had caught his eye for very long. He hadn't been with a woman in a long time. Maybe that was the problem. Branna was lovely. Being under the same roof with her was getting to him. Sexual frustration was ever at a boil, even when he was pissed at her.

"So, you and my mother seemed to be getting along. Did she give you the third degree?" Branna shook her head, "Not at all. She's a wonderful woman. She certainly loves you. She doesn't like your ex-wife much. Not that I can blame her."

Michael's eyes shot up. "What did she tell you?"

Branna gave him a wry grin, "Don't worry, she didn't tell me anything. Well, anything other than she never approved of her and that she hurt you. She told me about the O'Brien men, about them only having one true mate. She didn't seem to think Fiona was it."

Michael made a non-committal grunt. "Sounds like she told you a lot."

Branna could tell he wasn't happy about the direction her talk with his mother had taken. "I don't want you to think we were gossiping about you, Michael. It just sort of came up. She was talking about the Mullen side and then the O'Brien's. It just sort of segued into talking about Fiona. I'm sorry if she told me something she shouldn't have."

Michael knew she was being sincere. He gave a shrug. "It's not a secret around town. Boy and girl get married, he works a lot, she fucks around. He's the last one to know, and the only reason he takes his head out of the sand is because she tries to shag his cousin. Then it's off to the priest when he can't stand the humiliation any longer. The end."

Branna hadn't heard why they broke up. She was stunned. What kind of woman would cheat on a man like Michael? "I'm sorry, Michael. I didn't know. I'm assuming that cousin was Tadgh from the way she behaved around him. She is a disloyal bitch. You're better off without her."

Michael barked out a laugh. "You don't mince words do you?"

She gave him a direct look, "Why should I? I call it like I see it. My two encounters with her have been extremely unpleasant. I can't imagine living with her."

He was surprised. "Two encounters? When was the other?"

She answered him as she took her hair down. He was having a hard time concentrating when all of that gorgeous hair cascaded down from its restraint. To his disappointment she spun it back up into that stupid bun, hiding it from him.

She continued, "My first night. We didn't talk. I just couldn't figure out why I was getting a vitriol smile from some stunning red head across the room. She looked like she was mentally measuring me for a casket." Michael loved the way she worded things. She was smart and she was a smart ass, which was a combination he could appreciate.

"So, you had an annulment through the catholic church, based on her adultery?"

He shook his head. "No, in the end I wasn't willing to paint a scarlet letter on her chest. I took the blame, it was one of the reasons she agreed not to contest it. She could play the wounded party. Honestly, I just wanted it over."

Branna started to feel bad for bringing it up. "Michael, you don't have to talk about her. You don't owe me any explanation."

Michael appreciated her trying to make him more comfortable, but he wanted her to know. True, he didn't owe her anything. They weren't intimate, but he wanted her to know that his marriage hadn't failed because he was some slimy bastard that treated his wife poorly.

"No, it's ok. I appreciate that, but you'll hear it all eventually. It's a small town. Her reason for the annulment was based on the fact that I wouldn't give her children. She tried to get me to give her a baby, start a family. I refused. She knew our marriage was in trouble, thought a child would help. When I found out about her infidelity, that was the final straw. She just wanted to trap me. She knew I didn't want her getting pregnant, but that if she were, I wouldn't leave her. So, I agreed to be the bad guy, and we walked away with the church's blessing. And that is the end of my sad tale."

Branna couldn't believe that someone that had come from such a huge, loving family didn't want children. The thought made her sad. She didn't like Fiona, but she was surprised that Michael didn't want kids. It was easy, she supposed, for someone to romanticize a kid free existence. The thought of freedom from obligation, no baggage, it probably sounded appealing. He didn't know what it was like to have no one.

Her family tree was sparse. Some with no kids, others with one child. Add tragedy, disease, and God deciding he had it out for her, she had been left with no one.

Branna doubted she would ever fall in love or marry, but if she did, she wanted a big family. Was it just Fiona that made him not want kids? She hoped so, not for personal reasons. She had to admit she liked him, though. It would be sad if he never found love again and had the chance to start a family. He had good people behind him and some primo DNA. He would make beautiful babies.

"It's none of my business, Michael. I have no right to an opinion."

He gave her a knowing grin. "Yes, but you're going to give it to me anyway, aren't you?"

"Yes, I am. I'll be brief," she said with a grin. "You have trust issues. I am sure your experiences with Fiona are the cause of them. It's just, she's one woman. You have wonderful, loyal, smart, loving women in your life. Your mother and Brigid, they seem pretty incredible. Use them as your measuring tool for women, not Fiona. Don't let your ex-wife take what's left of your life away from you. You don't have to marry or fall in love again. God knows I am in no position to judge, considering how I live, but you can't go through life thinking every strong-minded woman is like Fiona. She wasn't strong. She was very, very weak and she didn't deserve you."

Michael wasn't struck stupid very often, but Branna had just done it. He was used to having to keep his lust at bay. Right now he just wanted to hug her. She was right, of course. Fiona didn't deserve him. He knew that deep down.

"Thank you, Branna. I guess I know that, but it's no easy thing. When someone's unfaithful, it hits you on another level. The betrayal is a blow to your ego, as shallow as that sounds. You question yourself."

She didn't know the half of it. He didn't tell her the other part of the annulment charges. She had accused him of withholding intimacies from her. Denying her love, neglecting the sexual aspect of their marriage, and withholding his seed as a way of defying God's law about the sanctity of "being fruitful and multiplying".

Her display had disgusted him. Always one to push his good graces, never feeling like she had drained enough out of him, she had even implied that perhaps he was impotent. It was all bullshit, of course. He'd refused to sleep with her because he didn't want to dip his quill in the community ink well. After he had learned that she'd slept with at least three men and tried with his cousin, he couldn't bear to touch her.

She didn't take it well. She was used to getting her way. He'd thought they'd had a good sex life. Fuck that, they'd had a great sex life. No one could ever accuse Michael O'Brien of not tending to his woman. Half the reason he had sought out those two flings after the annulment was to make sure he still had it. Immature, but he was a man. Those two women hadn't stuck around, but they'd been blown away by the end of the night.

Fiona had raged when he'd refused her attempt to manipulate him through sex. He moved into the guest room, refusing to even sleep next to her. Toward the end, he'd stayed most nights at Tadgh's flat. She had called him horrible things, told him that his lame attempts in the bedroom were the whole reason she had sought out a real man.

That line of thought made him look more closely at Branna. She'd sized Fiona up pretty quickly. She was smart, a good judge of character. She was also right about his attitude. It sucked. He had wonderful women in his life. Fiona had taken enough from him.

Christ, she was beautiful. Stormy eyes, long silky hair, a curvy little body. The thought of that little tussle in the garden stirred him up all over again. He wondered if all of that explosive energy and fire carried over into her bed play.

Who was he kidding? Of course it did. She didn't seem to do anything half way. He suddenly had the urge to hunt down every man she'd ever been with and...what had she said? Oh yes, measure them for a casket. He was shaken from his internal dialogue by Branna's voice.

"I'm sorry Michael. You got really quiet. I obviously overstepped. It really is none of my business."

He shook himself, "No Branna, you're spot on. She was a troubled woman. I'm glad to be rid of her. Other than the occasional collision in town, I've been enjoying the peace and quiet."

Branna chuckled, "Until some damn Yankee came and stole your house, you mean?"

He laughed a little at that, "Aye, well. That damn Yankee cooks her chops to perfection and she does her own laundry, so things could be worse."

Branna grinned, "Well knock me over with a feather. Was that a compliment? Pardon me while I swoon." She'd said it with a deep southern drawl and put her hand to her head like she was faint.

Michael barked out a laugh. As he walked by her, he grabbed the dishtowel and snapped it on her rump. She jumped and squeaked. She turned to him astonished, hands on her bum.

"Don't make me get the hose again."

He put his hands up in surrender. "Sorry Branna, I do love to make you squeak." He could have sworn her eyes flared a little.

He was thanking God that his shirttail was out, because his groin was throbbing. "I'm going to change out of my filthy uniform." He gave her an admonishing look. "Then I'll finish the scraping." He pointed, "Your color is back to normal, but you need to take a mug of water with you if you help."

She popped a salute like a seasoned soldier, "Yes, sir!" As he shut the door she heard him mumble, "Smart ass."

* * *

THE NEXT FEW days drifted by in lazy comfort. Michael worked a lot, due to storms and high winds. It also gave Branna an unwanted break from getting her painting done. She cleaned, jogged, painted the cabinetry. Michael noticed her muddy running shoes, one evening after work. "You should run with me, I have a good run mapped out."

She looked at his legs, then at his face. "I think I would hold you back. I'd be riding on your back after a mile at your pace."

Michael liked the idea of a sweaty, panting Branna O'Mara wrapping her legs around him, but he decided not to share that thought. She was in good shape. Small, but firm and well made. "Do you run often?"

She shook her head. "No, I used to take my friend Anna's yoga class. She taught on the military base." He was assaulted with mental pictures of Branna in yoga pants, ass in the air. *Down boy.*

Instead he scrunched his brow. "Never tried yoga. I'm not an exercise class type of bloke."

She rolled her eyes. "Men do yoga, too. Her class was full of Marines."

He laughed. "Oh yes, and if she looks anything like you, I am sure they were there strictly for the work out and not the spectator aspect of it."

She narrowed her eyes, "Was that a compliment? From you? About me?"

Michael's groin was at full salute, now. "Aye, maybe. I might have to see you during class to give a proper ruling on the matter," he said appreciatively.

She snorted. "I'm not that impressive, although seeing Anna bent over doing the downward dog might just make the airfare worth it. Blonde, fit, and perky."

He looked at her pointedly. "Don't underestimate your appeal," he said. It came out more like a warning than he'd meant it to, but maybe that was good. Then he walked into his bedroom before he said anything else stupid.

The highlight of the week was when her small household shipment came. Michael came home briefly, surprised by the boxes and furniture. "I know it's a mess, I am going to have it done by tonight." He waved a hand in dismissal. "Don't worry about it. With the weather reports I won't be home much. We will get a break tomorrow for about 12 hours." This made Branna think about the kayaks. Tadgh had offered to take her and she'd been thinking about it ever since. He knelt down next to her as she sat on the floor with a box between her legs. She was unpacking some sort of wooden figure.

"It's a Kokeshi doll," she said, answering his questioning gaze. "Most are just wood. This one has a scroll. My parents bought it when I was born." She unrolled it a bit. "They put my ink printed feet and hands on it, all of the doctor's and nurses and corpsman signed it at the hospital. Then as I would have a birthday, or when we moved, people would add to it."

He was listening intently, "You were born in Japan?" She nodded. "Yes, we moved when I was a toddler."

He eyed the desk and the recliner. "It was my father's chair. My mom hated it. Every time we moved it was victimized in some way by the movers. Holes, stains, tears. He loved it, though. The desk was my mother's. That little piece over there was something they picked up in Japan." Michael looked at the interesting piece. It had a lot little drawers with kanji lettering. "It's a sort of apothecary. I always liked it. I used to pull all of the drawers out. It made my mom nuts. She finally realized my dad had been hiding candy for me in the drawers."

Michael smiled as she talked. "You don't talk about your mother much."

Branna's face was tense, like she was suppressing an emotion. "She was a wonderful woman. She loved my dad a lot. Being a military wife is hard. It's never about you. You move, find new homes, new schools, new friends. You can't keep a career going due to the relocations and the bouts of single parenting. It is a selfless life. She never put herself first. She didn't seem to mind, though. She just never recovered when my dad died."

Michael's heart ached for her. He loved his parents so much. They'd been such an integral part of his life even in adulthood. He knew he would lose them one day, but the thought of it terrified him.

"Cancer?" he asked.

Branna nodded, "Breast cancer. Nasty stuff." That was all she said. He wondered if his mother had told her that she'd also battled breast cancer. She was private about it, but it was indeed nasty stuff. She'd fought like hell, and had been cancer free for ten years.

"Yes, I know a little bit about it. I'm sorry she lost her fight with it, I really am." Branna smiled, "Thank you, Michael. It was long. She held on for a long time. At the end, she was in so much pain she just wanted it to be over."

Branna shook herself, "Anyway, what brings you home?"

He knew when to drop the subject. "Just here to pick up some snacks and change my uniform. I got fish blood on these while inspecting a boat."

Branna had smelled the distinct odor, but had kept silent until now. "I wasn't going to say anything, but you stink Michael O'Brien.

Thank God I have the windows open!" she was plugging her nose and making gagging noises.

He gave her a false look of offense, "Oh, really? You know, after this trip down memory lane, you look like you could use a hug."

She stopped her mocking and started trying to unravel her legs and scurry away. He caught her by her bare foot and did a silent moan at the fact that for once, she was in shorts. Smooth shapely legs and cute little feet. "Oh no you don't!" She squealed, but he had her. "Yes, that's what you need. A nice big bear hug." He pulled her little foot and dragged her into his arms, falling back as she landed on top of him.

She was laughing and gagging and yelling peeeeyuuuu! When he grabbed her around the rib cage she shrieked with laughter, jumping wildly.

He just stopped. "Well, well, well. Is the little hellcat ticklish?" He looked up to the heavens. "Thank you, God"

She had a look of horror on her face, "Oh shit."

Then he attacked, and she screamed wildly, arms and legs flying as he mercilessly tickled her. He rolled and pinned her down. Arms above her head and legs pinned as he had done in the garden. Then he let her catch her breath.

"Well, now. Let's see. What other little secrets do you have? We've covered the ribs. How about the neck? She started pressing her chin down and squealing. He burst into laughter, "I haven't even touched you yet!" Then he did a little experiment. He kept pretending he was going to tickle her, just stopping before he made contact. She was a live wire, laughing and squirming. "It should be illegal to be this ticklish," he said with astonishment.

She could barely breathe, she was laughing so hard. "Tell me about it!" She said, choking.

"What about the little tummy?" He lightly tickled her tummy with his short nails. He didn't get the response he was expecting. She sucked in a breath and arched under his hand. He looked at her face, and felt like he'd been zapped with a lightning bolt. Any trace of laughter was gone, and for a moment, it was pure heat in her eyes. She snapped out of it, trying to conceal her reaction. He couldn't stop himself. He wanted more of that look from her. He lightly grazed his fingers over what was obviously an erogenous zone. She closed her eyes and her hips jolted. Sweet, soft, creamy hips that were showing from the waist of her shorts. He couldn't take is eyes of her as he thumbed her hipbone. Her back arched and her breast came up. Her eyes were dazed and held a little note of fear. Not of him, but of her own response.

"Jesus Christ, Branna." His voice was hoarse, his accent thick. At this he released her hands and legs. He pressed his leg between hers and she was clutching his biceps. He ran his hand up her abdomen to where her rib cage began. He was captivated by the raw heat that was rolling off of her. This buttoned up little stress bomb had her hair coming apart, splayed all over the floor and her lips were slightly parted.

Just as he thought about descending on that sweet mouth his walkie squawked. "O'Brien, you copy?" He jerked to the awareness that he was still on duty. She came out of her sexual haze as well.

Michael rolled off of her, grabbing the walkie off his belt. "O'Brien to Headquarters, I copy."

The radio operator was trying to suppress a grin as he talked. "FYI O'Mara, your mic kept getting keyed off and on. If you're done detaining the little hellcat, we are shipping off in ten." There was background noise of other men chuckling.

Michael was lying on his back, covering his eyes. His breathing was heavy and his face was red. Whether from exertion or from embarrassment, Branna didn't know. She was feeling all that and more. They hadn't done anything, really. Nothing that was beyond the point of no return. She was wondering, however, how simple horse play had ended in her panting and aroused to the point of dizziness.

Michael hopped up and took a deep breath. He keyed his radio. "Copy that, see you in ten."

Branna was standing as well. She was fiddling nervously in the kitchen when she noticed he was shaking. His back was to her, arms on hips, and he was fully shaking with suppressed laughter. Suddenly, she couldn't hold it in, the nervousness fueling her as she laughed hysterically. He turned to her and his face was all joy and mischief. She threw a dishtowel at him and said, "Go change your shirt, stinky."

He came out of his room after a minute with a new shirt and his extra boots on. It took him a few minutes to get a decent amount of shifting done so that he didn't leave the room or walk into the station with a visible hard on.

Branna was bending down, getting her rabbit food out of the produce drawer and he was juiced up all over again. She popped up when she heard him. She had a fresh shirt and pants on as well, a big USMC t-shirt and leggings. "Did my hug foul your clothes?"

She gave him a chiding look. "You're trouble, O'Brien."

He was thinking the same thing about her. "Aye, well I suppose I did get a little out of hand. I'm sorry if I…overstepped."

She blushed, "No more than I. Look, I know it isn't anything personal. You put any two healthy people of the opposite sex in close quarters like this. Well, I know you didn't mean anything by it. It was a bit of harmless horseplay."

Michael didn't say what he was thinking. It had everything to do with her, it was completely personal, and it was anything but harmless. He had the blue balls to prove it. Voicing that, however, was not going to get them anywhere. He didn't need complications, and she may have set her sights on his cousin. He needed to be more careful. He just seemed to throw good judgment out the window when they spent any idle time alone.

"Yes, well duty calls. I won't be home until after our session tonight. Are you coming to watch the show?"

She answered, "Yes, if I manage to get this put away. Be safe, Michael. The water is rough."

He softened at her concern, "Thanks, I always am." He checked his phone, "Shit, I've got to go."

She smiled, "Have fun at work. Prepare yourself for all of the naughty boys teasing you."

He grinned and gave a parting shot, "I'll just tell them ye can't keep your hands off me."

Branna gaped. "Don't you dare!" she screamed his name as he ran out the door.

As he drove back to meet the boat, he was trying to persuade himself to play it safe, while at the same time, flashes of her aroused body came to him, arching under his hands. They hadn't done anything, really. What kept wreaking havoc on his imagination was this. If she came that undone just from a few caresses on her belly, that smooth swell of lower belly he loved so much, and hips, what would she be like if he got serious? He was already haunted every night with thoughts of pulling her waistband down as he kissed and licked her warm lower belly, grazed his teeth on the soft, sensitive skin where her leg and hip came together.

If that walkie hadn't gone off, he may have tried to find out. His lust had almost overridden his good judgment. It was foolish, but he wanted her. She'd never openly expressed any desire for him in return. Yes, she had responded to him. Her response had been incredible. Maybe she was right, though. Maybe for her, it was merely proximity, and the sexual deprivation that goes along with living with a man she wasn't sleeping with.

He couldn't help praying that she didn't take that sexual frustration and turn it on his cousin. Tadgh denied it, but he could tell Tadgh wanted her. How could he not? If he was a good man, he would leave them both alone and let Tadgh have a chance with her. He wasn't feeling very giving right now, however. He was feeling some frustration himself and a very unhealthy territorial response.

CHAPTER 10

Gus O'Connors was packed. She was thrilled to see that James and Alex were still there and waved them over to sit with her. "Oh, we left for two nights to check out the scene in Dingle. We decided to head back, though, to check on our little Yank."

Branna hugged them both. "It's so good to see you again."

James, ever the blunt one, wanted some new scoop. "So, what's been happening with the big stud? Any sex yet?"

Alex elbowed him, "Must you be so crude? You're embarrassing her."

James was shameless; he didn't feel bad at all. "I'm sorry, darling. I can't help teasing you given you're overdue. How does someone as gorgeous as you stay a virgin this long?"

Because the universe was cruel, and prone to ganging up on Branna, Tadgh walked up right as he said it. She felt her face redden. Alex was admonishing James again, and Tadgh was staring at her with a stunned expression.

"Well, I'm not sure how that conversation started, but it ended with a bang." Tadgh said.

Which provoked James to add, "Or not, in this case."

"James!" Alex scolded.

Branna just put her head in her hands. What the hell? Was it written on her forehead? "Can we please not talk about my sex life, or lack there of, in mixed company?"

They all looked at Tadgh. "I think she just insulted our manhood, Alex," James said.

Alex replied, "You deserve it, you buffoon." He turned to Branna. "Your innocence is a rare thing. It is to be treasured, my dear. You will find the right man, and when you give yourself to him, you will be spectacular."

James nodded, unaffected by his partner's tongue lashing. "Absolutely. You know I am just teasing. You are beautiful and fiery. When you finally release all of the penned up passion you have simmering in your eyes, your man will never be the same. You, my love, are the kind of woman that people write plays about. I may not swing that way, but I know what I'm talking about."

Tadgh was looking at her. She could tell. She was so embarrassed. Then she felt his arm around her shoulders. He whispered in her ear. "Your secret is safe with me." She slumped in relief. Then he added, "Remind me again why I'm not trying to get in your knickers?"

That made her laugh and she put her head on his shoulder. James, never one to pass up an opening, replied, "Maybe she's not your type? I have friends."

Tadgh's jaw dropped, "That's a kind offer, but I don't swing your way."

James shrugged, "Fair enough."

Branna sometimes forgot just how much of a prude she was. The thought of Alex and James didn't bother her. It was just that when people started talking about sex, any kind of sex, she was out of her league. The fact that she had just been outed as the big V made her want to sniper crawl out of the pub and run for the hills.

Michael had been warming up in the back with his family. They sent him to see how big the crowd was and whether it was mostly tourists or locals. They adjusted the session depending on the breakdown. Tourists liked the popular tunes. "Whiskey in the Jar," "She

Moved Through the Fair," and God forbid, "Danny Boy." Every drunk, Boston tourist loved that fucking song.

Having Michael and Aidan home drew the local crowd. They needed the practice, anyway. Patrick's wedding was coming up in a couple of days. He had briefly considered inviting Branna, but he'd changed his mind. With the whole family under one roof and Caitlyn's clan, she would probably feel out of place.

It was an intimate affair, as a wedding should be. Fiona hadn't settled for that, of course. She had to have the big, obnoxious wedding with all the trimmings. No local music, even though she played. She had a DJ and hired an overpriced, out of town caterer. Michael hadn't known half the people in attendance. Bridezilla kept harping on about it being "her day" like he was some mannequin just propped up for the ceremony.

She had put her parents, his parents, and himself in debt to do it. Nothing made that witch happy. For the next two years, she had complained that she didn't get what she really wanted, which was a destination wedding on the French Riviera. Fiona's da was a bus driver. Her mother ran a small guesthouse that barely broke even. Where the hell she'd gotten her entitlement complex was beyond him. Too much television and not enough time at Mass, probably. Weddings were supposed to be about two people who loved each other being lifted up by family, church, and community. It wasn't supposed to be about showing up your friends and acting like royalty.

He scanned the pub, looking for Branna. He took guilty pleasure in performing for her. She liked the music, she made a point of telling him how much she liked his singing. He caught site of her. He growled lowly, before he could stop himself. Tadgh had his arm around her. Her head was on his shoulder. She had those two other men, the English man and the Italian sitting with her as well.

For God's sake, couldn't she find some women to hang out with? As soon as he'd thought it, he felt bad. She really hadn't had time to meet anyone. Tadgh had gone out of his way to be her friend. Did he really expect her to sit alone?

He really needed to try and find some girls for her to meet. He convinced himself that he had innocent motives for this, and that it had nothing to do with her spending so much time with his cousin. Still, she seemed to enjoy the male attention. A little comparison he tried not to make with Fiona.

Not that it mattered to him. She could date whomever she wanted. He just cringed at the thought of waking up to find Tadgh coming out of her bedroom. The thought made him mental, if he was honest with himself. He was in such deep shit.

Branna looked around the pub just in time to catch a look at Michael. He looked grim, and he was looking right at her. Actually, he was looking at Tadgh with his arm around her. Maybe she was imagining it, but he really seemed to have a hang up about her hanging around with Tadgh.

He denied it, so maybe she was being paranoid. They made eye contact and she felt a wave of heat go through her. He seemed to look right into her. Tadgh noticed her gaze and looked in the same direction. When he saw his cousin, he quickly retrieved his arm, giving him a casual wave.

Maybe he had said something to Tadgh. Something along the lines of "who's side are you on?" She hoped not. She couldn't afford to lose the few friends she had. James noticed the exchange.

"So Branna, what's shaking at the cottage? Is he leaving the toilet seat up, trying to poison your tea?" Branna was barely listening. She was feeling hot and a little queasy, but not in a bad way, and she couldn't help but let her gaze float back to Michael. She answered him when the question sunk in.

"Everything is fine. I got a car, started prepping the house for painting."

Tadgh piped in at this point. "She's been holding out on us boys. We're dining on oily pub fare, while we have a gourmet chef in our midst."

This got Alex's attention. "Ah, a woman who can cook. Always a good friend to have."

James swatted his hand dismissively. "I hate to cook. Alex does all of the cooking. I just open the wine."

Branna smiled shyly, "He's exaggerating. I can hold my own. I am rusty. I don't cook very often since it's just me."

Tadgh chuffed at this. "What she means is that she eats hamster food. Some kind of nutty bars that look like they should be wired to the side of a bird cage."

She elbowed him, "Don't you start on that, too. Michael practically force-fed me last week. I stayed outside too long with no water and he went all Army medic on me."

Tadgh gave her a strange look, "Did he now?"

James perked up at that, "It sounds like despite his protests, he is taking pretty good care of our girl."

She rolled her eyes, "Yeah, maybe. Don't tell him that." Then she put on her best Irish accent, "He'll get all fat headed about it, and they'll be no livin' wit him."

All three men burst out laughing. "Well done! We need you up on stage!" James exclaimed.

That made Tadgh look thoughtfully at her. "Michael mentioned that you played the piano. Do you sing as well?"

Branna shrugged noncommittally and started fiddling with her straw and sipping at her club soda. "You little chancer! You do sing!"

Branna was looking around, "Tadgh! Shh, lower your voice."

He gave her a challenging look, "Do you know any of the old tunes?"

She exhaled, "A few. Just don't say anything. These people really know their music. This Yank is staying in the audience, and off the stage."

Tadgh gave her a pleading look, "Throw me a bone, girl. I'd love to do a number with you. There's an open mic night at McDermott's."

She shook her head violently. "No way Tadgh, nada, forget it." She pinned him with a glare. "Shut your gob about this. I mean it."

"Okay, I'll drop it for now, but we will revisit this another time."

There was activity up on stage. Robby, Jenny, Michael, Brigid and Aidan were on tonight. Sean was helping set up. Branna saw Sorcha emerging from the back as well. They were starting in ten minutes, just enough time for her to grab another round of drinks. She excused herself and walked up to the bar. Jenny was on stage, so there was a man she didn't know tending bar. She ordered two gin and tonics, a Creans, and another club soda.

A chilly, but familiar voice spoke behind her. "Aren't the men supposed to be buying you drinks? Some girls just don't have the touch, I suppose."

Branna turned around. "Fiona, what is your problem?"

Fiona leaned on the bar and gave her a bitchy grin. "Me? I've not got a problem."

Branna was fed up with this bitch. "Let me guess, new girl in town takes two minutes of the spotlight off of you. So, you have to come hike your leg like a dog and mark your domain? Sound about right?"

Fiona bristled at this. "You don't know the first thing about me, this town, or your new housemate. I don't know what you think you're proving, popping in to town, expecting everyone to start falling all over themselves to help you. I see Tadgh has taken to following you around like a puppy. Are you shagging them both?"

Branna couldn't believe how rotten this woman was. "Let's get something straight, Fiona. My life is none of your business, and two timing is your thing, not mine. This is a small town, I am sure it hasn't been easy having your scandal under the community microscope, but leave me out of your shit. I grew up on military bases. I saw young wives like you all the time. Their men are off fighting, doing their duty. Meanwhile princess can't stand being alone, hates not being the center of the universe. Starts carousing the bars looking for a bit of attention."

Fiona was livid. She'd hit a nerve. "You can go fuck yourself with your assumptions," she said.

Branna put her hands up, "That's fine with me. Just remember, you approached me, but before you walk off in a snit, I have one more thing to add."

Fiona folded her arms in front of her chest and stood with one leg cocked out and straightened, a defensive pose. "I don't need any words of wisdom from the likes of you, Yank."

Branna lifted her shoulders, hands in her pockets. "Well, you're going to get them anyway. You had the world by the ass, Fiona. You had a wonderful man from a good family. I don't have to be shagging Michael to see who he is. He couldn't hide it if he tried. He's a good man. He's loyal and brave, smart and funny. He has a sense of duty that people like you will never understand. Any woman would be lucky to have him."

Fiona gave her a scathing once over."Don't forget good-looking and a great ass. Don't pretend you haven't noticed. I see the way you look at him. You wouldn't know the first thing about taking on a man like Michael." She leaned into Branna with an icy smile. "He's hung like a stallion, too, for all the good it did me. Did he tell you he didn't want children? Don't set your sights on him girl. He's not the keeping kind."

Suddenly Fiona stopped short. She was looking behind Branna with a shaken expression. "Good luck, little Branna. You'll need it. That's too much car for you." Then she turned and left the pub.

Branna looked behind her where Michael was standing. "How much of that did you hear?" Michael walked toward her, not taking his eyes from her. He took her chin in his hand. "Enough," was all he said. He rubbed his thumb along her jaw line. The feeling was hypnotic. Her joints loosened and heat pooled in her belly.

He leaned down and put his mouth to her ear. "Thank you," he whispered and then he kissed her temple. He released her and walked up toward the stage, leaving her there weak kneed and flushed. She watched him walk through the crowd, big and strong and confident. Fiona had been right about one thing. He had a great ass. A fact that didn't go unnoticed by every woman he walked past. Too much car indeed, but damn her if she wasn't thinking about a test drive.

* * *

THE NEXT WEEK PASSED QUICKLY. Branna worked on the exterior of the house, sometimes with Michael, sometimes without. She was eager to get it finished. The weather report was going to be sunny and dry for three more days before the rain started and didn't stop. Michael had given strict guidelines about how long she should work and how much water she should drink. Mostly she ignored him, falling into her old bad habits. Hamster food and coffee, but an occasional glass of water to ease her conscience.

He had also ordered her to stay off the ladder. It irritated her because he treated her like a child. She had the bottom areas and the trim painted, but she needed to get the rest done. He was on another twenty-four hour shift and she needed to keep the momentum going. He also had Patrick's wedding to worry about.

She had her initial appointment with Dr. Flynn. She sat in the examination room twitchy and anxious. She hated hospitals. This wasn't a hospital, just a family practice office, which was the only reason, she had agreed to this doctor. She jumped as the doctor knocked. She came in and introduced herself. "You must be Miss O'Mara. It is good to finally meet you. Dr. Troy called me and filled me in on everything. The only thing that is missing is the emergency contact. Who do you want me to put as your local contact in case of emergency? Branna cringed. She hated that question. After some deliberation, she decided Tadgh was the best option.

The doctor sat on her rolling stool and looked at her with frankness. "The hospital phobia, how serious is it?" Branna was really uncomfortable. "I looked in your chart. Your blood pressure is not high, but it is higher than previous readings. Are you feeling stressed?"

Branna blew out a breath, "I suppose. I'm sure the news of my little arrangement has reached your ears."

The doctor smiled, "Yes, well such is life in a small town. Now, when my office is open, we can usually get you in within a 48-hour period, but if you have an acute problem you can call me at home. It's a strange arrangement. I've never been put on retainer for house calls before, but your doctor assured me that you would die in your bed before you came to an emergency room."

Branna felt a little defensive, "It's not a phobia. I just don't like hospitals. I spent a little bit too much time as a spectator in my youth. Dr. Troy assured me that you'd agreed to my care plan, so here I am. I know they have socialized medicine in Ireland, but obviously you can't make free house calls to everyone. I don't intend on ever needing it. I am pretty healthy. I am sure any small problems can wait for your office hours."

Dr. Flynn listened patiently, then clapped her hands together. "Ok, dear. Let's get started then. BP, temperature and weight are all normal. I see that you had some urology concerns when you were younger?" Branna nodded, "Yes, but I've been fine for a long time, since I was a toddler. No concerns there."

The doctor kept reading, but gave instructions as she went. "Proper hydration is crucial if you want to keep that trend. Implement probiotics and go easy on the caffeine. It says here you haven't had a gynecological exam in a while. Is there a reason why not? I see a history of breast cancer on your mother's side."

The doctor removed her cheaters and looked at her. "Is that how she died?" Branna just nodded. "So, you have listed here that you are taking oral contraceptives, yet no yearly exams. Can I ask why not?"

Branna understood her confusion. "Yes, the pills are for regulating my overactive ovulation cycle. I started taking them two yeas ago. This just leveled things out. The reason the exams are infrequent is because, well, I'm not sexually active. I mean… not at all. Ever."

The doctor didn't change her expression, which pleased Branna. She hated the freakish stares when people found out she was a virgin and pushing 24 years old.

"So, no history of sexual activity?" Branna clarified, "Nope, never. I know that's odd."

The Dr. was direct. "Well, it's uncommon but refreshing. Do you need refills?" Branna shook her head. "I have a six month supply."

"Ok, Miss O'Mara, you seem to be healthy. When you need a refill on those pills give us a month notice. Also, if your activity status changes, you should come in for an exam. Until then, you have my number. I see that you saw a therapist at seventeen. Why did you stop?"

Branna sighed, "That was when my dad was killed. The school and my doctor thought it was a good idea and my mom made it happen."

Doc shook her head in acknowledgement, "I would have recommended the same. Did your mother go as well?"

Branna shook her head, "No, she was more the suffer in silence type."

Dr. Flynn raised one brow, "I see. Well, if you are feeling stressed, I can recommend a good therapist. You've had some big changes." Branna was shaking her head vigorously. "Fair enough. Okay, that's it. It was nice to finally meet you."

* * *

BRANNA PICKED UP HER PHONE. "Hi Tadgh, how are you?" She could tell that he was on speaker phone.

"I'm grand, Branna. I'm headed over to help get the wedding party set up for tomorrow. It got me thinking. I don't have a date. Normally I would poach one of the bridesmaids, but she only has Brigid. So, my beautiful, platonic friend, you should be my date. Alex and James are off to Dublin, so you need to be nice to me. I'm your only friend on this island."

Branna gasped, "You are a punk! Way to make me feel like a total loser!" Her tone was teasing. She knew he was only joking.

"I don't have anything to wear to a wedding," she offered weakly.

"Bollocks, you are as anal as they come. You must have an outfit for every situation. You love being prepared."

She laughed, "I am not anal! I happen to be quite serious. I don't have any party clothes. I got rid of a lot when I moved." She didn't feel the need to share with him that she also didn't have much of a social life.

Tadgh said, "Let me call you back in five minutes."

He didn't call back before she heard a knock at the door. It was Brigid. "Hello, Branna. I hear you have a wardrobe problem. Come on then, grab your bag." Branna was astonished that this wobbling little pregnant woman had just showed up and started bossing her around. She was a lot like her brother.

"I'm fine Brigid, really. I don't need to go to the wedding. Michael may not like it. He didn't invite me, after all."

Brigid turned that face on her, so much like Michael's. "Aye, he wouldn't have. He's playing at the party and he's also in the wedding and he wouldn't have been a very good host. So, I am inviting you and so is Tadgh. It's settled. Now, Caitlyn is Patrick's bride to be. She's about your size and has a little clothing addiction problem. I rang her on the way over. She's expecting us." Brigid started walking toward the door. She stopped when Branna didn't move. "You can paint later today. Right now we have business, girl. Chop chop."

They drove a few minutes to Caitlyn's home, making small talk. Branna decided pretty quickly that she liked Brigid. She also adored the bride to be. Caitlyn was easy going and funny and very sweet. The two women were like something off of reality TV. They immediately started throwing outfits at her, demanding she strip. "Well, Branna. You have quite a sweet little figure under those tidy clothes, don't you? You better not walk around in your knickers in front of my brother. Those O'Brien men like a nice round arse." Caitlyn covered her mouth, stifling a laugh.

Branna put her hands on her hips. "Where I'm from, we call this bootilicious." They giggled, the three of them like a gaggle of teenagers. She tried on several outfits before they really got serious. The winner was obvious when both the women gasped. "Holy God, would you look at her! The green makes her blue eyes glow." Brigid hopped off the bed and went behind her and started dismantling her bun. "What are you doing?" Branna asked. All she got back was a shush. She unfolded Branna's hair and draped it over her shoulders.

Brigid looked at Caitlyn. "A body like this and the eyes to go with it." She smacked Branna lightly on the shoulder, "Couldn't you have some flaw? A bald patch? Split ends? A spotty back?"

Branna looked at her like she was crazy. "What are you talking about?"

Brigid gave Caitlyn another look. Caitlyn shook her head, "She's got no bloody idea, has she?"

Branna looked at them both. "What! Stop being so cryptic! Is something wrong?" Brigid guided her over to the mirror.

The dress had a graduating hemline. Shorter in front, then gradually longer at the back. It was a beautiful, deep, emerald color. It was silk and the bodice was snug with a long waistline. It showed her curves all the way to the hips. Her pale skin looked translucent next to the green silk. Her dark hair was tousled and spilling down her back and shoulders.

The snug bodice held up the dress, but it also had thin spaghetti straps that accented her lean arms and décolletage. The front curved around her breast, dipping into her cleavage. The dress made her breasts look high and round. She just looked at herself for a moment, then at Brigid.

"You are a beauty. Your dance card will be filled all night." Branna blushed at their compliments. Brigid started putting things back on the hanger. Branna watched her bending and stretching with her baby bump and felt a pang of envy. Not that she wanted to be pregnant. It was just the idea of new life. Someone new to love, and be loved in return.

Branna asked, "So, do you have some gorgeous maternity dress picked out? Your hair is like your mother's and your face like your dad's. You would look good in any color." Brigid smiled and patted her tummy. "Well, the dresses at the bridal shop were awful. We went to Dublin and found something nice, since I'm her Matron of Honor."

"Oh yes, Tadgh mentioned you were in the wedding. How wonderful!"

Caitlyn laughed. "Well, several months ago when we were planning, she wasn't pregnant. We were dreaming of a hen party with cocktails and clubbing. Now we're sitting at home painting our toenails and drinking tea like a couple of old bitties."

Brigid added, "Aye, and me stuffing swollen feet in heels and waddling down the church row."

Branna had wanted to bring something up, but was hesitant.

Brigid said, "You've got questions, it's all over your face. Don't be shy, girl. You're among friends."

Branna looked at her in amazement. “What, do you read minds?”

Brigid just grinned slyly. “Of course, twin powers. Michael has eyes in the back of his head, and I read minds. We’re legends in these parts.”

Branna thought she was only half kidding. Michael did have eyes in the back of his head. “Your mother told me about the O’Brien men, about them only having one mate for life. She said they had a hard time coming to them. Was it like that with you, Caitlyn? When you met Patrick?”

Brigid looked at Caitlyn with a knowing grin. “You could say that,” she said with a throaty laugh.

Caitlyn was a lovely young woman. She had straight blonde hair, hazel green eyes that tipped up at the corners. She had freckles and beautiful, fair skin. She was nodding and laughing. “Aye, I almost broke his nose on our first date. On our fourth date he did break another lad’s nose. They’re a bit possessive. They don’t like other men trying to move in on their women. Of course, by the fourth date, I’d bewitched him body and soul with all of this.” She swept her hands down her waist and wiggled her butt. They all laughed.

Branna was intrigued. “Does it bother you? That level of intensity?”

Caitlyn dismissed the thought, “No, I’m just the same. I get a little touchy when I see other women ogling him. I’m sure you haven’t missed how the women respond to them. They’re a passionate bunch, the O’Brien men. Patrick was like a storm that came in and carried me off.”

Then she gave a devilish grin, “And the sex! Christ, I can’t get enough of him.”

At this point Brigid was covering her ears and saying her ABCs. Caitlyn was laughing at her. She wondered, not for the first time, what Michael would be like. She knew, really. He was a handful on a fully clothed day. She could only imagine what it would be like to get the fully unleashed desire of such a man. A girl could hurt herself on one of these O’Brien men.

As Branna kissed and hugged the two women goodbye, she was

feeling very content. She hadn't thought about how much she missed hanging out with other females until today. She had isolated herself for so long, working and taking care of her mother. She felt very happy at how her afternoon had gone. She had a gorgeous dress to wear and new friends. She found herself getting rather excited about the wedding. She had loved parties not so long ago. She'd just quit letting herself have fun.

It was time to get back to work, so she put her grubby t-shirt on. It was hot. She took a reusable water bottle out with her and started prepping to paint. She got the ladder and propped it. She climbed up and started to work. About two hours later she had finished a quarter of her water and one whole side of the house and part of the front. She was adjusting the ladder between the rose bushes. As she painted she realized one foot of the ladder was off alignment. She must have set it on a rock. The ladder was wobbly, but she didn't weigh a lot, so she let it be.

She was reaching up to pluck a leaf off the edge when she realized her mistake. Over she went, paint bucket flying. She followed, falling butt first into the rose bush. Luckily it broke her fall. Unluckily, she could feel thorns piercing her back. She could also feel a little stinging cut on her scalp where the ladder had come down on her head. She pushed the ladder off and grabbed the window sill to extricate herself from the thorny bush.

There was no way she was wearing that gorgeous dress if her face and arms and shoulders were all chewed up. She walked into the house with a doozy headache. The good news, she discovered, was the thorns had gotten her in the lower back and thighs. Nothing would show with her dress. She took her bloody t-shirt off and trousers off and tried cleaning the cuts, but she couldn't reach a lot of them. She was just walking from the kitchen sink to her bathroom when Michael walked through the front door.

He stopped abruptly, noticing her state of undress. Then shook his head and walked toward her. "Christ, you fell off the ladder didn't you?"

She was frantically grabbing a throw off of the couch to cover herself. "Why would you think that?" She smiled innocently. "I was just getting in the shower. You surprised me, obviously. I'll just be..." Before she could finish he was holding her tightly by her upper arms. "Don't try to bullshit me Branna," His face registered alarm. "Jesus, did you hit your head?"

She plastered her best fake smile. "More like something hit me. I'm fine Michael. The rose bush caught my fall. The ladder just bonked me on the head. It's a tiny cut."

He was looking at her scalp mumbling what she guessed were Gaelic expletives."Don't lie to me lass. That t-shirt has bloody spots all over the back. How hurt are you? I'll call Dr. Flynn." She said, "No, Michael. Listen to me. It was a little fall. I don't have anything but a few small cuts from the thorns. They just need cleaned. That's what I was trying to do when you came in." She could see that she'd scared him. He probably saw the ladder tipped over, the paint everywhere, and assumed the worst.

She put a hand on his face. "Calm down. It's nothing. I fell like this all the time as a kid, just like you did. I'm sorry I scared you."

Her hands on his face seem to stop the frenzy immediately. He closed his eyes and exhaled. "Let me see your back. You'll never clean them properly by yourself."

If Branna had gone back to the first day that she arrived in Doolin, and put herself back in that room, poking Michael in the chest, she would never have believed where she was now. She was sitting on his bed with the blanket pooled at her waist. He had taken some dressings and Q-tips from his en-suite bathroom. He had a warm, soapy rag, rubbing it down her back to clean the scratched areas. It wasn't as bad as he thought, he admitted that much. Her shirt was speckled with a little blood, but the various cuts were minor. He dried her by blotting another clean towel. Then he blew on the affected areas, getting them dry enough for the band-aids to stick.

Her skin came alive as he touched her. When he blew on her back, goose bumps appeared all over her. She marveled that someone in her position could be getting turned on, but the fact that his hands were on her, she was in his bed, and she was wearing nothing but a bra and panties was just a little more stimulation than her body could take. She was disgusted with herself.

He was all business. His concern was touching, but hot and heavy was not on his mind. He worked with silent, disconnected efficiency. She was also slightly disheartened that his first sight of her almost nude didn't seem to affect him at all.

Michael had finally calmed down after realizing Branna had fallen off the ladder. What he hadn't managed to calm down was his cock, which popped to full sail when he'd seen Branna in nothing but matching lace panties and bra. He had managed to hide his reaction and focus on making sure she was ok, but he had been painfully aroused ever since.

She had leaves in her hair and her bun was off kilter again. She had a blanket around her hips while he tended to her scratches. She was right. It wasn't serious. Even the cut on her scalp was minor, the ladder having just grazed her scalp on the way down. She was on his bed and the sun was lighting up her beautiful skin. "That takes care of your back for the most part." He only put a Band-Aid on one that was still seeping a little. "Let me see the back of your thighs."

Branna covered her shoulders with the throw and stood. He was sitting on the bed, feet on the floor, and her ass was in his face. She made sure her butt was covered, not needing up close scrutiny of any possible cellulite. She knew she had at least three spots on the legs that got hit. Two of them were high up on her leg. She was actually starting to blush. She felt the warm cloth go smoothly over her skin. He was as intimately positioned as a lover and it was driving her crazy. "You have a long one that goes between your legs." She grimaced thinking of her favorite sitcom that had coined the phrase *That's what she said.*

She stifled a laugh. "Did I say something funny?" Then he thought about what he'd said. He chuckled. "A dirty mind is a terrible thing to waste, Branna."

She could feel him now. He had the antibiotic salve on his fingertip instead of a Q-Tip. "I'm sorry, I'm out of clean swabs. I'll be quick."

Take your time, and be really thorough, she thought. He ran it slowly from the middle of her thigh to right where it ended between her legs. The soft skin of her inner thigh sending signals right to her center. How many times in the past weeks had she fantasized about him slipping his hand between her legs? She was pretty untried in the sex department, but she could imagine how it would feel. He had big, strong hands. Skilled musician's hands.

She mentally swatted her thoughts away. Jesus, she was turning into a complete perv. He was trying to help her, not seduce her. He had, in fact, kept his distance from her since the tickling incident.

She spoke with a shaky voice. "Yes, I did a little more damage trying to get out of the bush. I am just glad it won't show with my dress tomorrow. I have a few on my hands, but no one will see them." He froze. She remembered stupidly that he hadn't invited her. "Oh, I forgot to tell you. Actually, it just happened today. I am going with Tadgh to the wedding. Tadgh asked and so did Brigid."

He paused, "Did they?" She stiffened visibly. She pulled the blanket into position below her thighs as she exited the bedroom. "If you don't want me there, I understand. I can tell them I changed my mind." Her tone was light, but he could tell his cryptic response had hurt her feelings.

He jumped up, taking her by the elbow as he caught her part way to her bedroom. "Branna, you misunderstand me. I didn't ask you myself because, well, I'm the best man, and I'm performing at the reception. I guess I should have asked you anyway, but I was afraid of ignoring you." Just as he finished he noticed that he had separated the blanket in front by pulling her arm. He could see a blessed amount of creamy flesh swelling out of her white lacy bra.

He was about to lose his mind and drag her back into his bed. Rubbing that ointment on her thighs had driven him to lunacy. He wanted to put her hands flat against the wall while he knelt behind her, her back arched, legs spread while he pulled her to his mouth. It had taken every bit of strength he had not to forget her injuries and throw her down on the bed.

His lust must have shown on his face. She became aware she was showing him a good amount of cleavage and she closed the blanket.

"Ok, well if you are sure you don't mind. Caitlyn lent me a dress, and your sister might drag me out of the house by force if I try to cancel. She reminds me a lot of you."

He grinned, "Twins, double trouble."

Michael was painting and Branna was cleaning up the mess she'd made when Tadgh pulled up. Michael suppressed a growl as Branna's face lit up and she shot her hand up in a big wave. He really had to stop this jealousy crap. He loved Tadgh like a brother. He had no claims on her and they genuinely seemed well suited.

"What happened here? He didn't push you off the ladder, did he?" he jested.

"No, I did that fine all on my own," she answered lightly. Tadgh's face flashed to panic, "Christ, I was kidding. Are you hurt?" Tadgh pulled her up off the ground, forcing her to abandon her task.

His innocent comment chaffed and seeing Tadgh put his hands protectively on Branna made Michael's gut twist. "Do you honestly think I am such a prick that I'd have her out here helping if she was injured?" The harshness of his tone took both Tadgh and Branna back a little.

Tadgh hastened to reassure him, "No, Jesus. I'm sorry. Of course you wouldn't." He turned to Branna. "Did he take care of you, then?"

She said, "Yes, he did. All better. Just a few scratches and cuts on my back and thighs." As soon as she said it, she wished she could retract it. Tadgh gave his cousin a sideways glance. "Aye, I'm sure he was happy to help."

Branna needed to change the subject. "I wanted to thank you for sending Brigid over. I had a good time."

Tadgh said, "Well, if you swear you are ok, maybe you can take a break for a minute while we go over tomorrow's plan. Did you get a dress?"

Branna laughed, "They were relentless. Caitlyn has more clothes than a village of women. Patrick has his work cut out for him!"

Tadgh laughed at this, "Yes, I've heard. Patrick had to set the *I-don't-hold-purse-while-you-try-on-clothes* rule pretty early on in the relationship."

Branna said,"Thank you, by the way. It ended up being a great morning. I didn't realize how much I needed a little girl time. You knew just what I needed." At this she squeezed his upper arm.

"Well, I knew if anyone could get her way out of you, it was Brigid. She's pushy like her twin." Michael was painting and gritting his teeth. He just grunted at the jibe. He knew Tadgh was only playing around. He was more put out with himself. Why hadn't he asked her to the wedding? Why didn't he see that she needed some girlfriends? She'd isolated herself here, working on this bloody cottage, just peeking her head out when the sun went down. She liked the music and she played, but he never tried to pull her into a rehearsal and let her hang out with Jenny and Robby and his family. The only time he did give her attention was to argue or lust after her. Tadgh didn't mean to shame him, but he had.

"I'm glad you invited her Tadgh; she'll have fun." It was all he was capable of saying that wouldn't come out like a jealous, caustic comment. Tadgh wasn't the bad guy, here, but he still couldn't help resenting the shit out of him for getting a date with her tomorrow night.

* * *

BRANNA RAN out to the store while Michael cleaned up his paint supplies and took a shower. While they'd been painting, Ned Kelly had stopped by to check on their progress. He praised Branna for taking the time to clean the place up. To Michael's surprise, she had been quick to point out that he had split the cost with her, had everything delivered, and despite a hectic work schedule, had done just as much work on the place as she had. Why she did this was beyond him. She could have merely preened under his praise, gaining the upper hand.

He realized that he had misjudged her. She'd been genuinely offended that he thought her to be scheming. He knew now that he'd been wrong about the type of person she was. They'd been in a bubble for a couple of weeks. Not seeing Ned or Jack had made it easy to forget that they were on opposing sides. That thought hit him right in the gut. Somehow, the thought of getting rid of her was not sitting as well with him as it once had.

As if on cue, another reminder of what a lousy judge of character he was slapped him in the face. His phone was ringing. It was Brigid. She and Caitlyn were screaming on speaker phone. They were in the car. "Where is Branna? She isn't answering her bloody phone!" He looked over on the desk and it was on the charger by her laptop. "She left it, she won't be long, though. What are you two squeakin about?"

Brigid answered, "Well, we just so happen to be headed to Ennis for a spa treatment. Branna booked a hen party at the spa for the two of us. Pedicures and a pre-natal massage for me and pedi and a sugar scrub and massage for the bride. They called us all official like and told us our spa rooms would be waiting at six o'clock. God, we had microwave popcorn and home nail kits waiting for us. This is grand all together!"

Her tone immediately switched. "She's a darling girl, Michael. If you are mean to her I'll beat your ass!"

He laughed. His sister's Irish got thick when she was excited. She started mixing Gaelic and English in a bastardized language that was all her own. Being her twin, he understood every word. He used to joke with his brothers that he was the only one that was fluent in "Brigid".

"Well, I suppose I'll have to behave if I don't want three hens pecking at me."

Brigid huffed, "Make that four. Ma thinks she's a fine, lovely lass." She said the last while imitating her mother's voice. "You're screwed, brother. If you kick her out of that cottage we're adopting her! Tell her to call us!" Brigid abruptly hung up, as she always did. She blew in and out like the North wind, ruffling as many feathers as possible in a short duration.

Branna came home with her hands full of grocery bags. "That's a lot of hamster bars and rabbit food," he teased.

"Shut your gob," she shot back and it made him laugh. She was so cute when she was trying to sound local. "You worked hard today, and you patched me up. I decided to cook you dinner." She stopped abruptly, "You don't have plans do you? This will keep for later if you do."

He looked at her incredulously. "You mean to tell me that if I did have plans, you wouldn't cook all the food you just bought? You'd eat one of your bars and call it a night?"

She looked at him as if he was a bit slow. "Yes, I can't eat all of this. I have snacks I can eat. Do you have plans?"

He shook his head, amazed at her reasoning. "No, so get to work woman. I'm starved."

She shook some sort of leafy thing at him. "Watch it, Bub. I'll dirty every dish in the house and make you wash them."

He loved when she played tough with him. "Well, then I guess I should help."

She said, "No, you relax and have a drink. I have cider or beer. Any preference?"

He jumped up, "I'll get it." He came into the kitchen as Branna started her prep work. He dug around in the fridge and saw a bottle of French white wine. "Were you saving this?"

She looked at the bottle. "No, in fact I need a little for the sauce. The rest is up for grabs. Oh! I have my wine glasses now, and a cork screw!"

He dug it out of the drawer and took out two long stemmed wine glasses. As he poured, she noticed he had two glasses. She started to tell him not to worry about her when he shot her a look. "I don't drink alone, and you worked just as hard as I did." He handed her a glass and then clinked his to hers. "Slainte." He never took his eyes off her as he sipped. She drank and closed her eyes. "It is good. I don't drink alone either, for the same reason I don't cook a lot. Party of one is a little pathetic."

He wondered to himself what her life had been like in the states. She got the occasional text or calls from friends back home, but she didn't seem to have anyone as a permanent fixture. She was so giving. All that charity work and checking on her tenants. It was sad to think how many nights she'd spent alone since her mother had died.

"You never talk about your life after your parents passed. Do you have anyone serious at home?"

She shook her head, "No, not really. Just a couple of close friends. This is my home now, at least for the next two months it is."

There was no challenge in her voice. He sighed and that made her look up from her chopping. "It's okay, Michael. This time I've had here, is happier than I've been in a long time. I'm not going to try and cheat you out of this place. My cards are on the table. We'll just ride this out."

She gave him a sad smile. "If I get my walking papers in two months, I'll be ok. I'll find something. I've been taking care of myself for a while now. Let's just not spend the next two months fighting. I don't want that." She caressed his face with her eyes. "Despite my best efforts, I can't seem to stop myself from being your friend."

He felt like he'd been punched in the gut. He wanted this whole mess to go away. He just wanted to pull her in his arms. He wanted to be close enough to put his nose in her hair, comfort her with his body. It made him sick to think of her leaving.

She could feel his sadness. She turned to him, wine glass lifted and said softly, "Slainte, mo cara." He clinked his glass to hers, touched that she'd tried to learn his language. "Slainte, mo cara." Just in time to break the tension, her phone started ringing.

"Ah fuck me, I forgot to tell you to call Brigid!" he said.

Branna quickly picked it up. "So, where are you?" He could hear the two squealing over the phone. Branna was listening and laughing. "Your feet are soaking now? Did you get your massages yet? Oh, well you'll have to tell me how they were. I fell off the ladder today and my back is killing me. No, no. This is your night, just have fun and I will see you tomorrow. You're welcome. It's no big deal. Caitlyn needed her Hen Party."

She hung up grinning ear to ear. She smacked Michael on the ass without warning. He jumped and looked at her like she'd gone mad. "That is from Brigid for not giving me her message. She told me to smack your bum." She shot her eyebrows up, with a mischievous, little smile.

He moved toward her, "My sister had 29 years of practice trying to kick my arse. You're out of your league, little girl." She knew he was flirting with her.

She bumped his hip with hers. "Move over, pretty boy. I need to finish this, or we'll never eat." He moved to the other counter with his wine glass. She could feel his eyes on her.

Michael decided that watching Branna O'Mara cook for him might be the sexiest thing he'd ever seen. She was dressed in one of her starchy little outfits that downplayed her figure, but now he knew what she looked like in her bra and knickers. Her hair was braided down her back, not in her usual bun. He could see how long and shiny it was. He fought the impulse to snatch the tie out of it and start unraveling.

"What are you making?"

She looked over her shoulder. "Linguine with clam sauce. I got some local clams." He looked at the spread. Pine nuts, olives, fresh herbs, butter, olive oil, wine. She had some fresh tomato she sliced up and drizzled with the oil and a little salt. "I got some peach gelato too. I know it's starting to get colder at night, but it looked so good, I couldn't resist."

Michael couldn't believe the trouble she was going through. She ate for sustenance; she lived on meager rations with just enough nutrition to get by. Yet every once in a while she would whip up an exquisite feast. It was always for someone else, which made him think about the phone call.

"That was very nice, what you did for the girls." She just shrugged. "I didn't have time to shop for a wedding gift. It's no big deal."

He felt the need to point out the obvious. "From all the screeching on the phone, I think Brigid and Caitlyn thought it was a big deal. Why didn't you join them?"

She turned to him, a look of surprise on her face, as if the thought had never occurred to her. "It's not about me. It's for the bride and her best friend. I don't need to go." She turned and started chopping again.

She felt him come up behind her. He put his hands on her shoulders. "Where does your back hurt? And don't say you are fine, or I'll toss you back in that rose bush." She could hear his smile. He started rubbing her shoulders, digging his thumbs deep into where her blades met her back. The initial contact had startled her. She rarely had anyone touch her anymore. She melted as he worked her shoulders.

"Oh my God, that feels amazing." She moaned, and he gave a deep throaty laugh.

"That's what they all say." She went to turn on him and he pushed her back into place. "Stay still, woman."

He reached to the front of her and cupped his hand at her neck and jaw. He took the other hand and inched down her spine, kneading as he went. When he got to her lower back, he really worked it. Her head was completely bent back, leaning on his chest.

She let out a little grunt. "Did I hurt you?" He couldn't tell if he was doing it too hard, or if she loved it.

"God, no. Don't stop." That comment went straight to his groin. *Down boy, this is not about you.* He loved that she was letting him take care of her. She didn't seem to let anyone take care of her. He kept his lust at bay and just worked at making her feel better. She periodically made little noises as he rubbed her lower back. The noises were wreaking havoc with his imagination. He had to fight the impulse to give her the full treatment, happy ending and all, and keep his hands above the hips.

She lifted her head and sighed with relief. He slowly took his hand off her throat, caressing it as he retreated. "Better?" he whispered. His mouth was close to her ear.

She laughed a deep throaty laugh. "Any better and you'd be putting me to bed. Thank you. I didn't realize how tight my back was." She started working again. "I need to get this on the stove. Stop distracting me with those healing hands." She gestured to his hands with her chef knife.

The dinner was superb. They took the dining room chairs out on the porch and ate their gelato. It was supposed to rain tonight. "I hope it clears up by tomorrow afternoon," he said.

Branna replied lazily. He could tell she was getting tired. "It's good luck if it rains on your wedding day."

He was doubtful, "Really? It was sunny and warm when I got married. Who knew that was a sign of things to come." His tone was a little grim.

"Yep, Google it. It's good luck," she said. "Well, then. I hope it doesn't stop," he said.

"Me too, I love the rain," she said drowsily.

CHAPTER 11

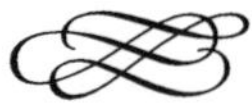

Michael heard her again. He'd been working a lot, but when he slept at the cottage, he occasionally heard the nightmares. It was like a shadow hanging over the cottage. He told himself to stay in bed. She liked to handle things herself, keep her pride in tact. He thought about the phone call with Brigid. She had been so happy to pamper them, but she admitted her back hurt and hadn't joined them for a massage. She always put other people first, and it had been a tangible pleasure to rub her back. He wanted to give her the full treatment. Lay her down and rub oil all over her. Rub and knead and pull until she was so relaxed she fell asleep. Not to seduce her, but to comfort her.

He couldn't stand it anymore. He got up and walked through the house. As he approached her room he heard sniffling. She was awake. He knocked. He heard her blankets shuffling and she finally spoke. "Come in." He eased the door open and she was at her dresser. She had a tissue wiping her nose. She had her back to him. "I'm OK, Michael. I'm sorry I woke you." Her voice was a little shaky, but she was trying to keep her bearing.

"Branna, turn around."

She lifted her chin and straightened her spine as she always did.

She turned around but she wouldn't meet his eyes. "It was just a dream. I'll be fine. You need your sleep."

He walked over to her and took her face in his hands. "Look at me, darlin'. Please." She finally did, and the sight of her puffy eyes and tight face told him that she was clenching so that her chin wouldn't tremble. "It's ok if you're not, you know. You don't have to be so bloody strong all the time."

She smiled, but it didn't light up her eyes. "You're wrong. I do have to be strong all the time. There's no one else left. It's just me." The look on his face made her stiffen.

She extracted herself from his hands. "Don't pity me Michael. It doesn't do any good and it makes me feel pathetic."

He sighed. "Maybe if you saw a counselor, talked to someone you didn't know…" She shook her head. "What about Father Peter? I could talk to him and see…"

She cut him off. "No priests, no church."

He looked surprised at her insistence. "I'm sorry, Branna. I just assumed you were a Catholic."

She walked past him into the living room. "I am a Catholic, born and raised. I just don't go anymore."

He knew he was pushing her, but he wanted to know. "Do you believe in God?"

She laughed bitterly, "Of course I do. Who else could inflict this much damage? You might know the fishes and loaves God, but I know the flood the earth, turn you to salt God. He's not listening, and I'm not talking, so I save my Sundays for something productive."

Michael just stood in silence hoping that she would keep talking. "Don't judge me Michael. You are among his blessed. You have a beautiful life, people who love you. Me? I was born with a target on my back. Grandparents died in their fifties and sixties, no aunts or uncles or cousins. All I had were my parents. You tell me how I am supposed to go to church and thank God when he chose me! Me!" she pointed to her chest. "He looked down from heaven and said *She's the one! She's my new Job!* He pointed that big finger down at me and he took it all! They say God loves everyone, but that's wrong. He doesn't love me,

Michael, and I don't love him!" She was shrieking at this point, tears pouring down her face.

He came toward her. He just wanted to wrap his arms around her. The pain in her face was absolutely gutting him. She shot her arms up. "Don't, I can't. I can't be touched right now." He stopped and she kept her arms up, trying to slow her breathing. "I can't afford to lean on you Michael. We both know where this is headed. In two months this will be over and I need to stand on my own two feet. The way my luck has been, you're pretty much a sure thing, so I wouldn't start packing." She swiped the tears from her face angrily.

Michael started pacing, running his fingers through his hair, mumbling expletives under his breath. "Michael, look at me." She was suddenly calm. She had shut down on him again. "I appreciate everything. I honestly do. This time here, it's more of a gift than I ever expected. This town, the people, it's a sort of heaven. I just need to take care of myself. It's not your job to comfort me. I am going outside to get some air, please don't follow me." At this she walked out the door into the rain. He walked over to the linen closet and took out a clean towel for her. Then he went back to bed.

* * *

BRANNA SLEPT LATE. Her tears had exhausted her, and she slept like the dead for the rest of the night. When she woke, Michael had left a note on the counter.

Off on wedding business. I'll see you at the church at 2. Save me a dance, mo cara. Michael

Oh man, she was really trying to keep her distance from him. He didn't make it easy, though. Last night she had wanted more than anything to walk into his embrace. She had to be careful, though. In two months she would lose. She would lose the house, or lose him. If she lost the house, she probably couldn't stay in Doolin. Either way Michael was out of her life. She'd briefly entertained the offer of letting him live there if Ned sold it to her. She knew, though, that his pride would never allow it. She understood; she would decline the same offer. Nope, in two months one of them was going. The newer townhouses were out of her price range. She would have to look in another county. She might have to go back to the states.

She shoved the whole line of thinking to the back of her mind. She munched on her dried fruit and grabbed her coffee. She needed a good long soak for her back and needed to devote some time to getting ready. Today was a special day and she was going to be happy.

Branna soaked in the bath longer than usual. The night had taken its toll. She just lay there soaking and daydreaming. She took her time getting ready. Lingering in the bathroom primping for hours was not something she did very often, but she hadn't really dressed up in a long time.

She spent a long while drying her hair and arranging it. She used a little more make-up than usual, accenting her eyes for an evening out. She didn't overdue it though. A little gloss and she was finally done. It was still warm enough to forgo the hose, so she put on the delicate sandals and looked in the mirror.

Not bad, O'Mara. She convinced herself repeatedly that she wasn't dressing up for anyone in particular. Before she left she dabbed a little rose oil behind her ears and on her wrists. Tadgh was helping with the set up, so she was meeting him at the church.

MICHAEL, Patrick, and Father Peter were at the front of the church. Michael had seated his mother at the front of the church with the rest of the family and they were pretty close to starting time. All he had to do was poke around the side of the church and walk his sister up to the front. Caitlyn's father was back with them, ready to give his daughter to the O'Brien clan. It was drizzling outside which had freaked her out. Then Michael told her what Branna had said about it being good luck for the marriage. She'd teared up and hugged him, Brigid started crying and hugged him, and then they both smacked him for ruining their make up. He was fairly certain that no matter how old he was, he would never understand women.

He was going over the last minute details with Father Peter when he heard Patrick whistle in that distinctly male way that indicates appreciation for the fairer sex. He looked up and lost his breath. "Bleeding Christ," he mumbled. Father Peter shot him a chastising look. "Oh, sorry Father."

The priest looked at what they both were seeing and even his eyebrows popped in appreciation. "Aye, well, we'll let that one slide."

Branna walked through the open doors of the sanctuary and several eyes were on her. Michael was pretty certain that he'd never seen a more beautiful sight in all of his 29 years. Her hair was completely down and cascading over her back and shoulders. Silky masses of dark waves spilled around her. She looked like something from a Celtic myth, beautiful and other worldly. The dress was emerald green. It hugged her everywhere that mattered, like it was made for her. It was shorter in the front and got longer in the back, but simply cut. Just enough to emphasize a perfect pair of legs.

There was no trace of the sad, defiant woman he'd been with last night. She looked around the church with a smile, taking in the flowers and all of the people dressed in their finery. She looked a little shy though, not sure where to go. He took a step toward her when Tadgh came beside her and took her hand. Tadgh was beaming as he looked at her, running his eyes up and down her in appreciation. She had a beautiful blush starting at her cheeks.

He thought he heard someone or something making a low growling sound. He looked up to see Patrick and Father Peter staring at him, then they both looked over at Tadgh and Branna. Apparently he was the one who had growled, and wasn't that a dandy way to start the wedding?

Father Peter looked at him thoughtfully, "When's the last time you made your confession, lad?"

Michael just nodded. "I'll come in Friday, Father."

He replied, "Aye, I'll block a little extra time for you." Patrick was suppressing a grin.

The church was beautiful. Tadgh had insisted she sit near the front with him. She felt odd. She didn't belong to either side, but since she was technically his date, she surrendered to his judgment and sat with the O'Briens. Everyone looked so wonderful. Michael's younger brother, Sean Jr. was the only one she hadn't met. He was as handsome as his father and brothers. He was tall for his age and a hopeless flirt. Yes, she would have been completely in love with him as a teenager.

Tadgh whispered in her ear, "Remind me again why I'm not trying to get in your knickers?"

She smacked him. "Shhhh, you are in a church!" She kept looking back at Michael. He seemed a bit stressed, but other than that he was sheer perfection. Clean cut, broad shoulders accented by his tuxedo. He looked like something from a Bond film.

Tadgh was as gorgeous as ever, and as mischievous. He leaned in again. "It's not nice to ogle another man when you're on a date, woman." His tone was teasing but she got embarrassed just the same.

"I wasn't ogling. I was looking at the flowers on the altar."

Tadgh scoffed, "Sell that to the tourists. If it matters at all, every time you look away, he's got his eyes on you. It's like watching a bloody tennis match."

She stiffened. "You're wrong. Michael doesn't look at me like that." Tadgh was silent, but she could feel his gaze. She turned to him, and he had a look of genuine incredulity.

"You really don't see it, do you?" he asked.

She sighed impatiently. "Shh, they're starting."

Branna hadn't been to a wedding since she was little. She'd been antsy and bored. The Catholic wedding mass was long for a child to sit through. This time around she was captivated. Caitlyn was stunning, and Patrick was beaming as she walked down the aisle. She watched the different players all doing their part. Brigid held her bouquet as they exchanged their vows. They spoke them in Gaelic, and Tadgh whispered the translation to her as they went along.

The mothers were crying, the husbands comforting them. The only time she looked away was at the start when she saw Caitlyn's father escort her down the aisle to her groom. *You'll never have this,* she thought. She didn't have a grandfather or brother or even an uncle to give her a way. Not that she would marry, she had accepted that sad fact slowly but surely. She couldn't watch Caitlyn's hand in her father's, or him lift her veil to present her to Patrick. She swallowed repeatedly and looked at her hands.

It was then that she felt a hand on hers. Tadgh squeezed her hand and she looked up at him. "It's ok, Branna. It's over." His face was filled with kindness, and it almost undid her. She looked at him with silent thanks in her eyes. He understood, somehow. He took her hand and kissed it.

Michael was trying to pay attention to the ceremony, and for the most part he succeeded. However, it occurred to him, as soon as Caitlyn's father started walking her down the aisle, that this must be absolute agony for Branna to watch. He was right. She kept her eyes ahead, instead watching Patrick. He knew her well enough, by now, to read her face. She was fighting for composure.

When they reached the front and Caitlyn's father handed her off, she had averted her eyes to her lap. He ached for her. He wanted to comfort her, but he couldn't. When he saw Tadgh take her hand, he was both grateful and jealous at the same time. She looked at his cousin with such tenderness. He was whispering to her, their eyes never leaving one another, and then he'd kissed her hand. Michael couldn't watch anymore.

The rustic hall where the reception took place was on the outskirts of town. It was traditional looking for the region and looked more like a house than a hall, being made of thatch and stone. The telltale signs were the lanterns and sprays of flowers and twigs flowing along the garden to the front door. It looked magical as the sun was setting low in the sky.

Branna could hear the sea from the isolated spot, along with the whispering insects and birds overhead. There were iron tables and chairs scattered through the garden for outdoor socializing. It had stopped raining, but it had rained just long enough to give Caitlyn and Patrick the luck they needed. They were so obviously in love with each other that if Branna believed in the old tale, she was sure that

Patrick O'Brien had found his mate. Tadgh was greeting the family inside, so she sat alone, breathing in the sea air.

She couldn't see the water, but she could hear it and smell it. She inhaled deeply. "You can smell it? The sea?" The voice startled Branna. Sorcha smiled, "Am I disturbing you?"

Branna quickly shook her head, "No, not at all. You look so lovely, Sorcha. Everyone does. It was a good day for a wedding."

Sorcha nodded, "Aye, another child married and happy. It's all a mother wants once she reaches a certain age. That and grand babes, lots and lots of grandchildren to fill her lap and her heart. But you didn't answer. Do you smell the sea?"

Branna thought it was an odd question, but she answered it. "Yes, of course."

Sorcha continued, "And do you hear it? Do you hear the water?"

Branna was starting to get the feeling Sorcha was teasing her. "Yes, I can't see it, but I hear it. Don't you?"

Sorcha didn't answer. "O'Mara, do you know what it means?" Branna thought she knew the gist of it. "I think it means water."

Sorcha shrugged, "No, not exactly. Close, but no. It's means *of the sea*. Branna O'Mara means raven of the sea. This place is special. It's not far from the cliffs, but far enough. It's only some who hear it and smell the ocean. The sea's in their blood. I saw you here, smelling the sea air, with your black hair blowing wild in the wind. You've flown home, wee raven. Haven't you?"

Branna swallowed hard. She looked down, fiddling with her dress. "I thought so. When I saw the Kelly place in the email, I remembered my father talking about County Clare. I thought it was a sign."

Sorcha listened intently. "And now? What do you think now?"

Branna couldn't look at her. Her eyes were welling up. "I've made such a mess of things. I've hurt Michael, ruined his plans. I wanted to belong somewhere so badly. When my mother left me, I was just in limbo. I wanted to go somewhere, be alone, find some peace. I thought I could make this work, but…" She stopped as Sorcha stood in front of her. She felt the woman's hands on her arms, pulling her up to standing. She looked at Sorcha with tears brimming.

"This is all going to sort itself out. Michael has broad shoulders, you don't worry yourself about him. As for your mother, well I know a little bit about that. More than I'd like." Branna watched as she pulled the neckline of her dress aside to reveal the top of her right breast. The scarring was visible.

"You? You had breast cancer?"

Sorcha adjusted her dress. "Yes, I did. Eleven years ago, when Seany was still small. Terrible, nasty time. My poor Sean was beside himself. He grabbed me and shook me. *You fight! You'll not leave me, ye hear? Me and the babes. I won't have it!*"

Branna had tears on her cheeks now. "You did fight. You fought for them. You stayed, even when it hurt. You're stronger than she was."

Sorcha shook her head, "Sometimes it's not enough, dear. Sometimes all the fighting isn't enough. I was lucky, they caught it early. She wouldn't have left you, otherwise."

Branna smiled sadly, "You're wrong, but thank you." She wiped her face and perked up. "This is your son's wedding, Sorcha. No more tears unless they're happy ones." She leaned in and hugged the small, beautiful woman. It was rare for her to initiate that kind of contact, but they both needed it. "It is time to party, Sorcha O'Brien. There's a handsome man in there waiting for you."

Sorcha smiled, "Aye, there's a line of 'em waiting for you, dear. I hope you've brought your dancing shoes."

Sorcha was right. Branna did need dancing shoes. After a while she abandoned the sandals to dance in her bare feet like the rest of the women. Tadgh rotated with the other musicians, sometimes playing, sometimes joining her on the dance floor. Michael played a lot, but she saw him dancing with his sister and his little niece in between drinking and eating. He even danced with Caitlyn, swinging her by Patrick just to tease him.

"Keep your hands where I can see them, brother!" Patrick yelled. Caitlyn laughed and Michael wiggled his eyebrows, planting a big kiss on her cheek. She also noticed that he tensed whenever she danced with Tadgh. She really hoped he wasn't annoyed that she was here. He hadn't invited her, after all.

When he'd danced with his little four-year-old niece, they'd started with her standing on his toes. She giggled, her curls popping up and down. She looked like a sweet little fae child. She was wild and beautiful and innocent. She lifted her arms for him to pick her up and he did, whirling her around as she squealed with delight. Then he settled her in his arms and she lay her head on his chest. He swayed to the music, cradling her lovingly in his big arms. Branna watched him and her chest ached. He was so natural with the child, so gentle. It was hard for her to grasp the notion that he didn't want children.

Brigid approached her and hooked an arm in hers. "He's good with her, isn't he?" She was embarrassed that she'd been caught red-handed watching him.

"Yes, he is. It's hard to believe he doesn't want any of his own, someday."

Brigid seemed surprised, "He told you that? That he never wanted children?"

Branna nodded, she spoke with a light tone. Brigid was smart and she didn't want her picking up on how she'd been mourning the fact. "He told me Fiona's charges during the annulment. He said he didn't want children."

Brigid looked at her sideways, "Aye, what a farce that was. As for the children, well perhaps with a different woman he might change his mind." Branna gave a non-committal hmph and changed the subject.

"The wedding was beautiful. Everyone seems so happy. It seems Patrick's found his mate."

Brigid smiled widely, "Yes, he has. Caitlyn is one of my best friends. I couldn't bear to part with her. If you don't get sisters one way, God gives them to you another, I suppose." Branna thought about that. "I always wanted a sister. Actually, I wanted sisters and brothers. You're lucky. I'm sure you know that."

Brigid put one arm around her and squeezed. "Go have fun. Why don't you go dance with that handsome brother of mine?"

Branna smiled, devilishly, "Which one?"

Brigid laughed. "True enough. Try getting through school with all the girls mooning over your big, gorgeous brothers. They were shameless. All my good friends took the vow. Thou shalt not shag thy Brigid's brothers."

Branna giggled, because Brigid's Irish was thick when she was making a point. "And did they stick to it?" She answered with a grim tone, "Aye, for the most part. O'Brien men can be rather persuasive, though. I think they snuck a couple past me, Fiona being the main culprit."

Branna's head whipped around to look at her, "She was your friend?" She nodded, "Yes, for a time. Just long enough to gain access to my twin. She's in the past now, for both of us. I'm more careful now. I protect what's mine. He's the brother of my heart. We shared the womb. I won't let another woman hurt him. He deserves to be loved. He deserves a true mate."

Brigid was looking at her intensely. It was making her fidgety, but she understood. "Good, I'm glad." She spoke quietly, looking at Michael as she did. "He's too good. Good people can get used. He needs you, Brigid. When I'm gone, I'll be happy knowing that you'll always take care of him." Brigid started to argue, but she put her hand up. "It's ok, Brigid. You and I are realists. There's no way Ned Kelly is going to kick a local boy out on his ass and sell that cottage to a Yank. I guess I've always known it."

She shook her head, almost as if to herself. "I should leave, I know I should. I should just end this." She paused, her voice breaking. "I just want to let myself have this for a little while longer." Brigid was silent; she looked at her and was taken back by Brigid's expression. She saw resolve and something else. Determination? That made no sense, but it's what she read in her face.

Just as she went to speak, Michael approached them. "You two look very serious, break it up. And you, little hellcat, owe me a dance." He crooked his finger at her in his teasing way.

Brigid gave her another squeeze, "Yes, Branna. Go enjoy yourself. I'm going to find that man of mine and pull him in to the coat closet." She looked positively unrepentant as her brother gagged and covered his ears in horror.

Michael took her hand and led her to the dance floor. The song the band was playing was slow and sweet. *The Lass of Glenshee.* She knew the song, well. He pulled her close, not speaking for a moment. She was stiff and nervous at first, but they each settled, getting used to the closeness. He towered over her, especially without her heels. Her head was under his chin, her cheek on his chest. He held her with one hand around her waist as he folded her tiny hand in his other. He curled their intertwined hands into his chest so that every inch of them was touching.

He was singing, very quietly, just for her and her body melted into him. She felt his big warm hand on her back, his thumb stroking her through her dress. He felt so familiar. She could smell him. Not cologne or soap, but him. His tie was loose around his open collar. He pulled her closer and they were touching thigh to chest. He smelled so good, she was intoxicated by it.

As the song ended, she went to pull away, not able to stand being so close. It was torture, not being with him, not being his.

He wouldn't let her go. "Please, one more," he said gently, pulling her to him again. "One more before you go back to him."

The band kept on with another slow song. She looked at him questioningly, "Do you mean Tadgh?" He pulled her close, putting his nose in her hair. She pushed his chest so she could look at him. "What exactly do you think is going on with me and Tadgh?"

He looked at her, "I think it's obvious. He's a lucky man."

She shook her head. "Nothing is going on, Michael. Tadgh and I are friends, that's all."

He looked at her more directly, "Are ye sure he knows that?"

She pulled back a little. "I'm not Fiona. I don't lie and I don't toy with men. Tadgh and I have been very clear about what we are, and what we aren't." She was getting irritated. "He's very loyal to you Michael. He loves you. I think you're probably his best friend in the world. He told me he wished I would find another house, and leave the cottage to you. He wants you to be happy. I'm not trying to come between you, Michael. I swear it."

Michael just stared at her, he said nothing, just stared at her and had stopped dead on the dance floor. He suddenly pulled her back to him, firmly, pressing his whole body to her. A wave of lust hit her so hard she actually felt her knees buckle. He held her tightly, moving his hand slowly up her back and sliding it into her hair. He swayed to the music. He groaned as he put his face in her neck. "Christ, you smell like roses." His fingers were deep in her hair, his palm pressing her scalp as he spoke in her ear. Her heart was pounding, and she was gripping his biceps.

"Do you think that's what this is about? The bloody house?" His soft lips grazed her ear as he spoke. She felt him thicken in his trousers, felt his arousal hard against her belly. She felt her body respond in kind. Hot and needy, heat pooled in her belly. He sensed it, too. He inhaled sharply and tilted her head back, forcing her to look at him. His face was pure animal hunger.

Just as Branna was about to either pass out or have her first orgasm, her lust was instantly quelled by a very drunk Jack McCain. "Well, well. You two seem to be getting on better. Glad to see you've called a truce for the lass's birthday." Michael jolted and looked at her. The question was in his eyes. Jack slurred on. "Yes, I get alerts for all my clients. I opened my email yesterday and saw it was your birthday, 24 years today!"

Branna was shushing him, "Mr. McCain. I wish you'd keep that to yourself. It's Caitlyn's day, Caitlyn and Patrick. We'll just keep that our little secret, ok?"

Jack swayed, "Ah, of course." He made a big gesture of putting a finger to his lips. "I'll be the pillar of discretion, Ms. O'Mara."

Just then his wife pulled him away. "Come dear, let the young people dance."

As they left Branna and Michael alone, the song ended. She removed herself from Michaels's embrace, completely rattled by her response to him. "Thank you for the dance, Michael." She smoothed his lapel. "You looked so beautiful up at the altar. I mean, you all did. Everyone was beautiful."

She turned and he took her elbow. "Why didn't you tell me it was your birthday?"

She smiled, "Today isn't about me. I've had a wonderful time. Today was a perfect day. It was everything I needed." She was smiling, and he knew she meant it. She walked away from him as happy as he'd ever seen her.

The party went on through the evening. Everyone ate, drank, danced, and seemed deliriously happy. Just as Branna went to sit down to rest her back, the crowd started to spread out, leaving the dance floor open and empty. The person on the mic shouted *O'Brien Set!* and everyone started hooting and clapping.

David and Aoife O'Brien walked to the center, followed by Sean and Sorcha. Next was Brigid and Finn and finally the bride and groom. Tadgh scurried over to her, grabbing her up. "Let's go. It's the O'Brien Set."

She stopped and he pulled, waging a little tug of war. "Tadgh, this looks like a family dance. I don't know this song! "

He assured her with a dismissive wave, "It'll be grand, come and I'll teach it to you. It's a sort of O'Brien mating song."

Branna dug her bare feet in, "Mating! What is this, the Middle Ages? Are you nuts?"

He laughed, "It's not all that. It'll be fun." She wouldn't budge. He sighed impatiently. "It's three songs mashed up to make the set. It starts out slow, then moves into a middle, faster bit, then the last is the most intense. It's a bit of a courtship song. Come, now and I'll teach it to you. Don't be such a chicken. You agreed to be my date, woman. You're not going to make me miss our family dance are you?"

He could tell he'd won. Branna sighed, "You know, you're manipulative."

He smiled, "I know, but it worked didn't it?"

As he drug her up to the front and they lined up with the others, next to Brigid and Finn. Branna could hear a few hoots and whistles. She was blushing. She could feel the heat in her cheeks. Tadgh leaned in. "I forgot one thing. We're not married or engaged, so you are fair game to any single O'Brien man. You might have someone cut in. It's a sort of game, a challenge. All the O'Brien men vying for the prettiest, single girl at the party." Branna's mouth dropped and she prepared to flee when the music started. She looked down at Brigid, who was snickering and refusing to look at her.

She'd been duped. She leaned in to Tadgh, "I'm going to tan your ass, later."

He gave a devilish laugh. "Promises, promises. I like it a little rough. Remind me again why I'm not trying to get in your knickers?" At this, Finn started snickering as well.

The music started as a slow plucking on the violin and the guitar. Another violin blended in and Tadgh started moving her through the steps. She was a fast learner, but she had never even seen the dance done. They walked around each other slowly, only their shoulders meeting. The pace was slow and seductive. Then he put a hand up. She could see Brigid and Finn out of the corner of her eye and Tadgh whispered the steps. She felt awkward, but not exactly hating the experience.

She couldn't look away or she'd miss a step, but she knew Michael was playing guitar. Jenny, Robby and another person she didn't know were on the other instruments. Michael wouldn't be cutting in, but she wondered, more to torture herself than anything, whether he would have.

Michael was gritting his teeth. He watched Tadgh dancing the O'Brien Set with Branna and was suppressing the urge to hit his cousin over the head with his guitar and throw her over his shoulder. He actually missed a key and had to recover his place.

Aidan was off stage, directly behind Michael. He heard him talking to Liam. "Look at Tadgh having all the fun. Christ, she is a beauty, especially with all that hair down. Well, tradition aside, Michael's shown no interest in her. I think it might be time I threw my hat in the ring. I'm cutting in."

Before Michael could say a word, Aidan hopped out of his seat, and headed toward Branna. Liam was sitting next to his empty chair. "Damn it all. He's too old for her. She needs a young, strong buck to show her some fun, not that stoic bastard. You certainly don't appreciate a girl of that caliber."

Michael and Liam watched as the dark horse, the eldest O'Brien walked up to Tadgh and removed Branna from his arms. His brother was as close to a monk as you could get, and if he did have a romantic interlude, it was short and sweet.

What the hell was he thinking making a move for Branna? He spent most of his time up north. Although, she was a military kid. She might like Aidan. That uniform appealed to a lot of women. He watched them as he tried to keep his tempo even. Branna seemed shocked at first, but then she was smiling at him. Aidan didn't take his eyes off her, a small smile curving his lips was all he ever wore, but she was getting it in full measure.

Michael's heart rate went up as the music moved into the next phase of the set. Aidan was whispering in her ear and she put her head back and laughed. Their hands were joined and they walked into each other, hands stretched above their heads. Branna would miss a step and giggle, glowing with exertion and happiness.

As Michael played, he spoke to Liam. "What the hell is he on about?" But he was talking to an empty chair. Liam was walking up to them to take his shot with Branna. The song was speeding up now, toward the final song. He grabbed her mid-swing and Aidan stepped back, shaking his head and laughing.

Michael was livid at himself. Why the bloody hell had he agreed to sit out for this song, play instead of dance? He'd never indicated in the slightest that he had feelings for Branna. He shouldn't be feeling the way he was right now. He loved his brothers and Tadgh, and he knew he was an idiot for the jealousy thrumming through his body. He glared at Aidan as he played.

Branna was giggling as Liam linked arms with her and swung her around. Every couple up there was smiling and happy. Everyone else was watching the bride and groom. He should be watching the bride and groom; this was Patrick's wedding day. He was a selfish prick.

Michael noticed that Aidan was watching them, his face blank of emotion. Then he saw him turn and nod ever so slightly at his little brother Seany. Sean Jr. nodded back and walked over and tapped Liam on the shoulder.

Branna laughed and he could read her lips, "Sorry Liam!" giggling as Seany took her through the last of the dance.

Sean, being fifteen, didn't know the steps much better than she, and they tripped over each other's feet with reckless abandon. As he hit the final notes of the song, he tried to think back to any time that the O'Brien Set had been danced so poorly. He just started chuckling to himself as everyone started milling around. He saw Sean Jr. walking arm in arm with Branna, head held high. Liam dropped to his knees in front of her. She took one finger and pushed his forehead. He fell over, clutching his chest. Michael watched her playing with his brothers and felt like a fool.

"We'd never take her from you, brother." He turned around and looked at Tadgh. "You know that. In your heart you know that. It's your head that's not getting the picture."

He turned away from him, "You don't know what you're talking about Tadgh, and you're one to talk. I see you. I see how you look at her."

Tadgh swore under his breath. "You're a fool. It doesn't matter what I think. It's what she thinks that matters. She doesn't care for me that way. I made peace with it early on. She's more like a sister now. Maybe this little spectacle will get through to that fat head of yours. Your brothers and I, we might be hands off, but damn it Michael. Surely you see it. Half the single lads in this town would give their left clacker for a chance at her. Every man who's met her is half in love with her already. Girls like her don't know how to do things half way. When she gives her heart away, she'll give it all away, forever. If you're not standing there ready to take it, someone else will." Tadgh slapped him on the back and then walked away.

After the fun of the O'Brien Set had died down, it was time for the father-daughter dance. Michael knew this was going to be a brutal ordeal for Branna and started scanning the room for her. He saw her discreetly duck out the door. He followed, God help him. He had been grateful for Tadgh at the church, but he wanted to comfort her.

She was standing outside, looking up at the moon. His body stirred as he looked at her. The breeze was causing her hair to flow back off her shoulders, her dress clinging to her. She noticed his approach and she turned away. It looked like she gave a brief sweep under her eyes.

"Getting some air after that dance?" She looked relieved, glad he hadn't pressed her about why she had really come out.

"Yes, it was exerting. Your brothers are all wonderful but they wore this Yank out." She put her face toward the breeze. "I like hearing the ocean at night, even if I can't see it. The air is so clean and wild."

Michael was surprised. "You hear it? Interesting. Do you smell the sea as well?"

She nodded her head. "Your mother asked me the same thing. Are you guys messing with me?"

He just shook his head. Michael took his middle finger and ran it lightly down her arm. "I would have liked to cut in, to the dance I mean. You're the most beautiful girl here."

He saw the goose bumps rise on her arm, and she shivered. Michael took off his tux coat and put it over her shoulders. She seemed surprised at the gesture. She pulled it closed and looked at him. "Thank you," she said softly.

He pulled the lapels and brought her close. "It's an Irish tradition. You must have a birthday kiss." Total bullshit, of course. There was no such tradition.

She was dazed, her breathing sporadic, and she was looking at his mouth. "Am I too late? Did you already get one from your date?" His tone was light but damn it, he wanted to know who's ass he had to kick if she had been kissed tonight.

She shook her head. "No, of course not. No one knows it's my birthday. Guess I'm not kissable, otherwise." She said it with a self-deprecating smile.

"You are wrong about that." He slid his palm in her hair, pulling her into him with his other hand around her waist. "Happy birthday, Branna." he said. He kissed her lightly, eyes open. He rubbed his lips lightly back and forth, their lips gliding and teasing over each other and he felt her get loose in his arms, liquid under his mouth. She liked the feel of him, he could tell. Her stormy blue eyes never left his. He didn't press for more. He backed away and the aroused look on her face was more than she could guard. *Good,* he thought. He wanted her needy and aroused and wanting more.

He fought the urge to grab her and take her mouth hard and demanding. "I'm glad you came, tonight. Even if I wasn't your date."

She smiled, "I'm glad you didn't mind."

He looked at her intensely. "I should have asked you. It was a mistake on my part. It won't be repeated." His tone was serious. A lick of heat went through her at the possessive tone.

"It's okay, Michael. I'm not family, I'm just a temporary, pesky roommate. I don't expect to be included." She looked around. "Tonight was amazing. More fun than I've had in a very long time." She smiled, mischievously, "And I got a kiss. It's been an even longer time for that."

She grabbed his attention with that remark. He wanted to know how long and who and what else the bastard got away with and why it had been her last. He started to pry but Robby yelled through the door, "You're up on the rotation, Michael!" Michael sighed. "Duty calls." Branna went to slide the coat off and he said, "Keep it. It looks good on you."

She smelled the lapel. "It smells like you," was all she said, but electricity shot right to his groin. She'd said it appreciatively and the thought that she knew his smell and liked it cranked him up. He wanted his smell all over her. "I'm going to turn in early. So, if I don't see you, be safe and have fun."

He fought the urge to kiss her again, given his completely fabricated excuse for the first one had already been used. Michael walked toward the door wishing, to his shame, that he could leave his brother's wedding and go home with her.

Branna left early, since she'd brought her own car. She had Tadgh and Michael's assurances that the family had arranged safe rides home for everyone. She was tired and she wanted to get a good night's sleep. Tomorrow it was going to be warm and sunny until a storm came in later in the afternoon. Kayak season was coming to an end, and she couldn't wait. Tonight had been so wonderful. Caitlyn and Patrick were so happy, everyone enjoyed themselves, and for a few hours she felt like part of a family. It was the best way to spend her birthday.

As Michael watched Branna leave, Tadgh came up beside him. "It was her birthday today. Did you know?" His tone was a little accusatory.

Tadgh swore under his breath, "No, of course not. There's no way she would tell anyone, especially today. How did you find out?"

Michael answered, "Jack spilled the beans."

Tadgh cheered up, "We'll have a do-over. Plan a night out or something." Michael nodded. "You didn't know, brother. We'll think of something, make a real night of it."

CHAPTER 12

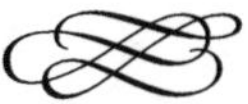

Michael got up later than usual. He wasn't hung over, but was fairly convinced Patrick and Tadgh had their head in matching toilets this morning. With the season changing, he never knew when he was going to get called on duty, so drinking more than a pint or two was out. He'd needed the sleep though. He had been up well past midnight.

Branna had been in bed by the time he got home, which he regretted. Dancing with her had been a perfect sort of torture. She smelled like the unique combination of roses and her own womanly scent. Just thinking of her in that emerald green dress, hair down her back, cheeks pink from dancing, made his blood stir. The light kiss he'd given her still burned on his lips. He came out of the bedroom, curious why he hadn't heard her milling around. She never slept late. That's when he saw her note.

Kayaking. Hope you had fun last night. B

He checked the weather on his phone. It was unseasonably warm and sunny right now, but a storm was rolling in at around four o'clock this afternoon. He didn't like the fact that she was headed out on the water this morning. He'd pulled too many clueless tourists out of the water after they'd failed to check the weather. He called her and it went to voice mail. Shit. He called Tadgh to see if she was with him. Tadgh answered the phone on the fifth ring, hung over as shit and at home. Jesus, surely she isn't going out alone? He threw his clothes on and jumped in his SUV.

Michael pulled up to the kayak rental place just in time to see the young, tan clerk pulling a kayak over to Branna's car. He hopped out and stood in front of him.

"Dia duit. Now, help me or get the feck out of the way."

Michael did neither. "She won't be needing that, you can turn right back around." The clerk lifted his eyebrows. Michael walked into the shop and there she was. She was wearing shorts and a swimsuit top, shrouded by a thin shirt. Her hair was braided down her back. She was surprised to see him.

"Just where do you think you're going this morning?" By this time the clerk had come back in the shop, having abandoned his load.

She looked at him like he was crazy. "Um, where does it look like I'm going? I left you a note."

He shook his head. "There's a storm coming in today. You can't take that little boat out on the water."

Her face started to show signs of irritation. "There's a storm coming seven hours from now. It's perfectly calm and sunny right now. I have a weather app too, Michael."

He exhaled with frustration, "Branna, you can't always be sure of that time line. You're just going to have to go another day. Do you know how many tourists I fish out of trouble every season? Forget it."

She raised her eyebrows and heard the clerk whistle through his teeth. That got Michael's attention turned on him. "What the hell are you doing letting her go out before a storm? It's totally fucking irresponsible!"

The clerk shrugged, unperturbed by his tone. "She's right, man. She knows to have it in by one or if the sky changes. It's coming to the end of the season. I can't go turning paying customers away coz their boyfriend comes in pitchin a fit."

Branna broke in, "He's not my boyfriend." The clerk turned a thousand-watt smile on her, "Well, then. Have you got a boyfriend?"

Michael was getting pissed. "What the hell does she know about reading a sky? She's not going!" He turned to her, "You're not going."

She put her hands on her hips and walked closer to him. "Now you listen to me Mister Big-Bad-Rescue-Swimmer! I'll have you know that I grew up on the beach. East Coast, West Coast, and Japan. I own a house on the freaking beach! I also grew up on military bases. If there was ever a bigger group of safety nuts in the world, it's the US Marines. If you take a crap, they have a safety manual for it." Her stare bore into him.

At this the clerk snickered and Michael shot him a look. She raged on, "I know a squall line and a rip tide and I also know a little something about pushy, arrogant, testosterone fed, jackass men!"

He cut her off, "Oh, aye. And how many of those little manuals talked about swim buddies?" He had her on that one. He pointed to the sign by the register.

We strongly recommend not boating alone. Use the buddy system!

She walked over to the sign, pulled it off the wall and walked back over. She gritted the next sentence out through her teeth. "It says recommend. It isn't a requirement." She shoved it in his chest.

Cue the clerk, "She's got you there, man." Branna smiled sweetly at him and he winked at her.

Michael was going to drown this prick. She continued as the paper sign floated to the floor. "My swim buddy is hung-over and probably has his head in the toilet. So, back off Michael!"

At this the clerk said, "You know, I get off in a couple of hours if you need..."

Michael snapped, "Would ye shut your gob, man!"

Branna continued. "Don't yell at him. You are not my father or my husband and even if you were!" she poked him in the chest, "I don't take orders! I'm going out kayaking and you can't actually do anything about it, so either help me get that skiff on the roof of my car or step out of my way." Five more pokes to the chest. The clerk was grinning like a Cheshire cat.

As much as he hated that fiery stubborn streak, he loved it just as much. God help him, she was fabulous when she was pissed. The corner of his mouth started twitching. He leaned into her, "You need turned over my knee, you stubborn little hellcat."

He spoke low and deep, which made Branna more nervous than if he'd yelled it. She put her face up to his and hissed, "Do your worst."

Michael did the only thing he could do. In one fluid motion, he threw her over his shoulder. She went wild. "PUT ME DOWN MICHAEL O'BRIEN!" The clerk was ecstatic. She was starting to kick, so Michael swatted her on the ass.

He looked at the clerk. "Make that two boats. Put 'em both on my truck," and walked out the door.

Michael walked outside, carrying his little ball of fire. He assured her that if she "behaved like a good lass" he would put her down, which caused a new string of kicks and insults. "You barely weigh seven stone, love. I can do this all day. Meanwhile your time on the water gets shorter and shorter." That point finally sunk in.

She got her bag out of the car while the clerk with the million-dollar smile helped Michael load the boats. As she went to get in the truck, the clerk came over. "I'll be gone by the time you get back. Here's my number in case you ever need a swim buddy." He winked at her and walked right past a glaring Michael.

Branna was grinning as she tucked the clerk's number in her bag. Michael watched her, "You know swim buddy is code for something a little more full contact? And besides, I thought you didn't date? "

She looked at him innocently, "Did I say that? Yes, I suppose I did. He is awfully pretty, I may need to change that policy and call…what was his name? Ah, Ryan." She'd taken a peek at the folded paper, just to needle him. Michael made a distinctly male snort of disapproval. She decided to let him off the hook. "I'm kidding. He is pretty, but he's not my type." Michael perked up, "Aye, well then, what about him makes him not your type?"

She ticked off the reasons on her thumb and fingers. "Let's see:

1. He cares more about a tan than dying of skin cancer.

2. He's too young. He looks about my age, which means he has the maturity of a 14 year old.

3. He perked up when I mentioned the beach house. Total gold digger.

4. He thought it was funny when you threw me over your shoulder."

"It was funny," Michael jibed. "What's number five?"

She paused and thought about it. "Yeah, I got nothing. He's a total POA."

He looked at her questioningly, "POA?"

She smiled, "Piece of ass."

Michael's jaw dropped as she looked innocently ahead at the road. He snatched his hand out and grabbed her knee, tickling her. She squealed, arms and legs going in every direction. He shook his head, "Piece of ass, indeed."

* * *

As Michael glided off the launch, alongside Branna's boat, he decided it was a beautiful day to go out. Deep down, he'd known she was right. The storm was coming in a lot later and there was no harm in a short, early morning row. "You know, if you had just offered to come out with me from the beginning, we could have avoided that whole scene." She was smiling and the sun was on her hair. He chuckled, "Now where's the fun in that?"

She looked at him, "What's that supposed to mean?" He looked at her intensely, a big smile still on his face. "Because, Branna O'Mara, you are spectacular when your blood is up. Fiery eyes, cheeks flushed with righteous indignation. It's gorgeous all together." She stopped rowing for a second, taken back by his directness. Then she shrugged, "Don't try to sweeten me up. I'm still mad at you."

He was grinning when he answered, "No you're not."

She narrowed her eyes at him. "Yes, I am."

He laughed, "No, Branna. You're not. Not really."

She kept stroking toward the cliffs. "How can you be so sure?"

He shrugged, "When you're really mad, you don't yell. You shut down. I hate it." He was more serious, now.

"Why would you hate that? I would think having me shut up was preferable."

He shook his head, "No, darlin, not at all. When you shut down like that, I know I've really hurt you. I'd rather have you rage at me then to know I've hurt you."

Branna stopped paddling, stunned at the admission. "You can be very sweet when you want to be, Michael."

He looked at her. His eyes were gentle and he seemed to be taking her in. He looked from her eyes to her mouth to her hair. "Aye, well." He started paddling again."Keep that to yourself. I have a reputation as an arrogant jackass to protect."

The morning was gloriously sunny and warm. The seals came out of a cove and starting swimming back and forth under the kayaks. The big alpha came barking out from the shore, giving them a tongue-lashing. Branna was wide eyed with amazement. He noticed she shut her eyes, concentrating. "What are you doing?" She opened them. "I don't have my camera. I'm taking a picture with my mind."

Michael marveled at what a contradiction she was. So small with childlike wonder in her eyes, but other times those eyes were like a fierce storm crashing on the shore. He wanted to see everything, every expression. It occurred to him during this revelation that it would kill him if she left Doolin. He couldn't quite grasp what he was feeling, or wouldn't. He just knew that the thought of her leaving in two months made his chest ache.

Her hair was blowing out of the braid, sprigs of black silk whipping around her beautiful face. She didn't have a stitch of make-up on. He noticed, analytically, that her beautiful pink lips looked parched. This snapped him out of his reverie.

"Branna, how much water have you had today?"

She rolled her eyes. "Not this again."

He cut her off with his boat, "How much?"

She smiled weakly. "I had a cup of coffee in the car, but I forgot to buy water." Then a thought occurred to her. "Because you distracted me in the shop!" She gave one nod, as if completely vindicated.

"Christ, girl. You need to take better care of yourself. You need to drink more water." He dug out his water bottle from his bag.

"I still can't believe you keep a spare pair of swim trunks and a twelve pack of water in your truck." She said resentfully. He smoothed his hand down his tight abs, "It takes some effort to keep this pretty boy image up."

She smirked, "I suppose you're right, you are pushing thirty. It's all down hill from there." Zing, contact.

He choked, "I'll have you know that O'Brien men are known for their longevity," he paused, "and their stamina." He smiled devilishly.

She shook her head. "Cocky bastard."

He threw back his head and laughed. She tried not to notice how his chest and abs flexed when he did it. Michael on any given day was a distraction. Half naked, shirtless Michael in swim trunks was almost more than her eyes could take. It wasn't any better when he was in the lead. Then it was miles and miles of strong back. All that primo real estate rippling as he turned his oar.

He shoved his water bottle at her. "Drink, woman. And if you say 'I'm fine' I'll throw that sweet little ass of yours over my shoulder again and take you straight home."

She snatched the bottle out of his hand. "I think you enjoyed that a little."

He barked out a laugh, "A little? Sweetheart, you have no idea."

He watched her drink deeply of his water. He liked taking care of her. She handed it back to him and he took a sip, loving that his lips were right where hers had just been. He tasted something. "I can taste your lips on here." He smacked his, inquiringly, "Orange is it?"

She covered her mouth, "Oh, my mango lip balm! I'm sorry!"

He looked sideways at her. "Don't apologize. You've improved the taste." Then he took another long drink.

That comment shot straight through her belly. Could he have any idea how beautiful she thought he was? She prayed not. She had no experience maneuvering the finer nuances of male on female relations. He'd been married for God's sake. She was way out of her league. She couldn't get that soft, lingering kiss out of her mind.

Not that it mattered… really… because of her no dating policy. She briefly considered the thought that if she just attacked him while he was getting out of the shower and threw her virginity at him….It wasn't really a date, right?

Michael took her close to some of the rocky shoreline where the current wasn't as strong. She loved it, the beauty and the roughness of the rocky surfaces. Little crabs and small fish intermingled with the mussels and oysters that clung to the rocks. "It is like a little village, isn't it?" she asked.

Michael laughed lightly, "Yes, well banging up against them is a little less neighborly. It's like getting thrown up against broken glass. Promise me you won't come out here alone."

Branna loved a good opening. "Well, I do have Ryan-from-the-kayak-shop's number now, so…" Michael was silent and she wondered if she'd pushed him a little too far. When she turned to look at him, it was just in time to get a string of green slimy seaweed tossed on her. She screeched in disgust. She peeled it off her neck and arm and gave a disgusted little shiver. Then she dipped it in the water and threw it back at him.

Michael just dodged it and chuckled. "I thought he wasn't your type." He said more seriously.

"Yes, I know. He's not."

He hesitated, then like an idiot he asked, "So what is your type?"

She looked at him, really looked. The quick, involuntary glances over his body made him want to paddle for shore, and drag her home. "I don't have a type. I didn't make much time for dating over the last couple of years." She left it at that, and so did he. "So, besides leggy redheads with an attitude problem, what's your type?"

He laughed, "Ouch. Well, I haven't been real social since that mess, but it isn't a particular physical type. Attractiveness is a combination for me. I've never been able to separate looks from personality. Fiona wasn't always the way she is now. She got worse as the years went by. I just refused to see it." He shook off that thought. "Anyway, it taught me a thing or two about what I want. It's the combination that speaks to me. Strength, beauty, loyalty, passion."

"Tall order. Does she exist, I wonder?" Branna asked. She could feel Michael's eyes on her. She just kept up with her smooth strokes, refusing to look at him.

"Yes, Branna. She does."

As Michael and Branna pulled up to the marina, someone shouted a "Dia duit" from a nearby boat. Branna looked up to see some men waving from a fishing boat. "Friends?" she asked. He nodded and yelled back, "Jamie! Brendan! How was the fishing?" They pulled up to the dock and Michael helped Branna out, pulling both the boats out at the launch. She followed him over to the fishing boat.

"Hello lad, the fishing was grand today, a big haul. Who is this lovely creature? Find yourself a Silkie did you?"

Branna looked between them. "Oh, aye Brendan. You shoulda seen her kin coming out to greet the boats. The bull barking at me to give her skin back. I think he fancied her," Michael said.

The man slapped his hand on his knee and laugh loudly. "I'll just bet he did! And who could blame him, aye Jamie?" He elbowed his son, whose ears were reddening as he admired Branna.

"What on earth are you two talking about?" She put her hand out to the man, "My name is Branna O'Mara."

He smiled at her, eyes sparkling. "So it is, raven of the sea. Welcome home, young Branna." He put his hand out, but it was the wrong hand. They shook awkwardly. "I'm afraid you've got me at a bit of a disadvantage." He put his other hand out, which had a prosthetic where his hand should be.

Michael thought that Branna might be squeamish at the sight. She surprised him when she did a little curtsy, shook his fake hand and said in a perfect Irish lilt. "Not at all, Brendan."

Brendan burst into laughter, again. "That was fine, girl! We'll make a proper Irish lass out of you in no time!"

"So what is a silkie?" she asked.

Brendan motioned for them to sit on the bench while he took up a stool on the back of the boat. "The tale goes that there are creatures in these waters. Neither completely beast, or completely human, silkies are an ancient breed, part seal and part human. The silkie females would swim ashore and shed their coats. On land they were beautiful, human women. Fine, white skin and hair as black as night. They had eyes like the stormy Irish sea."

He was a fine storyteller, and Branna was enthralled. His accent was thick and his face was lined by years of sun and wind. "So prized was their beauty, that many a young man risked the wrath of the Seal king to take a silkie bride. It's said that any man that can capture the skin of the silkie may keep her as his own."

Michael's attention was on the woman, his wild, black haired silkie. A sane part of his mind rejected the thought. *She's not yours.* But then Tadgh's words haunted him. *When she gives her heart away, she'll give it all away, forever. If you're not standing there ready to take it, someone else will.* He thought about the reactions of his brothers, Tadgh, Jamie, that pretty boy in the kayak shop, even Ned Kelly as old as he was could not resist her pull. The thought of her taking up with another man made him mental.

Brendan interrupted him from these thoughts. "How was the wedding? Did Patrick finally tie the knot?"

He nodded, "Yes, it was grand. They're headed to Paris for a short holiday."

Brendan smiled at this. "Good for him. A man needs a good woman. It's why we get up in the morning."

That stabbed at his heart a bit. "Aye, when it works, I suppose."

Brendan slapped him on the back, "Don't you worry about that old mess. It's in the past. Look to your future, lad."

Branna could tell Michael was getting uncomfortable, so she changed the subject. "So Brendan, if you don't mind me asking, how did it happen? Your arm, I mean."

He lifted as if to demonstrate. "Well, it is simple enough. Fishing boats are a dangerous workplace. I got it caught and mangled in the lines. The boat has these pulley systems, motorized to pull the nets. It happened a while ago."

She nodded and worked to keep any pitying looks from escaping. She'd worked with wounded men before, through her non-profit.

Pride was important. So was independence. She also noticed that the prosthetic he was using was seriously dated.

"You seem to be pretty self reliant. Surely you couldn't captain a fishing boat if it was affecting your work."

He smiled, "I do well enough, I suppose. As for this," He put his arm up, "it's rather useless, but I get on fine with the other hand. I've also got a good first mate. He does what he can to make up for my limitations." He slapped his son lovingly on the back.

She noticed he was smiling proudly at his son, but knew that it must hurt his pride to be dependent on him. "I've known a few wounded warriors, back in the states. The prosthetics nowadays are much better than even ten years ago. The market had to improve, with the war and all."

He nodded. "Oh, aye, and thank God for it. Those men deserve the best, don't they? Me, I'm a simple fisherman. The state doesn't have the kind of funding to be giving me such an upgrade."

Michael sat in silence as the two conversed. He had never heard so much come out of Brendan's mouth in one year, let alone a few minutes. She was like that, though. She had a disarming way about her. He could tell the wheels were turning, but he wasn't sure where she was headed.

"Yes, I see. I would imagine the cost is significant. Surely at your age, you mustn't be more than forty?"

He nodded, "Aye, around there."

Branna continued,"They have to replace it at some point."

He said, "Oh, yes. They're ever diligent with making their waiting lists. I checked into it, started saving to buy it myself. The one I need is a bit dear. I'm about half way there." Branna smiled, "I see. I am pretty familiar with the styles, having worked with the military men. Which one suits your needs?"

As they talked, Michael heard his phone go off. He grabbed it out of his dry bag. It was the station, "O'Brien." He listened as Branna watched him. "Right away, boss. It'll take me a bit to get home and get to Shannon." More listening, "I understand. As fast as I can, sir." He hung up. Brendan spoke, "It's a big one coming?" He nodded, "Yes, and it's sped up."

He looked at the boats. "Shit, we've gotta get moving. I need to load these boats."

Branna said, "Michael, take my keys. You can run to the shop faster from here. Take my car. I'll take care of the boats and drive your vehicle home."

Brendan interrupted, "No need to run. Grab your gear out of the truck, lad. I'll drive you to the shop while these two take care of the rest. By the look o'that sky, you need to move your arse." Michael switched keys with Branna and started off for Brendan's car.

"Michael!" He turned. "Be careful tonight," she said.

He smiled, "Don't worry, this is the fun stuff!" Then he ran off to save the day.

She grunted, "Men." By the time Branna dropped the kayaks off, paid her bill and started home, she was exhausted. Her back hurt again, maybe from rowing or maybe from lifting the boats. She kept watching the coastline as the front moved in. The chills came over her, thinking of Michael up in a chopper during high winds. She arrived at the cottage and dragged her sorry butt into the house. She stripped, ran a bath, and slipped into it for a nice long soak. It was lunchtime, but it felt much later.

BRANNA HAD FALLEN asleep on the couch in front of the fire. She woke with a start to someone knocking. She jumped up to find Brigid at the door. "Put some shoes on and grab a jumper. Michael's unit is at the cliffs!" Branna burst into action. She grabbed shoes and Michael's hoody that was hanging on a hook by the door, and she ran into the rain.

The wind was strong and the temperature had dropped. It was starting to rain in big sheets, whipping Brigid's small car. "Jesus, I thought this wasn't coming until four!" Branna said.

Brigid was breathing heavily, "Yes, it came in a couple hours early.

I sent Michael a text and he was headed out. Kayakers got caught out past the cliffs in the open water. They can't come near the shore or they'll get smashed to pieces on the rocks."

Branna's heart was pounding. "I know where it is, Michael and I were out there this morning."

Brigid shook her head, "Some people don't have the sense to keep checking the weather. They get out there and lose track of time. Then they don't know the currents and have a hard time getting to shore." Branna thought about Michael in the kayak shop, insisting that she not go out today, and that she should not go out alone. She was suddenly very grateful that he'd inserted himself in her plans.

As they pulled up to the cliffs, Brigid showed her a spot to get close without having to pay to get in the park. "Michael has a key to the gate, since they have to rappel down on occasion, but he's not here, so this is as good as we can get. Da and Finn should be here already." They hopped out of the car and ran up to the cliffs edge, railed off for safety. Their umbrellas barely helped at all. The storm was fierce.

Finn yelled at Brigid, "Damn woman, get your ass back to the house! You'll catch your death out here!"

Brigid glared at him, "Rain doesn't kill people. Angry wives kill people. Watch your tone, Finn Murphy or I'll box your ears." Branna suppressed a grin.

Just then Sean came around with a plastic poncho and put it around Brigid's shoulders."Don't be too hard on him, lass. He's just worried about you and the baby." He came over to Branna next. He took his big coat off and put it over her.

"Oh, no. I'm ok, you keep your coat!" Branna said.

He put his arm around her. "You look quite fetching in my son's jumper, but you're getting soaked, love. Let an old man take care of you." She blushed, both because he'd noticed she was wearing Michael's shirt and because he was anything but old. He was as strikingly handsome as his sons.

Finn had his arm around Brigid and pointed with the other hand. "There they are!"

Far off shore was the helicopter. The clouds had made the sky darker than usual. After a small amount of searching they lit up the kayakers. Their boats were flipped. One was hanging on and she couldn't see the other. The aircraft hung over them, waiting for something. It lowered just enough to keep out of reach of the huge swells. Someone in orange dropped from the helicopter at a free fall. "There they go!" Finn shouted.

Branna jumped out of her skin as she watched him drop. The helicopter swerved with a gust of wind then found its position again. Another swimmer dropped into the water. She dropped her face in her hands and started to tremble.

"Branna, dear. Look at me." She looked at Sean, his blue eyes were calm and confident. "This is what he does. This is who he is. They poached him right out of university. He's good at his job, one of the best."

She nodded, not able to speak. *So was my father. He was a good Marine.* How many times had she heard that? She took what Sean offered her. He was warm and safe and felt like the closest thing she'd had to a dad in a long time.

He held her and rubbed her back. "That's a good girl. Don't you worry."

They watched the extraction and she was truly amazed at the professionalism and skill of an organization that was almost all volunteer. As scared as she was, her heart was overflowing with pride as she watched those two kayakers get lifted to safety. She watched them pull Michael and the other rescue swimmer into the aircraft. As they walked back to the car, she was overwhelmed with relief. She couldn't stop the hot tears as they started to flow.

She got in the car as Finn hugged Brigid, kissed her, and helped her in the driver's seat. She just sat there for a minute, hands on the wheel. Branna looked at her and saw her eyes brimming with tears. She turned and took in the state of Branna's tear stained face. "They don't know what they do to us, do they? We get left behind while they're off playing the hero. That twin of mine is going to be the death of me." She put her head on the steering wheel. Branna pulled her to her and they hugged, crying together in silence.

When Brigid finally settled, she looked at Branna. "I couldn't bear it if you left."

Branna just stared out at the stormy sky. "I may have to Brigid, but it won't be because I want to. I just may not be able to stay. I'm not some wealthy Yank. I managed to pull this off with…" She swallowed. "My parents' life insurance. It was my nest egg. I didn't spend any of it because I knew I had to find a home. I just don't have unlimited funds. I know everyone thinks I am some real estate tycoon, but I actually earn a modest living." She looked at her, willing her to believe her. "This is the happiest I've been since my father died on that city street in Iraq. If I can't stay, remember that. Remember that I was happy, and that I am so grateful for that."

Brigid's tears were flowing again. "You love him, I know you do. I see it. I see everything."

Branna looked away, out at the sea again. "I can't love him. I watched love kill my mother." Her chin was trembling. "Love guts people, it can take everything. I can't love him." She was crying again. Silent tears rolled down her face.

Brigid started the car. "Love doesn't ask your permission, Branna. You can't stop this path you're on any easier than you could stop the tide from rolling in." Branna hoped to God she was wrong, because Michael was one tide that would certainly pull her under.

Just then, Brigid got a text. "They're headed back to the station. He's ok."

* * *

BRANNA DIDN'T DO WELL with waiting. She needed something to do. So, she did what most women do in a crisis. She cooked. She hopped in the car soaking wet and drove to the store. The people looked at her like she was crazy as she dripped through the store. She got home and got to work. She stoked the fire in the main room, then she went and made a fire in Michael's wood burner so that his room would be warm when he finally came home. She whipped up mashed potatoes, fried chicken, gravy, a cabbage salad, and made a homemade apple cake. She was pulling out the cake when she heard Michael's truck. It was late, way after dark. She opened the door just as he was getting out of the vehicle.

Michael pulled into the cottage driveway bone weary and exhausted. All he wanted was to see Branna's face. That rescue had gone textbook, but the sight of the young dark haired girl in the water, panicked and exhausted, screaming for her father had struck a brutal chord with him. She was surely sleeping at this hour, but she'd left the light on for him. Maybe he could just ease her door open and have a peek at her sweet face.

His father had called him at the station, needing to check on him. He understood the toll that critical incidents took on you, in the aftermath. Twenty-five years in the Garda, he'd raised some alpha males for sons. Him a rescue swimmer, Aidan in the Royal Army in the North, and Patrick scheduled for Garda training as soon as he came back from Paris. His poor mother was growing old before her time worrying about her sons. It wouldn't surprise him if she took Liam and Seany right to the priory before they got any bright ideas. When his da had called, he'd told him that they'd seen the rescue from the cliffside. Branna had been there. He remembered his father's retelling.

"She and your sister came running up to us. She'd just grabbed your college jumper, ran out with her shoes in her hand to hear Brigid tell it. Christ Michael, her face when they dropped you out of the helicopter. I'll never forget it. I tried to soothe her. Covered her up, told her how good you were at your job. I think she was thinking of her da. You know, being killed on the job? The lass near broke my heart."

Michael thanked him, was glad she'd had a strong man there to put his arms around her. She didn't ever ask for help, didn't like to show weakness. Her scars were deep though, deeper than he'd ever imagined that first day in the pub. The more he thought about it, the more he thought he should probably wake her up, just for a minute. Just to let her see that he was home. Just as he got out of the car and grabbed his bag, the door flew open. She stepped out onto the porch. She was clasping her hands in front of her, anxiety and relief tight on her face.

She was afraid to come to him, afraid to let her guard down, and didn't that speak volumes about his failures? He hadn't done much to earn her trust. He had to make the first move. He looked at her as he walked forward. He dropped his gear on the wet ground and opened his arms to her. A risk if she rejected the gesture, but her face flooded with relief and she ran to him, practically tackling him as she threw her arms around his neck. He picked her up off her feet as she ran her hands up his scalp. He couldn't see her face. She had her forehead pressed just above his ear, smelling his hair. "You smell like the sea," she whispered. She tightened her grip on him.

"It's ok Branna. I'm ok. It was just a little swim," he smiled as he whispered in her ear.

She pressed her face in his neck. "I saw you go in. I saw you rescue those people. Jesus, Michael." He gave her another squeeze and set her down. She backed away and smoothed her hair back. It was something she did when she was nervous.

"I'm sorry, I was just worried. You're probably exhausted. I wasn't..." She paused, embarrassed at her emotional display. "I wasn't planning on tackling you, I'm sorry. You must be tired. Come inside. I cooked. I made you some dinner. I know it's late but I thought you should eat before you go to bed." She was rambling, talking fast and not looking him in the face. She turned to lead him in and he grabbed her hand.

"Wait, I liked having you in my arms," he said softly. Michael pulled her close and wrapped his arms around her shoulders. He cradled her small head in his hand, bent down and smelled her hair. He kissed the top of her head. "Never apologize for caring, Branna. Sometimes it's ok to let yourself go a bit."

She melted into him. "I was scared. I know you are probably great at your job and that it was some kind of thrill ride, but seeing it happen, seeing you in action, it was a lot different from thinking you know something. Seeing it is scary as hell."

He just stayed silent a moment. "It was different this time. It felt different." She looked up at him, compelling him to continue. "It wasn't two men or a married couple on holiday. It was a man and his daughter." Branna gasped, covering her mouth. "She was only about sixteen, a little sprite of a thing with long dark hair. Christ, the foolish bastard. He could have killed them both!" he hissed. "She was hanging on to the upturned skiff, screaming for her da. She had a life preserver on, but he didn't. She watched him go under just before I landed."

Branna was watching him with a look of horror on her face. "I pulled him up, my partner sent him up while I tended to the girl. She was screaming and clutched to me. Not screaming for herself, mind you." He just shook his head. "Why aren't his eyes open? Why doesn't he hear me?" He looked down at her. "She wouldn't stop screaming for him. The medics got him breathing in the air. All I kept thinking of was you."

She stepped out of his arms and put her face in her hands. "I'm sorry, Michael. I was such an idiot today. I acted like a spoiled child. When I saw you jump in that water, I understood. I get it now, why you were so upset, why you didn't want me out there alone."

Michael was shaking his head. "No, love. That's not what I meant. She reminded me of you, the black hair, the sad eyes. I just kept thinking about you at that age, losing your da. I want to punch that fecking guy in the face. He wasn't off doing his duty. He didn't die in a war. He almost left that little girl with no father because he was too stupid to check the weather, check the time, too cocky to wear a life jacket!" He closed his eyes, "That screaming. Christ, Branna. All I wanted to do is come home and hold you. Tell you how sorry I am. Your father, Brian, he did a dangerous job."

She broke in weakly, "So do you."

He just looked at her and nodded. "Yes, I suppose I do. Not like him, but I try to serve in my own way and there is a risk in that service. He didn't die for nothing, though. You know that. He'd be so proud of you, Branna. His little raven, grown up to be a fine, strong woman." He tucked her loose strand of hair behind her ear. "I just wanted to come back here and tell you that."

She put her hand over his as he touched her face. She planted a kiss on his palm as she closed her eyes. She soaked in every nuance of the contact, then turned toward the house. "The food is still warm. Come in and let me feed you."

CHAPTER 13

As Michael walked into the cottage, a wave of smells overwhelmed his senses. "Good Lord, woman. What have you made? It smells gorgeous all together." Branna smiled. "Nothing healthy. You need the calorie dump. Southern fried chicken, gravy, mashed potatoes, a hot cabbage and bacon salad, biscuits,and an apple cake. Dig in and I'll start the tea." She motioned to the feast lying out on the counter.

Branna preened at Michael's unspoken praise. He sniffed and then ate and moaned with every dish he tried. "Holy hell, woman, you're a sorceress. This is witchery."

She laughed. "Not on the American Heart Association diet, but so good."

He stopped and looked at everything. Nothing had been touched from the dishes before he'd started gorging himself. He put the piece of chicken down. "You didn't feed yourself did you? When's the last time you ate?"

She shrugged, "I grabbed something earlier. Eat, I made it for you."

He sighed. "Come here, hen." He crooked his finger at her. She was too tired and too relieved to argue. He stepped away from the countertop. He put her back to the counter, trapping her in. He picked up his drumstick. "Bite." She raised one eyebrow and he suppressed a groan. Her eyes held mischief. She must be a witch. He looked at the small freckle at her temple. It was the only mark on her otherwise creamy, smooth face. A witch mark.

"If I am a hen, doesn't that make this cannibalism?"

He gave her a daring look. "Bite." He looked her up and down, slowly. "I know your weak spots. You've got them all over you." His tone was deep and playful. "I'm tired, but a little tussle might be just the thing to take the edge off. Shall I put down this chicken and have hellcat ribs for dinner?"

Her eyes widened. Then she narrowed them. "You think you're tough don't you?" and she took a bite. He watched her mouth. Feeding her was stirring him in a very primitive, masculine way.

"Damn, I am a genius in the kitchen!" she said.

He laughed. "Arrogant, little hellcat."

She smiled. He tried to feed her some more. She put her hand on his as he went back to the plate. "That is for you, Michael. You need it. I'll have some too. We'll share it." Disappointed that he wasn't going to feed her, he was still relieved as he watched her make a small plate for herself. She picked up both and walked to the table. She pulled out a chair for him. "Sit down before you fall down, love." He laughed at her perfect imitation of his mother.

He was stuffed. She'd made enough to feed his entire family and made him eat a second plate. "Jesus, girl. Maybe I'm lucky you don't cook every day. I'd be as fat as the sow at the fair."

She just glared at him, "Don't make me sick. It should be illegal to have a body like yours." As soon as she said it, she clamped her mouth shut. His eyes flared. "Did I say that out loud?" she asked. She was turning red.

He grinned devilishly, "Aye, you did. I'm glad you approve."

She scoffed at that, deciding that she'd already tipped her hand. "Please, Michael. You have a mirror. You know what you look like, pretty boy."

He stood up, his uniform shirt was totally unbuttoned and untucked, but he had a tight white t-shirt on under it. He stretched like a big cat, all smooth muscles and grace. He made a big, obnoxious spectacle of pulling his uniform shirt off. "I'm just going to go get out of these clothes and slip into something a little less…restricting." He was flexing and talking in a breathy voice.

She threw a biscuit at him. "Oh my God, stop! I'm getting the vapors!" She was speaking in a southern belle drawl, batting her eyes and fanning herself. He was laughing as he walked into his room. She noticed, however, that the torturing bastard took his white t-shirt off before he was out of sight.

* * *

MICHAEL DIDN'T SEEM to be stirring in his room. She had the apple cake cut for his dessert and was going to put a glob of ice-cream on it when he surfaced from changing. She called out to him."I made dessert, Romeo. Where for art thou?" He didn't answer. She walked across the room to his open door. He was out cold. His torso was on the bed, but his feet were hanging off. She'd seen her dad nap like this. No boots on the sheets, but too tired to unlace and remove them. She walked over and carefully started pulling them off.

He stirred instinctively and pulled his feet up on the bed. She took a quilt from the foot of the bed and covered him, reluctantly. With no shirt on, he was a vision. Strong, wide chest with just a dusting of golden hair, big, lean arms, tight abs. She remembered smelling him. He smelled like the sea and like earthy male and she had to resist the urge to crawl up his chest and bury her nose in his neck. She switched off his bed lamp and turned to leave when he caught her thigh with his big hand. He was still half asleep. "You made a fire for me."

She turned and smoothed his hair back. It was military cut, but she loved the soft feel of it. "Yes, Michael. Now get some sleep."

He mumbled, still mostly asleep. "I like when you touch my hair. Stay with me for a while." She was touched. She knew that if he had been wide awake, he would never have asked. She sat at the head of the bed and he put his head in her lap. It was oddly intimate. He was like an innocent little boy, dreamy and tired. She started grazing his scalp with her nails. "Thank you, " he mumbled, and drifted off to sleep.

Branna nodded off sitting up, back against Michael's headboard. He was in a deep sleep. She could feel his chest rise and fall. She thought about the conversation she'd had with Brigid in the car. Brigid was right. She felt the love flow out of her and into Michael as she cradled his head and stroked him. She'd tried to keep a level head, but every day she fell more in love with him. She thought not dating was the answer, a way to protect herself from entanglements. She couldn't quit feeling, though. She wasn't made that way. Fate had put her in the path of one of the most wonderful men she'd ever known, and she hadn't stood a chance.

It shook her to her core when he'd opened his arms to her. He'd needed her as much as she needed him at that moment, and that was the final nail in her coffin. Feeling his need. This had become so complicated. Layers and layers of complications not the least of which was that she had also fallen in love with his family. She missed her parents every single day with a suffering she wasn't sure she would ever really be free of. The thought of losing the O'Briens was just another ring of hell, but the simple truth was that you couldn't lose something that didn't belong to you.

As she sat there in the dark, listening to Michael breathe, she knew the heartbreaking ending. She whispered, so that she wouldn't wake him. "I won't take this place from you Michael. You deserve to be happy. I promise, I won't take it." She would stay until the end. She would let herself have the next two months with them. Then she would walk away.

She couldn't stay in this position. She was hot from the fire and his body heat. Her back was throbbing from falling asleep in that position. She eased her way out from under him, gentle enough so that he would stay asleep. He looked so peaceful. He slept like a man with a clear conscience and a blessed life. She placed a gentle kiss on his lips and left the room. A chill hit her as she left the warm room, and she began to shiver. She crawled into bed, curled up, and slept.

* * *

MICHAEL WOKE with the disorienting feeling of someone who hadn't actually gone to bed. He remembered coming in the room to change. He realized that someone had taken his boots off and tucked him into bed. Then he remembered the guilty pleasure of lying in her lap, having her stroke his head. Heaven. He wished she would have crawled in with him, fallen asleep curled in his arms. He did have a fuzzy memory of her sweet, warm mouth. She'd kissed him, a small, gentle kiss. Did it really happen? Christ, had he actually slept through that open door? He shook himself. *Easy, lad. She's been assured she was safe for the next three months.* The thought of pulling her down on his bed niggled at his mind, warring with his conscience.

What a torturous joke this had become. He'd never wanted a woman more than he wanted her and she was right in the next room, but he was bound by honor not to jump her. And make no mistake. He didn't just want a kiss. He wanted every last inch of her. Everything she had to give. If he'd been awake during that kiss, tasted that sweet mouth again, his control would have snapped. He would have rolled her under him and been all over her. He groaned at the thought of it. It was getting harder and harder to behave himself.

He got up and realized that it was early morning, before sun up. He walked to the kitchen to get some water when he realized her door was open. She always slept with it closed. He considered that she may have gone outside, but she'd been up late. She was probably so tired she forgot. He went to the room to check on her and close her door when he heard her whimpering. "Branna, wake up. You're dreaming," he said sadly. She didn't. He noticed she was restless, scissoring her legs, and her hair was stuck to her face.

"Branna, sweetheart please wake up." He said it louder, walking toward her. Still nothing. As he got closer to her, he noticed the shivering. He touched her face, "Holy God. Branna love, wake up. You have a fever." She was scalding to the touch. He turned on the side lamp and his heart started racing. Her eyes cracked just a bit. She was unfocused, delirious. Her lips were blue and her whole body was trembling. He ran out of the room and grabbed her phone. Dr. Flynn must be on it somewhere. He found her number and called. "Fuck!" he shouted. It was the voice mail for her office.

He did the only thing he could think of. He called his mother. "Jesus, thank God you answered! She's sick with a fever. I don't know what's wrong. She was fine!"

His mother spoke in a calm voice. "It's ok Michael. I'm on my way. Does she have a doctor? Maybe this is something she didn't tell you about."

He answered. "It's Mary Flynn. I've been with her most of yesterday and then last night, she didn't seem sick. Christ, Ma. I don't even have a bloody thermometer!"

"Calm down, Michael. I'll bring one. I am sending you Mary's home number now. We have it in case Brigid goes into labor. Call her, she may know what to do. Don't panic. Just put something cool on her head and keep her covered. Comfort her, try to get her talking."

Michael grabbed a clean dishtowel and filled the sink with water and ice. Then he wet the towel. As he went to her bedside his heart was splitting. His fiery, little hellcat looked so vulnerable. "Branna, I need to cool your head down." He put the towel on her head and she seized up and started batting it away. "It's Michael. Please, love, for once don't fight me."

All of the sudden she balled up and moaned, as if she were in pain. He slid behind her and put his back to the headboard. He pulled her between his legs, her back to his chest. He pulled the covers over them both. "Branna, dear. I've got you now. Let's put this on your head."

She turned sideways, burrowed in his chest. "Michael, please. It hurts." She sounded like a child.

"I know love, can you tell me where it hurts?" he asked.

She was gripping him, "I saw you. I saw you jump in the water. You couldn't save daddy. Daddy's gone." She was caught between past and present, delirious. "I can't leave yet. Please, I don't have to leave yet."

He was ripping in two. "No, Branna. You don't have to leave. You're right here with me in our cottage. Do you remember our cottage?" She groaned again. "Branna, I need to call your doctor.

Please just keep this on your head." He dialed, and after a couple of rings, Mary answered. He told her everything. "She says it hurts, but I don't know where. Mary, she's talking nonsense. Should I ring an ambulance?"

Dr. Flynn listened intently. "No, don't do that Michael. They'll take her to the hospital. I'm getting in my car right now. I can be there in fifteen minutes. Keep the cold rag on her head. Keep trying to figure out what she's feeling."

Michael argued, "Maybe she needs to go to the hospital. I can drive her! Since when do you make house calls?"

Dr. Flynn stayed calm, "Michael, I'm on my way. I have an arrangement with her. Just keep doing what you're doing, and I will be right there."

Michael yelled, "Arrangement? What the bloody hell does that mean?" but Mary had already hung up.He heard his mother come in. She came through the bedroom door just as Branna was groaning in pain, again.

"Ma, please, get the big bowl and fill it with cold water. This rag is already warm. Did you bring the thermometer?" She handed it to Michael and left for the kitchen. "Branna, open your mouth. Put this under your tongue." She did as he asked and he waited.

Sorcha came in with the bowl and took the dishtowel from his hand. As she placed it back on Branna's face, she spoke to her. Soothing, motherly words as she stroked her hair by her ear. "There, there. That's my sweet girl."

Branna spoke softly, shivering and weak. "Mommy? My back hurts mommy, please make it stop." Michael looked at Sorcha, tears brimming his eyes. He shut them, unable to bear the pain he felt. Sorcha stroked her and spoke in loving, soothing tones as her own tears fell.

As Michael thought about it, she never really talked to him about her mother. She talked about her father on occasion, but not her mother. Yet, when she was sick and delirious, it was her mother that she wanted. Would she ever quit breaking his heart? The thermometer beeped. "105.1. Ma, maybe we need to call an ambulance?"

Sorcha was thinking hard, staring at Branna. "What did Mary say?"

He shook his head, "She's on her way here. She seemed pretty insistent we not take her to the hospital. It was the oddest thing. She said she had an arrangement with her. National healthcare doesn't pay for house calls. What the hell isn't she telling me?" Just then, he heard the doctor knock and come in.

Dr. Flynn was all business. She took Sorcha's place at the bedside. He tried to move and Branna clutched him. "No! You said I didn't have to leave yet! Don't leave!"

The doctor raised her eyebrows. "How long has she been like this?"

Michael answered, "I don't know. I found her like this about 20 minutes ago."

She nodded, "Did you find out the source of the pain?"

Sorcha answered, "She says it's her back." Dr. Flynn nodded, "Michael, can you raise her up to sitting instead?"

He began maneuvering off the bed. "Branna, sweetheart. I'll not leave you. We need to let Dr. Flynn examine you. Can you let me sit in front? I won't leave, sweetheart. I promise." She submitted to the change of position, but Michael always kept contact. He sat in the middle of the bed and got down to her eye level.

She looked at him, brightening a little. "I made you some chicken."

He laughed, "Aye, girl. It was lovely. You're going to make me fat if you keep cooking those gorgeous meals."

She smiled and seemed to clear up a little. "I was scared for you."

He tucked her hair behind her ear. "I know the feeling. Now, let Dr. Flynn have a look at you. There's a lass." He held her hand and looked at his mother. He was taken back by her expression. She was watching them, tears in her eyes. He looked away, unnerved by what he saw. He could never fool his mother.

Sorcha watched her son as he cared for the young American. He spoke to her with such tenderness, handled her like a treasure. She watched Branna as well. Caught in the delirium that often accompanied a high fever, she never forgot who he was. She refused to break contact with him, and when they'd made eye contact, she'd cleared a bit, pulling out of her febrile ramblings. She watched them as he tethered Branna to the present and Branna actually started to answer the doctor's questions.

"Branna, how long have you had the fever?"

She took a bit to answer, "I think it started in the middle of the night. I was hot, then I was shivering." Her voice was weak, her body strung tight as a drum skin from the pain.

Mary looked at Michael, "What's her temp?" He told her. She shook her head. Just then Branna moaned and curled up again. "The pain seems to come and go," Michael offered.

The doctor looked puzzled. "How long has she been complaining?" He thought back over the last couple of days. "Since she fell off the ladder."

She looked at him sharply, "How bad of a fall?"

He answered as best he could. "I wasn't here, but I came home right after. The rose bush broke her fall. It happened Friday. Just scratches on her back, hips and the back of her thighs. I cleaned her up, put the antibiotic cream on the scratches." His ears were turning red as he felt his mother's gaze on him.

The doctor lifted her shirt in the back. "These are barely visible, no infection. Nothing to explain this fever or how much pain she's in." She tapped on one side of the lower back, then the other. At this Branna jerked and grunted.

"Does it hurt on your right side, Branna?" Branna silently nodded. The doctor took her hand and pulled the skin on the top. She was checking skin turgor, a quick check for dehydration. "Michael, I think I know what's going on here. Pyelonephritis, an infection in her right kidney. I need to get her to my office, run an IV and do an ultrasound."

Michael face was stricken. "Shouldn't she go to the hospital?"

She nodded, "Maybe, but I can't do that yet. She was very clear about her care plan. No hospitals unless it is life or death."

Michael looked at her as if she were daft. "What? That's ridiculous! Why the hell would you agree to that? If it's the money I'll pay the bloody bill!"

The doctor sighed, "It's not the money. Michael, there are things you don't understand. If I didn't agree to her terms, she wouldn't come in when she was sick. Do you understand? I had lengthy discussions with her stateside physician. I can't tell you any more. I've probably told you more than I should."

Mary turned to her patient, "Branna, look at me." Branna had closed her eyes when the pain had come. She looked at Mary. "I need to take you to my office. I can't run any tests from here."

Branna tensed in Michael's arms and started shaking her head. "No hospitals! I told you, no hospitals."

She patted her hand. "Not the hospital, just my office. Do you remember my office?"

Branna nodded her head, "Yes, I remember. You don't have any toys."

The doctor laughed, "So I've been told. I guess I'll have to budget that in, won't I?"

Branna nodded. "Kids don't like the doctor. Especially when their mommy is sick. You need to have toys."

Mary's face was sad. "Ok, but now we need to go. I am going to let Michael carry you to my car." Branna nodded, coming in and out of awareness. Michael bent and cradled Branna in his arms. It was so natural. She wrapped her arms around his neck.

She lay her head back and looked at him. "I'm sorry. I'm sorry for everything. You're good, Michael. You're so good and I'm sorry."

He squeezed her close, "No, Branna. You've got no reason to be sorry."

As they drove, Mary spoke to Sorcha. Branna was drifting in and out. She seemed to be soothed by Michael's embrace. He rode with her in his lap, her head tucked under his chin.

"It doesn't make sense. Usually Pyelonephritis is a complication of a UTI. She hasn't been treated for that. She would have come in. Those symptoms are very noticeable. I would have seen her in the urgent care last week. There's something else going on here. She shouldn't be in this much pain."

Sorcha nodded, "You think it's a stone, then?"

The doctor shrugged, "She doesn't have a history of them, but yes. It may be a stone."

Michael wasn't a medic. He was a swimmer. He followed some of what they were saying, but some of it he wasn't following. His mother had been a midwife before she got cancer. She hadn't worked for over ten years, but the doctor was conversing with her like a colleague. If he butted in, the doctor would snap out of it and start worrying about confidentiality again. She didn't understand that he needed to know everything. *She's mine.* The thought surprised him, but he couldn't deny it. She was so small in his arms. Like a little hot coal, burning with fever. She shook and he tightened his hold, planted kisses all over her head.

She leaned back, her face looking up to him. She put her hand on his face. "Don't be sad. I won't take it from you. I could never take it from you." He kissed her eyes feeling his own tears burning, "Just close your eyes, love. Rest and I'll take care of you," he whispered. *Because, you're mine.*

Branna was lying on the exam table, Michael holding her hand as the doctor asked him questions. She'd run an IV to give her fluids. "What's her diet like? What does a normal day look like?"

He shook his head in disgust. "Can you survive on coffee and blind ambition? She doesn't eat well. She has a few apples and carrots in the icebox, but she eats a lot of dried fruit and those stupid protein bars. Occasionally, when she cooks for someone else or goes out, she'll eat a real meal. She just nibbles. She eats enough to keep going, but it is like she can't be bothered to feed herself anything but quick and easy. She doesn't eat junk food, no crisps or biscuits or anything like that. Her meals are like something from a bird or rabbit cage."

The doctor wrote it all down, nodding as he talked. "How about hydration? Do you see her drink a lot of water? She seems very dehydrated. Her body is pulling it out of that IV bag like I just pulled her out of the desert."

He rubbed his hands on his face. "I've been on her about that. I came home to find her outside on her fifth hour of painting. Out in the heat with a cup of black coffee, damn close to heat stroke. She did it again yesterday. She went out kayaking with no water. She drinks a lot of coffee, but she doesn't drink enough water to keep a kitten alive."

The doctor stood up, "Ok, I need to do some tests. I think I know what's going on, but she needs to be tested to confirm it. It will only take a few minutes. Her fever is high and she's mentally altered. I need her emergency contact here. I at least need them on the phone."

Michael straightened up. "She's got no kin. I can be her emergency contact." The doctor shook her head. "I saw her almost a month ago, a few days after she arrived. She put…" she paused to look at her file. "She has Tadgh O'Brien down as the emergency contact. She said…" Mary cut off her sentence.

Michael tensed. "What, Mary?"

Mary cleared her throat. "She had just arrived. She was going to put Ned Kelly down, but she said something about not wanting to look conniving? I didn't understand it, but then she said it could be Tadgh. She said he was the only local person that…" She paused, then looked him in the eyes with a knowing look. "That didn't hate her."

Pain lanced through Michael. Pain and jealousy. Tadgh, again. Jesus, would they ever be out of this cycle? In her defense, she had a point about what she'd said. She'd seen the doctor right after that bloody awful trip to Dublin. She'd never switched the contact info to him, though. She'd lived with him for just over a month and she still had Tadgh down as the trusted one and only.

Michael whipped out his phone. Started thumbing through is contacts. "Michael, you can do that in the waiting room. We need some privacy." She looked at Sorcha who was looking at Michael with a distressed expression. "Sorcha, we need to work fast. I don't have time to call a nurse in for this. I just need some basic assistance, nothing medical. Do you mind?"

Sorcha answered, "I'm not going anywhere, Mary. Just tell me what you need."

Michael called Tadgh who was just getting up for work. "I'll be right there. Ten minutes, Michael. I will be there in ten minutes." Tadgh arrived in eight.

"Have they come out?" Michael just shook his head, not meeting Tadgh's gaze. Tadgh sighed and gave an impatient grunt. "This is no time for your misplaced jealousy. She filled that paperwork out after you chased her out of Dublin!" He calmed his voice, "A lot has changed since then, and well you know it. She wasn't going to make a special trip just to change her emergency contact." He smacked his cousin on the arm. "Snap out of it you broody fucker! You know I'll tell you everything as soon as she tells me."

Michael turned his back on him and ran his fingers through his hair. "I'm sorry Tadgh, you're right. I'm being a prick and you don't deserve it. You've been there for her way more than I have." He paused, breathing deeply, "You shoulda seen her. She was out of her head. Calling for her mother," his voice broke. "Begging me not to make her leave yet."

Tadgh put himself in front of Michael and took his face in his hands. "She's going to be ok, brother. She's tough. This might not be that serious."

Michael looked at him. "I love you, Tadgh. You know that. Like my own brother."

Tadgh put his forehead to Michael's. "I know, you stubborn bastard."

Dr. Flynn came out of the exam room and noted that the two boys she tended to as small lads had certainly grown up. They were a united front, double trouble. God help her when Brigid went into labor. She'd have O'Briens, Murphys and Mullens wearing ruts in the flooring.

"Okay Tadgh, I need to speak with you."

Tadgh put his hand up to stop her. "I'm going to tell him every word you say Mary. You know it and so do I. So, why don't we just cut the shite and get on with it."

Michael raised his brows, "Well said, brother."

Mary knew time was ticking. She resigned herself to violating privilege for the sake of expediency. "Ok, I was correct. She does have a pretty serious kidney infection. If it were a run of the mill lower UTI, I could treat her with oral antibiotics, but it isn't. Honestly,I'm not convinced that's how it started at all. She has a sizable kidney stone."

Tadgh cursed. "Can she pass it on her own?"

The doctor took off her glasses and rubbed the bridge of her nose. "No, I'm afraid not. There are several types of stones. Each one has its own set of causes and treatments. Her habit of eating those dehydrated, dense, high protein bars coupled with too much caffeine and chronic dehydration are bad enough. The two acute incidents of serious dehydration that you told me about were probably the final straw."

"She isn't taking in enough water to compensate for her diet and her caffeine intake is too high for someone as small as she is. The stone develops quickly. In this case, it caused enough irritation to form an infection. Given the stress she's been under, her resistance is low. Michael, how does she sleep? Have you been able to observe that at all?"

He had been looking at his feet, listening intently. "Nightmares a few times a week. She won't tell me what they're about. Probably her parents. Sometimes I hear her across the house. She must be sleep deprived. I should have made her come in. She's just so bloody independent."

Mary nodded, "Yes, well she's had to be, I'd imagine." She continued, "Pyelonephritis alone is serious. The kidneys filter blood. She can get septic if we don't get a handle on this infection. It could spread to her blood and to her other organs. We also need to get that stone out. Her body will keep trying to expel it and it is too big at this point. She will literally writhe in agony and get nowhere. I fed a high spectrum antibiotic into her IV and something for the pain, but she has to go to the hospital. There are a couple of ways I can handle this, but I need a urologist to weigh in on this. She made need surgery."

Michael cursed under his breath. He looked at Tadgh, "I need you to come with me. They may want you to sign something." Tadgh put his hand around Michael's neck. "I won't leave you or her."

The medicine made Branna groggy. She was drifting off as

Michael lifted her. He looked at Mary. "She's afraid of hospitals, is that it? Some sort of phobia?"

She nodded. "It's not that uncommon in people who watched their parents die slowly in a hospital. She lost both at a young age. It's amazing how well she's coping, considering." He slid in the back seat again, Tadgh and the doctor in the front.

Sorcha went home to talk to the rest of the family. They'd been texting and calling every five minutes. She stirred a little in his arms. He pulled her to him and smelled her sweaty hair. "It's all right, mo chroi. I'll not let any harm come to you."

CHAPTER 14

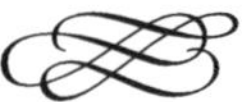

Tadgh watched his cousin caring for Branna. If he'd ever seen a man being eaten alive, he was seeing it now. God, how he loved her. She was clutched to him like no one else in the world existed. She loved him, too. The fact that neither one of them knew it, that these two stubborn lunatics had managed to fight it this long, amazed and bewildered him. Mary gave him a knowing look. "Only an O'Brien man could make falling in love look like a funeral pyre," Tadgh said, shaking his head.

Mary snorted, "Yes, so I've heard. Aren't you an O'Brien man?" He laughed. "Touché', Doc."

Branna stayed asleep as they drove to the University hospital in Galway. When they arrived, the nurses helped Michael out as Dr. Flynn held her IV bag. Branna stirred awake as Michael moved her to the gurney. She went wild. The nurses flew into action and had two male paramedics help them hold her down. Michael went mental.

"Don't hold her down! She's scared! You're going to make it worse you bloody eejits!"

Tadgh grabbed him in a bear hug and hissed in his ear. "She going to hurt herself if they don't! Calm the fuck down or they won't let you stay with her! You told her you wouldn't leave her."

Michael immediately snapped out of his spiral. The thought of them banning him from her shocked the stupid out of him. He walked along side as they wheeled her into the ER. The Urologist that Mary had called came up and started talking with her. She gave him the ultrasound disc and they ducked into an office with a computer.

Branna was crying. They took her to a curtained off area. "Are you the husband?" He looked blankly. "No, we're not related." The nurse nodded. "Ok, you two are going to have to go to that waiting area until we get her checked in."

Michael started to argue and Tadgh clamped his hand on Michael's arm and told the nurse, "This is Tadgh O'Brien. He's her emergency contact. Any access you can give him to her, you should. She's got no living kin. She's American. She'll cooperate if you let him in the room."

The nurse looked at them both. "If you're not kin, I need to let her have some privacy. I'll bring you in when I'm done taking care of a few things." Michael nodded.

"You are a crafty one aren't you?" Michael whispered.

Tadgh just smiled, "Just keep yourself under control. If you start losing your shit again, they'll kick you out, paperwork or no paperwork."

The nurse came after a few minutes and told Michael aka Tadgh that he could come see her now. He went behind the curtain and his blood went cold. Branna was completely shut down. She was looking off at nothing, tears pouring down her temple into her hairline, and her body trembled all over. She had padded cuffs binding her feet and wrists.

He went to her, touched the restraints. "Oh, God," he moaned. "You can't restrain her. Get her doctor. Please, just get the doctor now! You can't restrain her. She's afraid of hospitals, that's all. She's been fevered, she's scared. You're making it worse!" Tears were pooling in his eyes now. He quelled them. He had to keep it together for her sake.

The nurse gave him a pitying look. "We didn't want to. She was trying to get up, and she was trying pull her IV out of her arm. She was hurting herself."

He put his hand on her head, resting his forehead on hers. "She's just scared, I can calm her until they decide what to do. I know I can't stay with her the whole time, but at least until you sedate her." He looked at the nurse. "Please, ask her doctor. I can keep her calm."

She nodded, moved by his desperation. She left and came back with Dr. Flynn. "We'll take the restraints off. I'm sorry. You're right. It will make it worse, long term. Can you keep her calm, Michael?" Mary asked.

Michael exhaled, relief flooding him. "I can, I will." He got down eye level with Branna. "How's my little hellcat? Been naughty, I see."

She focused on his face. "Take me home. Please, I'm fine."

He smoothed her hair back. "So you keep telling me. You're sick, Branna. We won't keep you here any longer than we have to, okay? I'm going to untie you, and you can lie with me, if you promise to stay calm."

She had tears pouring freely. "It hurts. I'm scared. Please stay with me," she croaked.

He kissed her face all over. "I'll stay as long as they let me." He and the nurse started undoing her restraints. He slid in behind her as the nurse raised the top half of the gurney up to his back. He soothed her, whispering in Gaelic.

She clung to him and whispered, "Sing to me."

Michael couldn't deny her anything. He sang the two love songs they'd danced to at his brother's wedding. The nurse came beside them, adding some vials of liquid to her IV. All the tension left her body as she drifted off.

"I gave her another dose of antibiotics and a pain narcotic. I can't give her anything else until we get the okay from the anesthesiologist." Michael nodded.

The nurse said, "You aren't her husband, but you act like you are. You're very good with her. She's a lucky woman."

Michael shook his head, "You're wrong. I've been an arrogant jackass."

The nurse laughed. "Well, she's going to be fine Mr. O'Brien. So, you'll have a second shot at it. She doesn't seem like she's too eager to be rid of you. Just don't be so fat headed about everything and it'll all be grand."

He looked at her and grinned. "Your last name isn't Mullen, by any chance?"

Michael laid there with her, humming and whispering endearments in Gaelic. She wouldn't understand him, even if she woke, so he could feel free to be as much of a sap as he liked.

Tadgh sneaked in behind the curtain and sat on the only chair. He put his feet up so no one knew he was in there. "You know, it doesn't count if she can't understand you."

Michael looked sideways at him. "How much did you hear?"

Tadgh's gaze was appraising. "Enough, brother. I heard enough."

Michael cradled her head. Her face was turned up to him as she rested. He kissed her between her eyes and then on the corner of her mouth. She opened her eyes and touched his face. "Thank you."

He asked, "Whatever for?"

She exhaled deeply, "For touching me, holding me. I don't have anyone left who touches me. They all went away." He buried his face in her hair. She patted his head, in a drug induced stupor. "It's ok. I know I have to go." She was groggy and drifting in and out. "I never thought I'd get this. I'm grateful for the little while that I get this."

She looked over at Tadgh. "Hi."

He smiled. "Hello there, gorgeous. Making trouble again, I see."

She smiled back at him. "What do you say we tackle the big guy and get out of here? I'll even drink some whiskey."

He laughed, because he could tell she was stoned on pain meds, "You are incorrigible. Remind me again why I'm not trying to get in your knickers?"

She laughed weakly. "Because I am an emotionally damaged head case?"

Michael mumbled under his breath, "Because he's not suicidal." Branna looked up at him dreamily and closed her eyes again.

Both doctors came in and Tadgh tucked out the side before he was tossed out. Michael listened as they explained what would happen. They would break up the stone using sound waves. She would be put under sedation. If all went well, she would start passing the small pieces out almost immediately and she would not have to be kept overnight. Her fever was already starting to come down. "We have to take her back and prep her now."

He stopped them, "Wait, can I have a minute?" They nodded as they watched him pull his rosary out of his pocket. He knelt next to her, holding her hand in silence while he said a short prayer. Her eyes were closed, feeling the effects of the pain medication. He kissed her hand and whispered to her. "I know you're mad at Him, but He'll take care of you while you're away from me. Promise me you won't give Him too much trouble, aye?" He kissed her head and stood away from her. He nodded and they wheeled her away.

The procedure seemed to take forever, but in actuality, they were only gone for ninety minutes. Mary came out of the O.R. and her relief was palpable. "She's in recovery. She's doing really well. We should be able to take her home in about an hour. They want to watch her, make sure everything is working as it should."

Tadgh slapped Michael on the back. "I told you, brother. She's fine."

* * *

THE TWO BEAUTIFUL O'Brien cousins walked into the recovery area, and Branna watched as every female nurse on the floor gawked. Branna was tired and having residual pain. She felt like hissing at the nurses to put their eyes back in their heads. "What's the scowl for, Yank? Are you in pain?"

She looked at Tadgh. "No, not as much as before. I'm fine. A little thick headed from the fever and drugs, but my fever is down."

Michael said, "That wasn't her pain face, that was her angry, little hellcat face. Who's got your knickers in a bunch now, little Branna?"

She gave a crooked smile. "No one, I was just watching the show." He looked at Tadgh, confused. "You two are causing a wave of female hysteria throughout the hospital. Do you O'Brien men have to be so damned handsome?"

Tadgh puffed up his chest. "Really? Hmmm, maybe I'm feeling a bit faint. I may need my blood pressure checked. Which way were the young, hot ones?"

Branna pointed. "Head that way. A blonde with legs for miles. She seemed particularly enthralled with your backsides." He wiggled his eyebrows and left them.

Michael's eyes never left her. "You aren't going to race him to the blonde?" she teased.

He approached her bed and gave a slow shake of the head. "I think I have my hands full enough, don't you?" His eyes searched her face, as if he was reacquainting himself with her.

She spoke softly, "You were worried. I don't remember everything, but I remember you." Her voice broke, "I could feel you, pulling me back from the dreams." Tears started coming. "I could smell you and hear you. You sang to me." He kissed her head, and she closed her eyes. "Thank you. You could have just passed me off to the doctor. You didn't have to stay."

He kissed her cheeks and each of her eyes. "Yes, I did," he whispered, and he kissed her mouth.

Just as Michael closed his mouth on hers, he heard Dr. Flynn and the Urologist approaching. He reluctantly pulled away before they came into the room. Mary said, "You look like you are getting your strength back. Are you ready to go back to Doolin?"

Branna nodded, "Yes, please."

"Okay, there's some paperwork you need to sign. Michael, give my keys to Tadgh and have him pull my car around to the front of the hospital. I've got no bloody idea where he parked it."

As Michael returned from hunting Tadgh down, he shook his head. Tadgh had indeed found that blonde nurse. He found them in an empty area, behind a curtain. Tadgh had his fist in her hair, head pulled back as he nibbled her neck. He had his pelvis pressed to hers, but the clothes were still on. She looked like she was enjoying the ride. She'd actually whimpered when he pulled away.

"Sorry, love." He turned and adjusted himself, breathing deeply to corral his lust. "It's Tadgh O'Brien. I'm on the paperwork for room seven." He pulled her in and kissed the shit out of her. Michael turned his back again, not that they seemed worried about privacy. He marveled at how fast Tadgh worked.

"You have no shame, you know that?" Michael said, grinning at his randy cousin.

"Christ, man. What do you expect? We can't all have the angels fly down and deliver a girl like Branna. I'm stressed out. I need an outlet until I find Mrs. Right," he grinned.

Michael laughed, "Was that her, then?"

Tadgh scoffed at that, " Hell, no. You think Mrs. Right O'Brien is going to be some horny feckin' nurse that would shag me in a corner before she knew my name?"

Michael looked at him, "You realize, brother, that you're a total hypocrite?"

Tadgh sighed, "I have standards. No married lasses. I take what I can get. You snagged the best prospect in the last five years."

Michael shook his head, "Don't say that. I don't have any claims to her. I don't know what this is. Christ, it's tearing me apart, Tadgh. I don't know what she is. I just can't seem to keep away from her." He grabbed him by one arm and stopped. "You can't say anything to her, you hear? I live with her. She's stuck with me for two more months. Ned and Da told her she was safe around me. You can't put her in that position!"

Tadgh had always thought his cousin was smart, above the bar in the brains department. "Michael, pardon my bluntness but you are a feckin' eejit. Christ, don't you see how she looks at you?" He thought about that. "Aye, maybe you don't. She only gets that look when your head is turned, the same as you with her. You're both feckin eejits."

Michael glared at him. "This isn't as simple as all that."

Tadgh stopped abruptly. "That's where you're wrong, Michael. It is that simple. You don't have any claim on her, eh?" he poked him in the chest. "To hell with that bloody cottage! If you let her leave, I swear to Christ I will follow her and marry her before you have the time to change your fucking mind. I will have her under me getting a child in her before you can do a God damn thing about it!"

He pointed a finger in Michael's face. "I've given you time to come around, but maybe it is time I got in the game. Step back if you don't want her, Michael. I will sure as hell take her!"

Michael snapped, grabbing Tadgh by the shirt, and shoving him across the room. He slammed him into the wall. "You don't touch her! Do you hear me?"

Tadgh got deadly calm, "Tell me again how you don't know what she is, that you don't have a claim on her. Tell me again that you are ready to let her go, let some other man love her, be the one to touch her."

Michael backed away, putting his fist to his forehead. "What is she? Say it, you coward. Say it!" Tadgh yelled.

Michael pinned him with a stare and hissed, "She's mine."

Tadgh nodded and walked past him. "It's about fucking time."

* * *

THEY RODE HOME IN SILENCE, all exhausted. Tadgh drove so that Dr. Flynn could rest. She had cancelled her morning appointments, but she had to go into her office. Branna laid limply in Michael's arms. She'd been given oral pain meds and was still groggy. Michael held her, thinking about what had gone down between himself and Tadgh.

He knew Tadgh had deliberately provoked him. Jesus, what had come out of his mouth? He'd been ready to tear Tadgh's head off. He couldn't do this to her, he had to control himself. He wasn't sure how Branna actually felt. He held her closely, savoring the closeness. Things would change when she was recovered. He was so very glad she was okay, but he knew that the liberties that he'd taken while she was ill had to stop. He had to give her room to choose. She'd been sick, scared, and alone. It was natural that she would've taken what he offered. He just couldn't assume that he knew where this was headed.

Michael carried Branna's limp body into her room. She was passed out cold from the narcotics she'd been given. He put her down gently on her bed. "She's damn lucky you were here," Dr. Flynn commented.

"I barely know her really," he answered, looking down at his unlikely roommate. Then he went over to the dresser and took out her flannel pajamas. He handed them to Mary. "They were her father's. I think she feels close to him when she wears them. Could you put them on her?" he asked.

Mary looked at him thoughtfully. "You seem to know her pretty well, actually. I'll change her. Go get some sleep, Michael."

* * *

Branna woke in her bed. There was a fire glowing in her small hearth, and Brigid stirred from her reading. "How is our little Yank feeling?"

Branna smiled weakly. "I barely remember the ride home. When did you get here?"

Brigid got up, pregnant belly protruding with the effort. "A couple of hours ago. Michael went to the grocer. He had a list like he was feeding the Royal Army. He wouldn't go without someone here to watch you. He called off of work."

Branna looked embarrassed. "I've caused so much trouble, you don't have to stay. God, he should go to work."

Brigid looked at her, a look of incredulity on her face. "Are you daft, girl? You've had the whole family worried sick. Aidan and Patrick texting every two minutes, Liam trying to drive from Dublin, even Seany's been asking after you. Da and mom keep calling me, trying to take a shift."

Branna said softly, "Why? I'm not family. I'm no one."

Brigid sat next to her. She took her hand and patted it. "You're wrong. You don't believe that now, but you're wrong." She sat upright. "So, time to head to the water closet. Mary said I need to make sure that you're drinking and pissing."

Branna covered her mouth,."Please tell me that your brother didn't take me to the bathroom at any point during my memory lapse."

Brigid laughed, "God no. Between your doctors, nurses, Ma, and me, we've kept the lads out of your knickers."

* * *

BRANNA WAS SITTING on the edge of the bed later that day when Michael knocked. "Come in."

He walked in and said, "Do you need help?"

Branna shook her head. "No, I just got a little dizzy. I just need a minute."

Michael walked over, kneeling down next to her. "It's probably the drugs. Are you in pain?"

She shrugged. "It's nothing I can't handle. I just…" She paused.

"Tell me. What do you need, Branna?"

She blushed, "I want a bath. I smell like sweat."

He patted her leg. "You don't smell, but if you want a bath then I'll get it ready. I sent Brigid on her way, but I can get you part way in. If you want a bath, we'll figure it out."

She smiled. "I'm not an invalid. You should be at work. I've made a mess of things, again."

He took her chin in his hand. "Don't be so afraid to let someone take care of you."

Michael checked the temperature and smelled deeply of her rose and heather bath salts. He turned around, and there she was, her hair in a loose braid. He'd had Dr. Flynn put her in her father's pajamas, but she didn't have her tank top under them. The neck was low and he tried not to stare as the creamy swell of one breast was revealed. She was clear eyed, the haze of fever gone. She sniffed the scented steam and sighed, "I need this, thank you."

She was close now, looking at his face, then his mouth. He needed to leave. She was still recovering. "Do you need help getting in?"

She blushed. "Maybe just the legs, then I can handle the rest." She looked at him as she slipped her bottoms off. The top of the pajamas was long. He couldn't see anything above mid thigh.

"Just use me. Hold on while you step in." Her eyes never left him and he hardened in his trousers. He put his hands on her waist to steady her as she stepped into the water.

"I think I can take it from here." He started to walk toward the door. As he went to close it behind him, he looked up. She was turned to the side, unbuttoning her top. He closed the door as she pulled it over one shoulder.

Michael was breathing heavy on the other side of the door. He was mentally kicking his own ass. She was recovering, and she was also on pretty potent pain meds. She wasn't thinking clearly. Neither was he. All he could think about was laying her down in that tub, slipping his hand down in the water, and working her until she came against his hand. Slick and wet and deep. He was a pig. A shameful, randy pig.

Branna knew she must be feeling better. All it took was seeing Michael's big body bent over that tub and all the blood and fluid rushed to one area. At times she thought she felt some of that attraction returned from Michael, but her memory of the last two days was fuzzy. He certainly hadn't needed any persuading to leave the bathroom. She eased down into the warm water.

She had to stop mooning over him. It wasn't fair to either of them. He'd taken such good care of her. He'd cradled her and soothed her with such tenderness. The last thing Michael needed was her panting after him just because he'd been nice to her.

She needed to be his friend, concentrate on her work, and start thinking about what she was going to do when she got handed her eviction notice. Ned had been wonderful. He'd called periodically over the last month, checking on her. He didn't, however, do as he said he was going to do. Any inquiries he made were about her personally. He inquired about how she was settling in, never about the house. She couldn't figure out why on earth he was going through the motions for three months when he'd probably already made up his mind.

Branna stood up in the water, ready to get out. She reached for a towel and wrapped it around herself. The warm water had made her loopy. There was a knock. "Branna, I heard the water splash. Do you need help out of the bath? I put a towel down where you could reach it."

She answered, "I'm ok. Thank you." God, she hated this. Like some old, sickly woman. She felt better. Those painkillers were powerful, and she hated how she felt when she took them. She hadn't been horizontal this long since she was five and had the flu. She dressed, grunting with the effort. He cursed under his breath. "I'm coming in now, if you're decent."

Michael opened the door to the bathroom. He didn't know what had happened to that sweet, little, cooperative woman he'd put in the bath, but in her place was a prickly, wet little hellcat. "You are the most stubborn woman I have ever met."

She smiled. "Thank you."

She got up from the tub walked to the sink and picked up a bottle of pills. He watched her as she walked past him, went to the kitchen trash bin, and tossed them. Then she opened the front door, walked out on the porch and took a deep breath of fresh, cool air.

"What were those?" he asked from behind her.

She answered, "I kept my antibiotics. I don't need those." She pointed at the trash can. "They make me loopy. I would feel perfectly strong if I wasn't doped up on those pain meds. I'd rather suck it up."

He sighed. "Gee, I'd never guess you were raised by a jarhead."

She smiled, "Thank you, again."

She came back inside and headed for the kitchen. "Where is my coffee pot?" She needed a pick me up.

He folded his arms over his chest. "It's been confiscated."

She raised a brow. "By whom?"

He answered, "By me, Doctor's orders." Not really, but there were no half measures with this one.

Challenge sparked in her eyes. "I'll just get my other one."

He shook his head. "Also confiscated. You're going to go native. You can have tea for the next two days. If you behave yourself, you will get your fancy coffee pot back and one pod a day. You need to be re-trained."

She bristled. "I'm not a dog."

He shrugged. "Think of it as Olympic training if that helps. Olympic training for stubborn little peahens." He pointed at her. "You put yourself in that hospital bed. Not enough real food, not enough water, too much caffeine, not enough sleep."

Something occurred to her, and she opened the cabinet. It was full of groceries, unlike before. She poked around and then turned to him, "Where are my protein bars?"

He smiled sweetly at her. "If you go hiking or kayaking or somewhere else where they will come in handy, I will give you one. Other than that, you are going to eat real food."

She slammed the cabinet door. "You are not my lord and master. You are also not my nurse. I live my life my way. Period!"

He slammed his hand on the counter and she jerked. "You scared the hell out of me! Do you know what it was like to come in your room and find you like that? Your lips were blue, you couldn't stop shaking, you were talking out of your head! Christ, I almost dialed emergency services!" His accent was thick, he was warring between hurt and anger, pacing back and forth.

It finally got through to her what she'd put him through. "Michael," was all she said before he cut her off. "Don't say you're sorry and don't say you're fine. Just say you will listen to the doctor, and that you'll start taking care of yourself." His look was pleading.

Her anger deflated. She was being a prickly brat. The truth was that she felt weak and she hated it. She hadn't eaten in two days. Michael walked over to the bin and took the pills out. "Just take them before bed. They're not just for pain. These are anti-inflammatories. You can take something over the counter during the day."

She sighed. "Okay."

Michael jerked back, "Excuse me?"

She gave him a look. "I said okay. You're right. I'm being selfish and ungrateful. I owe it to you to do better." He cursed again. "What? I said okay!" her volume was going up again.

He growled. "That's what you think this is about? Forget me and forget everyone else! You owe it to yourself Branna! Why is that such a hard concept for you?"

She closed her eyes. "I understand that, I do. I know it doesn't seem like it, but I swear I am not trying to self destruct. I'm it. I'm all I have. No one else is going to take care of me. You're right, I need to do better. I will, starting with food. I haven't eaten since the chicken. I'm starving and it's making me weak and crabby. Are there any leftovers?"

He wanted to believe her. "I made dinner. Can't you smell it?" he asked, head cocked to one side.

"It smells delicious. I was playing dumb in case you didn't make enough," she said.

He moved closer and ran his palm down the back of her head. She had it bound up again. He pulled her face close to his. "Do you really think I'd just cook for myself?"

She shook her head. "No, you don't have a selfish bone in your body. It is just a habit, I guess."

He inched his face closer. "It's a defense mechanism. You're giving those up along with the coffee." He rubbed his thumb over her mouth and she exhaled lightly. He could feel her soft breath on his mouth.

She closed her eyes, just feeling him. "You know, it doesn't have to be my birthday," she said. Her eyes were open now and heavy lidded, focusing on his mouth. His eyes flared in response. He brought her to his mouth. Soft at first, then firmer, tasting her, sucking her lips in, nibbling. Lust roared through her as he slid his tongue deep. She let out a little moan.

Michael heard a little beep. It was his phone alarm. Time to take her medicine. He broke the kiss. "Christ, what am I doing? You're just out of the hospital."

She was breathing heavy. "Damn it if Marvin Gaye wasn't right. I feel way better."

He thought about it for a second and then understood the song reference. He barked out a laugh. He did another brush of her glossy, bottom lip, his eyes sparkling with desire. "Christ, you make me lose all sense. You need to eat. If you're feeling up to it, I'll take you to the cliffs for some fresh air. I've got a key, remember?" Her eyes widened with excitement. "You have to eat and take a Motrin and drink two glasses of water, then I'll take you."

After following Michael's orders to the letter, he drove her to the gate and sneaked her in to view the cliffs at night. She could barely see anything, but the sound and the feel of the place was intoxicating. She felt like she'd been transported. "When I see it like this, I can block out the modern world. I can pretend I am back hundreds of years, that my cottage is just over there." She motioned to the parking lot. "I could be here waiting for my husband or father to return from sea. I love the sounds and smells. I daydreamed about this place when I thought about coming here. Even the pictures stirred my blood."

Michael came behind her and wrapped her in a small blanket. He kept his arms around her. "Aye, and you look the part. Wild black hair in the wind, skin like ivory, eyes like the sea." He was quiet then, and she felt his fingers start unbraiding her hair. It went wild around both of them and she felt his arms come back around her. He put his face in her hair, lips by her ear. "I promised God that if you got better, I'd change how I treated you. I would see your presence here as a gift."

She turned to him. "You've never treated me poorly, Michael. I'll never forget this time here with you." She turned away and looked out at the black sea.

He stiffened; not liking the direction the conversation had taken, like she was planning a goodbye. He put his arm across her, turning her face back to his so that he could kiss her, showing her with his body, not his words, that he wanted her here. The roar of the water, the exhilarating wind, the darkness emboldened them. She turned and wrapped her hands around his forearms as he cradled her head in his big hands.

She kissed him with aching thoroughness, and he returned her kisses with the same barely restrained heat. He pulled her mouth to his and she opened for him tilting her face so he could take her mouth. She was on fire in his arms. Just before she pulled away, she sucked his bottom lip. He could barely see her face, but for the glow of the moon on her pale skin. He put his forehead to hers. "Christ, what are we going to do?"

* * *

BRANNA STAYED UP LATE READING. She'd slept so much in the last two days that she'd had trouble getting to sleep. She finally drifted off in the wee hours of the morning. She woke up in the late morning to find Michael working outside, raking and pulling the late season weeds. She came out on to the front porch with a blanket around her, and sat on the rocking chair that he'd put on the porch for her. She cradled her tea and watched him. He smiled, sweat on his forehead and the back of his neck. He straightened on his knees and looked at her cup. "It's tea, don't worry. I took my medicine and drank some water, too."

He smiled. "She can be taught."

Branna watched him and felt a stirring in her belly. His strong arms were flexing under his labors. He stood up, stretching, and she could see the trail of hair below his navel that disappeared down into his ragged, low slung jeans. He stilled and she noticed that he was looking at her. His face grew hungry. "You keep looking at me like that, hellcat, and I'm going to forget that you are sick and that I am a gentleman," he said.

His tone was teasing, but his look was not. She shrugged, "Do your worst, pretty boy."

A look of incredulity came across his gorgeous face and he laughed. He gave her a chiding look that said, *Don't toy with me little girl.* He took off his work gloves and stalked toward her. "I'm going to go take a shower. A cold one." As he closed the door, he heard her mischievous laughter.

Branna spent most of the day on her computer doing some work. She made a few phone calls and napped periodically, feeling the remnants of her illness slowly fading. Michael was working in the kitchen and had banned her from peeking at what he was making. When it was done, he came into her room. She'd nodded off again and woke to someone lifting her.

"Shhh, easy lass." She was cradled in his arms. "Dinner is ready."

She smiled as she put her head on his shoulder. "I can walk, you know."

He said, "I know, but you're almost better and I won't get to wait on you once you're up to full force."

She giggled. "Am I that difficult?"

He sat her down at the table. "Yes, you are a fierce, little beastie. Now sit like a good girl. It's time your education begins."

She said, "Now I'm intrigued. What sort of education?"

He looked at her sideways. "You're going to eat like a local."

She shook her head. "No blood pudding!"

He crinkled up his nose, "I'm with you on that one. Never could stomach it. I saw it made once and that was all it took." He started bringing dishes to the table.

He sat beside her, chair facing her. "Turn 'round and face me."

She obeyed. "Should I be scared?"

He shook his head. "No, love. This isn't greasy pub food. This is good, fresh, Irish cooking from local farms and dairies." He was taking a piece of fresh, soft bread and cutting into some sort of wedge that was covered in bright red sauce. "For the first, it's warm brie from Tipperary. Coated in bread crumbs, fried in local butter, and covered with warm red currant preserves and honey." He took the gooey concoction and spread it on the bread.

"Close your eyes."

She cocked one brow. "I've already seen it."

He said, "So you aren't distracted. Close them, and open your mouth."

She laughed, "I can feed myself."

He looked at her directly, "Yes, a fine job you've been doing."

She shut her eyes and opened her mouth. He slid it in and she bit down. When the buttery warm cheese and tart fruit sauce hit her mouth, she moaned. She chewed and swallowed and took his hand. She opened her mouth and took another bite. He watched her and couldn't keep the pleasure off his face.

He popped the rest in his mouth. She just lay back in her chair.

"Don't even tell me the caloric value of that dish. Just let me sit here in the afterglow," she said.

"Our food's not so bad is it? You ready for some more?"

She wiggled her brows. "Hit me, baby."

He laughed, "Christ, you are trouble. If I'd have known you could change moods this fast with a little food, I'd have done this a month ago."

Michael cut the next sample and lifted it to her open mouth. Seeing her little pink tongue was making all the blood rush to his groin. "Okay, this is veal with wild mushrooms in whiskey sauce."

She took a bite and both her hands gripped her thighs. She put her head back a little. "You are killing me. I can't even muster guilt over eating baby cow!" His smile was all smugness and mischief.

He thought about her reactions. She was sensitive. He remembered how ticklish she was, but also how sensitive she was to touch in general. Even when she'd been sick, she seemed to crave contact. She tasted and smelled and felt keenly. She was a musician at heart, which meant her hearing was attuned to pitch and subtleties of sound that a non-musician might not have. She was a live wire when it came to sensory input.

He knew that she would be the same with sex. Her heightened senses meant heightened pleasure. She was sensual by nature, although she suppressed it. She craved touch, but had denied herself that pleasure per her own admission. *I don't have anyone left who touches me. They all went away*. He'd venture a guess that there were droves of men in her old life that would have lined up to touch her, if she'd let them, plenty of them here as well. Yet, she had no one.

She was letting him touch her, though. She responded to him with such heat. He would love to stretch her limits. Take her past every place she'd been. He wanted her so badly it was like a sort of sickness. He wanted to wipe every ex-lover off the map, make her forget every man that had ever touched her.

Branna watched him take a bite of the veal and smile with satisfaction. She was trying to remember her vow in the bathtub to stop mooning over him, and just try to be his friend. This didn't feel like friends, though. She felt seduced. With food, of course, but damn if being fed by him wasn't turning her on. He was beautiful and sexy and she wanted him like she'd never wanted anything.

Michael fed her two more courses. Bacon sautéed shellfish with shallots, wine, and minced peppers. He took the meat out of a mussel shell with his fingers. She'd stopped closing her eyes. He didn't use the fork. He hand fed her. The seafood was fresh and dripping with butter. She thought, not for the first time since this meal began, that he had no idea how erotic this was for her. She had zero experience in seduction. Her dates had been awkward, adolescent torture sessions.

When he put the food in her mouth with his fingers, God help her, she turned her head, caught the tip of his thumb and closed her mouth as she sucked lightly. His eyes flared with lust. *Two can play at this game.* She smiled as she chewed. "That buttery sauce is heavenly."

He moved closer, watching her mouth as she chewed. "I'm not done with you. You can't miss the finale." And cue thoughts of screaming orgasms.

His accent was thick. "Sweet, juicy berries smothered with warm, sticky simple sugar finished with sweet cream." She just looked at him and the corner of his mouth came up. She did the same. He knew exactly what he was doing to her. She put her finger in the cream and then moved like a snake, wiping it across his face.

He was stunned. "You'd provoke me after the last ass kicking you got?" She was grinning ear to ear. It occurred to him, as his erection popped in his trousers, that she wanted to tussle with him. Like greased lightning he grabbed her under both knees and yanked her forward. He shot one hand under her shoulders, keeping her from falling as he knocked her chair away. He took her to the ground and she grabbed his arms. She squealed with delight. He pinned her down with his body and seized her by the ribs. He was positioned between her legs and there was no hiding his arousal. "You are a naughty little Yank. You need a lesson in Irish vengeance." He took her arms off his and pinned them above her head. Her eyes were wild, challenging. He had her pinned down and stretched out as intimately as a lover. He could tell that she could feel him. There was no trace of alarm. She liked where she was, liked that he was hard for her.

He reached above him to the cream on the table. She grinned and started wiggling her whole body, giggling underneath him. The movement made him hiss. He looked down at her, his frustration showing on his face. He put the cream on her nose. She thrashed her head back and forth. He ran a creamy finger down her neck and she put her head back, exhaling. "Are you going to eat like a good lass?" When she looked at him, he saw the first sign of surrender. She was getting overwhelmed, fear at her own response starting to cause her heart to pound.

He didn't care. He wanted her unbalanced, wild, feeling pushed. He took a warm, sticky berry and slid it in her mouth. She closed her mouth on his fingers and closed her eyes. He withdrew his fingers slowly and licked them. "Look at me." She opened her eyes. She was dazed, but not in a bad way. He slid his hand down to her lower belly. That smooth, creamy expanse below her navel. Then up again. He thumbed her navel. She arched for him, driving him further between her legs.

"I'm sorry, I need to touch you. Christ, I can't seem to stop from getting here, can I?" He let her arms go and she wrapped them around his shoulders. He settled on top of her as she dug her nails into his shoulders and her chest came up to his. His hand went to both hip bones and he thumbed the skin that stretched over them, tight and soft at the same time. She actually put her head back, moaning his name. He took her head in one hand and closed his mouth on hers. Not the chaste kiss of comfort he'd offered before. His kiss was confident and sensual. He caught her mouth and moaned as he tasted her. Lying between her legs took this whole thing to a new level. She was making desperate little noises. She put her fingers in his hair and whimpered as she took his kiss.

He pressed into her and she arched into him, wild and hot and needy. He slid his tongue in and she met him head on. He pulled his mouth from hers and looked at her. He slid one hand under her ass and pulled her into him. "Feel me, feel what you do to me."

She arched and pulled her knees up. She pulled his head down and stopped before their lips met. She traced the tip of her tongue on his lips. He watched her face as he slowly moved his hips. She hovered just under his lips, breathing deep and touching his lips but not quite kissing him. He rubbed himself right at her center. He knew she was close, that he had the right spot. Her breath was coming faster as he pressed the ridge of his cock right where she wanted him. She put her head back and her eyes rolled back as she moaned. He pulled her heat into him, mimicking sex. Her neck was exposed and he covered it with hot kisses, licking her as she rolled her hips under him.

"Give me your mouth, Branna." She lifted her head, closing the distance with a deep, slow kiss. He was vaguely aware when he heard pounding on the door. She broke the kiss and tried to get up. He pressed into her and lowered slowly. He took her earlobe in his teeth and he felt her heel dig into his ass. He pressed into her, making sure she felt every inch. More knocking. He jumped up and pulled her to him.

He glared at her, daring her to take one minute on the floor back. She didn't. She was as aroused as he was. He looked down at his hips and his problem was visible. He said, "I'm going to go in the other room and collect myself."

She grinned, "You don't want to answer the door like that?"

He looked her up and down, smiling. "You've got cream on your neck." He shot his hand to the back of her neck, the other one on her ass and ground her into him. He licked the cream and she whimpered as his hard length pressed into her belly. He let her go and walked out of the room.

She smoothed her clothes and hair, slowing her breathing. "Coming, just a minute," she croaked weakly.

Branna opened the door to Dr. Flynn. "You're looking better, did I wake you?" She was taking in Branna's disheveled appearance.

"I was just lying down." She left out where, and who'd been on top of her. The doctor put her bag down and had Branna sit. She needed to sit. Her knees were wobbly.

The doc felt her pulse. "A little high and you're flushed. How do you feel?"

Michael came out wearing a long tailed flannel that covered his pelvis. "She was just enjoying my lesson on Irish feasting after her nap." He was the picture of innocence.

The doctor looked at the table, "Wow, you need to teach my house keeper some of those tricks. She keeps making me curry." She resumed her exam. "What about fluids?"

Branna nodded, "I have had water by my bedside. He's a tyrant." The doctor kneaded her back. "Good, you deserve it. Any pain?"

She answered, "Not really, nothing like before. I feel way better."

The doctor listened to her heart. Then she took the stethoscope out of her ears and looked at her. "You're lucky. You have your marching orders. Introduce caffeine back in moderation. Eight bottles of water a day and finish all of your antibiotics. Other than that you seem perfect. The glory of youth, I suppose."

Branna nodded. "Thank you for everything. For coming here when I needed you. I know I need to pay some sort of bill."

The doctor shook her head. "I expedited your healthcare card. You don't owe me anything."

Branna argued, "No healthcare plan covers house calls."

The doctor took her glasses off. "Dr. Troy is one of my oldest friends. We did our residency together. I went to the states on an exchange program and worked at Walter Reed." She paused, considering her words. "We were close. I promised to take care of you."

Branna was surprised. They were around the same age. She was probably in her mid-fifties and unmarried. He was a retired Navy doctor in private practice and probably only a couple of years older. He was married with a couple of teenage kids. Branna had known him for years, but this was way before her time. Had they been lovers in their youth, before he'd married? Michael was looking at her and she could tell he was wondering the same thing. She was an attractive woman. She was fit, didn't seem to fuss with her looks, but she was pretty.

"Toys," she said. The doctor looked confused. "I'll set up a toy area in your waiting room. You have a little nook that would be perfect. I'll get some kid friendly art as well. You need toys." The doctor smiled, "So I've heard. I had them. When I moved offices, they were so beat up I just tossed them." Branna nodded as if it were settled.

"You know how to get your way, don't you?" Mary said.

"This is the right thing to do, Mary. Thank you for everything." The doctor got up and put her things away. "I want to see you in five days."

As the doctor left, Branna closed the door. She could feel Michael looking at her, willing her to meet his gaze. She was nervous. She'd been there with him one hundred percent on the floor. She wanted him. There was no doubt about that. In the wake of their interruption, she was feeling less bold, embarrassed even. He had driven her wild. She had moaned and pressed against him, mindless and needy. The thought of it, even now, was heating her up. Arousal warring with embarrassment.

She started putting food away, putting lids on the dishes and transferring them to the counter. His hand came over hers. He was behind her, and he looped an arm around her. "I can see you're going to need a little attention to get you pliable again." All of the air shot out of her lungs as she pressed back against him. He reached around her face and turned her head. He kept her pressed to him as he kissed her.

Michael was ready to explode. She was pressing back into him with that sweet little ass, and he was taking her mouth from behind. He needed to touch her. She was panting against his mouth, "Ah God, Branna. I need to touch you."

She pressed against him and reached for his mouth with hers. That was all the answer he needed. He slid his hand beneath her pullover. He could see her nipples through it. She wasn't wearing a bra. He slid up and filled his hand with one round, soft, perfect breast. Her hips did an involuntary jerk and he groaned against her mouth at the feel of her. He ran his finger over her nipple, tracing circles with the pad. She gasped and her knees buckled. He had an arm around her waist now, holding her in place. She was wearing thin leggings. The amount of fabric between them was minimal, and he felt her heat against him. He ground himself against her bottom as he flicked her nipple lightly, and she let out a strangled sound, breaking their kiss. He flipped her around and grabbed her face. She was flushed and breathing heavily. Her hair was messed up and her eyes were wild, like a summer storm.

He bent and covered her mouth. He held back, kissing lightly and nibbling her mouth. He could feel her frustration as he teased her. She was pushing for more, clawing his clothing, pulling him in closer. *Good.* Anticipation was part of the game. He wanted her out of her mind when he finally slipped his hand down and made her come that first time.

He picked her up by the thighs and laid her down on the other half of the table, dishes clinking. He stood between her legs and bent over her, covering her body. He felt her knees come up, and he groaned as he fit himself perfectly between her legs. "Can I touch you, Branna? It's making me crazed. I want to feel you."

"Yes, touch me," she groaned.

He slid his hand down to the waist of her leggings as he kissed her deeply. He could feel her breasts arching up, pressed against him. He slid his hand in and down until he felt her little, cotton panties. *Not yet.* He kept his hand over her panties as he finally touched her through the thin fabric. She reared off the table, and he caught her cry with his mouth. He rubbed her through the fabric as she writhed under him. She was so close, he couldn't wait to feel her fly apart.

"Michael, please." The raw need in her voice had him grinding himself against her. He needed to feel her with nothing in the way, feel her wet for him. He moved his hand to the elastic of her panties and slid his hand down. They both cried out as he finally touched her. Michael's body was strung as tight as a banjo string, and she was panting against his mouth. Her back was bowed, mouth open on a silent moan as she gulped for breath. Cue.Another.Feckin.Knock.

He cursed loudly. She broke from him, jumping off the table. She walked out of the room into the bathroom trying to arrange her clothing. Before she entered she leaned on the door jam, completely wobbly. The blood was thumping in his ears. She was completely undone. That starchy little Yank with her ironed shirts and her tidy hair was wild eyed and painfully aroused.

He had done that to her, and didn't that just jack him right back up. She stared over her shoulder, passion blazing in her sex flushed face, trying to catch her breath. His hand tingled from touching her. If he'd had a gun, he would have shot the visitor through the door.

CHAPTER 15

Michael adjusted himself painfully and barked out, "Who is it?"

A familiar voice came through the door. "It's the child minder." It was Tadgh.

"Come in," he snapped.

Tadgh came in and took one look at him and took a step back. "You've got murder on your mind, cousin. Did I interrupt something?" Michael was looking at his watch. "Shit! I lost track of time." At this, Branna exited the bathroom. Michael could tell she'd splashed cold water on her face. The tendrils of hair were wet around her face. Her mouth was swollen from kissing and she looked jumpy. Tadgh's brows shot up.

He couldn't call off again. She wasn't family. His work wouldn't permit it and they depended on him as the only full time swimmer. Tadgh was looking at her speculatively and Michael almost hissed at him like a snake. The thought of leaving her here with Tadgh in a state of complete sexual frustration made him reconsider a sick call.

Tadgh gave him a knowing look. "Duty calls, brother. Don't worry yourself. She is safe with me." He knew that double meaning, but it still chaffed. Tadgh was a handsome bastard, and hadn't Michael just cock blocked him at the hospital? If they both had an itch that needed scratching…

He looked at him. "Did your nurse call to reschedule that appointment?"

Tadgh smiled, "Aye, she did. I couldn't meet her tonight for obvious reasons."

Branna said, "I don't need a babysitter. The doctor was just here. I'm perfect. You both can leave me."

But the worry showed on his face. "Just humor me for one more day. I'll be back tomorrow evening. Brigid will be here in the morning to keep you company. Tadgh will sleep in my room," he said with a little more emphasis than was needed.

She started to argue, but he ran a finger along her cheek. "Please."

She sighed, seeing the residual worry that pained his face. "Okay. I agreed to do better." She turned to Tadgh, "No TV, sorry. Do you have something in mind to amuse ourselves tonight?"

Michael could tell by her tone that it was a completely innocent question. He marveled at how little she seemed to know about men, considering he'd had her hovering so close to orgasm three minutes earlier. Her body was made for sex. She was so small, but she fit him perfectly. She was soft and responsive and everything he wanted in a partner.

He noticed Tadgh had walked out and was coming back in from the car. He had his backpack and his guitar. "Are you going to serenade her, then?" he asked with a hint of resentment.

"No, brother. She doesn't just play the piano. She sings. Didn't she tell you?" Michael's eyes shot to hers.

She was blushing. "Not really, he's exaggerating. I can carry a tune, that's it." It irritated him that Tadgh knew things about her that he didn't.

Tadgh said, "Don't believe her. She knows the old tunes; she's been holding out on us."

Branna spoke lightly. "Maybe we can watch something on my computer. I think the signal is strong enough."

Tadgh would hear none of it. "Nope. We're playing my way tonight."

She dropped her jaw then laughed. "You O'Brien men just think might makes right." They looked at each other, then looked at her. They gave an "Aye," in unison. She rolled her eyes.

Branna watched Michael getting ready to leave. He looked miserable. He probably had double the problem she did. Men didn't do so well when they had to stop. She didn't know much, but she knew about blue balls. He also looked uncomfortable with his choice of babysitter.

He said, "I need to go. My clean uniform is at work and I need to get changed." He looked for his keys. He stopped and looked at Tadgh again, at the guitar, and at her.

She went to him, reaching up to put her arms around his neck. He lifted her off her feet, melting into her with a deep exhale. "Be careful," she whispered and he put her down. He bent down and brushed her lips lightly with his, not even really kissing her. Then he gave Tadgh a direct look that sent a clear message. *She's mine.*

* * *

MICHAEL WAS GONE and Tadgh was eating some of the food he'd made. He also shoved a plate under her nose, insisting she eat with him. "Holy Bride, if I'd known he could cook like this, I'd have kept him longer at my flat."

She was surprised. "He lived with you?"

He nodded. "Yes, off and on. It was after he found out about Fiona."

She nodded, understanding. "Was it bad? She seems very bitter."

He snorted. "She put him through hell. He did love her, but he was young. He thought it was more than it was, thought she was better than she was. She was a pain in the ass on a good day. Toward the end she was either screaming or shoving him or breaking things, or she was trying to…uh."

She tensed, "I get it."

He continued, "Yes, well. He didn't rise to either occasion. Couldn't touch her after he found out about everything. I can't blame him. O'Brien men don't share."

She cocked a brow. "They shouldn't have to. Any woman would be lucky to have any one of you O'Brien men. You're the kind of men that women dream about. The kind you start to think don't really exist."

He was surprised. "Jesus, I think that's the nicest thing any woman has ever said to me."

She smiled sadly. "Then you aren't picking the right kind of women. That nurse was hot, but she was a little obvious."

He laughed, "You pointed the way!"

She laughed with him. "I just figured you needed a little stress reliever. You can thank me after your re-scheduled appointment."

He barked out a laugh, "You picked up on that, eh?"

She winked at him and started packing up the food. "My parents were like that. They loved each other like something out of a fairy tale. They were separated a lot, but I have no doubt that they were utterly faithful. Not that it served them in the end."

Tadgh was surprised that she'd opened that door. He commented, hoping she would keep sharing. "Even a short life filled with that sort of love is better than not having it. Don't you think?"

She shrugged. "He died suddenly. No warning, no goodbyes. He expelled his last breath in some third world shit hole and she never saw him alive, again. Never felt his warm hands, never saw his sweet smile, never heard him sing," her voice was trembling as she fought for composure. Tadgh moved closer to her, rubbing her hand and her forearm, silent for fear that she'd stop talking. "The CATO Officer showed up at our door with the Chaplain. It's the two people you hope never show up on your doorstep. The ones that come to tell you that you're never going to be the same again. All we got was a flag, a cold body to bury, and a pot of money. We were lucky we lived off base or we would have been tossed out of family housing in the middle of it all. One day he is making jokes via e-mail and then he was gone. After that she was a walking corpse. She wanted to die, too."

Tadgh was heartbroken. He detected bitterness with regard to her mother, which wasn't rational but probably normal. "She had cancer, Branna. I'm sure she hated the thought of leaving you, especially after your da dying. I'm sure she fought to stay with you."

She looked at him very directly; he was taken back by the anger in her eyes. "You seem pretty sure for someone who doesn't know what he's talking about. Fought? Try suicide by cancer. It's like suicide by cop, but it takes a lot longer."

Tadgh was stunned, "What do you mean, Branna? Surely she tried? What are you saying?"

She looked at him, tears brimming. "I'm saying she didn't. She wanted to die and she let herself. I shouldn't have brought it up. I can't talk about her anymore." She was shoving things in the fridge when he came behind her. He tried to hug her and she resisted at first. Then she buried her head in his chest. "Don't tell anyone," she whispered.

He sighed in her hair as he held her. "You don't have to do this on your own. You have people who care."

She shook her head and backed away from him, "I can't let myself depend on people who may not be in my life in two months. I can't do that to myself."

He growled in frustration. "You aren't leaving. Fuck this cottage. If Michael gets it, you can live with me until we find you a place. You are not leaving!"

She held her bottom lip between her fingers, fighting emotion. "I can't stay somewhere I don't belong. I have to bow out gracefully and let him live his life."

"Branna, don't say that." Tadgh wanted to shake her.

She wrapped her arms protectively around herself. "Let's please not talk about this anymore." She gave him a pleading look "Play for me. I want to hear you play. Please?" He let out a weary sigh and walked out of the kitchen toward his guitar.

* * *

MICHAEL HAD NOT BEEN able to get Branna out of his mind all day. Brigid had sent him a text this morning, to tell him that she and Cora were at the cottage. He hoped that Cora wasn't disturbing her too much. Not everyone could tolerate an entire day with a four year old. As he got out of the car the sun was setting. When he walked through the front door, leftovers were out on the counter. Brigid smiled, chewing happily.

Branna was curled on the couch with Cora. Cora was sprawled on her chest, her tiny fingers twisted in Branna's hair, the other thumb in her mouth. She was sound asleep. Branna was reading papers that looked like they were printed from the computer. She looked up and put a finger to her lips, telling him to be quiet, then she kissed Cora between the eyes.

Michael felt warmth spread in his chest. How had he ever doubted that she and Cora would get on? He turned to his sister and she was watching him. A smile of knowing on her face. His twin saw right into his soul. She always had.

She whispered, "How was work?" It had been rather uneventful. She looked at Branna and lowered her whisper. "Tadgh told me to tell you that tonight's the do-over." He looked curiously. "Her birthday? He's got some plan cooked up. Finn and I got a sitter. She's going to drop him here and take Cora. Aidan came down and Patrick and Caitlyn are back from Paris. They're meeting us out. Even Ma and Da are coming. "

Michael raised a brow. Shit, his gift was coming tomorrow, bright and early. On cue Finn and the sitter walked in the open door. Finn walked over and kissed his wife deeply. "I missed you today," he crooned.

Brigid glowed. "Aye, maybe I'll take ye home from the pub tonight."

His eyes never left hers, "I'm counting on it."

Branna watched them and felt a pang of envy. They had one beautiful little girl, another on the way, and still totally in love. Not tired, married people love. Hot, steamy, romantic love. Finn was looking at her like he wanted everyone in the room to disappear. She blushed until she noticed Michael seemed to be watching them too. He looked at her and she smiled. He made a gag sound and stuck his finger down his throat. She laughed.

"I saw that Michael." Brigid said.

Finn came over and slid Cora out of her lap. The little girl looked at him drowsily. "Hello da. I was playin' office with Branna."

He smiled and said, "Hello pet. Did you have fun?"

She yawned and answered, "Yes, daddy. She wasn't so sad when we played. I think she likes me." He looked at his daughter and then at Branna. His warm, brown eyes held an apology for the child's candor.

The whole room was quiet. Thankfully, Tadgh walked in and broke the tension. "Well, Yank. You had enough time sitting on your bum. Up with you." She looked at him like he was nuts. "It's your birthday do-over." Branna stood and Michael noticed her attire. She had a loose braid, hair spilling in tendrils and wisps around her face and neck. She had a long Aran cabled sweater on. Not the chunky fisherman crew. This was wide at the top and plated around the neckline. The knit wasn't as heavy and it draped her curves perfectly, hanging off one, creamy shoulder. It was long enough to reach her knees and she had leggings on. It was lovely. The charcoal black sheep wool contrasted with her ivory skin.

"I don't need a do-over. Don't go to any trouble for my birthday, please." She was turning red.

Finn came back in the house empty handed. Brigid spoke up, "It's done, Branna. I have a child minder for Cora and plans are made. Don't rob me of a night out." Brigid was a manipulative genius.

Branna knew she was whipped. "Give me five minutes." She left the room with a scurry. Five minutes later, Michael was talking to Finn when he heard an appreciative whistle. She had the same long sweater on minus the leggings. She had high heels on the color of whiskey. Her legs were bare and she had a thin belt on which hiked the dress above her knee. Her legs looked splendid. She'd left her hair in the loose braid, thrown over one shoulder.

She looked sexy as hell. She'd even put a little red lip-gloss on her lips. "You work fast! You look gorgeous all together," Brigid said. "Off to McDermotts!"

Branna looked at Tadgh, "Thursday night Open Mic McDermott's?"

He grinned, "The very one."

She started to bolt back into the bedroom and he cut her off, scooping her over one shoulder. "Time is wasting, girl. I haven't got time to beg."

He looked at Michael who was tense. He didn't like someone else's hands on her. "Be ready to catch her in the back." Tadgh winked at him. Michael burst out laughing as Branna yelled curses at Tadgh. He was grinning. "Ah, I always did want a bratty, little sister. Shut your gob, hen." Brigid and Finn were laughing as they stuffed her in the backseat.

She was glaring at them both, having been dumped across Michael's lap. Tadgh got in the driver's seat. "You two are bullies."

Tadgh smiled at her in the rear mirror. "Aye."

Michael chuckled and agreed. "Aye."

She went to sit up and she felt his hand on her hip. "Easy, lass," he whispered to her.

She immediately calmed, looking at him with a whole other demeanor. "That's cheating."

He grinned devilishly at her. "Whatever works." He took a long look at her as she lay across his lap. He played with the hem of her dress where it was currently half way up her thigh. He whispered, his mouth on her ear. "You're so beautiful. You stop my heart to look at you. Happy Birthday. Your gift comes tomorrow. I couldn't get it delivered any faster. " He looked a little shy, but he instinctually ran his thumb over her hip, the effect was hypnotic.

She was feeling a slow burn, not like before. His hand felt like it belonged there, a familiarity coiling between them. "You didn't have to get me anything," she said.

He shrugged. "It's nothing really. It's just something I thought you needed."

Tadgh pulled into McDermott's and Branna shot up, afraid everyone would see them intimately entangled. She got out of the car and adjusted her skirt. They all walked in, and the place was pretty crowded with locals. Sorcha and Sean waved from a table that was set for a big group. She also saw James and Alex. She ran to them. Alex picked her up and twirled her. "Hello bella. Happy Birthday."

He put her down and she took one arm off him and pulled James to her. "You're back!"

James kissed her on the cheek. "Italy was wonderful, but we had to check on our girl."

She looked at them both. "How did you know?" Then she looked at Tadgh.

He lifted one shoulder, "You really need to put a lock code on your phone."

Next she walked over to Sorcha and Sean. "Hello. How is everyone?" Sorcha hugged her.

She whispered in her ear, "Thank you. I don't know how to begin to thank you."

Sorcha looked at her intensely. "You scared us, especially Michael. He was beside himself."

Branna's face showed regret. "I know. I'm sorry. I promise, Sorcha. Doctor's orders to the letter."

She smiled at Branna, rubbing her back motherly. "That's our girl." Sean reached over and took her head in one hand, planting a kiss on the top of her head. These two were going to make her cry. They were so affectionate, like she was their own daughter. She pushed the thought away. *Don't get used to this.*

Michael watched his family with Branna. They cared for her. His sister and Caitlyn giggled with her and whispered like old friends. When he'd seen his da kiss her on the top of her head, he felt it down to his marrow. She'd lost so much. He could sense her hesitation. She was afraid to let them in, afraid she would get it and then lose it. He understood. She felt like an outsider. This position Ned had put them in was like torture. What started out as an unorthodox real estate bargain had become beyond complicated. She was settling in, people were getting attached to her. He was getting attached to her.

The thought of her pressed against him, groaning as he touched her made the blood thump in his ears. Every time he told himself he was going to back off from her, he got in the same room with her, and it went right out the window. She had such a physical pull on him.

She wasn't manipulative or overtly seductive. At her age, she'd undoubtedly had at least a couple of lovers, but in some ways she seemed inexperienced with intimacy. She seemed surprised and even a little scared at her own sexual response to him. Who could blame her? It wasn't typical. He'd been married. He was pushing thirty. Yet, he had never felt such a physical and mental link to a woman. When he touched her, he felt them fuse together. Pulling apart from her was like ripping off a limb.

The evening started pretty soon after Aidan and Liam arrived. Everyone was shocked to see Liam, but his Friday classes were cancelled for some big event at the school. They were all there except for Sean Jr., who was too young to be hanging out at a pub on a school night.

"Don't think he didn't beg. Christ, he is as stubborn as his mother," said Sean.

Sorcha turned on her husband. "Oh is he, now?"

Sean grabbed her by the waist and kissed her on the mouth. "You know that's why I married you. You're pure trouble, woman."

All of the kids shouted, "Come on, Da! Control yourself in front of your children."

Branna was laughing and he looked at her and winked. "We like our women with a little backbone."

Branna went to the bar to get a round for the raucous O'Brien brothers. She included Tadgh in that group because he seemed more like a brother than a cousin. If she had any cousins living in the sparse branches of her family tree, she didn't know about them. She loved watching them all together.

As she waited for the five pints, James came up behind her. "Things have progressed." She looked at him innocently, but he wasn't fooled. "Don't give me that look, little girl. He can't take his eyes off you. Not that every man in the pub isn't drooling in their pints. That dress is divine. You are like a loaded gun around here."

She rolled her eyes. "You're crazy. It's nice of you to say, but I know what I am and what I'm not. Sex pot got left out of the DNA."

He laughed, shaking his head. "Fucking crikey. You really don't see it do you? Forget the fact that you are a total piece of ass." She gave him a look that said, *This coming from you?* He ignored her, forging on with his speech."Not only are you gorgeous and smart and funny. You have a glow that lights up everyone around you, despite all the shit you've been through. Hell, maybe because of it." He took her face in his hands and kissed her on the mouth. "You don't know what you are, but I see you. You are like an angel, love. Your time in the sun is coming. Don't be afraid of it. Please, don't run from it. Promise me. You can't push everyone away. Women like you need to be loved."

Branna had never seen James so serious. "I'm not sure what you think is happening here, but I hear what you're saying. I appreciate it. I just don't know what is going to happen. I do love you, though. I won't lose track of you or Alex."

James's face was sad. "Fair enough."

Michael was looking at Branna when James kissed her. He felt a snap. He swore he actually heard something break in his brain. What the hell was she playing at? She'd been all but fucking him on the dining room table the night before, and now she was letting that tidy little Brit kiss her. Did she think to share that kind of physical passion with him and then dismiss it once she got out at the pub?

He made a feral noise deep in his throat. Tadgh, Aidan, and Alex all looked at him then followed his gaze to Branna and James. "Problem, brother?" It was Aidan who asked.

"He's too old for her." He looked at Alex. "You can tell him I said that. Tell him to keep his fucking hands to himself."

Aidan looked at Tadgh incredulously. They burst out laughing at the same time. Alex was suppressing a grin under the rim of his glass.

Michael turned on them, visibly pissed. "What the hell is so funny?"

Tadgh looked at Alex. "Do you want to tell him or should I?"

Michael wasn't amused. Aidan shook his head. "Brother, we really need to work on your gay-dar."

Alex choked on his drink, spitting and laughing.

Michael looked at James. Great clothes, neat hair, buffed nails, expensive shoes. He looked right off Savile row. Then he looked over at Alex. The height of Italian men's fashion. "Oh, you and he?"

Alex smiled. "You don't get out of County Clare very often, I take it?" Michael's ears were burning red.

James approached and looked at Michael. "Christ, he's blushing. What have you been doing to the lad, Alex?" Michael started laughing, the tension leaving him. James looked at all the men who were snickering too. "Hmmm, this I have to hear."

CHAPTER 16

Branna was on her second trip with the pints when she ran smack into Fiona, barely missing dumping the beer all over both of them. "Come to play with the locals, eh? I must say, you work fast. Even Sean and Sorcha seem to be getting sucked in. You'll have to share your secret."

Branna looked at her. "My secret is that I'm not crazy. Crazy people don't play well with others." Fiona flinched at her words. She'd hit a nerve. She sighed, "I'm sorry Fiona, that was out of line."

Fiona shot her chin up. She was also looking around, nervously. Branna followed her gaze. The bar was filled with locals. A lot of the younger women and even some of the older ones were shooting looks at her. Now that she thought about it, she'd never seen her hanging out with anyone the times she'd been in the pub. She looked at her, understanding in her gaze. She was ostracized for the way she'd treated Michael. She'd also probably had a tryst or two with someone's husband. She remembered what Michael had said about not wanting to paint a scarlet letter on her chest. This was a tourist town, but under that it was also a very small community, and they had judged this woman and frozen her out of probably the only place she'd ever lived.

"I'll go." Branna said evenly. "I don't know why, but we seem to bring out the worst in each other."

Fiona smiled bitterly. "That's my special talent, bringing out the worst in people. You're no special case. So, are you singing tonight?"

Branna stiffened. "I hadn't planned on it, no."

Fiona gave her a saccharin smile. "Well, it's probably best. This isn't some karaoke bar, Yank. You don't want to embarrass yourself in front of the entire O'Brien clan." She turned and walked away. Branna took a couple of cleansing breaths. *Why do you let her get under your skin? Do not sink to her level.*

Branna delivered the last of the beers to the O'Brien men when she noticed the show was starting. The bartender had hopped up on stage to call the start of open mike night. "Who's going to start? Tadgh, get your ass up here or you're out of a job!"

Everyone hollered as Tadgh went up grabbing Aidan's guitar as he went. She loved listening to him. He didn't do a traditional song. He actually nailed his own, smooth rendition of *Angie* by the Rolling Stones. Everyone roared with applause.

Next, Sorcha and Brigid got up and did a duet with Aidan and Sean on their guitars. "Nead Na Lachan" was totally in Gaelic and they were spectacular. Patrick joined them on the whistle and Sean sang a small amount of back up. She was enthralled. The entire family was spectacular, and they complimented each other both with their singing and playing.

James swore under his breath, "It is like watching the VonTrap family singers. Do these people have any family that can't sing?"

Michael laughed. "Nope, how about you? When is your turn?"

Alex laughed, "He doesn't sing, ever. Neither do I. I'm a dancer. No singing, my friend. We leave that to the Irish."

Michael went up to the bar while some other locals were singing a bawdy favorite. *Girl's_When You're Young, Never Wed an Old Man*. The whole crowd was laughing. He ordered a club soda and cranberry for Branna and two gin and tonics for her unlikely foreign pals. He was laughing to himself again about the misunderstanding when Fiona came up beside him. "You've not gone up. Why not? Does the Yank have a short leash on you?"

He sighed. "Fio, I'm having a good time. You are the antidote for my good mood. Is that why you came over? To fuck up my perfectly good night?" He looked at her and she actually looked like she was going to tear up.

"Jesus, Fio. What do you want to hear?"

She stiffened. "Nothing, forget I'm even here. Just go sit back with your friends and family and your new little girlfriend. I see she's not singing tonight. Pity, you and I used to make some beautiful music together. It wasn't all bad, if you would just remember that."

His mouth was tight, "No, it wasn't all bad. Not until you took your show on the road without your husband." She looked past him over his shoulder. "Hello, little Yank. Don't mind us. Just reminiscing about old times." She gave Michael an overly familiar look and walked away.

Michael looked at Branna who was scowling at her. "What did you ever see in her?"

He sighed, "I don't really remember. I suppose it was youth, familiarity, the music. Whatever it was, it wasn't enough and it wasn't real. I don't wish her ill, but I don't miss her."

Branna shrugged, feeling a little petty. "I shouldn't have asked. It was a personal question. You don't have to explain."

He looked at her. "I want to explain. I want you to understand that I wasn't a bad husband."

She rubbed his face. "I never doubted that, ever."

Michael and his brothers were standing at the bar with Alex and James. She saw some sort of whiskey in their glasses. Apparently the boys had upgraded Alex from his gin and tonics. Aidan was sniffing it, trying to sell him on the finer nuances. James was watching, laughing. She was sitting at the table in a huff, thinking about that bitch Fiona. Tadgh noticed her stern expression. "What's got your knickers in a bunch?"

Branna was seething. Fiona was cashing in on the fact that she wasn't performing, insinuating she must be tone deaf and unable to play at all. Then Michael had innocently commented that one of the initial bonds between them had been their music. She brightened, "Nothing, why do you ask?"

Tadgh looked at her with humor and disgust warring on his face. "Wow, you are a horrible liar. Seriously horrible."

She narrowed her eyes. "You think you're clever don't you."

He wasn't put off in the least. "Very. Now, I know you, hen. You're stewin' about something. What's that fat headed cousin of mine done now?"

She shook her head quickly, "Oh, no. He's been wonderful actually. It's just…" she paused, and he looked at her in that unique Tadgh way that said *Spill it, girl.*

She gave him the short version, leaving out her seething jealousy and desire to dropkick Fiona out of the pub.

"Oh, I see. Aye, well, I have to say, she can sing. She's got that kind of sexy, smokey sound." He could see Branna's body language, he was getting under her skin. He continued, "That is the only time I saw them get along. She can't sing as well as you, but she can hold her own."

Branna said, "You can't possibly be sure of that. I only sang a little, last night."

He looked at her, all kidding aside. "Yes, I can. I hate to admit it but I was actually surprised when I heard you. There's not a trace of a Yank accent when you sing the old tunes."

She smiled. " My father had piles of CDs and sheet music. He was a bit of a fanatic."

He nodded. "Well, don't pay any attention to Fiona. Let her think what she wants, and Michael for that matter. You don't need to prove anything. Let them have their little memories."

She glared at him, "I know what you're doing. You are trying to manipulate me."

He leaned in shamelessly, "Aye, is it working?"

She folded her arms, "No." She cursed under her breath, "Yes."

He slapped his hands together, "About feckin time. The night's almost over!"

The music was at a lull. Brigid was talking with Finn and her parents. Michael was at the bar with his brothers. James and Alex were sitting down again. Michael noticed that Branna wasn't in her seat. Neither was Tadgh. He started looking around for them when he heard some hoots from the audience. Michael figured someone must be getting ready to sing.

When the music started, it was sweet piano dueling with guitar, "Dearthairín Ó Mo Chroí." It was Gaelic for "little brother of my heart". He knew the song, immediately. It was a popular song with the locals, an old war lament. It was also a soft spot for him. When his brother had gone off to fight with the Royal Army, he had trouble even listening to it.

It was beautiful and spoke of lonely despair, about losing everyone you ever loved. The back of his neck tingled as the singer began. He moved to the left a bit as a hush came over the pub, his brothers turning in unison. He saw her at the piano, playing flawlessly without sheet music. Tadgh was playing with her. She sounded like an angel. Sweet soprano and a perfect Irish lilt. The kind of devastating delicacy that could bring you to your knees.

I am a young fellow who has always loved rural sport-
The fairs and the patterns of Aran I used to resort,-
The true sons of Bacchus were always in my company,-
Til I lost my heart's treasure, my dearthháirín ó mo chroí

The pub was completely silent, the entire crowded room enthralled by her. Those who knew her were stunned, never realizing the depth of her talent and her ability to channel her sorrow through music.

The womb's turned to earth that gave birth to my brother and me,-
My father and mother have gone to eternity,-

She continued the haunting verses as the pub was silent. Her beautiful, intoxicating voice weaving it's magic through the room. Tadgh played along and he glanced at Michael. Then broke the eye contact, shaking his head sadly.

Michael felt a hand on his shoulder, turning to look at Aidan. "Did you know, brother?" He just shook his head. Aidan's face reflected his own. He looked at all of his brothers, Brigid, his parents, James and Alex. She was breaking their hearts. The song slay him anew as she sang of loss, of unending loneliness, of soul draining grief. The goose flesh spread all over him.

But now I'm alone like the desolate bird of the night,-
The world and it's beauties no longer afford me delight,
A dark narrow grave is the only sad refuge for me,-
Since I lost my heart's treasure my dearthháirín ó mo chroí

She finished the piano as sweetly as she'd begun it. Her fingers strong and sure, her face lifted up as she let the music flow through her. Tadgh's guitar weaved effortlessly, never losing pace with her as she pulled him along. A pang of jealousy hit him that was neither appropriate or controllable. As they finished, the pub was silent. She just looked at the piano, coming down from where ever she'd been.

The pub went berserk. They banged on the tables and cheered. Michael noticed that his father was looking at him. He was looking straight into him, his face fighting emotion. He just nodded at him once. Michael looked up and Tadgh was hugging her, kissing her on the cheek. He went up as she left the stage. She looked at him shyly and shrugged one shoulder. "I decided to join the fun."

Only Branna O'Mara could make light of that performance. He put one arm around her waist and lifted her as he put the other hand at the base of her skull. "You've been holding out on me, wee raven." Then he kissed the hell out of her. He heard his brothers start whistling and shouting. "What the hell took you so long?" and "About bloody time".

The pub occupants called for an encore, and Branna was embarrassed by the attention. She looked at Tadgh for reinforcements. "Nope, you're on your own darlin'. They don't give a shit about me."

She looked worried. She hadn't really thought past the one song. She looked at Michael and he said, "They won't quit until they've heard ye again. Go on, now."

She walked up toward the stage and everyone cheered and then settle to hear her play again. She decided she was pushing her luck with another traditional song. It was open mic night, so she decided to go with one of her favorites. It had strong percussion but delicate vocals, something special. She whispered on her way up to Patrick and Aidan. Patrick got up and grabbed the bodhrán, Aidan the guitar. She sat in silence and took a deep breath. Patrick started first, then Aidan, thumping out a steady beat. It took Michael a second to place the song. Her smooth acoustic version was different. Better. Dido's *Thank You.*

He heard Tadgh next to him mumbling incredulities to himself. She was unbelievable. He looked at him, forcing himself to look away from her face. "You didn't know, then?"

Tadgh shook his head, "No, Christ no. I mean, I knew she could sing. She sang along last night. When I played around, she joined in and she was amazing, but she was holding back. Feckin-A was she holding back. Remind me again why I'm not trying to get in her knickers?"

Michael leaned over, smiling sweetly. "Because I'll cut your balls off, brother."

Tadgh looked at her. "I'm thinking it might be worth it." Then he grinned at Michael. Michael punched him in the arm.

She sang and played and the effect was bewitching. Michael watched as she opened up, lost her inhibitions, like no one was in the room with her. She played because she loved it, not for the attention. Then she looked right at him and suddenly no one else was in the room. She suppressed a secret smile as she sang the lyrics.

Push the door, I'm home at last, and I'm soaking through and through
Then you handed me a towel and all I see is you.

He smiled as he remembered that first time she'd come out of the rain, covering her with a towel. That had been the first night. He'd wanted her even then. When she finished her song, the entire pub cheered just as loud as the first time.

Branna was red, she could feel it. When she was playing, she didn't think about everyone else. She just tuned them out. The applause embarrassed her and she tried to make a quick exit, but Caitlyn had grabbed a spare mic and caught her as she fled. "I've got some news, pipe down!" Everyone quieted and she continued. "Our lovely Branna, come from o'er the sea had a little secret. Putting aside the fact that she sings like an angel, that is." Everyone yelled in agreement.

"On my wedding day, she turned 24, but was too gracious to take the attention off the particularly smashing bride." Patrick was at the stage edge and pulled her down for a kiss. The crowd was loving it. Caitlyn fanned herself, "Well now, those O'Brien men can suck the thoughts right outta your head, can't they?"

Michael and all of his brothers cheered her on, agreeing wholeheartedly. Branna was laughing, now. Caitlyn was as good as any O'Brien at commanding the masses. "That aside, we've not given her a proper birthday until tonight. So, let's hear it in the Irish!" She put the mic out to face the pub as everyone yelled, "Lá Breithe Sona!" Then Caitlyn started singing.

Go raibh tú sona inniu,
Go raibh tú sona inniu,
Go raibh tú sona, a Shéamais,
Go raibh tú sona inniu!

Caitlyn threw her arms around Branna and tears stung her eyes. She remembered Anna calling and singing over the phone on her last birthday, in her sweet southern accent. Caitlyn reminded her of Anna. Not in the million pieces of clothing way, but in the confident, generous way.

As she stepped off the stage she saw the hasty exit of a certain redhead out the front door. She'd like to say she felt good about that, but she pitied Fiona. Before she could dwell on it, she was lifted off her feet. Michael had her cradled in his arms. He carried her to the table where his whole family was seated. He sat, keeping her in his lap, and she blushed as she caught Sorcha's eye. A cake appeared in front of her, some sort of fruity layer cake with one candle. "Ma made it," he whispered.

"Make a wish, darling girl," Sorcha said. She closed her eyes and then blew out the candle.

CHAPTER 17

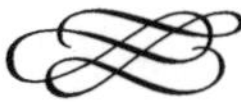

Michael was deliberately trying to slow his breathing. They were headed back to the cottage. Given the state they'd been in the last time they were alone, he knew he had to get a handle on his libido. There wouldn't be any interruptions if they got going again. If he got his hands on her, he would make love to her if she let him. He needed to slow down. It wasn't but days ago they'd been at each other's throats. Then she got sick and had needed him. He cared about her a lot. He had to take a step back and make sure he wasn't taking advantage of her. He wanted her so badly that he didn't trust himself if he put his hands on her again, let his mouth taste her again. At the pub he'd kissed her. Alone was a whole other thing. He wanted everything. He wanted inside her with a desperation that scared the hell out of him.

Michael was acting strange in the car. Branna could feel his tension. She hugged Tadgh. "Thank you for tonight."

He kissed her forehead. "You're welcome. Happy Birthday." Branna's heart raced as he drove away. They were alone. The thought of the last time he'd had her alone sent warm tingling through her body.

She wanted Michael. She might not have any experience, but she was sure about how she felt. He was a wonderful man that she was drawn to on a very physical level. She'd never felt this with any other man, and she wanted him to be her first lover. She couldn't predict the future. All she had was now, and now she wanted him. She was tired of being alone. If she couldn't have forever, she would take the physical intimacy. She walked into the house, thrumming with suppressed excitement.

Michael filled a glass of water from the kitchen sink and handed it to Branna. There was no lust boiling in his eyes, and she wondered if she'd misread how hot things had gotten the night before.

"You need to finish that and take your meds. Did you have fun tonight?" He sounded more like her mother than the seducer that had slipped his hand up her shirt. She nodded, a sinking feeling in the pit of her stomach. "I'll take the over the counter pain meds. I feel fine without the narcotics." She came closer to him and he turned around to close the cabinet.

She stepped back, "You're different."

He looked at her, puzzled. "What do you mean? I'm no different."

She turned and slowly walked into the living room. "You've pulled back from me, even since the pub. Did I do something wrong?" Her body language was strong, proud, but her eyes betrayed.

He took her hands in his, leaving distance between them. "Don't be silly. I'm just worried. You've been sick, you need to take your medicine and get some sleep."

She ran one hand from his chest to his shoulder. "I'm wide awake. I feel wonderful."

His breath caught and he backed away a few inches. She was so shocked that she jerked a little. She put her thumb and index finger on her forehead. "I'm sorry. I, um, I think I misread things. I'm just going to go to bed." She wouldn't look at him.

He got in front of her. "What are you talking about, misread?" His voice was rising.

"You don't have to explain. I understand, Michael. We just got out of hand last night. We got carried away. I obviously took it the wrong way. It was nothing personal." She was trying to play it cool but she was not making eye contact. "You're stuck here living with me and obviously it was a matter of any port in a storm," she said icily. Then she shrugged dismissively. "I get it. I'm sorry I made you uncomfortable."

She was turning red and her heart was thumping. She tried to go around him and he snatched her arm. "Nothing personal? Any port in a storm! For God's sake Branna, look at me."

She took a deep breath, planted a fake smile on her face and looked at him. "You were all wonderful to me tonight, really wonderful. Let's just forget this little encounter and call it a night." She pulled away.

"Branna!" he yelled this time. She jumped a little and looked at him.

She shouted at him, trading aggression for aggression."What? You can't leave me with a little dignity?"

Michael shook his head and then looked at her with such feral intensity that she took a half step back. "You think I don't want you? Are you fucking serious?" He turned and shoved his fingers in his hair. "You felt me o'er top of you. You felt what you did to me. Holy shit woman, I'm mad with it! For a month I've lain in that bed dreaming of nothing but what it would feel like to have you beneath me! If Tadgh hadn't interrupted us, I would have taken you right on that table!" He was breathing hard, his brogue was so thick she could barely understand him.

"Then why?" she demanded. "Why are you pulling away?"

He closed his eyes, trying to calm himself. "Ned and my da, they told you that you wouldn't have to worry about me. They trusted me, and you trusted them, and now I can't be alone with you for more that an hour without having my hands all over you! We need to slow this down! I care for you. God, I tried not to but you're…" he laughed bitterly. "You're you. You're beautiful and kind and smart and brave. God help me, when you sang tonight." He shut his eyes, overcome with desire and anger and tenderness all warring within him. He looked at her longingly, "You were like an angel. I didn't stand a chance. I don't want to take advantage of you, Branna. You're too important to me, to all of us."

She walked toward him and he put a hand up to keep her at a distance. "You need to stay away from me, Branna. I'm too raw right now. I'm past the ability to be a gentleman, now that I've felt you." He ground his jaw and then looked at her with raw lust showing in his face and she felt the heat stab her. "I'm close to the breaking point. I can't get the feel of you out of my head. You need to be the voice of reason, here."

His voice was raw and tense with wanting, and it was so powerful. She wanted him raw and losing control. She hadn't waited this long for polite and sanitary. She was so turned on that she was ready to do violence if they got interrupted again. She took another step, her intentions clear on her face.

"Branna, did you hear me? Go in your room, shut the door and I will leave you alone. If you touch me, I am going to be up that dress and inside you before you can take it back!" he hissed. That comment blasted through her. She stopped, breathing erratically. He thought she was heeding his warning. He exhaled and leaned against the counter with both arms, his body losing some tension.

She spoke, soft and demanding. "Do you remember what it felt like? Do you remember how I felt underneath you as you pressed into me?" She got closer and he couldn't take his eyes off her. "Did I feel unsure?"

His breathing started speeding up, his chest heaving like an animal getting ready to attack. He gripped the counter, keeping himself in place.

Before he could argue, she continued. "You are so beautiful. Strong and beautiful. When I look at you, all I can think about is how you feel. Outside on the ground, when we danced at the wedding, here on this floor," she paused and gave him a look that shot straight through him as she smoothed her hand on the table top, "on the table."

Michael sucked in a sharp breath. She was getting to him. *Good,* she thought. "When I lay in bed, I can still feel you. I feel your hands on me. I feel your mouth." She ran a small hand into the bottom of his shirt. She slid a soft touch from the button of his jeans up his abdomen. He leaned back. His breath stuttered and he rolled his hips. That was all it took.

He pulled her to him and covered her mouth with his. "I want you Michael. I know what I want." She said against his mouth.

He was mindless. He kissed her mouth, down her chin and devoured her neck as she breathed heavy against his ear. He started pulling the tie out and unbraiding her hair. He stopped and spread it out with his fingers. He ran his hands in it as he buried his face in all the silky tangle. "My Silkie," he whispered. He shuddered at the feel of her hair unbound for him.

He slid a hand up her bare leg feeling her warm hipbone. Her pelvis jerked at the contact. He backed her across the room, kissing the breath from her lungs, until he felt the door solid behind her. His hands were in her hair, his tongue deep in her mouth, his cock pressed against her. "I need inside you, Branna. I'm ready to lose my mind. I can't wait."

She pulled him to her mouth, sliding her tongue deep inside. Then she broke the kiss. "I don't want you to wait. I'm ready now." She was a little raw herself.

He dropped and slid to his knees in front of her, gliding his hands up as he hooked her panties with his fingers and slid them down her legs. His blue eyes never left hers. He slid his hands over her ass and groaned. "Branna, love. You have the sweetest little ass." She laughed nervously. He stood and kissed her, pressing her to the door. He took one hand from her ass and slid it down her belly. "I need to feel you." Her breath sped up as he came closer to her center. When he cupped her between her legs they both cried out.

"You are ready, aren't you?" He was half joking half choking, overwhelmed by her slick, willing body.

She looked at him and he saw that she was more serious than before. "I'm ready for this, for you."

She started slowly undoing his jeans. He was desperate for her. "We'll go slow the next time. I'll take my time the second and third time." He kissed her. "and the fourth and fifth."

She smiled against his mouth. "You're showing off."

He nodded, grinning as she kept opening his jeans. "Yes, I am. Are you impressed, yet?"

She started with a saucy comeback, but she was struck dumb when she wrapped her hand around him. She choked and looked down. Then she looked at him, a little alarm showing on her face. She'd never felt a man, but she knew they all weren't the same size.

"Maybe not like a stallion, but…" he jibed.

"You heard that?" she shouted.

He laughed and picked her up at the thighs, wrapping her legs around him. "Shhh, forget I said that. Concentrate on right now." She tried to make a comment and he kissed her into silence. He pressed the long length of himself at her core. "Oh God, you feel incredible." He gritted out the words. Then he took her face in one hand, thumb on her mouth as he closed in to kiss her again. He slid himself teasingly between her legs, his warm, hard flesh.

She broke the kiss as she gasped. She looked at him and his face was pure sex. Desire firing off out of every nerve in his body. She loved the feel of him, not inside her but pressing his whole length along her wet, sensitive skin. She went to his lips. She stopped just before the kiss and started moving her hips up and down, sliding along the ridge of him. Every nerve she had awakened as she felt him thick and ready. He just let her take control, sliding herself on him.

Michael was ready to explode. It was maddening and erotic to have her pleasuring herself on him, without actually being inside her. Her eyes were dazed and wild, and she put her head back and moaned, sliding up and down faster. He was afraid he was going to climax before he even entered her. He grabbed her hips. "You keep doing that and this is going to be shorter than we planned." He choked out the words.

"That's the point, isn't it?" She said it jokingly but he could hear the desperation in her voice. She was close to her own climax.

He gave a husky laugh, "Ladies first, always." He kissed her deeply and positioned himself right at her entrance, ready to push inside her. A moment of clarity hit him through the haze of arousal. What the hell had he been thinking? He broke the kiss, "Branna, I should be wearing a condom. I know I'm clean, but we should be using protection. I lost my head."

She was panting with anticipation. "I'm on the pill," she paused. "Not for anyone. I've been on it for a long time. I know I'm clean, too. It's okay, unless you want to stop."

He laughed against her mouth. "Not on your life." She felt him lift her hips to him. "Look at me, Branna. I want to see your eyes when I do this." His voice was strained and he rolled his r's, his brogue always thickest when emotions were high. She looked at him and he pressed. "Ah shit, you're tight." He winced. She pressed her hips, trying to help him. He made eye contact again. "That's it, love. Let me in."

Michael was mad with need as he held back. She was small and he was trying to go slow, but she was doing what she always did. Egging him on, pushing him. He reached between them and adjusted himself, then began rubbing her at the top of her sex. She bucked as he made the contact. She looked at him, and her eyes were wild, and a little alarmed. She pressed against the head of him as she arched. She was slick and ready, her eyes begging for more, and his control snapped. He gripped her hips and shoved inside her. She shut her eyes. He was in a couple of inches when he stopped cold. She wasn't overcome with passion, she was wincing in pain, a stifled whimper coming from her.

He pulled out and grabbed her face. "Branna, I'm sorry! Did I hurt you? Was it too soon?" She exhaled, recovering, then she kissed him hard.

He broke from her mouth and she got testy with him. "Don't stop. It's okay, just push!" She kissed him again and started pressing against him. He pulled his lips away and looked at her, seriousness and shock marring his face.

She averted her gaze. He spoke so gently as he pressed his forehead to hers. "Branna, sweetheart, are you a virgin?"

She looked at him impatiently. "I want this. It doesn't matter. I know you want me, too," she paused. "It's not a big deal. It's just a membrane. A stupid piece of skin." Her expression changed, her suppressed lust showing on her face. "I want you," she said and she pulled his mouth to hers.

He was fighting for control. She was pushing against him and kissing him so deeply; he could barely keep his head. He pulled his head back to look at her. He was incredulous that this beautiful, smart, sexy woman was still a virgin at twenty-four. It had been her choice, never giving herself to someone. There was no way it was from lack of opportunity. *Never giving herself until now.*

He touched her face so gently it immediately calmed her. He ran his thumb over her mouth, taking in every inch of her beautiful face. "If it was just a piece of skin, you wouldn't still have it. Why didn't you tell me?"

She grabbed him by the shirt with force. "Don't you dare stop this!" She shut her eyes. "I need this. We need this. This was my wish when I blew out those candles. I haven't let myself want anything for so long. I want you Michael." She kissed him gently. "Please, don't stop."

His heart was bursting. She'd waited this long, but chosen him as her first lover. He covered her mouth with his and put everything he had into the kiss. Then he said, "I won't stop, Branna. If you wanted to stop, I would. I just can't stop this on my own. I'm desperate for you." He settled her against him and started carrying her across the room.

Branna looked around, "What are you doing? We're moving?"

He walked slowly, enjoying the feel of her wrapped around him. "To bed, woman."

She laughed and kissed him. "No door? I liked the door," she whispered against his lips. He stopped and looked at her. Sensual curiosity mixed with an air of innocence that he still couldn't wrap his head around.

He smiled. "I liked the door too, but it might be a bit advanced for your first time." He grew serious. "You're so small. I don't want to hurt you." She felt so light in his arms.

She kissed his eyes, his head, his cheeks, and his mouth. "It's ok. It'll hurt and then it won't. Then it will be good, right?" He put her down. He took her face in his hands. He was so humbled by her. She realized he was trembling. "You're shaking. I thought I was the one who was supposed to be nervous."

He kissed her gently. "You waited. You saved yourself for the right time, the right man. I just want to deserve this."

She leaned in and sucked his earlobe, teasing the side of his neck with her tongue. "Then take me into that bedroom and give me the works."

He threw his head back and laughed. "For the love of God, hellcat. Have you no self preservation, pushing me like this?" Then he scooped her up in his arms.

Michael carried her into her bedroom and closed the door. He put her down and pressed her against it, taking her mouth with renewed enthusiasm. He started down her neck to her one bare shoulder. She sighed, "The door." She arched as he kissed her skin."I like the door."

Michael started taking her belt off. "I need to see you. I want to see all of you." It dropped to the floor. He slid her dress slowly up, exposing her where he'd already removed her panties. He watched as every inch was revealed. She had on a lacy, black, strapless bra. He put his mouth on the swells of her cleavage as he reached behind her and undid it. Once he removed it, she was completely nude in front of him. "You're the most beautiful thing I've ever seen. I can't believe I almost rushed through this."

What he really meant was that he couldn't believe he'd almost taken her virginity half clothed, shoved up against the front door. He was determined to remedy that near blunder. He rubbed his hands over her. Her small waist, her perfect bottom. He took a nipple in his mouth. She moaned and put her fingers in his hair. He swept her over to the bed. He slid his hands all over her as he moved his mouth to the other breast.

She groaned, "Oh wow, I really like the bed, too." He laughed, his breath tickling her skin. He propped up on one elbow and looked at her. Her skin was perfect and soft and smooth. "You're so beautiful. I just can't quit looking at you. You are perfection, lass."

He kissed her again and she pushed him off of her. "You're dressed. It's not fair. I want to see you."

He hopped off the bed. "You've seen me in my swim trunks. Don't act like you didn't look."

She smiled. "Oh, I looked. I didn't get the full show, though. I've waited long enough."

He pulled his shirt off. She couldn't take her eyes off him. He noticed she'd covered up a little. He slid the blanket away from her. "Fair is fair."

She blushed, not completely comfortable with her nudity. He slipped his jeans off. He was commando. Her eyes flared with admiration and more than a little panic. He slid next to her and pressed his finger to her brow, smoothing the crinkle. "Don't let this scare you. We'll take it slow."

She ran her hand down his chest and played with the soft hair that dusted his body. "I just…" she trailed off.

"What, Branna? Do you want to stop?"

She looked up at him shyly, "No, it's not that. I just don't want to disappoint you."

He looked at her in complete disbelief. "How on earth do you think that could ever happen?"

She shrugged one shoulder, "I know you weren't expecting a virgin. I don't know if I can…"

He stroked her belly and she arched. "Can what?"

She started turning red even as she gasped from his touch. "You know," she said breathlessly, trying to concentrate on his words and not his hands.

He stopped. "You mean climax?" Something dawned on him and he took her chin in his hand. "I understand you're a virgin, darlin' but have you ever had an orgasm?" She looked away and shook her head. He sat up. "How is that possible?"

She got antsy. "I'm not a freak, I just…"

He popped his hand over her mouth and put his chin on top of his hand, looking at her sweet face. How could she be unsure of herself? "I don't think you are a freak. I've seen you right on the verge more than once. Believe me, you're not going to have a problem." Her face changed, registered confusion. He continued, a devilish grin on his handsome face. "Showing is better than words, in this instance. You are made for this. You are not going to disappoint me, ever." He rolled on top of her and settled between her legs.

He kissed her, soft at first and then urgently. He rubbed himself against her. She arched with pleasure, feeling him slide against her. He raised above her, his face tight with passion. "You're made for me, and I you. We'll fit together. Do you know what it does to me to feel you like this? To know that I'm going to be the only man that's ever been inside you?" Branna's eyes were dreamy and unfocused, but her body had natural focus as she molded to him. She pulled her knees up, meeting his body as he slid against her. He arched deeply, putting his head back as he moaned.

She watched him. He was so beautiful. His eyes held lust and tenderness that warred within him in equal measure. He slid his hand between them, sliding his finger just where she needed him, first at the top, then inside. When she felt his penetration she clenched, putting her hand over his. She gave a husky little laugh and moved her hips.

His voice was rough as he spoke. "I want you like this, under me slow and sweet and deep," he said. She whimpered as he moved his finger deeper inside her. "Then behind you, hard and fast. I want you up against that damned door, pounding into you." He did a slow grind as he rubbed the ridge of himself against her inner thigh. "Then I want to taste you over and over again."

She started moving her hips, finding a rhythm of her own against his hand. "Then you'll take me on top, riding me until you come again." His brogue was thick and his voice hoarse. She almost couldn't take it. The visions he called forth were assaulting her. His musicians fingers were alternating between rubbing her and slipping deep and it was like nothing she'd ever felt before. The blood was pounding in her ears. "Michael!"

"Can you feel it? Just go with it. Don't fight it, love." She was so close, he almost had her there. "Let go. Give it to me, Branna. I can feel you." Her face was wild and dazed. He took her mouth just as he went deep with his finger and thumbed the top of her sex. She cried out. “That’s it, come for me,” he said. His voice was breathless and edgy.

She started gasping and bucking her hips under him, her muscles contracting, flying apart in his arms. He grabbed her hips with both hands and pushed inside her. She screamed, choking on her words. “Don’t stop! Please, Michael!” He watched her in the throes of her first orgasm and plunged past her barrier, deep inside. She gasped and he could tell that she was overwhelmed both by the contractions of her climax and the pain. He slid slowly to the hilt with one steady thrust, all the way in and stopped. He hovered over her, tense with the desire to cut loose.

He was shattered. “I’m in you, Branna.” *And you’re mine,* he thought. She was breathing hard. “Are you ok? Did I hurt you?”

She looked at him with amazement. “It hurt a little, but you waited. You waited until I was distracted.” Her blush was lovely. He was looking at her with such utter tenderness. Their hearts were pounding. He could feel his own and hers mingled together.

"Thank you, Michael,” she said as she touched his face, his mouth.

He closed his eyes and kissed her hand. He spoke gently, reverently. “It was beautiful watching you, feeling you,” he said softly. She pulled up to his mouth and kissed him. She felt him jerk a little. He hissed. She ran her hand slowly down his chest and abdomen. She knew he was holding back. She slid her hand over his ass and pulled. He instinctually pressed.

She gave a wicked giggle. “I can’t believe you fit that big monster in all the way.”

He looked at her and moved his hips, grinning. “You say the sweetest things.” He pulled back slowly and she closed her eyes, feeling him. Then he pressed back in slowly.

Branna was overwhelmed with a sense of fullness. Michael was flexing, watching her. He was straining with the effort of not hurting her, trying to be gentle. Then he lowered and she cradled his big body in her arms. She ran her hands all over him as he kissed her slow and deep, mimicking what he did to her below. She met him with her hips, grazing his scalp with her nails as she moaned in his ear. She didn’t want him holding back, she wanted all of him. She ground herself against him, reaching through the pain and finding pleasure as he pumped deep inside her.

He pulled her shoulders up and took her breast with his mouth as he rolled his hips. She moaned, uninhibited. He lay her back down and reached between them, touching her most sensitive flesh. He rubbed her as he slid in a little harder and deeper. He pressed her legs open, exposing her mercilessly as his control slipped. She groaned and dug her nails in his shoulders.

Michael knew he was pushing her. He was so deep in her that he couldn't go any further. She was with him though, lifting her hips to meet him. Her face was flushed, her lips flushed and wet from his kisses. When he started to rub the top of her, she closed her eyes and threw her head back. He drove in deep, feeling her muscles start to tense. He increased his pace, so deep he wasn't sure she could tolerate it.

She moaned his name. He felt her nails sting his flesh. She took all of him. He wanted to feel her come like this, so deep she forgot that they were two people instead of one. He was raging, feeling the animal need to spill in her. He'd always used condoms with Fiona, never being able to trust her to use birth control. He trusted Branna completely, and it shook him to his soul that she'd given him her virginity. "Branna." His voice was hoarse and desperate.

Branna looked at Michael and his face stopped her heart. He had such desperate emotion in his eyes. She felt a storm brewing deep inside her. It was an erotic mix of immense pleasure and pain. "I want to come inside you, mo chroí. Can I come inside you?" He was choking the words out.

She was breathless, so close to the edge. "Yes, I want to feel you. I want everything."

He sobbed on a moan and drove hard and fast and deep. He felt her break lose as she screamed, and her body released in racking spasms. With him so deep inside her, the intensity was so much higher. She arched and screamed as she felt him let go. His words were foreign and guttural.

Michael brought her head up to him as he released. She came so hard he felt her milking him as he spilled himself deep inside her. One hand on the back of her neck, one pulling her hips up to him, he had the longest, most intense orgasm of his life as she went wild underneath him. He gripped her small body and thrust into her with nothing between them. He started to come down feeling her trembling body beneath him. He also felt his own tremors. He pulled her close, keeping them joined. He kissed her thoroughly as her body jerked around him in the aftershocks. He looked at her and she smiled, tears brimming her eyes. He took her face in his hand. "What's wrong, mo chroí?"

She shook her head, "Nothing. I'm just overwhelmed. God, Michael I know it sounds silly to someone who's done this before." She paused and felt a little embarrassed.

He kissed her softly on the corner of her mouth. "Say it."

"I never expected it to be like that. I forgot everything but you. I never thought I could be that close to someone." She was having a hard time putting it into words, but he wanted to hear it. "I know that sounds corny and virginal and it was probably typical for someone with more experience."

He looked at her intently. "You're wrong. It's never been like this, ever. I felt your soul when I came inside you." His body shuddered. "I've always used a condom. I've never come inside a woman."

Her eyes teared again. "Really?" she asked.

"Never. Not even when I was married. I just needed to. I wanted to give you everything I had." He kissed her eyes. "Don't cry, Branna. You were perfect. It was so perfect. " He rubbed his hand over her abdomen and noticed blood on her thighs. She watched his gaze.

"I wish I didn't have to hurt you. I lost my head at the end. Was I too rough with you?"

She kissed his shoulder, tasting his skin with a light nibble. "Did it look like I was complaining?"

He grinned. "No, it looked like you were climaxing. Twice." His eyebrows were raised, his chest puffed up a little.

She smacked him. “Don’t get all fat headed about it.” She was putting on her Irish now, which he loved.

He laughed. “Oh, I’ll get as fat headed as I like! I should have a cape.” She was giggling and holding her stomach as he gave her ribs a little tickle. Then he pulled her into him. “That’s just the beginning, love. I’m kidding, you know. It wasn’t me. It was you. You felt safe and relaxed and you gave yourself over to it.” He kissed her softly. “You need a break, though. You’re going to be sore. I’ll run a bath for you, aye?”

She nodded. He got up off the bed and watched her as she stretched unashamed in the moonlight. “Christ, you are a beauty. You should see yourself, all flushed and satisfied. Makes me want to do it all over again.”

She smiled and noticed he was getting aroused again. “Does that thing ever go down?” He looked at it and smiled, “No, not for a while now. It won’t listen to reason.”

She looked at him questioningly. “How long?”

He leaned into her, hovering over her as he stood by the bed. “Since you knocked my sheet music off the stand and marched out of Gus’s like a wee hellcat.” She put her hands over her face, and laughed. He pulled them off and kissed her. “You are a handful, but I can’t get enough of you.”

CHAPTER 18

Branna reclined into the bath and it was heavenly. Michael washed her lovingly. "You should get in here with me. There is plenty of room."

He was washing her back, taking his time with her. He'd taken a quick shower while her bath filled. "Next time. If I slip in that tub behind you, we won't sleep for hours. You need to rest. You're getting your present tomorrow."

She was drifting off, head on her knees. That made her perk up a bit. "Ah, my mystery present?" She sighed as he sponged her back. "You gave me a wonderful gift already. Thank you, Michael. You were amazing. It was worth the wait."

He couldn't believe how backwards she had that. She was worth the wait. In twenty-nine years he had never felt the connection he'd experienced with her tonight. He stood her up and began toweling her off, planting soft kisses on her shoulder blades, her elbows, the small of her back. He wrapped another towel around her and picked her up, carrying her to her bed.

"Can I stay with you? I understand if you need your space."

She was touched that he seemed to be a little vulnerable. She kissed his face and smoothed her hand down his cheek. "Please stay. I want to sleep next to you." She slipped her panties on under her towel and then took her towel off to put on a little t-shirt and some tiny pink boxers. He hated seeing her cover up. She was being shy about her body in the aftermath. He knew that it was prudent, however. If she was pressed against him nude all night, he would have a hell of a time leaving her alone.

He slid his track pants off. "I don't sleep in anything." She smiled and looked him up and down. "That's okay, I like having my own private, Irish POA all nekkid in my bed."

He slid in between the sheets, laughing. "Yes, remind me to go back to the kayak shop and sort out the competition." He curled around her.

"You never had any competition, Michael," she said softly.

He squeezed her close. "You're wrong, Branna. I didn't give you the gift, you gave it to me. You gave me the most precious part of you, something you saved." He pulled her tight to him, humming softly as she drifted off. He drifted off with the thought that you could be completely shattered and truly healed all in the same moment.

* * *

MICHAEL WOKE to a light buzzing on the table. He had set his phone alarm on silent. He looked at her. She was facing him now, face turned up to his in sweet repose. A pang of guilt hit him. He had kept her up late. He wanted to kiss her, but he didn't want to wake her. Unlike her normal braid, her hair was spilled gloriously around the pillows. He slipped out of bed as he heard a truck pull up.

He came out shirtless, pulling his pants on, as Aidan slid the door open quietly. Aidan took in the scene, him coming out of Branna's room, and the lightbulb went off. He turned and spoke to his brothers, Finn, Tadgh, and Brigid who were approaching behind him. "Hold on a minute. I need to get Michael up." He stepped in and shut the door.

Michael gave him a look of gratitude, then ran to his room and put a shirt on. "Is she still sleeping?" asked Aidan.

He nodded."Thanks brother."

Aidan looked thoughtfully, "I did it for her. She's a good girl. I don't want her to feel embarrassed. Although, I'm glad you finally came to your senses." Aidan was grinning as he opened the door. "Shh, she's still asleep."

Michael marveled at his older brother. He was warrior to the core. A confirmed bachelor, never one for talking, but he hadn't hesitated to protect Branna's feelings. He had always been distant with Fiona. Never cruel, but indifferent. Aidan was giving quiet orders as Tadgh and the other lads were bringing in the gift.

He watched as Aidan walked over and pulled out a chair, depositing Brigid at the table. He pulled another chair up and put her little feet up on it. She reached up and kissed him on the cheek. He knelt down and patted her belly. It occurred to Michael, for the first time, that his eldest brother would be a wonderful husband. Aidan noticed him watching and stood up. He went outside to help unload.

Brigid smiled knowingly. "He doesn't like tarnishing that tough guy image."

Michael walked over to her and kissed her head. "Are your feet swollen, hen?"

She nodded. "Nothing to worry about." She looked at her twin, happily. "She'll love it, Michael." He hoped so. "She was marvelous last night, wasn't she? Like an angel. She's got a lot of secrets doesn't she?"

He nodded in agreement. "She's not exactly secretive. She just likes to stay in the background."

Brigid grew serious. "You can't let her leave, Michael."

He nodded again, "I know."

Michael slipped into Branna's room and she was still asleep. He leaned down and kissed her mouth softly. "Wake up, darling." Branna stirred and opened her eyes. She smiled when she saw him. "Your present is here. Time to get up."

She popped up like a little meerkat. She stretched and squeaked. She got an excited look on her face and scrambled off the bed. As she started to leave, he stopped her. She looked delicious, all sleep flushed and drowsy. Her hair looked like she'd spent the night making love, tousled and sexy. He pressed her against the door and kissed her deeply. When he'd sufficiently kissed her into a hazy stupor, he opened the door. He got behind her and covered her eyes with his hands, walking her out into the living room.

Michael's family watched as he walked Branna out of her room. He towered over her, a foot taller than her. He uncovered her eyes and whispered in her ear. "Open your eyes."

Branna couldn't imagine what was waiting for her. Had he cooked her breakfast? She opened her eyes and gasped. In an empty spot by her desk was a beautiful, antique spinet piano with a little bench. It was walnut with turned legs, lovely burled wood grain. It was so beautiful. She couldn't speak. She put a shaking hand out and touched the keys, hearing the sweet sound of a quality instrument.

She put the hand over her mouth, unable to stop the tears. She turned to Michael. He looked at her, a little alarmed. She threw her arms around him. "Thank you, Michael. I don't know what to say. It's the most beautiful gift I've ever received." She nestled into his neck, her tears soaking his skin.

He held her as she cried. "You need a piano. You need your music. Promise me you'll start playing again." She lifted her face to his, tears still flowing. "Don't cry, mo chroí," he soothed as he cradled her and kissed her tears away. She sniffled and wiped her face. He kissed her forehead and she turned around, realizing how many people were there.

"Did you all move this in here while I slept?"

Brigid came up and hugged her. "No reason to have all these big brothers if you can't make them lift the heavy stuff."

Branna looked at them, one at a time. Tadgh with his easy smile, Aidan with his quiet, commanding presence, Finn with his eyes always on his wife, warm and sensual. Patrick with his mischievous eyes, and Liam with his boyish good looks. She hugged all of them. She hugged Tadgh last. "Play us a song, love," he said softly.

Brigid clapped, "Yes! Play us a song, Yank!"

Aidan motioned to Patrick. "Let's get the tea on and start making these girls some breakfast."

Branna sat at the piano. “My friend Anna kept all of my sheet music, and my father’s. I didn’t think to bring it.”

Brigid brightened, “Well, now she can send it to you.”

Branna shrugged, “Maybe. I’d hate for her to send it if I can’t…” She stopped what she was going to say. “I mean, I’d hate to put her to any trouble. We’ll see.”

Michael tensed as Branna cut her sentence off. He knew what she was about to say. *If I can’t stay.* In the wake of last night’s union, the thought of her leaving Burren Way gave him the sweats. The thought that she might return to the states and leave Ireland all together was unthinkable. Brigid had told him about Branna’s financial restrictions. He’d foolishly assumed she could go buy another place nearby. What in the hell were they going to do?

Branna sat at the piano and her heart soared. She stroked it. “I always wanted a spinet. I love the feel of them.” She thought for a moment and then started. The song was spunky, an American artist. She started singing and Brigid was wiggling in her seat, so happy to be a part of the surprise.

Michael loved watching her play. This song was faster than what she’d played before. Tori Amos’s *Happy Phantom*. High, sexy vocals and Branna didn’t disappoint. She wiggled her little ass in those pink boxers as she played. She played the song with her whole body, hair swinging wildly down her back as she sang. He suddenly wanted to throw blinders on his brothers and Tadgh.

Aidan and Patrick were throwing together an easy breakfast for everyone. French Toast, fruit and cream, tea. Aidan watched the scene across the living room. “Do you see how he looks at her? Listen to his voice when he soothes her? He is so in love with her.” Patrick stopped what he was doing. “Was it like that with you and Caitlyn?” Aidan continued.

Patrick thought about it. “Aye, it was intense. The first time I’d ever thought I’d die from the wanting. Though, I suspect that wee lass in there might be the biggest heartbreaker I’ve ever known.”

Aidan looked at him, startled. “You think she’d break his heart, then?”

Patrick shook his head. "No brother, I think that her wounds are deep. Christ, the sorrow she's had? Sorting through those layers of pain when you love her as much as Michael does? It's the loving that'll break his heart, because he can't take it from her. The pain, aye? He can't take it from her."

Aidan understood, "But she loves him. Christ, how she looks at him. I can't fathom having a woman look at me like that." Patrick looked at his eldest brother and saw something that stopped him in his tracks. He saw longing. Aidan swore he wouldn't put a family through life in the military, but he was a family man to the core. He loved women and children. Why in the hell had he taken some stupid, unspoken vow not to marry?

As the men stood in the kitchen, Brigid spoke from behind them. "You could have that too, Aidan, if you'd only let yourself. A woman of your own, your mate to give you babies and love you the way Ma loves Da, the way I love Finn."

Aidan shook his head. "Don't you worry about me, sister. I'm content with my lot." Brigid and Patrick looked at each other. They weren't falling for it anymore.

Branna was floating as she walked away from her new piano and into her kitchen crowded full of beautiful O'Brien men and one Murphy. She looked at Brigid and shook her head. "Beautiful. Every one of them is beautiful. Do they all cook?"

Brigid nodded enthusiastically. "Ma taught them all. She said she wanted them to marry for love, not fall to one knee as soon as they found a woman that would do their wash." She looked at them with such affection. "They're all the best of men. I couldn't be prouder. Tadgh is just the same. When you grow up like we did, all in the same town, you scarcely distinguish between brothers and cousins. He stayed with us a lot, after his da was killed."

Branna's eyes shot to hers. Brigid was surprised to realize that she didn't know. "I thought he would have told you."

Branna was stunned. "How?"

Brigid was sad. "He was Da's brother, in the Garda like Da. He was killed in a motorcycle crash while he was on patrol. Tadgh was seven."

Branna had her hand over her mouth. "His mother took it hard, as you can imagine. Started drinking. She doesn't now, but when it happened, she lost her way for a few years. Now she's back on the island. He goes back and forth on the ferry to see her. She's a bit needy. That's why he's not going with Patrick."

Branna was shocked again. "Tadgh wanted to be a police officer?"

Brigid nodded. "Aye, his mother raged. She guilted him about leaving her. Said that he'd die and leave her just like his father did. She told him she'd never forgive him. Tadgh told everyone, right before you came, that he couldn't go." Brigid shook her head. "Three bloody jobs paying his rent and hers so that she'll keep speaking to him."

Branna thought about it. "I know about being alone. I'm afraid that at times I wasn't very understanding during my mother's illness. Tadgh should live his life, though. He can't let her guilt him into wasting his life waiting tables. He's smart. He would be a wonderful police officer."

Brigid nodded, agreeing with her. "Guilt is a terrible burden. You are right. He is smart, first in his class. He did well at university, too. Liked studying criminology and psychology. He was always one for puzzles. He could figure things out, you know? See things other people didn't. He's good at reading people. That's not something you can learn in a book."

Aidan came up to Brigid and Branna with plates of food and put them in front of them. Finn was currently in a headlock, courtesy of Patrick, and Tadgh was trying to shove a berry in his mouth. "Thank you Aidan. This looks lovely. What's the tussle about?"

Aidan and Brigid exchanged looks. "Finn hates blueberries. It's an ongoing struggle," he said with a smile.

She laughed, "How can you hate blueberries? They're like a little gift from the Baby Jesus."

Aidan barked out a laugh. "Agreed. The fun part is when he starts gagging."

Branna watched them with unhidden joy. "It must be fun having so many siblings."

Aidan looked at them and then back at her. "I suppose it is." Just then a loud pop happened from behind Aidan, and he lurched in front of Brigid. A fork was fisted in his hand like a weapon.

"Who wants a mimosa?" asked Michael. He looked at Aidan, then at the bottle in his hand.

Aidan snapped to attention and started carrying on like nothing had happened. He was sweating, though, and not making eye contact with anyone.

Brigid looked at Branna. "Aidan, when you're done stuffing me with all of this food can ye take me for a walk? The doctor said it's good for me."

He turned to her. "Yes, deirfiúr mo chroí. That husband of yours can do the washing up."

Branna protested. "No! You all have done so much. I'll do the dishes." He looked at her and she could still tell he was rattled. She knew the look well. The name had changed over the years, but combat stress looked the same no matter what you called it.

He looked over her face as an older brother or father would. "No, girl. You sit and let us take care of you." He leaned over and kissed her on the forehead.

He walked back into the kitchen and Branna watched him go. "What are we going to do with these boys?"

Brigid guffawed, "Welcome to life with the O'Brien men. Stubborn as a herd of oxen."

She grinned, "And you're not?" Brigid grinned, "Touché, deirfiúr." and they clinked forks before digging into the breakfast. Branna resisted the tears she felt prickling her eyes. Brigid had just called her sister.

After the breakfast was done, Michael watched Tadgh approach Branna with a little gift bag. He willed himself not to let the ugly green monster creep out. Tadgh loved him. He wouldn't betray him. Branna was a pure soul. She would never lead Tadgh on while sleeping with him. Tadgh had said it was like having a sister, and he needed to believe him.

"What's this?" Branna asked.

Tadgh was never shy, but he shrugged awkwardly. "It's a small thing. It's not a piano, but I think you'll like it."

She smiled. "You didn't have to do this."

He just gestured to the bag, "Shut your gob and open it."

When she did, she looked at him warmly, tears welling up again. "Summer Harvest. How did you know I wanted this?"

He just gave her a crooked smile. "I saw that you liked it, but when I went back the other day and asked the clerk if you'd bought it, she said no, that you only bought a little bar of soap. She assured me that was the one, said you had a budget to keep and were hesitant to buy it for yourself. So, I got it for you."

Branna hugged him. "You pay attention, you watch people and remember things. You're very smart. You know that, right?"

He shook his head. "It's nothing, just a little bottle of perfume."

She kissed him on the cheek then looked at him sadly. "Why didn't you tell me?" He just gave her a questioning glance. "About your dad, I mean. You never talk about yourself. You just listen."

He looked at her lovingly. "This isn't my story, love. It's yours."

She thought about that. "It's ours. All of us." She gestured to the occupants of Kelly Cottage, "We all intersected for a reason. I really believe that, however this ends."

He gave her an impatient look. "You're not…"

She put her hand up. "Shh, don't say it. You and I will talk later. We have more in common than I thought. It is about time I start listening, instead of feeling sorry for myself. You are this silent box of secrets and you are going to start spilling them. Later, though. Deal?"

He nodded, "Deal."

She smiled at him and said, "When are you taking me on a ferry ride?"

His face lit up. "I work tomorrow. Be on the dock at ten."

* * *

As the family piled into the borrowed van and cars, Michael and Branna waved and walked back into the cottage. Branna walked over to the piano and smoothed her hand over it. She fingered the keys lightly. Michael smoothed a hand over hers. "I could listen to you play all day," he said.

"You couldn't have found something more perfect. It's too much. I feel like it's too much." she said.

His heart was soaring. "I'm glad you like it. You will never guess where I got it."

"Where?"

He played around with the keys. "Brendan Sullivan, the fisherman you met last week. Says his mother played, but no one else plays and it was collecting dust. I gave him a fair price. I know he's saving for that arm and all." She looked at him and he could see the wheels turning again. "You're scheming, hen. I saw those papers you were working on when Cora was here."

She gave him a sneaky smile. "I might be working on something. I can't talk about it, though. It's a lot of moving parts and if I can't make it happen. I don't want to jinx it."

He kissed her nose. "You're too good to be true."

She went into the kitchen and poured a glass of water. Michael's chin dropped. "What?" she asked, looking at herself to see if she had some sort of bug crawling on her.

He stuttered, "Is that a glass of water? Are you drinking plain old ordinary water, on purpose?"

"Yes, I can be taught." She gave him a come hither look over the rim.

He stalked toward her, "Yes, I know. There is a lot I'd like to teach you."

She raised her eyebrows over the glass. She slid past him. "It's starting to rain. I think I need some air."

He chuckled deep in his throat. "Are you teasing me, hellcat?"

She just smiled and walked toward the door. "I like the rain." She swayed her hips as she walked outside.

Michael watched her out the window. She was soaked and squishing her feet in the mud. She looked up and saw him watching her. She walked toward the door, stopping to rinse her feet with a stream of water that poured off the roof. He opened it and covered her with a towel. "You're shivering."

She smiled. "I like the rain." She noticed that he'd started a fire in the hearth. He'd also spread pillows and quilts down in front of it. She gave him a sensually charged smile. "What time do you have to go to work?"

He grunted. "Four o'clock, so we have a few hours." He sat on the kitchen chair and drew her to him. He gently dried her off and stripped her. He was lazy about it, taking in every inch of her as he did it. He took her by the hand and drew her over to the fire. She thought he was going to come to her, but he didn't.

"Lie on your belly." She turned over and sighed. The warm fire and soft nest he'd made was heavenly. He knelt down beside her and she saw he had a bowl of something. He dipped his hand in it and rubbed it over both palms. He gently put his hands on her back and began to rub warm oil into her skin.

It smelled like something slightly familiar but she couldn't place it. "What is that smell? It's lovely."

He answered her softly, as if trying to keep her relaxed. "It is bergamot. It will help you relax."

Michael had wanted to do this since that night in the kitchen when he'd rubbed her back. He smoothed the oil all over her beautiful body. He kept his libido in check. It was difficult, but he wanted to take care of her, do this right. All the way until the happy ending. He rubbed her shoulders and back, her gorgeous ass and legs, even her hands and feet. His touch was firm, but not overly so. "You have to tell me when you want it harder, or when it's too rough. "

He felt her chuckle. She said, "That's what she said."

He paused and laughed huskily. "All in good time, hellcat. As hard as you like."

"You are a magician." She groaned. As he finished with the warm oil on her back she tried to push up.

"No, just roll over. I'm not finished." She did and he stifled a groan. She was perfection. Perfect and petite and just the right amount of curve. He rubbed her legs. As he came firmly up her thigh, he could tell she expected him to run his hand to the goal line. He didn't. He avoided, by a fraction of an inch, where she wanted him to go. He could tell her deep relaxation was mixed with a dreamy arousal. He rubbed her abdomen, over her sensitive belly and hips. Then he smoothed his hands over her breasts and chest and down her arms. He thumbed her pink nipples as they grew tight for him. He stopped by her face and kissed her lightly as her eyes fluttered open. Then he kissed between her breasts. He got up and stood at her feet. Slowly, he knelt and spread her legs at the knees. She propped up on her elbows, her face dreamy.

"You have too many clothes on," she said on an exhale. He ignored her and crawled between her legs. He started kissing her navel, her hips, and the tops of her thighs. Suddenly she understood, and she tensed.

He looked at her, eyes heavy with arousal. "Has anyone ever..." he trailed off, almost afraid to hear the answer. He knew, however. Deep down, he knew the answer. She just shook her head, swallowing hard. "Lay back then, let me do this. I need this like I need air." He dipped his head and she felt it. His warm mouth closed over her and she inhaled, choking on her breath as her head fell back.

She couldn't even moan. He stole her ability to speak. She lay back on the pillow and just felt him. He was thorough with his explorations until she was out of her mind from the pleasure. "Look at me, Branna." She almost couldn't bear it. She lowered her eyes and watched as he lightly placed his tongue at the top of her, where she was most sensitive. He began to flutter, concentrating solely on that spot that he knew would drive her wild. It was so erotic, not just the feel of him, but the fact that he loved what he was doing to her. Her hand went down into his hair as he intensified his efforts. A pulse was thumping in her ears and the tension climbed in her body as she watched him pleasure her. She flew apart, bowing off the floor, and he cupped her bottom, pulling her tight against his mouth and forcing her to ride out the pleasure.

Michael ground himself into the covers, trying to control his lust as she flew apart under his mouth. She'd been resplendent. Creamy thighs spread for him, hard nipples that arched from soft, beautiful breasts, and the feel of her breath coming shorter as she climbed to her release. She'd watched him, her sexual curiosity overriding her shyness. It had heightened the experience for both of them and she came wildly, head thrown back as she moaned and rolled her hips against his mouth.

It was all he had dreamed about over the last few weeks. He took an insane amount of pleasure in knowing that he was the only person on earth that knew the taste of her. It was such an intimacy and he had been thinking on it ever since he'd discovered how inexperienced she was. She lay there afterwards panting and addled, "That was incredible." She was jerking and shaking. He bit her inner thigh lightly.

"Yes, it was," he teased.

She was gripping his arms, pulling him up. "Michael," Branna's voice was desperate, her breathing heavy. "I need you, please."

He undressed quickly. He kissed his way up her belly, stopping to tease her breasts and hard nipples. Then he took her by the hips and flipped her back over on her belly. He kissed her from the base of her spine to the back of her neck. He lifted her knee on one side, cocking her hip up just enough. He slid into her from behind and they both cried out. She was so sensitive that she contracted, the aftershocks of her orgasm causing her muscles to fire off and tighten around him. He nibbled her ear, took her small hand under his and intertwined their fingers. He went slow as he rolled his hips. He'd never been so deep inside her and he didn't want to hurt her. She was so small, but damn it if she didn't curl her back like a cat, taking more of him.

He whispered in her ear, but she couldn't understand him. "Mo chuisle mo chroí," he was desperate, coming closer to his release. He squeezed her hand as he spoke. It wasn't his words, but hers that haunted him. *If I can't stay. If I can't stay.* The words tortured him. *It's ok. I know I have to go.*

Branna was completely absorbed in the feel of Michael. Not being able to see him, she was completely in tune with his body, his voice. He whispered in Gaelic and his voice was soft and desperate. He squeezed her hand. "Branna." He choked out her name and then cried out, growling as he came. He shuddered as he clutched her to him, so deep in her that she wasn't sure she could take anymore. He had one big thigh between her legs, the other to the outside, and she could feel his muscular hips shoved hard against her ass as he jerked and spilled inside her.

He kissed her face as he mumbled unintelligibly. It was a shattering intimacy, being completely aware as she felt him let go and shatter to pieces. She took his hand to her mouth and nibbled on his thumb. He trembled, spent behind her and breathing heavily into her hair. He was big and dominant and pure man, but when he let go, he was at her mercy, split open and raw. It was intoxicating. She felt sexy, powerful, and wanted.

Michael covered them both as he held Branna to his chest. He stroked her hair. Her body was soft and a little oily from her massage and he could smell himself on her skin. She was flushed and hazy, her curves molded to his muscles. He had used her bathroom to clean up before coming back to her, and he'd seen her oral contraceptives on the counter. He fought the insane urge to flush them down the toilet. He was shaking and completely spent. No woman had ever taken him so high.

It wasn't just physical. He felt like he'd joined with her on an irreversible level, like she'd marked his soul. He thought back to the confrontation he'd had with Tadgh, the morning in the hospital. Tadgh had threatened him. He said that if Michael let her go, he would hunt her down, marry her and have her pregnant before he could do anything about it. The threat had spurned blood lust in him. They had only known each other a few weeks, but the thought of someone else holding her, making love to her, marrying her and giving her children, made him mental.

"What did Tadgh get you?" Michael asked.

Branna lifted her head. "Oh, a bottle of perfume I liked from the Burren."

He kept his tone even. "Really? That was nice. Was it something you liked when he took you there?"

She nodded, "Yes, it smells lovely. It is like summer in a bottle."

He asked, curiously, "That place isn't expensive. Why didn't you just buy it?"

She shrugged, "I had just bought the car. I was trying to stick to a budget. Tadgh went back and got it a couple of days ago. He's like that. He pays attention, files information away. He would have been good in the Garda."

Michael was surprised. "He told you about that?"

She shook her head and sighed. "No, he doesn't talk about himself. You know him, always trying to make everyone else happy. He never told me his father died either. Brigid did."

Michael replied, "Yes, I suppose I should have told you. It hasn't been easy for him. You are right about him. He reminds me of you in that way, always taking care of other people." She started to argue and he cut her off. "Please, woman. You won't buy yourself a wee bottle of perfume, but you sent Brigid and Caitlyn to the day spa. Now you are cooking something up for Brendan Sullivan. Don't get me wrong. It's wonderful. Just don't forget you deserve good things as well. A good life somewhere that makes you happy."

She was silent, the implication hanging between them. "I'm happy right now. I am happy in this place, wrapped in your arms, today. That's all I can think about right now and I am grateful for it." He tilted her head up to his and kissed her.

MICHAEL WAS LEAVING for work when Branna emerged from her bedroom wearing her starchy, buttoned down clothes. "I'm headed out. I won't be home until tomorrow evening. What are you doing tonight?" he asked.

She approached him and hugged him and nipped his ear with her teeth. "Nothing. I have a quick appointment with Dr. Flynn to discuss the toy area and get a check up. Then I have to run errands. After that I will come home, read my book, and turn in early."

He kissed her on the nose, holding her close. "Don't forget to eat. I made some tuna salad, chopped up some fruit for a nice bit of sweet. There is cheese, some good bread that Ma baked, fresh juice. Promise me you will eat something healthy."

She looked at him and ran her hand over his chest like she was petting a big cat. "I promise. Oh, and don't be surprised if I am gone tomorrow when you get home. Tadgh is working on the ferry tomorrow and is going to take me on the island during his lunch break. I may decide to stay and explore. I haven't really seen a whole lot since I got here."

Michael couldn't believe he hadn't taken the time to think about how little she'd seen of her new home. She moved to Ireland and had been on one miserable, short trip to Dublin, the Burren, and kayaking. That was it. "Well, have fun and be careful. Take a jumper. It gets colder on the islands."

Her eyebrows lifted. "You know, I haven't lived anywhere that gets cold in..." She thought. "I guess since we lived in Virginia. I barely remember it. I guess I am going to need some winter clothes. I can't outfit myself in Aran wool every day, but I guess I may need to start thinking about the cold weather." An idea was brewing in Michael's head that he kept to himself for now.

* * *

BRANNA WALKED into Jack McCain's office and smiled at Miriam. "How's the travel agency going?"

Miriam rolled her eyes, "Stifled by the bloody internet as usual."

Branna laughed, "Well, I won't forget you if I plan a trip. I promise."

Miriam lit up, "Thank you, Branna. I would love to help you!"

Jack McCain came up to the front. "I thought I heard you, come to my office, dear. Miriam, hold my calls."

Branna followed him and sat down across from his desk. "So, how is the search going?"

Jack gave her a bleak look. "Scarce. I have three potentials. Are you ready to go look?"

She nodded. "Jack, please keep this to yourself. I just need to think about where I am going to end up if this doesn't happen for me. You know my situation."

Jack gave her a sad smile, "Yes, I know. I'm responsible for a big bit of the trouble you are facing. I will do everything I can." She didn't argue. He was right.

After three houses, Branna was clinically depressed. The first had been a "charming cottage needing a little TLC". It was about 30 minutes from Doolin. When she walked in the front door, the smell almost knocked her down. She looked at the floor and noticed the stone and mortar was disintegrating around the edges. The kitchen was a freestanding sink with no cabinetry and old plumbing. The stove was small, dirty, and rusty, and it had a suspicious looking propane tank attached to it. The faucet was dripping along a path of rust stain. She looked up and saw the reason for the stench. Mold. The thatch and parts of the wall had black mold. The fireplace had loose stones and bird droppings, obviously in need of repair and chimney sweeping.

She went into the one bathroom and there were spider webs and archaic plumbing. The light fixture was a bulb free hanging from the ceiling. "This is the same price range as Ned's cottage. Are they delusional?"

Jack had a look of distaste on his face, obviously disliking the smell as well. "Aye, they are. I could try to get them down on the price a bit."

She shook her head. "This mold is a game stopper. This is hard to get rid of and you have to hire professionals." She remembered her dad telling her that a black mold infestation was reason to walk.

The next two properties were in Ennis. They were cookie cutter in neat little lower priced neighborhoods. Every house was the same, every street the same. They were just the sort of house she didn't want. Bumper to bumper neighbors, no potential for improvement, not a good investment. The interior was no better. She hated them. Small, no personality, thin walls, and a view of the street and the neighbor's house, which looked identical. They weren't cheap, either.

They stretched her budget and came with additional monthly community fees.

She left Jack with the instructions that he was going to start looking on the outskirts of Dingle, Kerry, and Galway. Not too far from Doolin, but very expensive areas. He didn't seem optimistic. Who didn't want to live in the Ring of Kerry? He suggested other areas but they took her from the sea. That thought made her ache. She pulled into the cottage and just stared at it through the windshield. Michael was at work, so she let herself cry.

CHAPTER 19

Branna woke up early and went for a long walk. She could hear the sea, smell it on the breeze. The sun was out and the morning was chilly. She had a slicker on in case the weather changed today. She pulled out her soft, well-worn jeans, her Sanuks, and a soft long sleeved t-shirt. She was going to be playing on the islands today and she needed her play clothes.

As she headed to the marina, she was nervous about talking to Brendan. She had made some major progress with her project, but she needed to bring him on board. She had first wanted to see if she could pull this off before she got his hopes up. Now she needed to convince a humble, proud, alpha male that it was okay to let people help him. This was the hardest part, but she'd danced this reel many times. She had to make him understand.

"Hello, young Branna. Welcome back!" Brendan was smiling ear to ear. Jamie gave her a wave and a shy smile. He helped her aboard and they walked to his father who was struggling to bait a trap.

"So you use nets and traps. Interesting. I grew up around the sea. It is interesting to see how everyone does things."

He smiled at her appreciatively. "Beautiful and smart. Michael's a lucky man." She noticed Jamie's face darkened a little at that.

"Oh, I'm not Michael's…um."

Brendan cut her off with a hardy laugh. "Don't even try it lass. I see the way he looks at you."

She blushed, "How does he look at me?" she said, embarrassed but too curious not to ask.

He stopped his work and looked at her. "He looks at you like you're his," he said simply. That made her tummy do a little jump.

"I don't think so," she said softly, "but enough about that. I have something to talk to you about."

She told him. Not every detail, but what he needed to know. When she was done he just stared at her. So did Jamie. "Lass, I cannot take your money."

She shook her head. "It's not just my money. This non-profit is not taxed. I can't run it from here and I don't have a beneficiary on the books to receive anything. The US has so many military charities. I have this final pot of money that I need to find a home for. If I just take it into my own accounts, I have to pay taxes. My government will take half of it."

Brendan scowled, "Aye, they love to stick their hands in your pockets don't they? Still sweetheart, that money was supposed to be for men hurt in service of their country. I don't deserve it, they do."

Branna's spine stiffened. "And why not? Don't you serve your country?"

He looked puzzled. "No, lass. I told you. I fish. I've not gone to war."

She shook her head vigorously. "You are so wrong. You fish, yes, but for who? Do you eat it all yourself? You feed people, Brendan. You feed these people! Is there any more noble pursuit than to fill a child's belly? You might not go to war, but you serve this community every day that you go out on that boat. You and Jamie, you risk your lives doing a pretty dangerous job to put local fish on these tables."

She motioned to the town around them as she spoke. "You aren't getting rich doing it. You do it because someone has to." She leaned into him from her seat. "There are many ways to serve, Brendan.

Don't discount your contribution just because you don't have a uniform. You are important to this place."

His face softened and he spoke softly, "My how fierce you are, and a bigger heart I've ne'er seen."

She knelt next to him and took his hand. "This is your chance to gain a little more independence with a great piece of modern technology. I have connections in that community. If you will let me, I can do this. Let me do this for you. Let us," She motioned around her. "Let them say thank you for your service. Don't let misplaced humility or pride get in my way, Brendan Sullivan." Her tone turned stern. "I will get my way on this and you deserve this."

She could tell when she'd turned the corner. He ran his rough hand across her face. "I would have loved to have had a daughter. You near break my heart, girl."

She squeezed his hand. "Thank you. Thank you for letting me do this." She looked up at Jamie and his eyes were brimming with tears. He just nodded, not wanting to draw his father's attention.

* * *

"Permission to come aboard!" Branna yelled as she walked down the dock.

Tadgh smiled and took her hand, leading her onto the deck of the Doolin Ferry boat. "What has my little Yank been up to this morning?"

She smiled, "Well, breakfast then a quick stop at The Sea Mistress."

He gave her an odd look. "Brendan?"

She nodded. "Long story, I will fill you in at some point. I may need your help. Just let me work on it a little more." He worked as he talked, handing lines over to a man on the deck. "So where are we headed? The big island?"

He shook his head, "No, Inis Oirr. It's smaller, but you'll love it. There are ruins and a shipwreck."

Branna clapped her hands and squeaked a little. "I have my good camera and comfortable shoes. Bring it on!"

He looked at her appraisingly. "I noticed. No stiff little button downs today, eh?"

She noticed his gaze drifted a little to her sliver of belly that was showing at her waistband. "Did you just check me out, Tadgh O'Brien?"

He laughed unapologetically. "Aye, I did. I'm a man, lass. Remind me again why I'm not trying to get in your knickers?"

She put an arm around his shoulders. She looked out over the water. "Because, she's out there Tadgh. She's just not me. You know it as well as I do."

He smiled sadly. "Maybe. She hasn't shown up in Doolin on my day off, unfortunately. I only get one about every two weeks." She put her forehead to his cheek, squeezing him. "You can't live your life for other people. You are working yourself to death. You are too young for this. Promise me you won't limit yourself."

He sighed. "Brigid has been talking to you, hasn't she?"

She looked at him. "I wish you had. Don't you trust me? I've told you things. Things even Michael doesn't know. Can't you lean on me for a change?"

He looked at her as he steered the boat. "I love you, you know that. Not like...well, not like that, but I do love you. You are so very dear to me, Branna. Please don't leave."

She stiffened. His mouth tightened. "Don't deny it. I know you. You won't take that cottage from him. Even if Ned lets you have it."

She shook herself. "Let's not talk about this now. Let's just pretend we are two tourists going on an adventure." She could feel his gaze burning into her.

"Find a way to stay. You can't leave. I won't have it!"

She sighed. "I'm trying, Tadgh. I just don't know if I can. Please, understand. I don't have anyone other than a friend in North Carolina. This is my home. I wouldn't leave if I could avoid it."

* * *

Branna had a wonderful day. Tadgh took her to meet his mother. She was nice enough, but she felt a little resentment that the woman seemed to manipulate her son. She saw the co-dependence as plain as day. Her complaining about the house he was paying to rent. Pointing out what a good lad he was and telling him that he was all she had in the world.

"Ma, how's the knitting going?"

She grunted. "Sales are slow. My stuff is as good as any sold in the shop, I don't know what the problem is."

He gave her a look that said he knew exactly what the problem was. He went over and snubbed her cigarette out in the tray. "Your finished product smells like these bloody fags. Smoke outside and your business will go up."

She just gave him a snort. "You sound like your da, God rest his soul." She crossed herself.

Branna decided to break the tension. "I bet they just need airing out, once you get them home. May I see your inventory, Mrs. O'Brien? I don't have any warm clothes for winter. I came from the South."

Tadgh's mother brightened at that, "Of course you can."

Tadgh gave her a grateful look.

"I would love these mittens and this scarf. I love the weave. Do you have any black wool?"

Tadgh's mother dug in the baskets. "Call me Katie, love. Here's a hat, the slouchy, beanie type that's popular with the young folks."

Branna smiled, "That's perfect! Do you think you could make a cream sweater in this pattern? I want one of the long cardigans I've seen in the catalogs around here." Tadgh's mother knew exactly what she was talking about and pulled out a catalog. "Yes, that is it exactly."

Katie was ecstatic. "I promise, I'll use new wool and I'll smoke outside while I make it."

Tadgh was shaking his head as they walked to the only small eatery on the island. "You are unbelievable. You made her feel so good. How do you do it?"

She looked at him, "Do what?"

He rubbed his hand over the back of her head. He noticed she'd worn her hair down. She looked so young and beautiful. "Cast your spells. You made her so happy." He kissed her on the head. "Thank you. She's a sorry excuse for a mother, most days. I won't lie. I love her, though. Thank you for being so kind to her."

Once Tadgh left for his boat, Branna explored on her own. She walked along the stone wall encompassing O'Brien castle. The sheep were mingling in the greenery on one end. She took photos and read the pamphlets on the history of the island.

She was startled from her reverie by a horse drawn carriage that appeared around the stone walls that lined the island. "Dia Duit. You are gorgeous, aren't you? You can sit up front with me." The carriage was filled with American senior citizens, all smiling with their cameras and day packs. He drove her and the other passengers to the shipwreck. "Are you staying long? Do you have a man here with you?" The driver was cute. About her age with a ponytail and dimples.

"I live in Doolin, actually," she answered.

He was taken back. "In the Kelly cottage?"

She jumped in her seat. "Has word spread this far?" She put her face in her hands.

"Oh, aye. We've heard of the raven that's flown over the sea," he said mischievously. "Other's deny it, say you're a silkie woman, come looking for a mate." She was staring at him with her mouth open a little, stunned into silence. He looked at her mouth, shamelessly flirting with her. "Have you found him yet?"

Branna jumped out of the seat of the carriage as soon as it stopped. She tipped him and he flashed those dimples at her. "Come back to my island if you don't have any luck on the mainland." Damn. She was definitely going to have to get Anna over here.

Branna got home to the cottage and saw Michael's truck. She went in the front door and found him, sound asleep on her father's recliner. The sight of him, boots shed, uniform askew, passed out from exhaustion on the old leather chair, made her chest ache. She kissed him softly on the mouth and he woke. "Hello, beautiful. Did you have fun today?" She walked over to the kitchen, talking about her day. His ears went deaf as soon as he looked at her. She had low slung, ratty jeans on, and a tiny t-shirt that barely came to the waist of her pants. There was a patch on her ass where the jeans had been repaired.

He got up and walked slowly toward her, watching as she bent over in the fridge. "You look different today." His voice was husky from sleep and a stirring arousal. Her hair was down and wild around her shoulders. He pulled her to him and smelled it. "You smell like the sea. Like wind and sun and water."

She returned his embrace. "You should come with me next time." He kissed her neck and she wiggled in his arms. He loved how ticklish she was.

She stepped away. "You haven't eaten. I'll make something." She started pulling out knives, the cutting board.

He came up behind her. "I've never seen you in jeans. God, woman. All I can think about is getting inside them, bending you over that butcher block."

She arched into him. "You need to eat." He slid his hand down her belly, lifting the hem of her shirt to feel the skin of her abdomen.

"I'll tell you what. If I slide my hand in here and you're not agreeable, I will let you cook." Branna sucked in a breath, bucking her hips. She started panting, arching her back. "If you are slippery and ready for me, dinner can wait," he said in her ear. When he slid his hand in her jeans, he knew he'd won.

BRANNA WAS PREPARING a quick dinner while Michael showered. It was late. He'd enjoyed the rewards of his little experiment, twice. The first time, he had indeed bent her over the butcher block. He never rushed. He always made sure she was fully satisfied. The thought of it made her tingle all over. He emerged from his room with wet hair, dressed in a pair of shorts and t-shirt. She'd started a fire in the hearth, so he went to start one in her room. After that he went to start one in his. "Why are you making a fire in there?"

He looked at her shyly. "I didn't want to assume."

She walked over to him. “Do you want to stay in your own room?”

He shook his head. “Not at all.”

She wrapped her arms around him. “Then save the fuel. I’ll warm you.”

Michael fiddled with Branna’s iPod while she worked in the kitchen. He saw a playlist named “Three Months”. He hit the list and his gut clenched when he saw the songs. They were all familiar. All songs she’d either heard them sing during the sessions at the pub, or songs they’d done on open mic night. He closed his eyes at the last. The songs that they’d danced to at the wedding. *Three Months*. She was documenting their time with music. A wave of panic seized him at the thought of coming to the end of that time period. Christ, how could he let her go? Did she really think he’d just toss her out? He didn’t know where this was headed, but he knew that three months would not be enough. He would show her. Words weren’t enough. He’d show her with his actions how he felt about her.

Michael and Branna enjoyed a light dinner together. He stopped her as she started cleaning up. “I have a surprise for you,” Michael said.

Branna smiled. “Another one? That beautiful piano wasn’t enough?”

He continued, “Well, this is for both of us, really. That is, if you’re game. I can undo it if you aren’t.”

She sat up straight, “Now I’m intrigued. What’s the surprise?”

He was fiddling with his food, a little nervous. “I took eight days off of work. I have plenty of time saved. I thought maybe it was time for you to see Ireland. I booked a holiday for us starting three days from now.” She shot out of her seat and launched herself into his lap. She straddled him in the chair and kissed his face all over.

“Oh, Michael! Thank you! Where are we going? Holy shit, I am so excited!” She just kept kissing his face.

He cupped her ass in his hands and laughed. “I love this kind of gratitude.”

When she calmed down, he continued. “Well, we will start in Dublin. I decided we needed a second crack at that.”

She beamed, "Yes, we do. Are we staying with Liam?"

He looked at her, astonished. "Hell no, woman. I'm not staying with my brother and his nasty roommate, sleeping on the beer stained couch. I booked hotels and guest houses everywhere but Belfast. We'll stay with Aidan that night. He has a guest room."

She was wiggling with excitement. "Newgrange, Trim, up to the North to see Aidan in Belfast, then along the Antrim Coast to Donegal and down to Galway." He threaded his hand in her hair and brushed her lips with his. "We'll explore, eat, and make love. A real vacation."

Branna just took his face in her hands. "You are so good to me."

She kissed him deeply. She went to hop up. "I need to pack!"

He grabbed her hips. "Hold, lass. I like you just where you are." He started trying to nibble through her shirt. She ran her fingers through his hair and rolled her hips. "You just had me twice."

He stopped what he was doing and looked at her, challenge in his gaze. "You think I can't go for a third?" When he said it, his accent was heavy, all hard Ts and rolled Rs.

She gave him a wry look, "Well, you are a bit older than I am."

He choked on a laugh and pulled her pelvis into his hardness. "You have a thing or two to learn about O'Brien men."

She leaned over, pressed her mouth to his ear. "Where will you have me now, O'Brien?"

He turned and kissed her hard. "Right on this feckin chair."

As Michael sorted laundry for the impromptu holiday, he thought about Branna. She had come to him a virgin, but she was so sensuous. Maybe that came with the fact that she wasn't some immature teenager when she'd shed her virginity, but a grown woman who was ready to embrace her sexuality. He'd never craved a woman like this before. The more he had her, the more he wanted her.

When he'd slipped his hand between her legs, she'd been drenched with arousal. He teased her until she'd begged him to get inside her. She'd been soft and submissive and whimpering as he bent her over the butcher block, pulled her pants down to her knees and shoved into her. She arched up, curling her lower back as she let her release roll through her. He fisted her hair in the back so he could see her face as she climaxed, smiling and dazed as he felt her grip him, riding out the orgasm with delicious leisure. Then she'd been wild as he pounded into her against the door. She screamed and bucked her hips against him as he took her hard. When he'd had her the third time, she'd straddled him on that chair, head thrown back, riding him as she dug her nails in his shoulders. Hungry and intense, she'd done the taking.

He couldn't get enough of her. Her lovemaking was like the changing coastal weather. Sometimes warm and calm, sometimes wild and stormy. She took everything he gave her. She held nothing back, giving her whole body, mind, and soul to him when they made love.

The fact that she'd never had another lover both elated and puzzled him. They were perfect together. He'd taken a few experienced women to his bed. Even his ex-wife had been with a few men before him. The fact that Branna had already learned to read her own body as well as his, spoke to the rare gift that was between them. Theirs was a deep connection, not due merely to physical attraction, but to the emotional bond that had forged between them. He felt fiercely protective of her. It scared him sometimes, the thought of her out there in the world, somewhere without him. He knew it was too soon to feel that way, but he couldn't help it.

Passion sated, the edge was off both Michael and Branna as they crawled into bed. Branna had her little pink boxers and mini-tee on as she slipped in next to him. Michael reached for her, pulling her shirt over her head. "Don't worry lass, I'm not gonna jump you again. I just like the feel of you." He pull her over his chest and nestled her head under his chin. He kissed her head. "Dublin has all of the good shopping. I'll take you out to the shopping district while we are there. You can get some winter clothes."

She nodded and replied, "Great, but this isn't a shopping trip. I know that. My experience is that shopping should be the smallest part of a trip. It isn't about stuff. It's about learning. Art, architecture, gardens, food, people. That is what I love."

He tilted her head up. "A woman who doesn't like to shop? Caitlyn would be scandalized." He kissed her nose as she giggled.

"Probably. I just know some things about life that she doesn't," she said.

He perked up, "Oh, and what is that?"

She was quiet for a few moments, and then she answered. "I know about loss. Experiences mean more than things. Shopping doesn't make memories."

Michael pulled her closer, absorbing what she'd said. "Then memories it is," he said. "Sleep, now. We'll see Miriam tomorrow to finalize it all."

CHAPTER 20

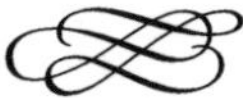

The drive to Dublin went markedly better the second time around. Branna worked, though. With the local phone she'd acquired, her reception was great and this was the time for her to get cracking on her final philanthropic hoorah. Brendan Sullivan had agreed to take this help, and she was going to make it work if it killed her. Her first phone call was to a Boston medical facility. She had Navy friends up there in the medical community that put her in touch with exactly what she needed. She found a doctor to collaborate with Mary Flynn.

He was second generation Irish-American and had grown up in Southie not far from her father. The details of Brendan's case had fascinated him. He wanted to know all of the every day tasks that Brendan would be doing as a fisherman if he had two arms, then what he was able to do with his current prosthetic. New England had a thriving fishing community, he had never considered working with injured fisherman to get them back to work. Next was her big challenge.

"You're really going to try and do this? Those prosthetics are thousands of dollars." Michael asked in amazement.

She smiled. "Do or not do, there is no try."

He laughed, "Is that some great American business tycoon's advice?" She shook her head, "Nope, Yoda. Star Wars Trilogy."

When they pulled into the small hotel near St. Stephen's Green, Branna was bopping up and down in her seat. "Where are we going first? I want to see the river! Can we see the Book of Kells? Holy crap I can't believe we are here!"

He moaned. "Stop, you are making me sad."

She asked, "Why would my happiness make you sad?" He sighed. "Because I had you here already, and instead of taking you to all of those places, I chased you off with tears in your eyes."

She took his hand and patted him. She gave him a look of complete sincerity. "That was the evil, mistrustful, prickish Michael. I exorcised that demon with my charm and wit and sexy body."

Michael burst out laughing and grabbed her head, kissing her. "That you did." They went into the lobby and checked in. The room was small and had no windows. "Sorry love, this is what was open last minute. Well, open and affordable."

She replied with a wave of her hand, "It's clean, perfectly located, there's a head down the hall, and…" she wiggled her brows at him. "It has a bed. We don't need anything else. Besides, we won't be here much. I am going to walk this town like a madwoman."

Michael should stop being surprised by Branna. If he had taken Fiona to this little, plain room with no en-suite WC she would have walked back out to the car. He took her hands in his and asked her, "Ok, so where to first?"

She knew where and answered without hesitation. "Trinity College, then Christ Church."

Branna was hands down the best traveling companion he'd ever had. She loved everything about the experience. She talked to people, took pictures, asked questions. When she went into the Long Room in Trinity College she was speechless. She just stared, fingers over her lips, absorbing every detail.

She would shut her eyes and he knew she was taking a mental picture, trying to store the vision. Her eyes were full of amazement and wonder as she bent silently over the old manuscripts held at Trinity. She sighed, "*The Book of Kells*. My father told me about this. He loved the artwork. He used to doodle it on the paper margins of my history notes. I would get to school and find it. *Remember your own history*. That's what he marked below the sketching."

"Your father sounds like a wonderful man. What about your mother?"

She shrugged, "She was Irish, too. She never really got into it like he did. She never dug around for her family records or tried to find out where her people were from. She just said that was dad's thing. She humored him, letting him play his music, read his books. She was supportive." She paused, "She just didn't have her own journey. She was on his journey. Does that make sense?"

Michael understood. Women were like that. Not all of them, but a lot of women abandoned all of their dreams and derailed when a husband and kids came into the picture. "Well then, lunch and then Christ Church?" She nodded excitedly.

They had lunch at a local pub that Michael liked. "Just try it. Open up."

She got a look of distaste on her face. "It's fried fish."

He sighed, "It's fish and chips and it's delicious. Just take a bite. So many of these pubs aren't Irish owned anymore. Their food is for shite. This is done right. Crispy heaven." He shook his head at her, "If you can't eat fish and chips then you don't have a lick of Irish blood in you."

She took a bite and was surprised how crispy and airy the breading was. The fish was firm and white and fresh. She looked at him, trying to play it off. Then she snatched the whole filet out of his hand. He just grinned victoriously. "I told you. Why do you doubt me?"

She pushed her vegetable soup at him, "You can have that."

Christ Church was beautiful. Michael watched as Branna ran her hand over the tomb of Richard the Strongbow. "I've read these stories so many times. It's like I know the people." Next was the Viking Ireland museum next to the church called Dublinia.

"You know that this museum is for children?" he mocked.

She just turned to him, grabbed his shirt and pulled him to the ticket booth. “So channel your inner child.”

Michael watched Branna with pleasure. She went through all of the sections of the family museum, commenting and reading up on Viking Ireland. She took pictures, asked questions, and she played. She got to the interactive section where the children were making rubbings of the runes, and she sat down with them, telling them how pretty their pictures were. She put the Viking helmet on, grabbed a shield and played shield maiden with two little sisters. It struck him as he watched her that she would be a wonderful mother. She didn't have siblings, but she'd had a good life when she was small. That much was obvious. She knew how to play. He never grew tired of watching her.

As Branna and Michael sat across from Liam in Temple Bar, Branna was giggling and shaking her head. Liam gave her a patient look, “Branna, darlin, I came into this crowded tourist trap for you. Now it is time to pay the piper. Ye cannot live in Ireland if you won't even try it.”

She smiled mischievously, “How about Baileys? That has whiskey in it.”

He gave her an indulgent smile, “Baileys is for breakfast and for pussies.”

Michael swatted him on the head with the bar menu. “It is! You told me that when I was twelve!” Branna straightened her spine.

Liam knew he had her. She had an ego as big as any O'Brien's. “Well, lass. If you can't handle a little dram of whiskey, I can see if they've got some juice boxes in the back. Do you need a straw?”

She gave him the evil eye, “I know what you're doing.”

He smiled innocently, “I just offered to get you a drink, girl. I understand completely. Moving to America often waters down the blood line, makes the next generation weak from too much McDonalds.”

She swatted his arm. “Give me the drink.”

Michael was shaking his head laughing. Branna had met her match. Liam could've gotten Mother Theresa drunk. She smelled it and her brows shot up. She exhaled, readying herself. Michael put his hand on her arm. "This isn't Tequila on spring break. Don't shoot it. Take your time. Sip it. Smell it. Let it slide over your whole mouth. Good whiskey is like good sex. Take your time and pay attention."

Liam whistled. "Damn, brother. You need to write that down. I need to remember that for the lasses." Michael winked at him.

Branna toasted them, "Here's mud in your eye" and took her first sip.

Michael and Liam watched her expectantly. She winced a little from the intensity of it. Michael and Liam took a sip as well. "Let it sink in, wash over you, slide down to your belly."

She closed her eyes concentrating. "There are a few tastes. It's hard to describe. Sweet, smokey, tangy. It's comforting, though. Like rubbing your muscles when you're sore."

Liam looked at her questioningly. "How so?"

She thought about it. "Well, it hurts a little, but then it feels good. Soothing."

He smiled, "There's a good lass." He clinked her glass. "Now you're a local." She beamed, and Michael took her chin and kissed her.

Branna excused herself to the restroom and the two brothers sat together. Liam had a pint and his brother a club soda. "One drink? Where is Michael O'Brien? Get ye away changeling!" Michael laughed. His brother had a way with words.

"I have to walk back to the hotel, not stumble. I've got Branna with me. I need to have my wits."

Liam stared at his brother, "Jesus. You really have it bad for her don't you? You're like Da with Mam. Protective and serious." He wasn't joking. He looked intensely at Michael. Then his face changed. "Aye, I'm sure it's got nothing to do with the fact that you need your wits once you get back to that hotel room and have her all to yourself."

Michael's silence spoke volumes. He suppressed a grin. Liam snorted in disgust, jealousy plain on his face. "Drink your bubbly water, ye lucky fucker."

As they walked back to the hotel, Branna was smiling widely. Michael spoke, “You had a good day.”

Not a question, but she answered it. “Yes, it was wonderful. I can’t believe this was only the first day.”

He put his arm around her small shoulders. “So I’m forgiven for making a cock-up of it the first time?”

She stopped and looked up at him. “You were forgiven that night, when you apologized. Now I just have to show proper gratitude.” She leaned into him and very discretely pressed her palm to his groin. He hissed and jerked in her hand. “Does that thing ever go down?” She started walking again, swaying her hips to catch his eye.

His voice was smooth and low. “Not when you’re near me. Never when you’re near me.”

They used the communal bathrooms to clean up and ready for bed. Michael was already in the room when Branna came in wearing a robe. He was in bed, reading. He looked up and she had that look in her eye. He put his book aside. “Something on your mind, hellcat?” he crooned.

She approached and undid the tie to her robe. She slid it off her shoulders and let it fall. She had on a lilac lace bra and a matching set of very small panties. So small in fact that he ground his teeth, “Turn around.” She did and he popped up on his knees, eyes wide. A silky, lacy, little lilac thong sweeping down and disappearing. Her ass was spectacular. Her black hair was spreading down to her tail bone.

He crooked his finger at her. His face was utterly reverent, as he looked her up and down. She climbed up on the bed, kneeling as he was, close but not touching. He put one hand at the small of her back and his breath shuddered. “You are so beautiful.” He kissed her soft and deep as he slid both hands under her arms to her shoulder blades. He pulled her to him then slowly slid his hands down her back and over her gorgeous bottom. “You have the most beautiful, perfect ass.”

He felt her press him over onto the bed. She sat up and slid his boxers off and then just looked at him. He was hard and ready, and his chest was pumping with labored breath. “Christ, O’Brien. You are beautiful." She ran her hand up his arm, over his shoulder, then down his chest. She ran a nail over his hard nipple and he hissed.

He pulled her on top of him. He kissed her as he ran his hands all over her body. She never undressed, she just rolled her hips on top of him until he was on the verge of losing his mind. She pushed his hands on the bed and pinned them to the mattress, and she intensified what she did to his mouth. Then she started inching down, kissing his chest. She nipped his nipples as she reached down to stroke him. "Branna!" He bit out.

"Just lay back. I want you in my mouth, Michael." He cursed in what she could only assume was Gaelic. She nibbled his abs as she worked her way down.

"You're killing me." He felt her smile as she kissed him. "God, your hair is everywhere. I can feel it everywhere," he groaned.

She talked softly as she kissed him, "I want all of you." She paused, "I've never done this. I want to."

He was watching her, breathing hard. "You don't have to."

She looked at him, doubt creeping on her face. "Don't you want me to?"

His laughter was deep and husky. "Do I want your sweet, little mouth on my cock? Did you actually just ask me that?" Before he could continue, she put her hand around him and licked the tip. All his breath flew out of him as his hips jerked. She gave her own husky laugh. She ran her tongue from the base all the way up the length of him. He moaned and she felt powerful. He was completely at her mercy.

Michael watched as she knelt over him, on all fours, in that lilac ensemble. Her breasts were heavy and round and hanging down right behind his erection. Her hair was slung over one shoulder and tickling his thigh. She slowly took him in her mouth, her head going down as her ass tilted up in that thong. He grabbed the pillow above his head and squeezed his eyes shut. Was it possible to go blind from watching something this hot? She came back up and sank down again, cupping his balls in her other hand.

He bowed off the bed. "Branna, I need you. Come up here." He was going to come if she kept it up, and he needed to finish inside her.

She stopped at the top. "You have me. I'm right here." Then she circled the tip, following up with running her closed lips down the ridge of him and back up.

"Branna!" He could hear the pillow case tearing. "I need inside you, come up here!"

She just gave an evil little laugh and started again. Her blue eyes were full of arousal and mischief as she looked up from her task, and he knew he couldn't keep this up, as exquisite as the torture was. He gathered her hair in his hands and watched her. He was groaning, a sheen of sweat breaking out all over him with the effort of not letting go.

He sat up and grabbed her, throwing her on her back. She giggled as he flipped her over and started nibbling her ass. "You are learning fast, but I'm still bigger than you." He bit her ass and she squeaked. He tipped her back over on her back, slipped her thong off, lifted one of her knees up and drove into her. He took her head and cradled it, kissing her. "Look at me, darlin. I want to see your eyes when you come," he whispered.

THE NEXT DAY Michael and Branna left the room for breakfast. As they walked out of the room, their neighbors came out as well. It was two women who looked to be sisters. They both gave Michael an appraising look. Branna scowled a little, not thinking they'd notice. Michael went into the men's bathroom while she went into the women's. The girls followed her, did their business, and they all ended up at the sink together. "You can hardly blame us, neighbor."

She looked at the one sister. They were American by the sounds of it. The other one finished her thought. "Thin walls." Branna choked out a laugh and covered her face. "You've got nothing to be shy about, girl. We heard him too, he was even louder than you. Bravo." They gave her a little golf clap and she giggled, red-faced and horrified.

They all three walked out giggling; Branna's face the color of a tomato. Michael was waiting for her. "What's all the fun about, then?" he asked.

Both the women stopped and looked at her. The older of the two spoke, "He's Irish, too? Forget what I said. We hate you." All three giggled again. The younger waved, staring at Michael as they left.

"What the hell was that all about?"

Branna rubbed her upper lip. "Apparently they were impressed with our audio performance last night. Thin walls."

He chuckled. "Well, you are a screamer. You're welcome."

She nudged him, "They said you were louder. You're welcome."

He laughed and smacked her butt as they walked down the hallway. "Did you just throw down a challenge?"

* * *

After a morning visit to St. Patrick's Cathedral and the surrounding gardens, they packed up the car and headed to County Meath. Newgrange and the Hill of Tara were on the day's agenda, lunch and then Trim Castle where they would spend the night. "I decided to spend the night in Trim instead of Dublin. I think you'll like this place. It's a lot different." Branna just stared out the window, admiring sheep, houses, trees, anything that caught her eye. It thrilled him that she loved his beautiful Eire as much as he did.

When the bus pulled up to the passage tomb at Newgrange, Branna was speechless. She walked up slowly, taking every detail in as she went. The tour guide was an older gentleman with a long red and white beard. She put a shaking hand on the entrance stone. Swirling carvings of Neolithic man. Michael watched her as she hung on every word of the tour guide's lesson.

She stood inside the tomb, dark and otherworldly. Her breathing was shallow, her body trancelike. "You feel it? You feel the stones and those who placed them here?" She just looked at him, dazed. "What is your name, girl?" he asked.

"It's Branna."

He nodded, "Aye, Brannaugh, the raven. Many Celtic Goddesses are associated with the raven. The Vikings as well. It is a symbol of war and darkness and specifically of death in battle. Does that mean anything to you?" Michael tried to cut him off, but then to his horror saw Branna go over. The guide caught her right before her head hit the stone.

"Is she claustrophobic?" The woman talking was a concerned older woman. Michael had carried her out of the tomb and she was already coming to awareness.

The guide spoke. "It's something I said. That's right, isn't it?"

Michael looked at him, about to tear his head off. "Her father was killed in battle in Iraq. Jesus, did you have to be so honest?"

The man didn't waiver, "It was him who named her. He's the blood tie to this place. He brought her here. She's come home." Michael looked at him oddly. "She'll stay," the man said simply. The hair on Michael's neck stood up on end.

"Michael, I'm ok. I just got a little woozy. I swear, I'd tell you if I wasn't."

He looked her over, still concerned. "Have you ever fainted before?"

She shook her head. "Never, I ate and had plenty of water. I don't know what happened. I'm sorry I scared everyone. Is the tour over?" He kissed her head. "This one is, yes."

Branna seemed completely fine after the incident at Newgrange, but they skipped The Hill of Tara and drove straight to Trim. They opted for an Indian place for lunch. "This is gorgeous, try this one." Michael put his fork in Branna's mouth and she chewed with pleasure. "It's hard to find good Indian food in the South. This is like nothing I've ever had before, though. It's delicious."

They ate and rehydrated before taking the Trim Castle tour. "So this is a Norman castle. Hugh de Lacy, not so loved by the locals, I take it."

Michael shook his head. "Definitely not. Then the modern day war started when the government okayed a 3 story hotel right across from it."

Branna nodded, "I see their point. We're not staying there, I take it? Being locals and all." He smiled at that. "What? I drank whiskey. Liam said I'm in the club!"

He pulled her in for a kiss. "Yes, you are at that."

Branna was exhausted by the time the tour was over. When Michael took her to the hotel, she was stunned. Not a hotel, but an eighteenth century house with stoned arches and lush gardens. There were also views of the River Boyne and the castle. The room was furnished in antiques with down bedding and colorful artwork. She walked over to the window and spread the shutters. They had a view of the beautiful gardens that were filled with end of the season blooms.

She turned to Michael, eyes misting. "This is wonderful. You didn't have to do this. I would have stayed anywhere as long as we were together."

He went to the window and looked out, then he pulled her to him. "That's why you deserve it." He kissed her on the head, content to hold her.

She sighed. "The breeze is nice and it's so peaceful. Let's take a nap." They curled together in the bed, a breeze flowing through the room, and slept.

Michael returned to the room after his trip to town. As he came to the door, he heard her. He knew the sounds, unfortunately. She was having another nightmare. The room had become darker. It was still light out, but the day had clouded over and it was dinnertime. Her covers were off. He checked her head, no fever. "Branna, love. It's me. Wake up, Branna."

She jolted and gasped. She started to tear up when she saw him. She grabbed him and clutched his shirt. She just smelled him, trembling in his arms. "You're here."

He rubbed her back slowly. "Yes, darling. It's all right. I'm here. Do you want to tell me about it?" She looked at him, wiping her tears. She shook her head. "One of these days you are going to learn to trust me," he said sadly.

She could tell it hurt him when she wouldn't talk to him, but she couldn't. The dream was awful. Her father was there and she was so happy to see him. Then she looked at his feet. There was blood on his boots and a raven was on the ground. It squawked at her. Her father looked at her, "Does he know? Fly to your nest, Raven. You need your nest."

Branna was shaking in his arms. She was starting to worry him. First she fainted, then she came home and slept in the afternoon which she never did. Now another nightmare, and it had been a bad one from the looks of her. "It's ok, it was just a dream, Michael. I smell food. What did you bring?"

He pulled her off the bed. "I thought we could picnic in the garden. I bought some wine." He kissed her, pulling her back from her nightmare.

She pressed her forehead to his as he bent down. She closed her eyes and just felt him. His head, his face, his strong shoulders. "Thank you."

They dressed warmly and took a spare blanket out to enjoy the gardens. There were iron chaise lounges outside and chairs and tables. He had a selection of soups, salads, and fresh bread. Michael bought a white burgundy, which they drank out of juice glasses. "Where did you get the dishes?"

He grinned. "Nicked them from the breakfast area." They ate in peaceable silence. "How are you feeling? Any dizziness?"

She shook her head, "No, I feel fine. The nap did me good. Where to next? To see Aidan?"

Michael brightened, "Yes. I haven't been to see him up at his place since he got back. I'm looking forward to it. It's hard when there are so many people around."

"What branch is Aidan serving? I thought the Irish Army kept it local, like our National Guard."

He nodded in agreement. "Aye, they do mostly. He's part of the Royal Irish Regiment. My mother and grandparents are Northern Irish. Catholics of course, just in the North. My ma moved down when she married Da. We spent time up here with family though, through our childhood. Aidan always liked the city. I think he was ready to break away a little. Being the oldest of six is a big responsibility. I think this was his way of grabbing a little independence, though he visits a lot when he lives in the North. When he was with 1st Battalion, we didn't see him as much. He was in England and deployed a lot."

He continued, "Aidan went to school up there, stayed in Ma's old flat. When your 9-11 attacks happened, things changed. There was a ceasefire in '94, but when that happened in America, then the bombing on the London Tube, there seemed to be a genuine shift. Maybe they realized that we needed to stop fighting amongst ourselves and see the real evil." Michael shook his head, "Ma begged him not to, but he enlisted about a year and a half after the Prime Minister publicly announced that the UK would be fighting alongside the Americans."

"He was living at the Belfast flat at the time, just finished his seventh semester of school. One semester away from his degree and he just left school and did it. Finished college on the internet that next year and became an officer. The Brits were taking casualties just like the Americans. He never felt that division with the British or the Protestants like they did a few decades back. He didn't think about whether the guy next to him was Welsh or English or a Scot or an Irishman. All he knew was that they needed strong leaders, men willing to fight, and he went."

Michael shrugged, "He said he had to, and I didn't question it. Da understood, too. He was Garda for twenty-five years. It's hard to stand by and do nothing when you might be able to help. This was his fourth deployment. I don't know anyone who has gone more than him. He just seems born to it."

Branna asked, "How often does that happen? The incident with the champagne?"

His eyes grew sad. "A few times that I've seen. Loud noises, crowds, strange things like men with backpacks. You can see the change in him. He gets tense, starts sweating. He hides it pretty well, but if you pay attention you can tell. He gets headaches and has nightmares, too. Don't tell Ma. I tried to talk to him about it. He says he's fine, just adjusting to being back."

Branna put her fork down. "Sorcha knows, believe me. That is her first born, and nothing gets past her when it comes to her children."

When they finished cleaning up, Michael pulled her down onto the chaise lounge. "Take me to bed, hellcat. I need you."

She stretched languorously over him. "What exactly do you need?" she purred as she teased his mouth. "Tell me in vivid detail." He pulled her head back and told her, in vivid detail. Then he pulled her mouth back down to his and she roared to life. They barely made it to their room.

* * *

THE DRIVE UP to Belfast was beautiful. Michael explained a little bit about the peace lines and the ceasefire. The wall and gate in Alexander Park had been painted with symbols of peace, hope and healing. The collisions in that notorious area had lessened significantly. "Ma's flat, now Aidan's, is on Springfield. It's in West Belfast" He paused, "Listen, you need to stay with me or Aidan. There's more crime in Belfast. It's just how things are. He's in a nice enough building since the re-urbanization. She never lived in one of the really bad areas by Divis flats, but they had their problems during the Troubles. No one was safe on either side of the conflict. You just can't take your safety for granted. This isn't Fisher Street or even Temple Bar. Do you understand? It's a beautiful city, but it's a city. Drugs, thugs, crime."

Branna squeezed his hand. "I understand."

Branna was amazed when they arrived in Belfast. It seemed like a regular bustling city until you took a closer look. There were indeed walls and gates erected through the big city. They were peace walls now, but they were segregation walls not so long ago. It gave her a chill to think about what Sorcha's life had been like as a girl. How on earth had she met Sean? That was a story she was looking very forward to getting the details on someday.

Michael noticed her tense as she looked at the segregation walls. "It's intense, I know. It's hard to imagine, Irishmen killing Irishmen. This was a brutal place to live for a long time. Ma lived there during some of the worst times. Car bombings, IRA collisions with the government. My grandparents had moved to a small house outside the city, and she took the flat while she went to school. She didn't want to stop her studies or leave her friends, and they let her stay, which they now admit was not the best idea."

"Protestants and Catholics beating each other in the street, rumor has it she had a brush with what they think were the Shankill Butchers." Branna could see the hair standing up on Michael's arm, and she shivered. "During the worst of it, my father showed up in the middle of the riots, practically dragged her out of the city, and took her over the border. She'd tell it better than I, but I think her words compared him to a barbarian caveman."

Branna stifled a giggle. She really did need to hear the whole story. Michael continued, "I never remembered any of that, though. The violence, that is. It was later and we just hung out at Grans, oblivious the way children are."

Branna looked out the window and thought about this city she was seeing for the first time. She wished she could step into the past, see it through Sorcha's eyes. She hadn't even been born yet and Sorcha's very own O'Brien mate had whisked her out of the turmoil and danger to claim her. They were still together. *What an amazing love story,* she thought, longing for something she knew she shouldn't want.

They arrived at Aidan's place just before lunch. Michael had a key, so they went into his flat before he was home. "He should be here shortly. He took a half day off, but it's a little drive."

Branna was surprised, "He doesn't work in Belfast?"

Michael shook his head, "No, the unit is posted about 40 minutes away in Portadown. He lives here because we already had the property. No reason to rent down there when he can live here cheaply. My parents tried to refuse the rent, but he insisted. He told them he'd move elsewhere if they didn't take the money."

She smiled at that. "Yes, pride is a thing with men."

Michael looked at her with a mocking grin, "Right, I forgot. Thank God for level headed women." She nodded, agreeing. Then he put on a fake American accent and put one hand on his hip and another pointing. In falsetto, he mocked, "You don't know the first thing about O'Mara women. I will eat your lunch!"

Branna suppressed a begrudging grin. Then she turned and poked his chest. "Don't forget it." He grabbed her hand and pulled her in, kissing her. "You are spectacular when you're in a temper." They heard the door unlatch and Aidan walked in.

Branna's heart lurched in her chest as Aidan came through the door. He was in his cammies, hat and rucksack in his hands. He dropped his bag by the door, hung his beret up on a hook and walked in. He gave Michael a big bear hug. "Good to see you so soon, again." He turned to Branna, warmth in his face. She took note again how much he looked like Michael. His eyes had no ring of green, but instead clear and blue like Sean's.

They were only two years apart. He was about an inch taller and more muscular, his face a little older, not by the lines, but by the eyes. She knew the look well. Eyes that had seen horrible things had a different look about them, shadows. Michael's eyes were more innocent. Aidan's eyes were the mix of a twenty-five year police veteran and a mother who grew up a Catholic in Belfast.

"Hello, Branna. How's your holiday going?" his eyes were kind.

She brightened and answered, "Wonderful. Everything has been wonderful." He kissed her cheek, "Glad you came to see me. How about Michael takes your things in the spare room and you and I mix up a bit of lunch?" She nodded. Aidan started milling around the kitchen when he stopped. Branna was looking at his boots. He stopped, putting down the pan he was holding. "Christ, lass. I didn't think. I'll go change."

She shook her head vigorously, "No! Please. I was just…" She paused, not sure whether to open the door. "I was thinking about a dream I had last night, it's not you. I love your uniform. You look so handsome. Leave it on. I was always so proud to see my dad in his uniform."

He looked at her and she could tell he was still debating. "What kind of dream?"

She shuddered. "Not a good one. It's just subconscious stuff, boiling over. Anytime you have life kick the shit out of you, it is bound to back up on you some way, right?"

He understood. "Yes, I understand that very well. Now, I'm done for the day. If you give me a minute, I'm going to go ahead and change. I don't want to soil my uniform. It is still pretty clean and I hate doing the wash. Chop those herbs and I'll be right back."

Aidan was changing his clothes in his room and his chest ached. He'd made the lame excuse about the wash, but he knew it hurt Branna to see him milling around the house in his uniform. Michael had told him about the nightmares. Whatever she saw on his boots, he was going to lay it to rest for the day.

Ten years in the infantry had taught him one thing. A wife and children at home was heartache waiting to happen. He watched his friends mourn every day, opening letters from their wives and colored artwork from their kids. His regiment hadn't taken a lot of casualties. He'd worked with other units, though. Americans, English, even some time with his Afghani counterparts. He'd even worked with the US Marines like her father. He'd seen dead fathers, dead husbands, dead sons. He was never going to put a woman he loved through that, or give her children to orphan. Never.

* * *

BRANNA AND MICHAEL spent the afternoon touring Belfast castle. There was an antique shop near the castle, and they stopped to browse. Michael noticed that Branna seemed to like several items, but she never bought anything.

He remembered the conversation Brigid had told him about. Branna had told her that she made a modest living, but that she'd made this move to Ireland on a very specific budget. She wasn't paying rent right now, but she seemed hesitant to buy herself any unnecessary items. Her winter clothes shopping had been efficient and practical. She didn't want to browse the big designers or tarry in the shops. She wasn't materialistic, he realized. How had he ever thought her a greedy Yank with a fat wallet?

He noticed that she was looking at a lot of teacups. She was a coffee drinker, but he had put her on a one cup a day regiment, and she'd developed a taste for tea. When she moved on, he went over to take a look. The one she seemed to admire was bone china with a pattern from *The Book of Kells*. He took it discreetly to the cashier, and then he hid it under his spare jumper in the daypack.

After meeting Aidan for early dinner, they headed back to the flat. Branna did some work while the men drank and smoked cigars on the balcony. It was five hours earlier on the East Coast. When she screeched, both men jumped up and ran into the apartment.

"What's wrong?" Michael looked at her face, "Oh, well then. What's right?" She was dancing around the kitchen with the phone in her hand. She stopped. "I did it. Brendan's arm, I freaking did it!" She leapt in Michael's arms.

"What's she talking about? Brendan Sullivan, the fisherman?" Aidan asked.

Michael was laughing and nodded. "How the hell did you pull it off? You were thousands short."

She was beaming. "You, my dear, are in the presence of genius."

Michael rolled his eyes, "Aye, you keep telling me. So?"

"Well, as you know Brendan thought he had about half saved for the prosthetic. Unfortunately, it was a little more like a third, but the prosthetic I can get in the states is far superior. He'd need to pay a doctor, though. So, you know I got the doctor in Boston on board. He agreed to let Mary do the x-rays and send the measurements. There are a few costs, but he is doing a big chunk of it pro-bono. He wants the press exposure for his practice, wants to reach out to the fishing community in New England. There was still the problem of the other two-thirds. My foundation has another huge chunk to add, but I needed to run it through a US non-profit. I can't just give it to Brendan. I have to be able to have it be a legitimate charitable donation. Plus I need help with the rest of the cost."

She continued, "I called the Boston Irish American Society where my dad was a lifetime member. He stayed tight with the group. They even sent flowers to his..." She paused and shook herself. "Anyway, I told them all about Brendan. They have a non-profit attached to their club. They agreed to channel my donation through them before I close the foundation." She started jumping up and down now. "They also agreed to donate a good chunk of money toward the balance of his medical equipment!"

Michael and Aidan were incredulous. "Why would some group in Boston do that for a Doolin fisherman?"

She smiled, "Well, that's where the pitch comes in. Listen and learn, boys." She grinned, spreading her hands out as she told them. "I started telling them all about the town. They put me on conference call with two other board members. I told them how much he did for the community, about him being on a wait list and that his son worked the boat for him to help with his disability. I told them how humble he was, saying that he didn't deserve the help. That he hadn't gone to war and served the way the soldiers had. Then I told them how I convinced him. I swear I think one guy started crying." She took a deep breath. "So, they agreed. They agreed, with the promise that Brendan would come and have a drink with them at the club, tell his story. They want a re-cap of the Silkie Tale as well. I think they are going to try and bring in some funds that night. When they started thinking about the buzz it would cause if they were hosting a real Irish fisherman, wounded fishing the Clare Coast, well, these Irish American Society types eat this crap up! Oh!" she was doing the little dance again, "and they are taking him and his wife to a Boston Celtics game! One of the donors has box seats!"

Michael laughed, "Brendan will love that. He loves to weave a tale. They'll be enthralled. Not sure how he feels about American basketball, he's a rugby man, but I'm sure a night out for the two of them would be grand."

She was excited, nodding with agreement. "Exactly, now I only have to get the rest to pay for lodgings in Boston and about a thousand more for the arm."

Michael pointed out a deficit. "What about air tickets?" She just shrugged. "I have frequent flyer miles. I was going to donate them." He looked at her, his eyes burning with emotion. "You've done enough, Branna. Let us see if we can sort it out another way. You may need those miles."

She just looked down. "I don't have anyone to visit, unless I need them for," she hesitated, "for a return ticket. We have them if we need them."

Michael and Aidan were silent. It was obvious why she might need a return ticket. They all knew it. Aidan broke the tension. "So, how did you convince Brendan."

She blushed, "I just reminded him of who he was."

"And who is he?" he asked.

She told them everything she'd said to Brendan that day on the boat. "Holy God, woman. You've nearly got me tearing up." Aidan remarked. She smiled shyly. Aidan looked at her admiringly. "You're really good at this." He turned to Michael.

Michael was staring at her, pride gleaming in his eyes. "Yes, she is. You see the good in people. You help them to see it in themselves. You help people that don't like asking for help, and you let them keep their pride." She squirmed under his praise, but he continued. "You also find some way of bewitching doctors, Boston socialites, and volunteers to come on board."

She shrugged, "I told you. People are good. You just have to ask."

"So, what's the plan? It seems like you are talking maybe another three or four thousand. How are you going to pull it off? You can't take your own money, lass. You know Brendan will never stand for it and you can't lie to him."

She exhaled, "That's where you locals come in."

CHAPTER 21

Branna promised to ease off work unless they were on down time. They were on vacation. She did make a call to Ned, Sorcha, Jamie, and Tadgh telling them all that had transpired and her plans for the rest of the fundraising. The next few days flew by in a blur of good meals, beautiful ruins, seaside towns, and nights making love in their room. Branna reflected that she hadn't been this happy since she was a small child. The happiness was different in that she saw things with an adult heart and mind, remembered them more readily than a child's waning attention allowed. If she had nothing else after the next six weeks, she'd had these eight days.

Branna was so glad to be home. As much fun as they'd had, she missed the cottage and the people of her new home town. "Ma is insisting I bring you to dinner. She caught wind of our..." He blushed, "Well, you know, and then we skipped town. She's ready to box my ears."

Branna's eyes widened. "Oh, shit. I never thought of that Michael. They're good Catholics. What will they think of me?"

Michael chuffed a laugh. "She's got four grown sons and a married, pregnant daughter. She's seen it all. Besides, I have it on good authority my father plucked that rose before the nuptials."

Branna covered her mouth. "No."

He smiled, "Yes. Don't underestimate O'Brien men when they see something they want. He had every intention of marrying her, of course. He said he knew he loved her the first day. She was a bit of a handful, though. Convincing her was the tough part."

Branna rolled her eyes. "Please, Michael. I've seen your father. She was done for as soon as she looked up into those blue eyes. She just wasn't admitting it."

Michael walked over to her and pulled her close to him, forcing her to look up at him. "Is that so?" She nervously looked away, but he lifted her chin and caught her eyes again. Then he rubbed his lips to hers, back and forth, never breaking eye contact.

* * *

"You are brilliant, Branna. I can't believe the work you've done." Sorcha took Branna in her arms and hugged her. "You've got a big heart, dear. We'll do anything we can to help." Branna was smiling, absorbing the motherly approval she so missed. Branna felt a tug on her shirt.

It was Cora. She swept her into her arms. "Hello, monkey. Have you been a good girl?"

Cora nodded dramatically. "Yes, I showed Da what a good office helper I was. I took all of the papers and rearranged them all better." She struggled when she tried to say "rearranged" and Branna thought she was the most adorable little girl on earth.

Branna stifled a giggle and she looked at Brigid. Brigid gave her a look that suggested that "better" was a relative term. "Well, you must help me with the big party. We are going to get Mr. Sullivan a better arm."

Cora's eyes widened. "I thought he was a pirate, like on Peter Pan, but he said he was no' a pirate. He said he was a fisherman like Peter from the Bible."

Branna smiled at Sorcha, "That's very right. Do you want to be my big helper? I need to decorate and I need you to make some pretty pictures for me. Can you do that? "

Cora nodded, "Oh, yes. I'm good with my colors."

Branna kissed her face, "Okay, just leave your daddy's papers alone. I'll get you some really big paper!"

Cora clapped her hands and wiggled down. "Mama! Mama! Guess what!"

Michael watched Branna with Cora, his heart stirring. "She's good with the wee ones." Sean said next to him.

Michael came out of his reverie. "Yes, I suppose she is."

Sean's voice was low and serious. "Have you told her yet?"

Michael looked at him curiously, "Told her what?"

Sean answered, "That's she's the one."

Michael sighed, "Da, don't start. I haven't known her that long. There's a lot that complicates this situation."

His father looked at him, his impatience showing on his face. "Bullocks. I took one look at your mother and knew. Fiona was a diversion, a wrong turn. Don't screw up your one chance to have a true mate. You love her, I see it. The problem is she doesn't."

Michael looked away, and he watched Branna. "She knows I care for her."

Sean scoffed, "What the hell does that mean? You care for a dog or a wee kitten. You love a woman like that. You love her with everything you've got." He pointed at her. "You've not made yourself clear, because she's still got that look about her."

Michael was getting irritated, "What look?"

Sean exhaled, "Like she's taking notes, trying to remember us all. Like she knows the goodbye is coming!" Michael thought about the iPod playlist, *3 Months.* He walked over to his sister, leaving his father cursing under his breath.

Branna was playing thumb wars with Seany when Michael motioned for them to go. She messed up his hair and he blushed. As they walked outside, Michael nudged her. "You know that's a fifteen year old lad's way of getting to hold your hand?"

She laughed, "Did it work for you?"

He raised his eyebrows. "Who do ye think taught him that trick?"

* * *

Branna and Michael were getting ready for bed when he started making some herbal tea. Branna came in the kitchen and he asked, "Can you open that cabinet and hand me two cups, please?" She opened the cabinet and stopped. Resting in the front was *The Book of Kells* teacup she'd loved so much in the shop in Belfast. She pulled it down and turned to him.

He was leaning against the counter. "You seemed to like it, but you rarely buy yourself anything."

She hugged him. He pulled her close and smelled her hair. She knew he liked it down. She had shed the tight buns and braids everyday. She still did it sometimes, which he didn't mind either. Having her run around town with all that hair flowing would certainly turn heads. "You are so beautiful, Branna. Will you sing for me? Play a song while I make the tea?"

Michael loved listening to her play. The fact that she loved the piano he bought her was gift enough, but when she played and sang it was like she was giving him a gift. She was playing a Kate Bush song. He brought the tea in and rested it on the piano ledge. She finished and took a couple of sips. "I like my new cup. I like my new piano, too. You're spoiling me."

He smiled, "I like getting things for you. You're always grateful."

"I got you something, too. I was waiting to give it to you."

He leaned in and his eyes were hooded, "Is it another one of those little outfits like that night in Dublin?"

She rolled her eyes, "That's not a present."

He chuckled deep in his throat, "You are so wrong."

She went into her room. She hesitated just out of reach of him, "It's nothing big. It's a small thing, actually. I just liked it, and I thought of you when I saw it. But now I'm thinking it might be kind of silly. Your gifts are so beautiful."

He cut her off. "Come here, hen." She walked over to him like a child, hiding something behind her back. "Look at me." She looked at him, and she was a little red in the cheeks. "Branna, you are so beautiful and so kind. Anything you gave me would be a treasure. Now, let's have it."

She pulled a parcel from behind her. When he pulled the gift out of his bag, he had to fight the tears. It was a resin picture frame shaped a lot like their cottage. In it was a framed picture of them. She'd had Liam take their picture at Temple Bar. He'd not seen the photos yet. It wasn't them posing, like he remembered. It was afterward. She had her head back, laughing. His head was turned toward her face, his mouth by her ear smiling. Liam had taken it without them knowing. They looked really happy.

"I didn't know he took it until I thumbed through the photos. I printed it at a local camera place after I got the frame." She paused, swallowing hard. "I just wanted you to have it in case..."

He lurched out of the seat, pulled her off her feet. His hand was cradling her head, his mouth by her ear. "Don't say it." His voice broke. She nodded, unable to speak. He held her desperately. "I love it. It's the most precious gift anyone's ever given me."

* * *

THE NEXT MORNING Michael and Branna got up early. He showered for work while she made him breakfast. He sat down to eat while she was cleaning up. Her laptop was open and she had the memory card in, downloading their photos. The download stopped and the first picture popped up. It wasn't of Dublin or anywhere he had been with her. It was a photo of a dingy cottage. He scrolled through, seeing a cottage that was moldy and falling apart. His skin prickled as he saw the next few. A row house, shitty and plain. Then another similar to the second and they were all dated a few days before their trip. "Branna, what are these photos? Some sort of cottage and two row houses? These aren't from our trip."

Branna froze. Her face was still; she seemed to be figuring out how to answer. "I didn't mean for you to see those. I forgot about them, actually."

"When were you going to tell me you were house hunting?" Silence. He stood up, "How long have you been looking? What the fuck is going on Branna?"

She was clenching her jaw. "I started looking a couple of weeks ago."

He cursed, "Why? Nothing's been decided yet."

She gave him a pleading look. "I don't have family to fall back on Michael. I have to start looking now. Besides, I can't do it," she said.

He looked up from his pacing. "Do what?"

She came around the kitchen counter. "I can't take this cottage from you. You deserve it. You've lived in this town all of your life, your family is here. I'll tell Ned."

Michael slammed his hand on the table. "No, you won't tell him anything!"

She took a breath, calm to his fury. "Michael, you have to understand. Jack was helping me for you. So that you can be free of this stupid deal."

He pointed at the photo. "That place is for shite. None of them are something you would normally even consider. Am I right? It's not fair to you. Where else did you look? How far away?"

Tears were pricking her eyes as she swallowed hard, and calmly answered him. "He's searching some of the smaller towns around Dingle, Kerry, and Galway. I haven't talked to him for a few days, but it wasn't going well. If we can't find anything, I'll try inland."

He shook his head. "What if he doesn't find something?" More silence. "You listen to me, Branna O'Mara. You are not leaving!"

Her throat ached, and she could hear the strain in her voice, but she was not going to make this worse by breaking down. "I might have to, Michael. I don't want to leave. I've been so happy here. I just, I don't have unlimited choices. I made this mess and I know that. I'll be fine. I will land on my feet, like I always do. Please don't make it worse."

He stalked toward her and grabbed her face, kissing her hard. "I will make it worse," he growled at her mouth. He kissed her deep, pressing himself into her. She whimpered under his mouth. "Michael, please." Her resolve melted away, and in the wake, the tears overtook her.

He looked at her, faces inches apart. "Please what? Please let you be some bloody martyr? Can you walk away so easily?" Her face had tears pouring down it. His anger deflated in a shuddering breath. His kisses turned softer. Branna was touching his face, soothing him with her hands and mouth. "We wait. We wait for Ned. Then we sort out the particulars. I want you here with me, longer than six weeks. You're not leaving." He pressed his forehead to hers. "Don't do anything out of fear, Branna. Just wait."

She took a trembling breath, "Okay. I'll wait."

* * *

THE NEXT FEW days went by in a frenzy of phone calls, visits to shops and business. Branna walked into the local ancestry shop and heard the bell ding. She started browsing, looking at the different crests and lineage that were framed and adorning the walls. "Well, look what the cat dragged in." Deep, smokey Irish lilt. Shit.

She stifled the wave of dread, keeping her face even. "Hello Fiona, I didn't know you worked here. I'm sorry to bother you. Could I maybe talk to the owner?"

Fiona's posture was defensive, her eyes held a nasty gaze. "Sorry, he's on holiday. It is me or nothing. Have a nice day."

She turned to walk back into the office and Branna spoke. "Well, could you help me?"

Fiona turned, impatience obvious on her face. "Why would I do that?"

Branna said, "It's not for me, actually. It's for Brendan Sullivan."

Fiona's face changed, "Yes, I've heard about that. Some sort of charity dinner and auction. You've made quite a buzz around town, little Yank."

Branna said, "Why is it when some people call me that, it comes out like a nickname, and when you say it, it comes out like an insult? Forget I asked." Branna turned to leave.

"Wait, don't go getting your knickers in a bunch. I just," Fiona paused. "I've been on the town shit list for so long, my people skills are rusty."

Branna's face softened. "You don't have to explain, I see it. I actually do need help if you have a few minutes."

"So, what do you need for the event?"

Branna thought about it. "Well, we don't want too many live auction items. We need a couple of big ticket items. My idea was to patch a handmade quilt together. I wanted some of the squares to be different Aran wool weaves. Katie O'Brien is going to do them. I just want something else for the other patches. I want it to be a real jaw dropper. I saw this place and thought maybe we could do crests of the different families, try transferring them on to fabric."

Fiona thought about it. "We could do it. I know a place that has the equipment, I just don't know about that, though. Two hundred years ago you might have had eight to ten clans here, but now." She shook her head. "You're limiting yourself to a few big families."

Branna was listening to her, but she couldn't take her eyes off the photo that was on the wall behind the desk. She'd seen a couple out in the store as well. "I think you're right. I'm sorry, I know this is off subject, but who did these photos?"

Fiona stiffened. "It's just a local artist."

Branna was mesmerized. It was of an old man shucking oysters on the dock. "It's breathtaking. Is this the same artist that took the photos out in the shop?"

Fiona nodded silently. Branna got up and walked out, looking at a series of photos taken around town. They weren't touristy. The photo of the cliffs was stunning. It had a child, looking out over the sea. The cliffs were the backdrop, but the child was the star of the show. Beautiful chestnut curls, perfect skin. Just the profile, and the child was holding a man's hand. Just the arm and a small bit of the man showing. Recognition struck her. "This is Cora. Is that Finn?"

Again, Fiona just nodded. Branna looked where the artist signed. Just three letters.

"Fio. It's you. You are the artist." Branna said.

Fiona shrugged. "Yes, I suppose your opinion of them just decreased."

Branna recognized her defensiveness for what it was. "Actually my opinion of you just increased. I thought you were an evil shrew. Now I realize you are a talented, evil shrew."

Fiona laughed out loud. "All right, Yank. Let's get back to the issue at hand. The quilt, what are we going to do about that?"

Branna looked at the photos. "Do you have a portfolio?"

Fiona blushed, "Yes, I have it behind the counter."

Branna started flipping through the book and she had to give a grudging respect. "These are amazing, Fiona. They're not touristy or typical. You haven't captured *Doolin the ferry stop on the way to Aran*. You've captured the real town, the local people and places. It's so organic. Who is this man? You have several of him."

Fiona grinned. "Well, that's Connor O'Flay. He's the local eccentric."

Branna wondered if they were looking at the same guy. "He looks like a normal, older guy."

Fiona's face held mischief. "Look again. Every picture he has a different flannel shirt on. He must own fifty. For the last thirty years he has worn nothing but flannel shirts. Says he likes the feel of 'em. If he is at Sunday mass, he buttons the top button. If it is a funeral or a wedding, he adds a tie."

An idea came to Branna. "Holy crap, Fiona. You are a genius! Can you print photos to fabric?"

She nodded. "Aye, not here, but there's a camera shop that can do it. Why? Oh! I see where you're going with this."

Branna was envisioning the project. "We need it to reflect the local vibe, we need it to celebrate life here and the work that Brendan Sullivan does. It has to be special. Will you help?"

Fiona asked, "Why are you doing this? You should hate me."

Branna sighed, "You weren't a good wife, but that's not my business. Your past transgressions are your damage, not mine. You're not a bad person."

Fiona's voice was soft. "You can't know that."

Branna straightened, voice strong. "Yes, I can. If you were all bad Michael wouldn't have fallen in love with you and married you. More importantly, a bad person wouldn't be able to see the beauty in the stray dogs, twisted nets, and flannel shirt wearing old men of this town. I need you on this Fiona. I think we could do something really extraordinary. Are you in?"

Fiona nodded, "Yes Yank, I'm in."

MICHAEL WAS CLEANING his gear when Branna walked in from her busy day. He stopped what he was doing and went to her, lifting her off her feet. He kissed her soundly. "Hello, mo chroi. I've missed you. I haven't see enough of you this week." She wrapped her legs around his waist and he walked back to the counter, resting her bottom on it so that she was eye to eye with him. "So, how was your trip down to Dingle?"

She smiled, her face excited. "Actually, I sold out." Michael took a step back. "To who?" She was doing a little wiggly thing with her ass that was distracting him. "The fishermen, mostly and a few pub employees. They all knew him since that's where he docks the boat most nights. They were all so nice, so happy to hear about his new arm."

"So, what's the total? You have the church women cooking. You've got free entertainment. The hall was donated, right?" She nodded. "Yes, your dad took care of that." He tucked her hair behind her ear, "I wish I could have helped more. Work has been busy. I'll be there, though. Did you put my ticket aside?"

She said, "Of course. Your family is sitting together. Our total after costs is at about 2900 euro." His eyes popped up. "That's a hefty sum. You're going to need another thousand, right? I hope that auction goes well." She gave a confident nod. "Aye, it'll be grand." He laughed as he always did when she tried to speak the local accent. Just as he went in for another kiss, someone knocked. Branna hopped off the counter as he went to the door.

"Hello, Ned. Please come in. Have you brought Diane?" Ned Kelly walked in and Branna was caught between joy and dread. She hadn't seen him in a while. She liked the old man. He was, however, a walking, talking reminder of the situation they were facing.

"God bless all here." He took his hat off and bowed his head.

"Come in, please. Would you like some tea?" Branna said.

He smiled in his easy way, "I'd love it, if you'll join me. I'm sorry I didn't call. I was just thinking about the two of you and before I knew it I was headed down the road."

Michael sat with Ned at the table while Branna brought some cookies and tea accouterment. "How have you both been? I heard you went on holiday." Branna blushed. It was a small town.

"Yes, we did," said Michael. "Well, I am glad to see you two getting along. I've heard about all the work you've been doing for Brendan Sullivan. I remember when it happened, poor soul. Nasty business for a Sunday afternoon."

"It's not just me, Ned. It's been a community effort." Ned looked at Michael giving him a knowing smile.

"She's too modest, Ned. You should've heard her on the phone with that Boston doctor. She's bewitched the entire Irish half of Boston to pull this off, and they've never even laid eyes on her or Brendan."

Ned smacked the table and laughed, "That's our girl. Well, the city council has put together a donation. I'll be there with bells on, and so will Diane."

Branna brought the tea and joined them at the table. Ned spoke hesitantly, "I did feel I need to check in with you both about the house. I haven't been here as much as I should. I just need to know, now that we are coming up on the last month, whether you are both committed to this. Any change of heart?"

Branna started to speak and Michael cut her off. "We're both still in Ned, we're in it until the end. Then it's your choice. I'll abide by whatever you decide. There won't be bad blood between us, any of us."

Ned put a hand on his shoulder. "You've always been such a good lad. Now we have Branna, our little Raven flown over the sea. All right then. We'll play this out."

As Michael showed Ned out, Branna's heart was pounding. She should stop him, tell him that things had changed, that she wanted Michael to have the cottage. Michael slashed his hand across the air, anticipating her thoughts. Ned got in his car and Michael shut the door.

"Michael, you have to think about this."

He shook his head and descended on her, taking her mouth in one swift move. He was all over her, and then he swept her up into his arms and took her into his bedroom. When he laid her out, he loomed over her, his gaze intense. "I need you. I need inside you."

She didn't answer, she just pulled her top off.

Michael made short work of her jeans and panties. He was single minded, trying to strike that little visit from both of their minds. His mouth was searching, licking and tasting her skin. Then he opened his pants, freeing himself. He hissed as he pushed inside her. "You're wet. God, I need this! I need you!" He had her hands pinned to the bed under his, both were raised above her head. He surged his hips, and he groaned as she raised herself up to meet him.

Branna felt the need rolling off Michael. He was fully dressed and she was completely undressed as he took her with a desperation she'd not felt from him before. The effect was dizzying, erotic, bringing her close to the edge within seconds. His passion was dominating and possessive. He was kissing the hell out of her, but when she moaned into his mouth he broke the kiss. He looked at her, his face intense. He ground the words out as he thrust into her. "Tá tú mianach! Mo chuisle, mo chroí. You're mine. Do you hear me?" Branna exploded around him. He increased the pace as she convulsed uncontrollably, caught in the maelstrom.

When they lay entangled, completely sated and exhausted, Michael cradled her, repeating his Gaelic endearments. He pulled the covers over them as he held her to him. He thought, *I love you. I love you so much it's ripping my heart out. Stay with me.*

Why couldn't he say it aloud? She'd never said it to him, but he thought maybe she did. It wasn't just the sex. He'd loved her since he watched her that first night, as she spread her arms wide and tipped her face to the rain. Why couldn't he tell her? It was simple. He was a bloody coward.

Fiona had done such a number on his ego during the last year of their marriage. He knew Branna cared for him. He also knew that the physical aspect of their relationship was mind blowing. He just couldn't help thinking she had one foot and one eye turned toward the exit at all times. She kept things from him. The house-hunting aside, he'd heard Branna talking to Aidan about her dream. She talked to Brigid, Tadgh, his mother.

He couldn't break through that wall she had extracted when it came to her plans, her fears, or her parents. She'd never completely told him what happened to her dad and he knew there was more to the story with her mother. She didn't trust him. Voicing his feelings would leave him dangerously exposed. If he told her he loved her and she left, he didn't think he would recover. Branna could break him in a way Fiona never could have.

* * *

BRANNA WAS DREAMING. She knew that on some level. The sky was dark. She was standing in the field in front of the passage tomb. She had painted symbols on her body. She looked down at herself and raised her shirt. There was a rune painted on her abdomen. She didn't recognize it. She approached the entrance, seeing something on the entrance stone. The stone was long and carved with swirls, just as she remembered it. As she approached, a bird started from the stone and squawked loudly at her, flying out of what she now could see was a nest. She looked down and the nest contained two eggs. She looked up from the stone to see her father in the entrance to the tomb. "You must stay, Raven. Stay in your nest."

She reached for him. He was wearing his uniform. There was blood on his boots and uniform. She touched his face. "Daddy, I need you."

He kissed her hand. "It's okay, Branna. Just don't leave your nest. I have to go now. I have to find your mother. I can't find your mother."

Branna lurched up from the bed gasping. She was choking on a sob. Michael rushed in to find her clutching her head, racked with sobs. "Oh, God! No, Daddy!"

Michael scooped her into his lap. "Branna, love, it's ok. I'm sorry I left you. Shhh, it's ok." He wiped her hair out of her face, kissing her forehead as he comforted her. "Please Branna, tell me how to help you."

She just clutched to his shirt breathing deeply and trying to come out of the hysteria and panic that had hold of her. "You're doing it." She gripped him, burying her face in his chest. "This is what I need."

CHAPTER 22

The night was finally here. Branna ran around spinning circles around everyone as the team of volunteers helped her ready everything. The musicians were starting to pour in with their instruments. The place smelled of fresh, beautiful, local cooking. It also smelled of flowers, the table arrangements going out. Branna said, "Brigid, the flowers are gorgeous. You were so smart to use the vases from Caitlyn's wedding."

Brigid grinned with pride. "Caitlyn and her parents helped with the flowers. The florist let them have them at cost if we agreed to do the labor. I can't believe you pulled this off in two weeks, Branna. You're a miracle worker."

She was beaming. "I had a lot of help. Everyone has been so wonderful. It's amazing really. We have people coming from Aran and Dingle as well." Just as she was going to continue, she saw Jamie and Fiona walk in together. Brigid gave a derisive grunt. Branna mumbled under her breath, smiling. "He who is without sin. Google it." Brigid snorted.

"Hello! Do you have it?" Branna was ready to lose her lunch from nerves. This had to be something great.

"Yes, it's done. Jamie has been helping me with the slide show as well. We drove by and picked up the finished product from the church." Fiona was nervous, shooting looks around her as she felt some not so warm vibes coming at her. Branna noticed that there were some women shooting looks her way, but at least Brigid was playing nice.

"Come in the back so I can see it," Branna said. Brigid tried to follow. "Nope, you have to wait." When Brigid started to protest, Branna just pinched the air and gave her a "chsss."

Brigid's jaw dropped. "Did you just Caesar Milan me?"

Branna smiled. "Stay. There's a good girl," and patted her head. Jamie carried the box back with the women and Branna closed the door behind them. "Ok, let's see."

When Jamie and Fiona pulled the quilt out and unfolded it, Branna's hand shot over her mouth. She was afraid she would scream. Her eyes shot to Fiona's. "It is perfect."

Jamie smiled at them both. "You women are amazing. I still can't believe this is happening. Da keeps preparing us, saying it isn't a done deal. It is, though, isn't it? You did it."

Branna just nodded. She was struck stupid by the masterpiece in front of her. "The smaller items on silent auction have bridged the gap significantly. Those items will go for at least half the value if not more. By the looks of it, we will need about 800 euro."

Jamie's eyes bulged. "Do you think this will really bring all that?"

They could tell by her face that it was doubtful. People were only going to pay so much for a quilt no matter how beautiful it was."I have frequent flyer miles. I can buy one of their tickets with that if need be. We're ok."

Jamie shook his head, "You've done enough. Maybe Ma can stay back."

Branna shook her head adamantly. "No, he needs her there. You know that. He'll be in a strange town, people will be poking at him, he has a speaking engagement. He needs his wing man…or woman in this case."

Jamie nodded. "I've got savings. I was saving for some computer classes but…"

Branna interrupted him. "No, you know your dad wouldn't take it. You have to give him his pride. Let him stay your provider, your hero for a little longer. Do you understand?" Jamie did. "We will make the money stretch. We didn't come this far to let a few hundred dollars bugger the deal." Fiona just listened in silence. Branna could see the wheels turning in her mind.

As Branna went to leave the room, Fiona stopped her. "You can't tell them I took the photos."

Jamie cursed. "We talked about this, Fio," he said.

"Aye, we did. You just didn't hear me, Jamie." Fiona turned back to her. "Brendan needs this money. If they know I had part in it, you'll see it in the bidding. They'd never admit it, but it will hurt you. You know it will."

Branna shook her head. "That isn't fair. They should know that you did something good."

Fiona gave her a crooked smile. "They'll never see me as anything but Hester Prynne, jumped off the page. I deserve as much. You need to shut your gob, say it was someone out of Galway or something. Don't do it, Branna. You're almost there. This isn't about me."

She was probably right. They all knew it. Jamie turned his back on them and paced away, hands on his hips. Fiona spoke as if the matter was settled. "I have to go take care of something, but I'll be back. Where did you put me? Not next to some brood of nasty hens, I hope."

Branna laughed. "I wouldn't do that to you. Not after all of your hard work. You are next to Ned Kelly. He loves everyone."

* * *

The evening was going smashingly. The silent auction had several items, and the small things added up, but Branna was a little worried. There was no way, despite what she said, that the quilt was going to go for eight hundred euro. She'd be lucky to get half that. She had a contingency plan, but what she really wanted was for the community to get there on their own.

As she stood there watching, doing some hand wringing, she felt a little missile hit her legs from behind. It was Cora. She smiled at Michael as she picked up the little fireball. "You looked like you needed some Cora therapy."

She snuggled the little girl in her arms, kissing her and rocking her. "Just what I needed. How is Miss Cora today? Did you see your pictures?"

Cora had gone on a coloring frenzy. Brigid said it was all she wanted to do after being handed her assignment. With a little guiding hand, the pictures she'd made were wonderful in that uniquely child-like way. Big heads on stick bodies. Curly ocean waves, bright orange and purple fish, she even tried to draw The Sea Mistress. Brigid had made cardboard frames for all of them, Finn spray painted the frames silver and blue. Cora was beaming with pride. "Mr. Sullivan said I should be painting in Paris, France. I don't really know what that means, but he liked 'em fine." Michael was giggling under his hand.

Everyone was dancing and eating and singing along. The rotating band schedule was making sure that everyone got a break. People could pay a euro to request a song. Each band that had a CD had donated one to another auction basket. "Time to start the ceremonies." Branna handed Cora off and walked up toward a podium area they had set up near the stage. The band stopped playing and she took a microphone.

"If I could get everyone's attention, we are going to have you sit down and take a little bit of time to celebrate why we are here today. Jamie has put together a slide show for us, and I know you are going to love it."

Everyone hastened to their seats, excited to see what was coming. Fiona dimmed the lights discretely while Jamie pulled a screen down and started with the show. The music was simple, flute and whistle. As the photos started to roll, Branna felt tears prick her eyes. It started with old photos. Brendan was young and handsome and had two strong arms. He and his wife first, then came the ones of Jamie as a baby. The pictures rolled on as Brendan's life progressed. The first one of him coming home from the hospital made everyone sigh a little. His arm was bandaged, there was a sign up. "Welcome Home Da!" Jamie was about eight from the looks of him.

As the pictures turned present day, Branna saw Fiona's hand in them. That unique way she had of taking perfect moments, unposed and natural. Jamie and his dad on the boat, Brendan mending a net, Brendan looking out at the sea, one hand resting on the edge of the boat. The slide show ended and there was a lot of eye wiping and sniffling going on in the room.

Some of the fishermen gave a whoop and everyone clapped. Brendan was blushing like a schoolgirl from the attention. Branna walked up to the front and spoke. "I've talked to many of you tonight about how you know Brendan, but I'm new to this town. I was wondering if there was anyone here who would like to say something?"

It was a risk to go open mic, but she needed to keep this feeling of community and enthusiasm going. A crusty looking fisherman stood up. He was older, one of the more successful men with a fleet of boats. Branna walked over and gave him the microphone.

"Fishing is a tough living. It's competitive, too. Many a year we barely squeaked by, other years the fish were jumping in the boat like Christ himself was with us. I've know Brendan a long time. He was never one to let money get in the way of being a good man. He never put his crew in danger, even if it meant losing a good haul." The fishermen of the crowd all grunted approvingly, words of agreement milling throughout the room.

He continued, "How many of you over the years have had Brendan lend you a part for your boat, or give you aid when you had trouble on the water, loaned you petrol in a pinch?"

A booming *Aye!* came bursting from the men. "How many of you remember when the *Sea Foam* went down? He was the first one out there, helping pull men out of the water."

Louder still the men answered with a resounding, *Aye!* He shrugged. "Most men would figure they only had one good hand, so they wouldn't offer it up. But Brendan? He offered that one good hand, freely. Always our brother."

He walked over to Brendan. "You go, man. Go to Boston. I know you've been fretting over closing up the season, about leaving the lad alone to work the crew. I'm donating a man, your choice of any man on my crew. I'll keep his wages going. You choose, and he'll show up that morning you leave. He'll help young Jamie until you return."

Branna choked down her tears. The crowd went wild with applause as the two fisherman embraced. A couple of other men walked up to them, offering to donate some labor as well. Branna was amazed at the gesture. It was something she hadn't even thought of, but that is how it worked. People were good; you just had to ask for help.

Branna felt a hand on her shoulder. It was Father Peter. She normally steered clear of him, not wanting the inevitable questions of why she wasn't attending mass. "You've done a good thing, lass. You may not be on amicable terms with the Almighty right now, but I see him working through you."

She looked away, not wanting him to see her discomfort. Obviously Michael had dropped the dime on her. "You've taken these few fishes and loaves and they've multiplied." Branna just looked at him, not sure what to say. She just gave him a weak smile and a nod. "You may not be talking to him, lass, but he's talking to you. God bless you, girl. You have taught even this old priest a thing or two tonight."

After the dinner guests settled, Branna spoke to the crowd again. "As you know, the silent auction has ended, and I would like to thank everyone who donated and everyone who bid. Now it is time for our live auction. There is only one very special item up for auction, but believe me when I tell you that you've never seen anything like it."

Jamie and Sean Jr. came out with the bundle. When Branna nodded, they unrolled the exquisite quilt. The guests gasped in unison. The young men did as she had instructed and started to walk through the room with it.

"Several people's efforts went into the making of this beautiful quilt." Branna said. "If you look at the knitted patches, there are several local weaves done by our own Katie O'Brien." People clapped and Branna could see Tadgh put his arm around his mother, kissing her head as she smiled proudly.

"The photos were taken by a local photographer, and as you can see, the heart of this town is in every shot." As the boys carried the quilt through the crowd, the people were in awe. The picture of Brendan leaning on the boat was in the middle. All around in alternating squares, however, were other local shots. Robby and Jenny on stage, the stray Labrador that hung out in front of the bakery, children walking to school, Tadgh steering the ferry boat, rows of fishing boats docked alongside one another. There was a particularly poignant photo of Aidan in uniform, his father embracing him with tears coming down his face. Obviously a homecoming shot. There was one of the front of the church and one panoramic view of Fisher Street. The collage of photos was breathtaking. When it passed Brendan, his face twisted, fighting the tears.

"The last part of the quilt was donated by a long time resident of this town. If you see the different patches that cover the back and alternate in the front, they are all different squares of softly worn flannel. Connor O'Flay, would you like to stand up and give a demonstration?"

Connor was a big boisterous man. He had a corduroy sports jacket over his flannel shirt. He removed it and twirled around to the raucous laughter of the entire room. There was a perfect square cut out of the back of his shirt.

"Connor was nice enough to let us dismantle several of his large collection of flannel shirts in an effort to make this quilt truly one of a kind." Everyone was cheering as Connor took a bow. Branna continued, "I would like to thank the women's group at the church for assembling the squares and constructing this true piece of art. Our guest auctioneer is Sean O'Brien. Sean would you like to come up and get this auction rolling?"

Sean came up to the podium and smiled broadly at the crowd. He was perfect as the auctioneer. He wasn't a politician, but a man of service and family values. He was also alpha-dog to the core, a tribal leader of sorts. "What a grand evening it has been. It warms my heart, truly, to see all of you here today. Brendan is an important part of this town. He's fed us for decades, given fish to those he thought in need, helped his brother fisherman out on the water. Even donating fish to the church fry up during Lent. He's been a good father, a good husband, and a dear friend. So, what do you say we get him to Boston?" Everyone applauded.

"Who would like to start the bidding at one hundred euro?" One of the fisher wives raised her hand. "Can I get one hundred and fifty?" Jack McCain raised his hand. "Anyone for two hundred?" The bidding continued to go up until it was at 400 euro. Sean was great at working the crowd, pitting the bidders against each other in good fun. "Do I hear four fifty?"

The room was quiet, everyone looking around. "Anyone for four-fifty?"

Ned Kelly raised his hand and said, "Four-fifty!" Everyone was chatting excitedly.

"All right, now this is getting fun. Do I have a bidder for five hundred euro?" Quiet.

Then Connor O'Flay stood up and said, "I'll bid five hundred euro!"

The crowd gasped. "Do I have any bids for Five fifty? Any bids? Going once, going twice, sold for five hundred euro!"

Everyone cheered as Connor walked up to the stage to get his quilt. He stopped and looked at everyone. "Well, I had to get my shirts back somehow!" and everyone exploded with laughter.

Branna was telling everyone that dessert and tea was being served when Fiona pulled her aside. The musicians started playing again and the room was buzzing. Branna slipped in the back to talk to her. "Is something wrong? Don't be disappointed. The quilt got more than I thought, actually."

Fiona nodded, "Yes, I suppose it did well, didn't it? It was a grand idea."

Branna squeezed her arm. "It wouldn't have happened without you. You know that."

Fiona shrugged, "Yes, but you are still short. I was wondering if perhaps you'd like to auction off one more item?"

Branna laughed, "Sure, but I am fresh out of donations. Should we auction off Tadgh?"

Fiona laughed, "No, Father Peter would probably not sign off on that one, though we'd get a dear price for him. Actually, I have something for you. It may not catch much, but I thought it might help."

Branna looked at her, confused until she saw what she pulled out from behind a cabinet. "Oh! Fiona, I couldn't let you do that. That picture is beautiful. The size, the detail, the framing, you must have spent a fortune getting it printed and framed! That is gallery quality, Fiona. It's too much."

Fiona just looked at her. "Are you daft? It's not in a gallery, is it? It's hidden in the office in that bloody shop not doing anything for anyone. I don't imagine you'll get more than fifty euro for it, but maybe it could get more. Maybe you could put it toward the airfare?"

Branna knew this was important to Fiona. She had left specifically to get it in case they fell short of their goal. "Fiona, this is so nice. You have done so much, the slide show, the quilt, this picture. I feel like I am taking advantage of you."

Fiona gave her a wry smile. "This shrew has a lot of making up to do with the Almighty. Let me do this, please."

That *please* cost her a little, Branna knew. "Okay. Thank you. Jesus, thank you so much. I'm going to go get Sean." Fiona went to duck out and Branna said, "No, stay with it. Make sure no one comes in."

Branna brought Sean back to see their last minute donation. As he came in, Fiona tried to leave, but Branna caught her arm. "Sean, this is it."

His eyebrows popped up and he whistled. "That is a very generous donation. Christ, that's Jimmy McDaniels. He died six months ago." He looked at Fiona and started understanding the secrecy. "You? Did you take this photo, lass?" She just nodded silently. Sean was not a dumb man, so he quickly put it all together. "The quilt and the slide show, that was you too, wasn't it?" Branna actually felt sorry for Fiona, she looked so uncomfortable.

"Lass, look at me." Fiona looked up, barely resisting the urge to flee. "You've done a good thing. I'm proud of you." Her bottom lip started to tremble. He kissed her on the forehead and backed away. He looked at Branna, giving Fiona time to collect herself. "Why didn't you say it was her?"

Branna sighed, "She was adamant. She said if people knew it was her work, that it would affect the bidding."

Sean rubbed the spot between his brows. "I see, well as unfortunate as that is, she might be right. Now, are we ready to go get that last bit of funds?"

* * *

BRANNA TOOK TO THE MICROPHONE, again. "Excuse me, I hate to interrupt your dessert but we have a surprise!" Everyone stopped and looked expectantly. "We have a last minute auction donation. It is an extremely generous donation and I know you are going to love it." Jamie turned the large framed photo around and the audience all responded with oohs and ahhhs.

"Notice the photographer has managed to catch the man unaware while working on the dock. There is nothing artificial or contrived or posed about the picture. He'd just given that seagull a broken oyster, and so both man and beast do their jobs with no care for the one taking the photo. It's our beautiful seaside town in its simplest moment. Isn't it amazing?" Everyone applauded, shaking their heads in agreement. Many of them commented about the man in the photo, and his recent passing. "Now, we are just a hair from meeting our goal, so let's take this up to the auction block, shall we?"

Michael was watching Branna work the crowd side by side with his father and he couldn't have been prouder. The photo she'd pulled out of thin air was magnificent. His da went up to the podium and started the auction up again. "This is a fine piece of local photography, can I get a starting bid of fifty euro?" The bidding went up quickly. Branna looked over at Fiona, who was biting her thumbnail. "Can I get two hundred?" Everyone stopped and looked around, which was what happened when the bid started getting high.

Jack McCain raised his hand. "Two hundred euro!" The crowd was getting excited.

"Two twenty-five!" Branna looked over and it was Michael bidding. He gave her a wink. She cringed inwardly at having kept the photographer's identity from him. She was hoping he was just driving the bid up.

"Two fifty!" It was Diane Kelly. Jack raised her. "Three hundred euro!" The crowd was gasping. Diane hesitated, so her father bid. "I'll bid three hundred and fifty euro," he said calmly.

Jack was laughing and motioning that he was out of the bidding. "Going once, going twice, sold!" Sean bellowed. The crowd cheered as the auction came to an end.

Branna started thanking everyone, and she gave a special thanks to Cora for her lovely pictures. Before she stepped off the stage she paused. She looked at Sean, giving him a wordless request. He nodded ever so slightly.

She cleared her throat and continued. "I would like to thank one more very special donor. The local photographer that helped put the slideshow together was also responsible for the beautiful photos on the quilt and the stunning photo we just auctioned off. Although the fundraising efforts have gone smashingly, those two items put us over the edge and paid for the airfare to Boston for Brendan and his wife." Everyone was paying close attention, glancing around to see if anyone was approaching the stage. "Fiona, would you please come up here?"

The jaws were dropping all over the room and you could have heard a pin drop. Fiona was stark white, looking toward the exit in the back of the room. Michael was stunned as well. But as he looked at the two women, one his past, the other his present, he started to understand that Branna O'Mara was never going to stop surprising him.

Fiona looked like a deer in the headlights. It struck him that he'd never really considered how isolated she'd been from these people since their marriage fell apart. Instead of being angry with her, he pitied her. As if mirroring his thoughts, he watched his mother walk to the back of the room and gently take his ex-wife by the hand. She walked her up to the stage and Branna took Fiona's other hand.

Branna took Fiona's hand and whispered out of the corner of her mouth, "How ya holdin' up Hester?"

Fiona stifled a giggle and whispered back, "You are so dead, Yank."

Branna addressed the crowd. "I would like to thank Fiona for sharing her wonderful gift with us and with Brendan. This is a community that takes care of its own. Thank you, Fiona, for all of the time and effort you put into these creations."

Branna could see someone immediately stand and start clapping. It was Michael, and she looked at him with utter gratitude and love in her eyes. She felt Fiona jerk, stunned by the gesture. The clapping was contagious as everyone joined in. Even Brigid begrudgingly caved as her daughter jumped up and down, encouraging her to clap.

* * *

"ARE you going for sainthood or something?" Branna turned from her clean up duties to see Michael standing with his hands on his hips. "You've been holding out on me, hen."

She smiled and gave a shrug. "It was business. I needed her for these projects and she is really talented. I know I should have told you, but she was very clear she wanted to remain anonymous."

He laughed, "So you and Da ambushed her at the end?"

She lifted one shoulder, "Exactly."

As Michael collected their things, eager to get Branna home, he heard a familiar voice behind him. "She's good for you." He turned around to see Fiona. Her normal prickly demeanor was gone. "She seems to care for you a great deal. I'm happy for you." Michael nodded. She continued, "I wasn't the one for you. We both know that. Even if I hadn't done what I did, I wasn't the one."

Michael sighed. "What do you want Fiona?"

She jerked a little at his tone and his face softened. "I'm sorry. You did a good thing. I need to take a stab at playing a little nicer, I suppose. Old habit."

She just smiled, "It's not like I haven't given you enough reasons. I guess we both need some work. I just wanted to tell you that I'm doing better now. I went back to Mary, and this time when she asked me to see a psychiatrist, I went."

Michael was shocked, but he stayed silent. "She's suspected I was bi-polar for a few years now. It started in my early twenties. I just couldn't see it. I wouldn't see it. Anyway, I am on medicine now and I am doing better. The medicine and the counseling is really making me see things differently. A lot of the thoughts I used to have, the impulsiveness, and the mood swings, it's all starting to level out. It's only been a few weeks, but I already feel more stable. I just wanted to tell you that, and that it wasn't you. All those awful things I said to you, the way I treated you. It wasn't you. I'm sorry, Michael. I'm so sorry for everything, and I'm so glad you're finally happy."

It took him a minute to speak, "Why didn't you ever tell me?"

She shrugged, "If I didn't want to admit it to myself, I could hardly admit it to you. I'm not making excuses. The anger and spite I directed at you, the infidelity, I won't make excuses for that. I've learned a lot, though. It took one failed marriage to do that, but I hope we're both wiser. Anyway, I just wanted you to know."

Michael stopped her mid stride as she went for the door. He stood in front of her and gave her a chaste hug. "I forgive you, Fio. I honestly do."

Fiona suppressed a sob, putting her hand over her mouth as her head was on his shoulder. "Thank you, Michael. I know I don't deserve it, but thank you."

CHAPTER 23

Michael woke to the sound of rain on the window. The peat was glowing in the fireplace and Branna was warm and earthy, spooned against him. She was sound asleep, finally letting herself go after the enormous task she'd taken on was finished. Michael thought about the evening that had transpired. She had a way of spreading light, like a fire but less destructive, more healing. It spread just the same.

He also thought about Fio. It was because of Branna that he was able to see Fiona for the damaged woman that she was. She wanted to be forgiven. He suspected that the olive branch Branna had offered her had been more like a life preserver, pulling her back to the community, giving her a purpose other than being the fodder for gossips. He'd been so proud of Branna throughout the night. But when she'd stood on that stage, chin up, defying everyone's preconceptions about Fiona, demanding silently that they forgive her, he realized that she had the purest heart of anyone he'd ever known. He'd finally been able to put the old wound to rest. "Gráim thú," he whispered as he pulled her close, "mo chuisle." *I love you, my pulse.*

Branna woke to the strumming of Michael's guitar. She heard something familiar in the tune, but couldn't place it. She got up and headed for the bathroom. As she finished her business, she went to the sink, a prickling tension nagging at her. She pulled out her birth control pack. She had started the placebo pills Sunday. Usually her cycle started between Tuesday night and Wednesday morning. It was Friday morning and she had not started her period. This was the first month when it had ever really been on the radar, considering that after twelve years of cycling, they finally started to matter. She told herself that it was probably stress or the illness. *You are on the pill, don't be paranoid.* She took the next placebo and returned the pack to its place. She refused to panic.

* * *

IT WAS SATURDAY NIGHT. The pub was slow, the tourist season having waned a bit. Branna was sitting with Tadgh and Michael's parents, who were not playing tonight. Liam was in town for the weekend, and she was excited to see him join his family on the stage. "So what are Liam's magical properties?" Sean looked at her oddly.

"She means talents. Gamer-dork speak." Tadgh teased.

She dropped her jaw. "I am not a gamer dork!"

He laughed, "Whatever, Galadriel, Queen of the Fairies."

Before she could stop herself, she corrected him. "Elves, she was queen of the…"

He raised a brow. "Busted."

She covered her face. "Okay, for a small amount of time in junior high."

Sean interrupted, smiling at the two. "To answer your question, Branna, he plays the fiddle, the guitar, and the octave mandolin."

Branna clapped her hands, "Is he playing the mandolin tonight?" Sean stood a few inches, peering behind the stage chairs. "He's got it with him, so probably."

Sorcha was watching Branna. She could feel her gaze. She met her eye. "You look beautiful tonight, dear. Radiant, even. My son must be taking good care of you."

Robby, Patrick, Jenny, Liam and Michael were playing tonight.

They did a few fun numbers. Liam had a wonderful voice as expected. He did a version of "The Limerick Rake" that had the pub males laughing and toasting. Michael addressed the crowd afterwards. "How many of you have heard of the fundraiser our little Yank hosted Friday?" The crowd started shouting and drumming on the tables. Sean reached an arm around her and kissed her temple.

"Well, now. We don't make a habit of doing American tunes, but we do know a couple of songs. So, how about a little tribute tonight to our brothers and sisters in the parish to the West?" Everyone cheered in agreement. "We don't get our Trinity College Rake here very often, so we are going to get a real treat listening to him on the mandolin." There was more cheering, especially from the ladies in the crowd.

Branna was blushing. She was touched that they were going to do an American song, curious as to what it was. When they started, the dread welled up in her chest. It was a song by Nickel Creek called *The Lighthouse Tale.*

Tadgh felt Branna stiffen beside him. He looked at her hands and she was gripping her napkin, white knuckled. He thought about what could have set her off, and realized exactly what song Michael was doing. He cursed internally. He excused himself and once he was behind her, he started making subtle slashing with his hands for Michael to cut the song off. Michael, confused, looked at him like he was an idiot and kept playing. Sean saw it, though. Tadgh sat down, riding it out. As the song continued, his heart broke as he watched Branna. Fake smile plastered on her face. He subtly reached over and put a hand over hers. She gripped it, releasing the napkin.

I am a lighthouse, worn by the weather and the waves.

I keep my lamp lit, to warn the sailors on their way.

I'll tell a story, paint you a picture from my past.

I was so happy, but joy in this life seldom lasts.

The song was written from the perspective of the lighthouse, a unique point of view. The lighthouse loves his keeper, lives vicariously through him. Sees him live, fall in love, and marry and revels in the joy and happiness of the couple. As with most tales, it takes a tragic turn. Branna's body is covered with goose bumps but her chin is up and her gaze is steady. Everything she telegraphed to the average onlooker would say *I'm fine.* She couldn't fool Michael, though.

He watched her ship fight,

But in vain against the wild and terrible wind.

In me so helpless, as dashed against the rock she met her end.

Branna was struggling to keep it together. Michael was almost done with the song, but he had no idea what had put her in such a state. When he'd seen Tadgh reach over and take her hand after trying to cut the song off, he knew something was up. He couldn't just stop in the middle with a pub full of people watching.He found himself wishing he knew a few more American folk songs, because this one had obviously been a bad move. As he sang the last verses he watched her eyes dart down to her hands and wondered if she was hiding tears. Tadgh was whispering to her. The fact that he immediately knew what was wrong made Michael mental. What the fuck was he missing?

Branna tried to hit the disconnect button in her brain, that would deafen her to the last verse. She was weak deep down, however. The torture of her memories, and the idea that love could destroy, that knowledge kept her safe. This was good in a way. She'd let herself forget for a while, and so she let the wound fester anew. She would remind herself why she couldn't love completely, ever. That part of her had died with her mother.

I saw him crying, watched as he buried her in the sand.

And then he climbed my tower, and off of the edge of me he ran.

After the song, Branna's body loosened a bit, but the blood was pounding in her ears. "Are you okay? Do you need something?" Branna answered after a deep breath. "Some water, please." Tadgh looked at her doubtfully. "Maybe something stronger? Christ, Branna. You didn't tell him? What you told me about your mother, you still didn't tell him did you?"

She just shook her head. She considered his offer of something stronger, and after a wave of dread hit her, she decided to error on the side of caution and forgo the alcohol.

"Water is fine, thanks. I'm okay. Don't say anything Tadgh. Please, promise me." Tadgh growled quietly. They were speaking quietly but Sorcha and Sean were sitting at the table. The issue had not escaped them.

Tadgh approached the bar as he heard Michael announce a short break. He wasn't sure Michael had picked up on it, but his cousin was smart. After he'd motioned to him not to play that song, he'd been watching them. "Tell me what I did?"

Tadgh winced and turned to Michael. "I don't know what you mean. I was just playing around." Tadgh's tone was light, he'd almost convinced himself.

Michael's face turned quietly aggressive. "Do not ever lie to me when it comes to her. I know her body. I read her eyes. I know her fucking soul."

Tadgh shut his eyes. "She's ok. Just let it go." Michael was seething and Tadgh knew instantly that it was the stupidest thing he could have said.

"First you lie, then you tell me to butt out. Strike three and I will throttle you, cousin."

Tadgh's eyes shot to his, his own anger spiking. "I suggest you stow the bullying impulse before you talk to her. If you need to know something, she needs to tell you. I made a promise to her not to repeat a confidence and you aren't going to bully it out of me, either. She should have told you, I agree. If you know her fucking soul, then you know it must be pretty bad if she is this clamped down about it. Don't screw this up further. She needs you. If you hurt her, I will throttle you, cousin." Tadgh walked away, leaving Michael at the bar alone.

Michael went up to the band and told them to start again without him for a few songs. His dad came up to fill in on guitar. "Whatever it is son, it's bad. You need to watch yourself. Don't be part of the problem. She tried to play it off but she's near made herself ill with the effort." Michael looked back to the table and Branna's chair was empty. "She said she was going to the ladies room," Sorcha offered. He went to the hall where the ladies room was and the door was open and the light was off. He squeezed through the pub to the street and saw taillights headed toward the cottage.

Michael pulled into the cottage drive with his blood thumping in his ears. He slammed the car door and went in the house. When he came in, he startled Branna and she dropped the glass she was holding. It smashed everywhere. She didn't look well. She stepped to the side and winced. "Branna, don't move!" He walked over in his heavy shoes, picked her up and carried her out of the kitchen. She was trembling. "Did you cut yourself?"

She said, "I'm okay. I was just tired. You can go back, Michael. You and Liam were wonderful."

Ignoring her, he placed her on the couch. She indeed had a piece of glass in her foot, but nothing major. He pulled it out and propped her foot on the coffee table. He got a washcloth with soapy cold water and wiped her foot. Then he swept the glass up. He didn't say anything else to her. Storming in the house had obviously made her mental state worse. Tadgh and his father had both warned him, but he had let himself get pissed off when he realized she'd left.

He put the broom away and went to her. He sat on the coffee table across from her, all anger having fled him when he'd felt her trembling in his arms. "Branna sweetheart, tell me why you are so upset. I don't know what I've done, but I swear I didn't mean to upset you. Was it the song?"

She looked at him, chin up, a fake ass smile on her face. "It was beautiful. Please, Michael. It's nothing. I loved your song."

Michael's face showed a bit of impatience. "You are not one for theatrics, Branna. You are downright stoic when you are in pain. You remind me of that fat headed brother of mine. But I know you, girl. I know your body as well as my own." She didn't say anything.

He grunted in frustration. "You won't tell me, but you'd tell Tadgh? Explain to me what you find so unworthy about me?"

Her eyes widened. "Don't say that. Don't ever say that. That isn't it. Can't we just drop it? I just get tangled up in my head, sometimes. I'm fine, Michael. Let's just go back to the pub."

He got up and started pacing, running his hand through his hair. A sure sign he was getting upset. She knew his body language, too. "You talk to my mother, Brigid, Tadgh, especially Tadgh. Why?" His voice was getting louder. "Why them?" She was shaking her head now, jaw tight. He sat down hard on the table and grabbed her arms. "Why?"

She shouted at him, "Because they're safer!"

He was shocked by the answer, dropping his grip on her immediately. "You're afraid of me?" he asked.

"No! Never, Michael. Please, this isn't your fault."

He pushed, "Why? Why are they safe to talk to and I am not? Why, Branna?"

She was at her breaking point. She jumped off the couch. He stood as well and she met his face with aggression. "Because I don't feel about them the way that I feel about you! God, I swore I wouldn't do this!" she shouted. "I didn't date, I didn't have sex, I didn't let anybody in until you! I can't do this!"

She was holding her head now, crying. "Branna, please! Talk to me. Tell me why tonight? What the hell does that song have to do with this? Talk to me God dammit!"

Branna's composure snapped. She smashed both her hands on his chest. "She killed herself! You want to know everything? She killed herself! That's why that song upset me! He died and she couldn't go on!" Michael was stunned into silence. She was screeching, shoving her palms against his chest in anger.

He eased toward her and she backed up. "Your mother? Is that who she is? You told me she had cancer." She was hugging herself, face soaked with tears. "Please let me hold you, Branna."

He eased toward her and she stepped on her cut foot. She snatched it up, over correcting and almost fell over as she felt his arms close around her. He held her as she hyperventilated. "Please, mo chroí. Let me bear some of this for you."

He saw the transition, like a switch. She straightened her spine, shot her chin up as she detangled from his arms. "I don't need you to bear anything. I have done fine on my own. If I say I'm fine, I am."

Michael walked to her and cupped her defiant chin. "Don't. Don't you shut down on me."

Before he knew what was happening she went wild. She pulled his mouth down hard to hers, ripped his shirt out of his jeans, and began fumbling with his zipper. "I don't want to talk. This is what I want."

He grabbed her hands and pinned her to the wall. "Branna, stop. This isn't what you need. You need to talk to me."

She pushed her head away from the wall and caught his mouth with hers, and he kissed her back despite himself. "Don't tell me what I need," she growled and deepened the kiss.

Michael was warring with himself. He was fully aroused but trying to resist her aggressive advances. He was hurt and angry and scared. Scared for her. Part of him wanted to throw her down and roger her until she was too weak to argue. But she was on the edge of some sort of pit, looking down at her despair and ready to jump into it body and soul. He was no shrink but somehow he knew that until he broke down her defenses, she wasn't going to share whatever pain she was choking down.

He let go of her wrists and she launched herself on him. Their coupling was hard, fast, and she was completely undone as she took him right there on the floor. Clothes removed fast, buttons flying off in haste. She was slamming herself down hard on him, not keeping eye contact. Like the sea against the rocky shore, she smashed herself against him. She was there, but not there. That's when he turned the tables on her.

He rolled over and pinned her down. She bucked underneath him. He knew she was having trouble finding her release. He also knew why. He knew her, inside and out. He pinned her hands above her head with one hand at her wrists. He pinned her hips down with his. He was inside her to the hilt. She was thrashing her head back and forth, caught up in some battle with her head, her heart, and her body. He spoke softly. "Branna, look at me."

She bucked under him. "Don't stop!"

He put his free hand to her chin to settle her head. She looked at him, fear warring with anger. He was cool water and she was scorching heat. He rubbed his thumb over her bottom lip. She tried to look away but he held her chin and reeled her in with his eyes. "Look at me, mo chroí." She did, and he kissed her softly, with utter tenderness. Her eyes were glazed, hysteria giving way to a sort of hypnotic peace. His eyes held mercy, understanding, deep intimacy. His message was clear. He would give her all of him, but he wanted her there with him. He would not be used in a blur of sex. If lovemaking was her balm, they would make love, not rut like two strangers. They would climb out of this together.

She gasped as he moved his hips, never breaking eye contact as tears spilled down her temples. He descended on her mouth and kissed her slow and deep. He lifted her pelvis as he slowly rolled his hips. He looked into her soul with everything he had. Her eyes held the unfocused ecstasy that always preceded her climax. "That's it, darlin. Let go." He intensified with a deep grind of his hips, holding back his own climax, willing her to release herself to him.

Her shallow breaths peaked to a gasp. She arched her neck and closed her eyes and he pulled her to him. "Stay with me, love. Look at me." His tender command ripped a scream from her as he dove deep into her releasing body, and into her eyes where she could hide nothing from him.

When he finally joined her, she clung to him. He tethered her with his body and with his heart and she finally backed away from that pit. The tears were silent. When she looked at him, he saw regret. "I'm sorry," she croaked.

"Shhh, don't be. We rode out of this storm together," he whispered.

* * *

SHE TOLD HIM. "My mother knew. She knew way before the diagnosis." She was calmer now. He had her sit with him on the couch. He cradled her small body against his chest, wrapped in a quilt, not forcing her to look at him anymore. He thought she'd open up that way. He was right. Holy God, was he right.

"I heard them. My friend Anna and her father and brother lived next door for a little while. He was a single dad. More importantly, he was the man that pulled my father out of the line of fire. He'd taken a sniper round to the shoulder in the process. They were clearing buildings in Fallujah. My father got hit in the neck. He bled out in his best friend's arms. Gunny Falk, Anna's father, came home wounded with my father's remains. He wouldn't leave him. After that he stayed in touch, checked on my mother. I think he felt responsible, even though he wasn't. In hindsight, I think he may have been in love with her. Not while my father was alive, but after. Shared grief and all that. He was a single dad, and my mother was very beautiful. Anyway..."

Michael just softly stroked her arm as she talked. He didn't want to spook her into silence. "I heard them fighting. Anna and I were out on the beach, but we came up to the door and they didn't know we could hear them. They never fought, ever. They were best friends. He was pleading with her. *'How long have you known? How could you do this Meghan? How could you do this to Branna?'* I didn't understand at first, but they kept at it. She was so calm, it was eerie. *She'll be fine, I arranged everything.* He was so angry with her. *You think that makes a fuck load of difference to her? The money? Jesus Christ, Meghan! You're orphaning her because you let this cancer go!* He demanded to know how long ago she had found the lump. Two years. She'd been dodging mammograms and check ups for two years, crawling into a hole that she wouldn't be able to get out of, if she waited long enough. If she'd been treated immediately, she would have had a full recovery." She stopped, taking a few necessary breaths.

"Finally, she passed out. She fainted in the kitchen from the toll it was taking on her body. I called the ambulance when I couldn't wake her. That's when everything started, when she got officially diagnosed. The doctor noticed she hadn't been to her check ups in two years, and hadn't had a mammogram in five. She was high risk. Her mother and her grandmother died from breast cancer. She should have had one every year, but she stopped getting them right after my father died."

Michael felt fear spike in his gut. He interrupted. "That is genetic, Branna. Jesus, have you been tested?"

She nodded. "Of course. My mother was adamant that I get the gene work up done. Fortunately, my father's DNA was the winner. I don't carry the gene. Can you believe the hypocrisy?" Her tone was bitter. "She got me tested, showed me how to do self breast exams, all while she was ignoring the warning signs that she was being savaged by the same disease."

Michael hated the bitter tone in her voice but damn it all, he couldn't blame her. She went on, "I overheard this little chat between Gunny Falk and my mother when she had already been diagnosed. Apparently she was doing very little to stave off the cancer. Just enough to make it look like she was trying, just enough to prolong her death. She'd let them cut it out, even though it wasn't a long term solution. It was an aggressive cancer, she needed aggressive treatments. She refused it. She did holistic treatments, fucking meditation, herbs. It was all bullshit of course. She needed chemo and radiation and a double mastectomy. She knew it. She wasn't going to let anything get in the way of a good old fashioned death wish."

"She wanted me to be old enough to take over the business, have a livelihood, dodge inheritance tax. Five years from when she signed the houses over to me, she needed to hold on until then. She actually thought that if she set me up financially, the guilt over what she was doing would be washed away. She drug her death out over three years, suffering horribly, all for sake of securing my financial future. At the end, she cried. I confronted her about what I had heard. She begged me to forgive her."

She looked at Michael. "All I took from the experience is that this was what true love did to you. When my father died, she died. She just kept breathing for six more years. Imagine a knife in the heart that takes six years to finally bleed out."

Michael cursed under his breath. Branna shot up out of his arms and started walking away. "Now you know the truth. It wasn't you that was unworthy, Michael, it was me. It's always been me. You may not realize it now, but my mother was right. Some people just aren't enough."

He got up and followed her. "What are you talking about? This wasn't your fault. What your mother did was wrong. You're not like her. Brian O'Mara's daughter would never do something like that. My heart goes out to your mother, God knows the pain must have been unbearable, but she should have fought like my mother did. She should have fought to stay with you."

Branna looked at him, a bitter smile on her face. "Sorcha has Sean and six wonderful children. My mother only had me. I wasn't worth the fight. After daddy was gone, she had nothing left to live for."

The look on her face was calm acceptance. He asked, "Branna, for God's sake tell me you don't believe that?"

She turned, walking toward the bathroom. "I've told you, Michael. That's what you wanted. Now you know everything. I don't want to talk about this anymore."

He caught her by the arm. "We are certainly not done talking about this! Look at me." She shot him an angry look. "Get as pissed as you like, Hellcat. I can take it. What I can't take is this distorted self worth. You are worth walking through hell and back for, and this was not your fault!" He cupped her face with his hands, willing her to believe his words. "Your mother probably needed to be treated for depression. She was sick, both in body and mind. She wasn't thinking clearly. This was not about you." She said nothing.

"Why did you move here?" He asked the question out of the blue, a non sequitur that had her shaking her head.

"I don't know what you mean. You know why," she said sharply.

Michael asked again, "Why did you come to Ireland? You had friends in the states. They weren't family but they were something. Why, Branna?" She started pulling away from him. "No, I want to know why. I never followed the logic, but this thing with your mother changes things. You had people who cared about you, Anna and her father, at the very least. Why, Branna? Why move to some secluded place in another country where you have no one?" His tone was forceful. He wanted an answer.

"Don't you get it?" She shouted. "My mother was gone! They all leave, eventually. That is life in the military, Michael! They move, they leave! No one is forever. If I left first, then…" She paused, not wanting to finish.

"Then what?" He asked. He had to push her. She couldn't keep this awful poison inside her. It was killing her.

"Then it's my choice!" she shouted at him, breaking his hold. "This was my choice!" She was choking, racked with sobs. "If I came here where no one knows me, it was my choice. I left!" She pounded on her chest. "I could leave and choose to be alone! Then it's my choice to have no one! I was supposed to come here and choose to be alone. No one needed to know that I didn't really want to be alone!" He grabbed her and held her as she sobbed. "It's my choice! I left!" she screamed.

"You're not alone, Branna. Don't you know that by now?" he said softly, kissing her hair and trying to comfort her.

She started to struggle, "No, I can't. I can't depend on that. I can't depend on you!"

He wouldn't let her go. "You might push, but I'm strong. I'm strong enough, Branna. If I could take this cup from you, I would." His voice broke, fighting the tears. "I can't take it from you. I can love you, though. Please, mo chroi. Please, let me love you."

She stopped resisting and went limp, sobbing uncontrollably. "Oh God, Michael. I miss her so much. I was used to the separations with my dad. She was the one constant, even with all the moving. She was everything to me, and she just left me!"

Michael held her with silent tears pouring down his face. She'd let her anger at her mother shield her from grieving. All he could do was hold her, and let the grief wash through her. "It was all for nothing." Her voice was strained and trembling. "They're not together. He comes to me. He comes to me in my dreams. He can't find her. Oh God, what if she's not with him, Michael? What if she's in Hell for letting herself die? What if God's punishing her!" She was hysterical.

He took her head in his hands. "No, Branna! Don't even think that. She was a good woman. You know that deep down. Don't think it for a minute. We'll talk to Father Peter, they're just dreams, darling." He rocked her as she cried. She choked on her sobs until she exhausted herself.

Michael was ripped down the center, gutted by these confessions. He knew she'd been hurt, but the pain inside her would have crumbled the strongest of men. How in the hell had she kept it together? In her mind, God was to be feared. The big bad boogey man that took everything from her. She'd had no one and nothing to comfort her. Not even her faith. The only family she had left in the world had willingly abandoned her. The sorrow and rejection coupled with survivor guilt was tearing her up.

* * *

BRANNA WAS FALLING asleep in Michael's arms. He only let go of her long enough to get ready for bed, and then he held tightly to her. He held her like their lives depended on it, and she finally started to drift off. As she nodded off, he whispered to her, stroking her hair and kissing her head. "Mo chuisle mo chroí."

She whispered hoarsely, "I'm not the only one with secrets. You know I can't understand Gaelic."

He pulled her chin up so she could look at him. "You are the pulse of my heart," and he kissed her softly.

CHAPTER 24

Branna got up at o'dark thirty and drove to Ennis, not wanting Michael with her. She stopped at a 24 hour mart, praying they had what she needed. She went home and he was still asleep, the sun having not come up yet. She went to the bathroom and took out the test. She needed to start a new packet of pills, but if she was pregnant, she shouldn't take them. She sat in the bathroom, desperate and afraid. Michael's words rang through her head. *Her reason for the annulment was based on the fact that I wouldn't give her children. She wanted to trap me. She knew I didn't want her getting pregnant, but if she did, I wouldn't leave her.* Then she heard Fiona's bitter tone. *Did he tell you he didn't want children?*

She'd assured him that she had the birth control covered. Pills were supposed to be super safe. What the hell was going on? God, the ninety days were ticking down and she ends up pregnant? He would think she lied, that she was trying to trap him into letting her stay. The thought of it was like a wave of horror through her body and mind as she fumbled with the test.

One line negative, two lines positive. Wait two minutes. It didn't take two minutes. Branna looked in horror as both lines appeared one right after the other. Tears started rolling. She couldn't figure out why she'd been so weak, so tired, so emotional. She'd never fainted in her life. Now she understood.

Panic tackled her. She had to get off her ass. Michael might wake up. He used her bathroom half the time now that he was staying in her room. She gathered the box, the wrapper, directions, and the telltale stick.

Michael woke to a noise outside. He heard the garbage can lid. He stretched and got out of bed. He didn't like waking up without Branna, especially after last night. He walked into the main room as she was coming through the front door. She jumped and clutched her chest.

"Sorry. I just heard you outside and thought I'd get up." She blanched, noticeably. "Are you ok?" he asked.

She shook herself. "Yes, sorry. You just startled me. I was taking the garbage out."

He looked at the time. "The garbage pick-up isn't for a week. They came Friday."

She smiled. "I put some leftovers in there and I didn't want it to smell up the house."

He yawned. "Come back to bed, Hellcat. I don't have mass for a couple of hours. Let me hold you."

She walked into his arms. He leaned away enough to look at her. "You're shivering, come get back in bed."

She snuggled against him. "Michael, I was thinking I would like to go to mass with you today, if that's ok."

Michael froze. "Of course you can come. It would make me happy. Any reason for the change of heart?"

She exhaled. "I figured it was time I started talking to him again, even if it was to yell at him."

Michael laughed softly, his chest rumbling in her ear. "That's fine, girl. He can take it. We both can."

* * *

THE CHURCH WAS CROWDED. Branna and Michael sat with the family and they were thrilled to see Branna join them. As they all went up for communion, Branna stayed back. She hadn't been to confession in two years. When they all started piling out of the church, each stopped and shook hands with the priest. Branna put her hand out. "Good morning, Father Peter."

He gave her a warm smile. "Good morning, Miss O'Mara. I am so very glad to see you with us this morning. I see you didn't take the sacraments."

She smiled nervously. "It's been a while since my last confession."

He gave her an understanding look, "Well, then. If you wish, I will be here hearing confessions on Wednesday." She nodded. "Is Brendan all set to leave Saturday?"

Branna had tried to escape but the priest was downright chatty. She answered, "Yes, I believe so. It was a lovely sermon, Father. I don't want to hold the line up. Thank you again." She fled nervously, afraid of anymore questions. As she left for the parking lot, she saw Mary Flynn. She ran over while Michael was distracted.

"Hello, Branna. How are you feeling?" Branna smiled weakly. "Hi, Mary. I was going to ask you, do you think you could fit me in tomorrow morning if I come in early?"

Mary was surprised. "Of course. Is it urgent? Do we need to go now?"

She shook her head. "Tomorrow will suffice." Mary assured her that she would confirm an early morning appointment with her via text later today.

The O'Brien clan decided to go to brunch. An Fulacht Fia in Ballyvaughan was an upscale place nearby. The large group of O'Briens sat at brunch chatting and eating and drinking mimosas. "Don't you want a mimosa, Branna?" It was Liam asking. "Or did I convert you to whiskey? I can get you an Irish coffee." Branna shook her head. "No, it's a bit early for me. Thank you, though. Juice is fine." Michael looked at her place setting. "No coffee? Are you feeling okay? Is this some sort of sign of the Apocalypse?"

She smacked him. "Don't be a wise guy. I had some tea earlier." She lied.

Sorcha watched the dark haired beauty down the table. Michael doted on her, so did her other sons. She laughed and teased like a sister with Brigid. Something was niggling at her about Branna, however. She couldn't put her finger on it but something was different.

Branna nibbled her eggs and toast. She had a nervous stomach, the secret she kept was weighing on her. She wasn't a dishonest person. She had prayed so hard at church. *Please let the test be wrong. Please let the test be wrong. I will start coming to church. I will do more charity work. Please, I don't want to leave. Please let the test be wrong.*

She heard a ruckus down the table. It was Finn. "You sneaky little chancer! You know, don't you?" Brigid was blushing, trying to give an innocent look. "When did you sneak off and get an ultrasound?"

Michael looked at Brigid. "You told me they couldn't see, that the baby was turned."

Brigid looked at him like she was going to flog him. "It was. I went back last month." She hid her face, laughing.

"You are so weak. I thought we were going to wait!" Finn scolded her, but not with any real fervor.

Branna felt a little nudging under her arm. Cora wiggled in and sat in her lap. She watched with mirth as Finn and Brigid and the brothers all argued whether she should spill the beans. Michael butted into the conversation, "Oh, for God's sake. You know it's a boy. Getting a girl child in this family is like seeing Halley's Comet. You got Cora. Now we have to go another seventy-five years."

Sorcha laughed at this. "Well, she's got Mullen in her. I got Brigid, she got Cora twenty-five years later. It's not quite that dire." Branna was listening, but inside she was feeling like snakes were coiling in her stomach. This baby talk was freaking her out.

She held Cora, smelled her curly hair. It smelled like baby shampoo and something uniquely childlike. Cora touched her face. "I love you Auntie Branna. I had a dream about you."

Branna thought that was sweet. "You did? A good one, I hope."

Cora smiled, her cheeks dimpling. "Yes, it was very good. I was at your house playing with your baby birds. You had a nest with cute little black baby birds. There was a man there, too. He was dressed like Uncle Aidan."

The hair stood up on Branna's neck, echoes of her own dream flashing in her mind. *Does he know?* She remembered his words in the dream. *"Fly to your nest, Raven. You need your nest." Oh, God. Have you been trying to tell me, Daddy?*

Branna started sweating. "Michael, can you take Cora. I need to go to the ladies room."

Michael looked at her. "Are you ok?"

She nodded. "I'm fine." She got up and left. Michael heard a ruckus behind him, people gasping. He turned around as he saw Branna go to the floor.

"It's okay, Michael. I'm sorry I spoiled brunch."

Michael had her in the lounge of the restaurant, Sorcha and Sean beside them. "You aren't okay. You need to see Mary. This is the second time, Branna. You could have really hurt yourself."

Sean was shocked. "She fainted before?"

Michael nodded, "Aye, on our holiday. I should have made her go see Mary as soon as we got home."

Branna squeezed his hand. "I am seeing her tomorrow. I told her about the episode at Newgrange. She thinks I may be anemic or have low blood pressure. I will be fine. I just need to get some food in me and then some fresh air."

Michael looked doubtfully at her. "I'll take you first thing tomorrow."

She shook her head. No way could he go with her. "You have to work. I will be fine, Michael. I probably just need some supplements, a little more red meat. You aren't calling off work just to babysit. Now let's go finish breakfast, okay? I totally feel better." Branna was smiling, laying it on thick. What the hell had just happened? She was actually a little shaken by the fact that she had fainted twice in the last couple weeks. She faked her way through brunch, however. All eyes floating to her. The microscope treatment was giving her the sweats again.

They spent the rest of Sunday relaxing. They read, played a little music, played in bed. Michael had gone right to the store after brunch and bought some beautiful beef steaks, determined to get Branna's strength up. When he tried to buy some of her favorite wine, she declined. "Are you still feeling off?"

Branna answered lightly. "No, not at all. I just want to hydrate today. I don't know what the problem is, but it can't hurt to be careful." Michael saw the wisdom, forgoing the alcohol.

"I can feed myself, you know." Branna was propped on Michael's lap as he fed her steak and vegetables and a gorgeous dessert of nuts, berries, and honey drizzled over shortbread. "I like feeding you. It makes me feel good. I like when you lick the honey off my fingers, too." He was watching her mouth. She got off his lap and picked up the honey jar. Slowly she walked backward toward the bedroom.

Michael was thoroughly enjoying his dessert. Branna started by dabbing honey on him and licking it off, but he turned the tables on her. He rubbed a small amount of sticky honey on her nipple and she inhaled sharply. "Branna, your breasts are lovely. I swear since I've been feeding you, they've gotten even more so. They're gorgeous all together." He sealed his mouth over her nipple and she groaned his name. She put her hand behind his head, encouraging him to keep going, harder.

"Don't stop, Michael." She whispered with desperation. She straddled him with haste and slid herself down on his arousal right as he drew her nipple deep into his mouth and she came violently and immediately. Her breasts were sore and sensitive. She was feeling edgy and aroused and feeling him suck her as she impaled herself on him swept her over the edge instantly. She rode out the spasms as she jerked up and down on him, then put her hands on his chest and pushed him down on the bed. He laid back and looked up at her as she undulated, riding him slow and with purpose.

That had to be a record, was all Michael could think. He'd never seen Branna peak so fast. She was riding him, headed for another explosion and he was mesmerized. Unlike the night she'd broken down, she was smiling at him, playful as she took her pleasure. She was one hundred percent with him. She was confident, beautiful, and if it was possible for her body to look more beautiful than the first time he'd seen it, it did. Her hips were smooth and curvy, her breasts heavy and full. She wasn't one to take control during sex, more submissive. Damn it if she wasn't the hottest thing he'd ever seen. She knew right where she was headed, working her hips and her internal muscles until she seized up and threw her head back as she cried out, grinding hard as she came for him again. He couldn't get enough of watching her.

As she came down from the high, she looked at him, breathing heavy. "Behind me." He almost exploded right then. He flipped her over and she was on her hands and knees. She looked back at him, ass tipped up, waiting as he drove into her. Just when he thought he couldn't hold out anymore, he felt her clamp down. She started screaming unabashedly as she bucked against him, her hair flying everywhere. He clutched her shoulder and shoved hard into her as she arched and spasmed, a cry ripped from her gasping throat. She sent his own orgasm ripping through him like a freight train.

Both Michael and Branna lay in bed, panting, sweat-soaked, and exhausted. "I saw stars. I actually saw fucking stars." Michael's joints had turned to jell-o.

Branna gave a wicked, little giggle. "I'm sorry, I don't know what got into me."

Michael laughed incredulously, "Don't ever apologize for throwing me down and fucking me senseless, Hellcat." She hid her face in his chest and laughed.

* * *

BRANNA DROVE herself to the doctor's office right after Michael left for work. "The doctor is ready Miss O'Mara."

Mary brought her into the exam room. "Michael texted me last night to make sure you were set up this morning. He said you've had two fainting spells. Can you tell me anything else? Any other symptoms?"

Branna looked down at her hands. "I haven't gotten my period, Mary."

Dr. Flynn froze. "Um, I see. That hadn't occurred to me, although I suppose it should have. Did something about your activity status change?" Branna nodded. "Michael, I am assuming?" Another nod. Mary exhaled. "Okay, well let's not panic. Have you been taking your oral contraception?"

Branna answered, "Yes, of course. We didn't use anything else because I have been on the pill for two years. I just can't think of any other explanation other than…" She couldn't say it.

"Did you have any days where you missed a pill?" Mary asked.

Branna thought about it. "Just the morning you took me to the hospital. I usually take it before breakfast. By the time I was coherent and vertical it was the next morning. I doubled up, just like the packet said. I didn't think one day would matter."

Dr. Flynn was looking a little pale. "Jesus, Branna. I should have grabbed your pills on the way to the hospital. We left from my office and I didn't think about it. I thought you were a virgin. It didn't even occur to me."

Branna blushed. "I was, then. It happened that next week. I didn't think one pill would matter. The packet said to use another method if you missed two pills. I only missed one," she repeated.

Mary got up and started typing in the computer, nervously. "Most times it wouldn't, but we had you on some serious antibiotics, two different heavy hitters. Those can, in rare instances, diminish the effectiveness of birth control. Again, it is rare. There's debate about it, actually, but combine the drugs, the trauma to your body, the fact that you were taking them due to an overly healthy ovulation cycle, and you missed a pill, you could have ovulated during the month." Branna was rubbing her temples, trying not to freak out. "We can't speculate, we need to do a test."

Branna looked up at her, tears welling. "I did one." Mary's

eyebrows shot up. "Maybe it is wrong, I've heard they can be wrong," she said with a pleading look in her eyes.

Dr. Flynn took her hand. "We'll do the blood test. I have to be honest with you, Branna. False negatives happen, but false positives don't happen that often. Those tests are pretty accurate." Branna started trembling. "Does he know?"

She looked up, panic in her eyes. "No! God, Mary you can't tell him! He doesn't want children." She was starting to get worked up.

"Branna, he's a good man. He obviously cares for you. He'll do the right thing."

Branna shook her head, "You can't tell him."

Mary sat up a little straighter. "Branna, I know things are different in America, but this is Ireland. Catholic Ireland. Your options aren't," she paused. "You don't have as many here."

Branna looked at her, confused then shocked. "Oh my God, Mary I would never! This isn't a planned pregnancy, but I would never! Michael's feelings aside, this is my baby. This is the only family I have!" Branna shocked herself stupid. She put her hand over her mouth. She thought about what she'd just said. She stiffened her spine. "I have means. I can do this. I don't need someone marrying me out of obligation. I can go somewhere else, somewhere more affordable. I'm having this baby."

Mary's face was gentle, relief and sadness warring in her eyes. "If you are pregnant, it is his baby, too."

Branna's face tightened. "He told me part of the grounds for his annulment was that he wouldn't give Fiona children. He was very clear that she'd tried to trap him with a baby. I can't tell him, Mary. Neither can you. Promise me you will abide by your oath. Michael cannot know."

Mary came back into the office with the results of the blood test. "I think you already knew this, but it is positive. There is something else a little odd."

Fear stabbed Branna. "Is something wrong with the baby?"

Mary hastened to reassure her. "No, not as far as I know, but your HCG levels are high. That is the pregnancy hormone. You are only four weeks along, it shouldn't be this high unless…" She didn't have to finish.

"Unless it's more than one." Branna said softly.

"You knew?" Mary asked. She didn't, but she thought back to her dream, two eggs in the nest. Cora dreamed of baby birds, not a bird. Her father had come to her twice and once to Cora, he'd known about the babies. She was carrying twins, just like Michael and Brigid. She put her hands over her face and wept.

* * *

It was morning, and Michael was coming home from a twenty-four hour shift when he saw Branna up and buzzing around the kitchen. She'd made them both breakfast and she was wearing her da's pajamas. It made his heart ache. Did she wear them when she was sad or scared? Was it because she had slept alone, warding herself against her nightmares?

"You've made quite a spread. Vegetable omelet, sausages, and when did you start drinking orange juice?"

She just shrugged. "I need to do better with my diet. First a kidney stone, now anemia."

He pulled her to him. "That makes me happy to see. I might even let you have two cups of coffee."

She kissed him on the cheek. "Very sweet, but I am trying to give it up completely. New leaf and all. The juice is fine. Now, I have buttered you up with this big feast for a reason. I have some news."

* * *

"I still don't understand why you have to go with him." Michael was being whiney. He knew it. "Haven't you done enough? A trip to America?"

Branna was washing the dishes. "I spoke to my accountant. I need to be stateside when I make the final donation, in country or it will mess up the tax-exempt status. I can't run an American charity from another country. I will get penalized way more than airfare and a couple of nights in a hotel." She was lying. She hated it. There was no such rule, but she knew he didn't know the first thing about American tax law.

"I need to go. I wish I didn't have to, but this is important for Brendan. It's probably better that I'm there to make sure everything goes well, anyway. We worked too hard to get him to this point. Plus I can check on my renters."

Michael turned her around, away from her task. "You've been ill. Add jet lag to it and you might get to Boston and faint or something. I don't like it."

She hugged him trying to be reassuring. "I'm ok. Mary gave me some supplements." Not a lie, just leaving out the "pre-natal" prefix. "She said I need extra iron. I've been taking them for two days and I already feel way stronger." She hugged him tightly. "I wouldn't leave you if I could help it. I swear." Also not a lie. She fought back the tears.

CHAPTER 25

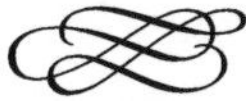

The next few days flew by. Thursday morning, she was on her way to meet Brendan, solidify the time frame for their departure. As she walked down the dock, the smell of dead fish hit her strongly in the gut. She made it to the dock's edge just in time to lose her breakfast. Toast and juice was all she could tolerate this morning. She retched violently over the dockside into the water. Little fish came up, nibbling at their recycled breakfast which sent her hurling another round. "Christ, lass. What's the matter?" *Oh shit.*

She wiped her mouth, straightening herself and blotting tears from her eyes from the straining. "Hi, Tadgh. Sorry you had to see that. I took my supplement on an empty stomach. Dr. Flynn warned me this would happen, but I kind of forgot until it was too late."

He smiled crookedly. "Well, I've lost my lunch a time or two in this same spot. It was the supplemental drink that was the culprit."

Branna laughed, nervously. "I'm fine. I need to remember to have something to eat before I take them. Don't tell Michael. He's already freaking out that I'm going to Boston." Tadgh didn't like it. She could tell by his face. "I promise you. That was all it was. Relax. You O'Brien men worry too much."

* * *

BRANNA AND MICHAEL had dinner at Brigid's house. She'd made some thick and rich beef stew and Sorcha had sent over some fresh bread. Branna brought the dessert. The nausea had subsided and she was famished. "What do you call this again?" Finn asked.

"Redneck Trifle! It's an American institution. Vanilla wafers, pudding, and bananas. You layer it like a trifle, and it is tasty!" Finn looked doubtful. "Just taste it. There aren't any blueberries, so you'll love it."

Finn made a face at Cora. "Blueberries, ew!"

"Da, mother says you're a nutter. Blueberries are verra good."

Michael swept Cora into his arms. "That's my girl. You eat your berries like a good little bear cub. You'll grow big and strong and fierce."

She took his face in her chubby hands. "I want to be a big bear like you, Uncle Michael."

He set her down. "You want to be a big, scary bear like me?"

Branna could tell this was a familiar game. "Yes, I want to eat all the little girls who won't go to bed!" She was wiggling, jumping up and down in anticipation.

"Oh, you mean like this?" Michael put his hands up like claws and growled, and little Cora squealed and ran. Michael chased her for a bit, growling to her delight. He finally caught her and tickled her, pretending to bite her limbs.

Branna's heart was breaking. "Sing the Fox Song for me, Uncle Michael. Please, I promise I'll go to bed. Sing the Fox Song!"

Michael and Finn got their instruments. "Wait, you play the fiddle too?" Branna asked. She liked Finn. He was the dark Irish of the group. Soft brown eyes, longish dark hair pulled back in a ponytail. He was big and lean like the O'Brien men. He towered over his wife. He looked more like a Pict warrior than an IT guy.

He smiled. "Yes, just not on stage. It's how I met Brigid." She looked at Brigid who was rolling her eyes.

They started warming up, tuning their instruments. Branna asked, "So, what's the story?"

Brigid was cleaning up and wiped her hands on a towel. "That fat headed lout was at a music festival. Musicians from around the country meet up for a little healthy competition. I caught him stealing my violin case with my violin in it."

Finn barked out a laugh. "Lies. She had it right near mine, I took hers on accident." He shrugged innocently.

Michael piped in. "Lies. She had her name in huge letters in plain view. He wanted to talk to her, and he couldn't get the balls up to say hello."

Finn was smiling unapologetically. "Well, it worked didn't it? I've got a second child on her. You could learn a thing or two from me." Brigid walked over to Finn and kissed him. He put his hand on her belly, kissed it. "I love you, mo chroí."

Branna felt tears threatening. God, she really was never going to have this. She was never going to look at Michael and know that he was overjoyed at the prospect of her carrying his child. Finn had been so natural. *I love you, mo chroí.*

She knew Michael cared for her, but deep down he wasn't sure he loved her. One thing he was sure about was that he didn't want children. He had never come right out and asked her to permanently move in with him. He'd said he wanted her around more than six weeks. He'd said they would wait, figure it out with Ned. He also had never said he loved her. Sure, when she'd had her meltdown, he said he could love her, if she'd let him. He'd said it in a desperate moment when he didn't know how to comfort her. He'd never said it before, and he hadn't said it since.

She just couldn't stay and watch his family guilt him into marrying her. Force him to have children he didn't want. He'd grow to resent her. He'd once called her conniving. He'd think she trapped him. She had lost so much in her young life. She wanted to leave while he still cared for her, wanted her. She had to leave before he noticed she wasn't getting her period, before she started to show.

"Branna!" She was jolted out of her lamentations.

"Sorry, daydreaming. What was that?"

Brigid looked at her strangely. "You looked like you were thinking about something sad. Are you upset about going to Boston?"

Branna shook herself. "Honestly, I wish I could avoid it, but I can't. I'm fine, really." She could tell Brigid was getting ready to probe a little deeper, but luckily the show was starting.

Michael was on the guitar and Finn on the violin. Cora was brimming with excitement. "We need Uncle Liam with his wee guitar!" Michael laughed, "That's a mandolin, sweet."

Finn said, "Darling, Uncle Liam's in Dublin chasing women."

Brigid scolded, "Finn, don't be telling her that! Cora, Uncle Liam is at school. Can you just let daddy and Uncle Michael play?"

Cora settled for the evening's entertainment, and they started playing. Branna knew this song. "The Fox" was a sweet little folk song her father used to sing to her. Cora was bopping up and down and swinging her little legs off the chair as they sang. Michael moved in close to her and she giggled as he sang to her.

Then the fox and his wife without any strife
cut up the goose with a fork and knife.
They never had such a supper in their life
and the little ones chewed on the bones-o, bones-o, bones-o

Branna was overcome with a wave of sorrow. She turned into the kitchen to stifle her crying and bumped straight into Brigid.

"What is wrong? Tell me." Brigid was holding her elbows, willing her to make eye contact. Branna sharpened up and put on a brave face.

"I think it's PMS. I've been missing my dad and I'm just a bit emotional." Only half a lie, God forgive her.

"Dessert time!" Brigid called everyone over.

Cora hopped in Branna's lap. "Auntie Branna will you make this for your children?" Branna froze, they all did.

Brigid broke the tension. "Cora, Branna doesn't have any children. Maybe she could teach you to make it for your little brother."

Everyone's head popped up. "I told you it was a boy! Halley's Comet isn't due back for decades!" Michael pointed and shouted.

Finn grabbed her and pulled her close. "A son? Oh, Brigid. You've given me everything." His voice cracked. She kissed him and it was like no one else was in the room.

"You're not mad that I spilled the beans?" She was smiling under his mouth.

He shook his head. "Christ, girl. I was ready to tie you up and tickle it out of you. It's been killing me." He kissed her again. "I have a son. First my little angel," he went and picked Cora off of Branna's lap, "and now a boy. I'm the happiest man alive."

Michael looked at Branna and tears were coming down her cheeks. He took her hand and squeezed it. "They're very happy, aren't they?" he said. She just nodded, too choked up to speak.

* * *

BRANNA MET Tadgh for lunch the next day. "I just missed you. I wanted a little time with you before I left."

Her eyes were sad, and Tadgh knew her. "Is something wrong, hen?"

She shook her head. "I just love it here. I love my new life. I'm not ready to fly off to Boston, even for a few days. I'll be fine." He squeezed her hand across the table. "Take care of Michael while I'm gone. Don't let him mope around," she said. Tadgh just nodded, looking at her strangely.

"You know, Tadgh. You can't let someone else's fears run your life. You know you can't keep this up."

He sighed, "Branna."

She stopped him, "Hear me out. You're so smart, Tadgh. I think you could do good things as a police officer. If men like you don't stand up and volunteer to help, then the world loses. I know you love this town, but this town will always be here for you. Your family will always be here for you. You have to be bold. See it through. Promise me you'll think about that."

As they left lunch, Branna hugged Tadgh fiercely. "I wish I'd had a brother like you." She whispered. He returned her hug. "I guess that puts to rest any ideas about me getting in your knickers." Branna laughed. "You are incorrigible," she admonished. Then she grew serious. "She's out there Tadgh. She will be quite something when you meet her."

* * *

"HELLO BRANNA, dear! What brings you here?" Sean kissed Branna and brought her in the house.

"I just wanted to make sure I saw you before I headed to Boston."

Sean smiled, "Well, Sorcha is up north. Her parents came home early from their holiday with the flu." He noticed the stricken look on her face. "She'll be back when you return. Come in and have a cup of tea with me." She sat at the counter while Sean worked on the tea and took out some cookies. "Sorcha made these before she left. She knows I like lemon."

Branna took a bite, and the citrus was soothing. She was having trouble keeping down her lunch.

"Would you like something more substantial? I have some tripe soup in the fridge I could reheat." That did it. She lurched for the bathroom and lost her entire lunch. "Branna, dear, can I help you? Some water, perhaps?" She came out after rinsing her mouth. "I'm sorry, Sean. These iron supplements that Mary put me on are really doing a number on my stomach."

As Branna left Sean and Sorcha's house, she hugged him. "You're the closest thing I've had to a dad for a long time. I love you."

Sean cupped the back of her head and kissed the crown. "Aye, lass. You are very dear to Sorcha and me. We love you like our own. You come back around when you get back. Sorcha will be sorry she missed you."

* * *

BRANNA USED this week to say her goodbyes. She'd done a little more visiting. She said goodbye to Patrick and then Caitlyn joined her at the spa. They got a manicure, giggling and gossiping like sisters. She was like the walking dead most moments. She was packed. She had a suitcase hidden in her trunk. She had the smaller suitcase in her bedroom, packed with the essentials. In the bigger one she'd taken her Kokeshi doll, her photo albums, and some of her clothes. She'd also packed the camera, which was full of pictures of the cottage, Michael sleeping, other things. She also tucked away her teacup.

She sat by the fire, wrapped in a blanket. She thought about how her relationship had evolved with this town, these people, and especially Michael since she'd shown up here that day in August. The thought of leaving was killing her. They would go on. They all would. They had each other.

The thought of leaving Michael was like a suffocating, unbearable pain in her chest. She knew that even if she stayed, and found another place to live, that it would never be the same. Her pregnancy aside, the spell would be broken. Once he had the house to himself and his life wasn't on hold anymore, he wouldn't feel the same way. She was here, sharing close quarters, and he had succumbed to the proximity and temptation. Once she moved out, he would realize that she was just some pathetic, lonely American girl. Once the immediacy of the situation was gone, maybe he wouldn't remember why they had come together.

On top of that, she was indeed pregnant. She was pregnant with twins. The man who wanted no children would have two. His family would pressure him into marrying her. Everyone would think she'd trapped him. She couldn't do it. She couldn't watch the most wonderful time in her life turn sour. She had to do this. She had to leave.

When Michael came home with a bouquet of white and lavender roses, he found her staring into the fire. "I know you can't take them, but I'll keep them fresh until you get back. I just wanted to get you something." Branna looked at him and couldn't hold back the tears. He held her as she cried. "I'm sorry, Branna. This is my fault. I made you feel guilty for going to Boston. I'm a selfish prat. Don't cry, darlin. It's only for a few days."

She looked at his beautiful face, memorizing it. *Will they look like him?* She started crying again. "I don't know what's wrong with me. I'm sorry. The flowers are beautiful."

He stroked her back. "Let's eat something and turn in early, mo chroi. Let's make the most of tonight, okay?"

Branna touched every inch of Michael. She needed this. She was going to have to live off of it for the rest of her life. This was the man who had awakened her sexuality, taught her, emboldened her. She'd never have physical passion like this again. She needed to pay attention and savor every moment. As if he sensed some underlying desperation, he was completely in tune with her. Slow, deliberate moves, long, deep kisses. He drank her in, kissing and tasting and touching every inch of her. Their bodies so intertwined that they were one flesh, one soul. Branna let the experience cut her heart to ribbons, because she knew that on some level she deserved it. He had no idea that this would be the end.

He would be angry when he found out she'd left, but he would have the cottage. He'd have his family. He would be okay. He was too wonderful to stay alone for long. She needed this one night with him where he was still completely hers.

BRENDAN and his wife chatted non-stop as they flew from Dublin to Boston. Neither had been to the US and they were very excited. Branna was glad for the distraction. She was avoiding the inevitable crushing reality of life back in the states. No family, no Michael, no pubs full of lively characters and beautiful music. She finally drifted to sleep half way over the Atlantic.

Branna was standing in the rain. She was on the beach, looking over the Atlantic. She lifted her shirt. The same rune was painted on her belly. It was swollen with impending motherhood. Her father was next to her. "What are you doing, Branna? You need to go back to your nest." She woke, looking around the airplane. She took an old receipt out of her purse and sketched the rune on the back. It looked like a square that was turned to look like a diamond, two lines branching out at the bottom like legs. She laid her head back and stared out the plane window. *Oh, Daddy. You don't understand. You weren't there to watch her die.*

Boston was a chaotic whirlwind of appointments, speaking engagements, and a Celtics game that Branna gracefully bowed out of. Brendan's prosthetic was amazing. His wife cried, thanking Branna for all that she had done. The doctor in Boston had assured him that he would Skype and walk Dr. Flynn's prosthetic colleague through any adjustments or re-fittings and send parts at wholesale if we couldn't get them in Ireland. The mission was a success.

As they left for the airport, Branna informed them she had to take a different airline. "Well, then I suppose we'll see you again over the ocean." Brendan was smiling. She hated lying to him. "Ok, Brendan if you could give this to Michael when you get home, please?" She handed him a sealed envelope. He looked at her strangely. "I am taking a long route and I may get stuck in Germany. I just want him to have that itinerary since my phone doesn't work out of country. Make sure he gets it right away."

She was lying of course. She wasn't going back over the Atlantic. She hugged him and walked toward the United terminal, toward her flight to North Carolina. The flight took several hours, with one stop in Charlotte. When she got into the terminal and went to get her luggage, she saw Anna waiting for her. She approached her, looked at her only close friend on this continent, and her face crumpled. Anna dropped her purse on the ground and hugged her.

CHAPTER 26

Michael was waiting in Dublin when Brendan got off the plane with his wife. He and Liam were waiting by the pick up area when they came out. He was supposed to wait for Branna at home, but he drove up last minute, excited to see her. Michael looked around. "Where is Branna?" Brendan and his wife looked at each other and then at him. "She was on a different flight. She didn't tell you? She gets in later tonight."

Michael sighed. "No, she didn't. I assumed she was on your flight. I suppose we can go get some dinner and come back. Did she give you her flight information?" Brendan dug in his carry-on. "Aye, she said to give you this." Brendan and his wife walked to the luggage carousel to grab their bags.

Michael opened the letter. He'd had a bad feeling ever since she'd left, but it got exponentially worse when she'd not come home with Brendan. Alarms were going off in his head. He opened the page and a key was taped to it.

Dearest Michael, Please, don't hate me. I just couldn't. The cottage is yours, as it always

should have been. I'll never forget you, and I want you to be happy. Be happy enough for both of us.

Love, Branna

Michael's hand was trembling as he peeled the cottage key off of the paper. Liam took the paper out of his hand as he turned and walked out of the airport.

Michael called her phone. It was disconnected. He also called her old phone number that Tadgh had from her first week. Also disconnected. "She wouldn't leave for no reason. What the hell happened?"

Michael looked at his brother. "Do I look like I was expecting this?" He banged his head against the seat. "We were happy. God, Liam. I don't know. She was happy."

The next week went by in a haze. Upon returning to the cottage, he looked around. Her little wooden doll was gone, most of her clothes, her photos. Michael dodged calls from his family, worked overtime. He was in Shannon when the call came in for air rescue. Perfect distraction. He sat in the briefing room as his commanding officer addressed the rescue team. "Alright, this is serious. We have multiple passengers in the water. They are getting the shit pounded out of them on the rocks. Stay sharp!"

As they loaded the gear, Officer in Charge pulled Michael aside. "Is your head clear?" Michael started to argue. "Shut it, O'Brien. You've been an insufferable prick all week. You've been working too much and you look like shit. I need you in the game. Finish this and you are off for the rest of the week. Before you open that gob of yours and say something stupid, that's an order. You need to clear your head."

* * *

BRANNA WOKE WITH A GASP. Her heart was pounding and she was shaking. She jumped as a knock came on her bedroom door.

"Branna, can I come in?" It was Anna. Anna sat on the end of the bed. "Another bad dream?" Branna just nodded. "Was it about your dad again? The birds?"

Branna took a deep breath. Anna knew everything there was to know about her. She'd missed that connection. "No, it was different. It was about Michael. He was in the water and there was blood. I'm okay. I'm sorry for waking you."

Anna took her hand. "I was up. You know me."

Branna laughed a little, trying to lighten her mood. "The vacationers move out in the morning, then I have the other half for a couple of weeks. I'm sorry I didn't give you any warning. You didn't have to boot a boyfriend out of here did you?"

Anna snorted. "Are you kidding? You know me, I kick them out right after I'm done with them." They both laughed, now. She was kidding of course. As beautiful as Anna was, she dated almost as little as Branna had. "You know I love having you with me, Branna. You can stay forever, even with the babies. I just don't like the circumstances. I never took you for a quitter."

Branna bristled. "I explained everything to you, Anna. This is for the best. Michael doesn't want kids. I don't want to be a pity wife. End of story."

Anna shook her head. "Not buying it, little sister. You didn't tell him did you?" Branna was silent. "Well, you never could lie, so thanks for that. Now, what the hell were you thinking?" Branna's eyes shot up, irritation flickering. "Don't look at me like that, missy. He may not want kids, but not telling him? Sneaking away? That reeks of cowardice."

Branna wrapped her arms around herself, not meeting her friend's eyes. Anna gave a little frustrated grunt. "You know I love you. I'll raise those little rug-rats with you like something off of Lifetime for Women if that's what you want. I just want you to be happy. You look like you lost your best friend. If you loved him that much, he must have done something pretty bad to make you just leave like this."

Branna eyes were so sad. "He didn't do anything. This is just how it has to be. I can do this. I can start over with my babies."

Anna corrected. "Our babies. Don't you mean our? They're his babies, too. Whether you tell him or not, they're his blood. You'll look at them every day and remember him, and someday you will have to explain why they don't have a daddy. Even if he hurt you, even if he's a big jerk, you should tell him. At least make him support them."

Branna just looked away and said softly, "He's not a jerk. I just don't want his money. This is how I have to do it."

Anna gave a capitulating sigh. "Okay, I'm in. I'm here with you, sister. We can tell the neighbors we're lesbians and these are our love children." She elbowed Branna, trying to make her laugh. "Either that or you could take my brother up on his offer."

Branna rolled her eyes and Anna giggled. Anna's older brother Erik was a cocky Marine pilot and a divorcee at twenty-six. He was a good enough guy, but had never been Branna's type. He had been scandalized at the thought of Branna being a single mother. He also had a thing for her. He'd actually offered to marry her, raise the children with her, give her security. A lot of girls would have jumped at the chance. He was as good looking as the rest of the family. She just couldn't marry someone she didn't love. "What? You don't want to marry God's gift to the world?"

They both started giggling and pretty soon they were tangled on the bed, tears of laughter coming down their faces.

* * *

Brigid and Finn were eating at her parents' house when the call came in. Sean's face was grim as he took the call. "What's happened?" Sorcha's face was etched with fear. "Is it Michael or Aidan? God, deliver me from sons!"

Sean said, "Easy. It's Michael. He's all right. He got a panicked swimmer, lost control and they flew into the rocks. He shielded the man and took the bashing. He hit his head, banged up his arm. His CO said they took him to the local hospital."

Brigid cursed under her breath. She said, "He's all right, Ma. I'd feel it if he wasn't." Sorcha took a deep breath, taking some comfort in that. Brigid and Michael had a strong twin connection.

CHAPTER 27

Michael sat in the cottage, glass in his hand, half empty bottle sitting on the table. When he'd taken a cup out to make some tea, he'd noticed one more missing item. Her Book of Kells teacup. He'd grabbed the whiskey bottle instead.

He heard knocking and ignored it. There was more knocking, then the door opened. "I didn't invite you in."

Brigid's voice was stern. "Well, that's a bloody shame, because I don't give a shit."

He sighed, "Brigid, I'm not in the mood."

She snatched the bottle off the table. "I can see that. Did you take your pain medicine with this?"

He shook his head. "I'm drunk, not suicidal. Go away, peahen."

Brigid's heart broke as she looked at him. Arm in a sling, stitches at his crown, he was broken in every way. Anger surged in her. She knew how much Branna loved him. This could not be over.

Brigid walked over and smacked his foot off its prop. "Snap out of it! We lost her too! What the hell are you going to do about it?"

He jumped up and screamed at her. "What in the hell do you want me to do? She left me. She didn't give two shits how much it hurt everyone! She lied, she sneaked, and she took off! She disconnected her phones, she changed her email. She doesn't want me!" He walked over, picked up the picture she'd given him and threw it against the wall. It smashed to pieces. He picked up the piano bench and started to smash it over the piano.

"Michael, don't!" He froze, mid-swing. "Don't do it." She pleaded. "You don't know what's going on. Don't do something you can't take back."

He dropped the bench and held his head with both hands. "I don't know how to do this, Brigid. I don't know how to live here without her."

She put her hand on his shoulder. "Turn around, Michael." She was gutted by his expression when he did. "Oh, Michael. You can't do this. You can't give up. I know she loves you. This can't be over."

After two cups of tea and a shower, Michael started cleaning up the mess in the house. He hadn't done a dish or swept or done anything for a week. Brigid's voice rang in his head. *You can start by taking a bloody shower and cleaning the house up. There's garbage all over the garden. Some animals got into it, and it's strewn all over.*

He went outside to clean up the mess. He had forgotten to take the garbage to the street and it had been piling up. He was startled by the culprits. Ravens, jet black ravens brazenly squawking at him. *Oh, the irony.* He started shooing them, stomping his foot. One stayed, picking at a piece of paper. It cawed at him. "Bugger off!" The raven took flight, swooping over his head. He went over to look at what it had been pecking at. It was a receipt. The 24 hour drug store in Ennis. The birds had knocked the bin over. He started picking up bits of trash.

Then he found something that stopped him cold. A ripped piece of packaging. *Over 99% Accurate. Early Results.* He started rifling through the pile of garbage that was half out of the bin like a man possessed. He found the drug store bag and remembered the receipt. He unfolded the wadded up paper. *PregTst 15.00 EU.* It was dated the day they'd gone to mass and brunch. The day she fainted. She'd shopped in the wee hours of the morning, the day before she went to the doctor.

He dug until he found it. It was concealed in toilet tissue. A flash-back assaulted his brain. He had woken to her out in the garbage bin at the break of dawn. She had visibly paled when she saw he was awake, made up some excuse why she'd been taking the trash out so early.

* * *

"I NEED to speak to Dr. Flynn." The nurse was prickly. She didn't like his bossy tone, but Michael didn't give a shit. "She's with a patient, Michael. You are going to have to make an appointment." He cursed under his breath. "I'm not sick. I need to speak with her. It won't take long."

Mary emerged from her office. "Michael, you need to lower your voice. Come into my office."

He walked back and she shut the door. "She's gone, Mary. She's gone back to America and I can't get ahold of her."

Mary's face blanched. "Bloody fucking hell." Michael's brows raised. Mary never cursed, at least not in front of him.

He continued, pulling the telltale stick out of his pocket. "I found this in the trash. She tried to hide it outside."

Mary sighed. "I can't discuss this with you, Michael. I'm sorry."

"God damn it, Mary! Don't give me that shit! Is she pregnant? Did she leave Ireland carrying my child?"

Mary shot him a warning look. "Don't you get high handed with me, Michael O'Brien. I took care of you when you were still pissing the bed. You will not bully me on this. She has rights."

He put his face in his hands, then slid them up and through his hair. "And I don't?"

The sweet, professional, controlled Doc Mary tightened her jaw, picked up a stack of medical journals, and threw them across the room. She muttered under her breath, "What a bloody cock-up."

She gave him a pitying look. "Find her, Michael. For God's sake, find her."

* * *

MICHAEL KNEW ALL he needed to know. The fact that Mary was so closed lipped and that Branna had run scared confirmed it. She had to be pregnant. The only question now was who else knew? Brigid would have told him. He went to the only person she might have felt safe telling. A person who for the last week had gone radio silence. He walked into Gus's back rehearsal room.

Tadgh was rehearsing with Aidan, Sean, Sorcha, Brigid and Patrick. Aidan had heard about the accident and about Branna. Aidan had caught wind of everything and come in for the weekend to be with the family. Michael stood in front of Tadgh and slammed the pregnancy test down in front of him. Tadgh looked at it, confused.

Brigid and Sorcha recognized what it was. "Where did you get that, Michael? Bloody hell, is that Branna's?" It was Brigid talking, but Michael's eyes never left Tadgh's.

"Did you know?"

Tadgh stood up. "Jesus, is that what I think it is?"

Michael's voice boomed, "Did you know?"

Tadgh looked at him in shock. "No! Of course not! What the hell are you on about? Are you saying she's pregnant?"

Michael got deadly calm, "It would appear so. Is it mine, Tadgh?" The punch came out of thin air. Tadgh gave Michael a right hook and knocked him on his ass.

"Whoa!" someone yelled. The brothers flew into action. Aidan grabbed Michael and Patrick grabbed Tadgh. Sean jumped in the middle, the women were screeching.

"That's enough!" Sean bellowed.

Tadgh put his hands up, "Oh, Christ. Uncle Sean, I'm sorry."

Sean glared at Michael. "Don't apologize. He deserved it."

"What the fuck kind of question was that, you bastard?" Tadgh was done attacking, but he was livid. "You know very well that you're the only one she's been with. Ever."

Everyone in the room gave their own muttered expletives under their breath, but Brigid was ever the blunt one. "Jesus Christ, Michael. You took her virginity? How could you say such a thing?"

Michael's anger deflated. He slumped in Aidan's grasp. "Fucking hell, Tadgh. What did

I say, brother? Da is right. I did deserve it. I'm out of my bloody mind right now."

Tadgh went to him, took his face in his hands. "Never again. Do you hear me? Never. This is not about us, or your bloody misguided insecurities. What does that test say?"

Sorcha was the one that answered, "She's pregnant."

"The puking. Damn it all to hell." Michael looked at Tadgh.

"You saw her throw up?"

He nodded. "On the docks. She said it was the new vitamins Mary had given her."

Sean spoke then, "She threw up at the house as well, when I offered her tripe soup."

Brigid grunted, "Aye, that would do it."

Sean continued, "When she came to say goodbye. She gave me the same excuse. She said the iron pills were upsetting her stomach."

Michael started thinking about all the other signs he missed. "Jesus, the fainting. And no coffee. No coffee and no wine. She started drinking orange juice."

Brigid spoke then. "For the folic acid, Michael. She's drinking it for the baby."

Patrick spoke then. "She's been stopping to see everyone. She hugged me, told me to take care of Caitlyn. She's been saying goodbye. Christ, the poor girl. She seemed so sad, even though she was trying to hide it."

Michael slammed his fist on the table. "Why? Why would she leave? Why would she keep this from me?"

Brigid cleared her throat, treading carefully. "Because you told her you didn't want children, Michael. I'd imagine that's why she left so suddenly. She didn't think you would want the baby."

Michael said, "What? I did no such thing!"

She raised a brow. "Really, because she seemed pretty convinced. She told me before this all happened and before you were together. She said that you told her Fiona's grounds for annulment were because you wouldn't give her children. At the wedding, she was watching you with Cora. She said she couldn't believe a man who was so good with children didn't want any of his own. What exactly did you say to her, Michael?"

He thought about it. "I told her Fiona wanted to have a baby. That I refused to give her children." He exhaled and shook his head, "That she wanted to trap me with a baby when she knew we were having problems. She wanted to make sure I'd never leave her by getting pregnant." He shook his head, "I didn't mean I never wanted kids. I just didn't want them with Fiona."

Tadgh gave him a candid look, "Did you tell her that? Because you can bet your ass that isn't the version Fiona told her."

Michael cursed and flipped over a chair. Brigid continued, "She would have never stayed if she thought we'd all gang up on you and make you marry her. And we would have!" she said with a little more pluck than was needed.

"You don't think..." Aidan's voice trailed off.

"What?" Michael asked.

Aidan rubbed his neck. "I don't know how to say this without it coming out awful. I'm fond of Branna, you'd know her better than I, but..." he hesitated. "America, women have more options. When they get pregnant, they have more options."

Fear washed through Michael and he swayed, grabbing a chair to balance himself. The thought of her terminating the pregnancy hadn't even crossed his mind. Is that why Mary wouldn't tell him? "Oh, Jesus."

"No!" Brigid shouted. She got in front of her twin. "You saw her with Cora. You said yourself she wouldn't even have a cup of coffee! If she was going to do something like that, she wouldn't bother. She'd sneak off quickly, do it, and come back. She's a Catholic, Michael."

He thought about it. She had asked to come to mass with him right after she'd bought that pregnancy test. "I'd like to think she wouldn't, but what if she gets over there and changes her mind? What if she gets scared and alone and panics and does something rash?"

Tadgh got eye to eye with him now. "Then you'll forgive her.

You'll forgive her and bring her home. Brigid is right, though. She wouldn't. She's got no family left. That baby is the only tie to the two families she's ever had. That baby is the only tie to you." Tadgh throat was tight with emotion. "Don't you know how much she loves you? How much she loves all of us? She wouldn't. You know her." Michael looked at him, straightening up. He nodded, too choked up to speak.

"Did you tell her how much you loved her? Did you tell her that she had a home here, with you?" It was his father's voice now.

Michael answered defensively, "I did, sort of. Not exactly in those words, but we were getting there. I thought I had more time. She knew how I felt."

His father got in closer, almost aggressively. "Really? Because no one else seems to know. How the hell do you feel about her, Michael? I can tell you if you had made it clear to her, she wouldn't have gotten on that bloody plane!"

"I love her, Da! Okay? I love her so much it rips my guts out! I watch her suffer, I wake her from nightmares and it rips my guts out." His eyes were ruined. "You wouldn't have had to force me. I'd count myself lucky to be her husband. I just...God I thought I had more time. She's everything to me and I fucked it up. Is that what you want to hear? I would burn that fucking cottage to the ground before I would live there without her!" His voice was shaking.

Sorcha's pleading voice broke in, "Sean, please."

Sean grabbed Michael and held him. "Yes, that is exactly what I want to hear." He pulled away and started pacing. "We have to find her. She's carrying your child. She needs you," his voice broke as he became emotional. "She needs a mother." He looked at Sorcha, tears welling in his eyes. She put her hand over her mouth, the tears free flowing silently from her. Sean cleared his voice. "She needs a family." Aidan and Patrick and Tadgh grunted in agreement. He put his hand on the back of Michael's head and pulled him close, nose to nose. "That child needs a da and a grandda. We'll find her. When we do, you will go get her and bring her back. You will bring her back if you have to tie that little hellcat to a rowboat and row across the Atlantic. You will be on the first flight out of here when we figure out where the hell she's gone."

* * *

JENNY BROUGHT in a pot of tea. Jack McCain had joined them with all of the financial statements from Branna's home application. Sean was looking at the spread. "How many states does she own property?"

Michael answered, "Five. She's got two in California, one in Florida, one in Virginia, one in North Carolina, one in Boston."

Sean nodded. The *Holy shit that's a lot of ground to cover* going unsaid. "Would she go to the Boston one since it's close?" Patrick asked.

Michael shook his head. "Those tenants are an older couple, they've been there for years. She told me she had them all rented. It's one of the reasons she was so upset when she got here. She had no empty house to go back to."

Tadgh chimed in, "She wouldn't go there because it was the most obvious choice. She's taken measures to go under the radar. God help me, I don't understand why. How could she not understand that you would have taken care of her?" He instantly answered his own question. "Because love killed her mother. She's not running from your feelings, she's running from hers."

Michael said, "She's not her mother. She's strong. She just keeps forgetting it."

Sean thought about it. "We are looking at this the wrong way. She's alone, pregnant, scared. She has to have someone. Who would she go to?"

Michael looked at Tadgh and they both spoke. "Anna."

Aidan asked, "The one in North Carolina?"

Michael nodded, "Anna Falk. Her father was a Gunnery Sgt. when Branna's father was killed. He pulled him out of the line of fire, took a sniper round, too. I don't know what rank he is now, but there can't be that many Falks in that area. They were the closest thing she had to family in the states."

Tadgh nodded, "The beach house is a duplex, the other side is a holiday rental. That's where she would go, you're right. I'm going with you."

Aidan interrupted. "No, he gets stupid about you and Branna." Michael started to argue. "Need I remind you why you got knocked on your ass?" Michael put his hands up in surrender.

"Aidan, do you still have friends in the American Marines?" Sean asked.

"Aye, I have one that is stationed right at Camp Lejeune. I'll go." He looked at Michael, "I'll go with you, brother."

Michael looked at Patrick with a bit of regret. "I'm going to miss seeing you off." Patrick waved a dismissive hand. "Go get her, Michael. We'll say our goodbyes and I'll see you in a few weeks. Don't come home without her. Caitlyn has been beside herself. Go get our girl."

Aidan got off the phone. "Okay. He is taking a drive out to Topsail Island. Apparently it's right out the back gate of the base. He is going to see if he can get an eye on anyone. He'll park and walk down the shore. It's a public beach. He can get pretty close to the house. He said he'd put a blanket on the beach and stay out there from dusk until dawn if he had to. As soon as we have confirmation, we buy tickets into Jacksonville. We have a place to stay if she tosses you out on your ass."

Michael smirked. He was clear headed. He would find her. He thought about the ravens picking at that garbage. The hair stood up on his neck. He was supposed to find her.

Michael went to Tadgh who was standing by the bar, hand wringing and looking across at the liquor. They'd been planning and investigating for hours, on the phone to the states, on the internet. Everyone was exhausted. "I'm sorry. I didn't mean it. I don't know why I said it. I just get jealous. Not because I think you would do that, or her really, but because she tells you things. She tells you things that she doesn't tell me."

Tadgh looked at him. "Do you tell Aidan and Brigid things you don't tell anyone else?" Michael nodded. "She's got to have someone, like a brother. She moved away from Anna. She told me that she was the closest thing to a sister she'd ever had. She needed someone. So did I. Losing our father's, it was sort of a bond between us." And didn't that just put a fresh wave of guilt through Michael's chest.

Michael had one more question. "Why haven't you called me? If you didn't know, then why?"

Tadgh sighed. "I was pissed off at you, Michael. I figured she left because you were too much of a coward to tell her you loved her. I couldn't see you yet. I love her too, Michael. Not the way you do, but I love her. This is killing me. I miss her so much it's like a hole in my chest."

Michael hugged him. "I love you, Tadgh. I should have been there more for both of you. I'll never doubt you again, brother. I can't say I won't get jealous. I am a jackass when it comes to her, but I am going to try and do better."

Tadgh just grinned indulgently. "I love you, too. You're my best friend, Michael. Don't you know that?"

Michael shrugged a shoulder. "Yes, I suppose I do. Branna was right, you know. You would be a good police officer. You and Da, I've been watching you. You're right in step with him. You can't waste your time here anymore. I'll take care of Aunt Katie."

Tadgh just stared at himself in the bar mirror and didn't answer. Just then, Michael heard Aidan yell from the other room. "She's there!"

* * *

Michael was walking along the cliffside, the wind was blowing and the sky was dark. The crashing waves roared beneath him and he looked out at the jagged, rocky cliff. He remembered kissing her here. Wrapped in a blanket and in his arms, they had kissed like they were the only two people in the world. He was distracted by a mound of black birds, cawing in the wind, leaping and soaring in and out of a pile of clothing. Then he saw it. Long black hair draped over a huddled figure. Amidst the cawing of the ravens he heard a baby crying.

He ran to them, screaming and shooing the birds away. Branna was huddled, clutching the baby protectively, tears streaming down her face. She looked utterly ruined. "It's okay. Mommy will take care of you. Mommy loves you."

Michael was screaming, but she couldn't hear him. He knelt by them, yelling to no avail. He couldn't touch her, couldn't hold her, couldn't even get her to look up. He looked past her and saw a man. A man in a military uniform, familiar blue eyes, and tightly cut hair that was as black as night. There was sadness etched in his face as he watched Branna. His boots were bloody. He looked as helpless as Michael felt. He looked at Michael, looking him up and down as if sizing him up. His jaw tensed, judgement in his eyes. He looked back at the woman and child.

She just kept rocking the baby as its chubby little hand came out of the wrapping, reaching toward Michael. The baby cried inconsolably. "Mommy will always want you. You'll never be alone."

Michael shot upright in his bed screaming. He gripped his head in his hands. His head was splitting open, both due to the head injury and the crippling despair he'd felt in the dream. "Oh, God. Oh, God! Hang on, Branna. Please, I'm so sorry!" He was moaning the words as Aidan leapt through the doorway.

"Jesus Christ," was all his brother could say.

Michael swung his legs off the bed, his head hung low as he bent over the edge. He was gasping, trying to steady his breath. "It was Branna, her and the baby. Oh, God. They were so alone! She's alone!"

Aidan put a hand on his neck and tried to calm him. "They're not alone, brother. We'll find them. Do you hear me?" He squeezed Michael's neck. "Look at me." Michael lifted his head and looked into those blue eyes. So strong, so much like their Da's eyes. "We will find her and bring her home."

CHAPTER 28

Jacksonville, North Carolina-Home to Marine Corps Base Camp Lejeune

The O'Brien brothers got off the small plane in Jacksonville tired and bedraggled. They had grabbed the first flight out of Dublin that they could afford the next day. It was not, however the most direct flight. Michael's head was throbbing at his stitches and his arm hurt. He was completely sleep deprived, haunted by horrible, stress-induced dreams and the nagging fear that Branna had done something irreversible. He winced as he adjusted his carry-on.

"You should have kept it wrapped. Where the hell is your sling?" Aidan could tell he was in pain.

"It's fine. I need two arms to handle the luggage. I'll need two arms to hold her down while you tie her up." Both men started laughing. Fatigue and worry spilling into a case of hysteria that only came out in two ways for O'Brien men. Laughing and fighting. Just as they grabbed their checked bags, Aidan's friend approached.

"You two look like shit."

Aidan turned around and embraced the man. "Christ, it is good to see you. Captain Denario, meet my brother, Michael."

The men shook hands. "Call me John. So, are you ladies going to freshen up first? I can take you to my house, get some coffee in you and let you shower."

Michael shook his head. "I need to see her. I need to go now. I can't thank you enough for everything you've done."

Denario slapped him on the back. "Are you kidding? My wife is beside herself. She said this is like something out of a romance novel. I swore her to silence. I don't know everything, but I know enough. She's the daughter of a Marine killed in action. You let her get away. We are prepared to remedy that if you are." Michael nodded.

"We don't leave orphaned Marine kids to fend for themselves. I'm at your disposal." Then he grew serious. "Hear this, though. She won't be forced into anything. I hope you brushed up on your sweet talk, my friend." Michael just gave him a weary smile. He liked this guy.

"Anna Falk is daughter to Sgt. Major Hans Falk. He's kind of a legend. It's probably fortunate for you that he's currently stationed in Virginia. His son is a pilot at Cherry Point, about an hour from here. He won't be bothering you either. Now, you two need wheels. Just let me swing by the house. Aidan can grab our other car and take you to her." Michael shook his hand again. "Thanks for the intel and the transport. I won't forget this."

Michael and Aidan pulled into the driveway and both their hearts were racing. "Don't screw this up brother. Keep that temper under control. She'll meet you head on."

Michael sighed, "It's not like I plan it out that way."

Aidan just looked at him. "You can't come home without her. She needs to come home."

Michael answered quietly as he stared at the house. "Aye."

"Ok, according to what Denario found out, Anna is on the left. He said it looks like there aren't any holiday renters on the right and that she is staying there, but he isn't sure. She might be staying with Anna on the other side. So, you go right and I'll go left."

They got out of the car. It was warm for mid-November, but there was a breeze. He could hear the ocean. The appeal to live here must be strong, though he imagined the tourist season was worse than in Doolin. *God, please let me be enough.*

The men separated, walking to each pathway toward the front doors of the duplex. Aidan rang the door bell. He could hear someone running down the stairs. When the door swung open, he lost his breath. A green eyed, fair-haired Goddess answered. "Bleeding Christ," he said, before he could stop himself. She looked at him like he was insane and went to shut the door. "Anna! Anna Falk? Please don't shut the door, lass."

She swung it back open. Her eyes narrowed. "O'Brien?" Aidan nodded. He was getting ready to tell her exactly which O'Brien when she slammed the damned door right in his face. He could hear her marching away and he started beating on the door. His temper surged the longer he knocked. "Fuck it." He opened the door right as she reappeared.

"I didn't invite you in, buddy. Back up, before I back you up."

Aidan's brows shot up. Interesting. She had a sweet southern accent and she was marvelously pissed. He looked her up and down, not hiding his appraisal.

"Don't you dare look at me that way. I'll smack your eyeballs back in your head. God, she said you were a good guy!" She started to slam the door again and he caught it solidly with his palm.

His eyes narrowed. "Don't make assumptions."

Just then Michael came next to him. "Aidan, she's not answering. Is she over here?" Michael looked at Anna, then at Aidan. Steam seemed to be coming out of both of their ears. He shook his head. "Are you Anna? Anna Falk?"

She looked at him and then at Aidan. "You're Michael?"

He nodded. "Is she with you? Jesus, tell me she is still here." Anna looked at Michael's face. She saw desperation, sadness, relief.

Her expression softened. "You love her." It wasn't a question.

"I swear, she didn't tell me. She just took off and went out of contact. I need to find her. I've come to bring her home. Please tell me where she is, Anna. She's scared, but I know she loves me, too."

Anna thought for a moment. He could see indecision in her face. She sighed, "She's out for a walk. She went that way," she pointed.

"She took a phone with her in case she started feeling poorly. If you walk down the beach, you'll find her."

Michael went to run down to the beach when she called back to him. "Michael!" He turned. "She's nursing some pretty serious wounds. If you worsen that situation, then you and I are going to tango. Understood?" Michael's eyebrows shot up. So did Aidan's. She sounded as sweet as a summer peach, but under that pretty little drawl was pure hard ass.

Aidan waited to see Anna's face turn to him. She looked at him, a hint of contrition showing before she changed to a defensive stance. "How the heck was I supposed to know?"

He smiled sweetly. "Well, I guess the answer is that you couldn't know for sure. That's why you keep your wee gob shut until you find out all of the facts."

She put her hands on her hips. "I'm assuming my gob is referring to my mouth?" she said saucily. He looked at her mouth, nodding once.

She betrayed herself with one corner of her mouth coming up, suppressing a grin. "You're not one for over disclosure are you? The stoic older brother, Royal Irish Regiment. Now it makes sense."

His eyes flared. She didn't give him a chance to respond. "The door should be unlocked. Good luck to your brother, Aidan. That little lady might be my best friend, but she is a handful. He has his work cut out for him." Then she shut the door, but not before doing her own quick head to toe appraisal.

* * *

MICHAEL WALKED about a half mile before he saw her. Small frame, hair bound up behind her head, wisps swirling. She was staring out into the water, over the Atlantic. Was she thinking of him, he wondered? Her hand smoothed over her flat belly and relief hit him. Relief, anger, guilt, hurt, and a stirring arousal all warred within him. He sped up, walking with purpose.

Branna was deep in thought. She missed Michael so much she felt like there was an anchor on her chest. She thought about what Anna had said. *What have I done?* She smoothed her hand over her abdomen instinctually, as if she could shield them from her own personal agony. She saw motion to her right and turned.

She wasn't sure she wasn't hallucinating. She put her hand over her mouth. He approached her. She started to shake. "Are you real?" she said weakly as the tears started to flow. He looked at her, not touching her. The pain in his face sliced through her. "I'm sorry, Michael. I shouldn't have done it the way I did. Please forgive me. I just," She swallowed hard, "I know this is best. You shouldn't have come all the way here. This is best for everyone." She turned and looked at the water.

Michael came a few steps closer. "Oh, really? How magnanimous of you to decide that for everyone. So, what was your plan, exactly? Come here and start over, again? Casually ignore me and change your phone number. Was it that simple for you? Maybe find a new man? Let him love you, let him raise my child?" His voice was starting to get angry.

Her eyes flew to his. He knew. She didn't bother with denials. She could see it in his eyes. Somehow, he knew. "I found it. I found the test you buried under piles of garbage. How could you leave me when you knew you were pregnant?" His tone was accusatory.

She walked past him. "Michael, I had to. You were very clear that you didn't want children. There really wasn't anything left to say given my condition."

She breezed past him and he yelled at her. "I never said that! Never!"

She flipped around, anger starting to take over. "You did. You told me all about how you didn't want to give Fiona children. How Fiona tried to trap you with a baby! Even Fiona made sure to warn me that you never wanted kids! So, day ninety was fast approaching and all the sudden I'm pregnant? I couldn't stand the thought of you resenting me! That you might think I contrived this to trap you into keeping me at the cottage. You know your family would have forced you to take responsibility. I couldn't be that unfair to you. I won't live like that. I won't let you trap yourself out of obligation."

He grabbed her. "Obligation? You gutted me when you left! Do you hear me?" He let go and backed away. He ran his fingers over his short hair, overcome with too many emotions at once. "I've had a lot of time to think about this, Branna. Fourteen hours on a plane as a matter of fact. You heard what you wanted to hear. You're afraid. You love me and it scares the shit out of you! You ran because you knew how much I loved you. You took me as your lover after years of letting nothing and no one into your life. No love, no passion, no pain, no pleasure. Then you gave me this gift. You unlocked yourself and gave me all of you. Your body, your soul, passion like I never thought was possible. Then you snatched it away like it meant nothing! Left with a note and a key taped to it like you'd checked out of a guesthouse. Even if you weren't pregnant, you were eyeing the exit, because you were getting spooked!"

She shook her head. "Don't give me your selfless excuses," he spat out. "This was about self preservation. You took yourself and our child across the ocean because you were scared of ending up like your mother!" He started pacing as he always did when he was upset. "God, do you have any idea what you put me through? What you put my family through? Mary wasn't talking. For all I knew, you came here to get rid of it!"

Branna gasped, her hand flying to her belly. Then she leaned toward him. She put her hand out, trembling as she touched his chest over the top of his heart. He covered it with his, pressing tightly. There was such pain in his eyes. "Michael, I would never. How could you think that for one minute?"

A tear came down one of his cheeks and the look on his face just shattered her. "People make a lot of bad decisions when they're afraid."

She pulled away, putting her hand back over her belly. "They are the only family I have. They are everything to me."

He looked at her strangely, then realization came to his face. It hit him that she'd used the plural. "Oh, God. Twins? It's twins?" He put his hand in his hair, a look of incredulity on his face.

She stiffened, misunderstanding. "I know it is a big responsibility, twins are a lot of work. I can do it, though. I can work from home!" she sputtered defensively.

Irritation flickered on his face. "Stop it! Stop acting like I don't want them!" He noticed his raised voice was causing a stir from the beach house behind them. Someone was looking through a glass door. He lowered his tone, "You have it all wrong. I don't know what Fiona told you, but I didn't want kids with her. I never said I didn't want children at all. Jesus, when Brigid told me why you left, that you ran because you thought I wouldn't want our child, that I wouldn't want you anymore."

He gritted out a frustrated growl. "Christ, I'm so sorry. I never realized how that talk about Fiona must have come across. I'm sorry you felt like you couldn't share this with me, that I wouldn't be happy. You dealt with this alone and that's my fault. I should have told you before you left for Boston. I love you, Branna. I'd fill my house with children if they were ours."

He pointed at her stomach speaking low and confidently, "Those are my babies, too. You are getting on that plane, coming home, and fixing up that cottage for our family. You will not continue this foolish, destructive path you are on."

She looked down at the ground, wrapping her arms around herself in that self-protecting, defensive way she always did. He snapped, "No! You will not shut down on me, Branna!" He took her in his arms and kissed the ever-loving shit out of her. She didn't fight him. Her physical capitulation was instant. He pulled her pelvis to his as he took her mouth. He could feel the bond weaving between them, feel her body start to yield to him. Her hand curled around his neck, as she slipped her tongue deep in his mouth, letting out a little moan. Her intensity grew into a wildness. She pulled at him, kissing him fiercely, not able to get close enough to him.

God, she'd missed him. Had she really just believed the worst so that she had an excuse to run? She didn't have to think hard about it.

She had. The depths of her feelings had been scary enough, but when she realized the depth of his, it had scared the hell out of her. That night he'd pulled her off the edge, tethering her to him, pulling her out of her grief. He'd known just what she needed. More than she had known herself. He'd comforted her on the most elemental level both with his body and his love and smashed through her barriers.

She'd begun erecting them when her father died but they'd fortified during her mother's slow decline. Michael had seen right to the heart of her and ripped her out of the pit of despair she'd grown so accustomed to. That happily ever after seemed a little bit too tangible, too achievable. Then she'd gotten pregnant and the thought of him rejecting her had been maddening. The thought of him not rejecting her had been equally maddening.

He broke the kiss and looked at her. His eyes were fierce. "You're mine, Branna." He kissed her again, and it was hot, possessive. It was a kiss that claimed. Then he pulled her face back to meet his eyes. "Can you honestly tell me you don't want me?" Her head was tilted back but their entire bodies were fused. She was completely intoxicated by the completeness of the contact. "That you don't love me? Would you take our children and live away from me? Jesus Christ, Branna. Do you think I could live in that cottage without you? That's our place. I've known it since the first day. Can you really walk away from me so easily?" His eyes were wounded.

Her face crumpled. She raised her mouth and kissed him again, small healing kisses all over his face as he slowly relinquished his grip on her. "God, no. I'm sorry, Michael. I was just afraid."

He met her eyes. "So was I. I'd failed so horribly with Fiona. I was afraid of making another mess and hurting us both. I was a bloody, fucking coward." He kissed down her neck. "God, I missed you, lass. I love you. I should have told you every day, every hour how much I loved you. I know you love me, too. I feel it when you look at me, when you touch me. I feel it every time we make love. I need to hear it, Branna. Say it, please." He was desperate, covering her face with kisses. She could feel the ache in his voice.

She was crying, her voice shaking. "I love you, too. I tried not to, but I love you more than anything. I swear I didn't get pregnant on purpose." She pulled away and her face was tight, her prideful chin up. "It was the illness, I missed a pill the day of my surgery, plus the antibiotics they put me on. I didn't mean for it to happen. You don't have to do this. This was my mistake."

Michael put a hand up. "Stop. Don't ever call our children a mistake. I understand, Branna. Don't apologize and don't talk about being alone. You will never be alone again. Not while I draw breath. I want this. I want them and you."

Branna blinked, "Don't say that to make me feel better, Michael. I don't want you to resent me. You might, later."

He kissed her into silence. "Christ woman, would you shut your gob and kiss me." He slanted his mouth over hers and moaned as he tasted her. "I felt it. That first night, I felt your soul. I told you. You gave yourself to me and I came inside you. God, the perfection."

He'd known from the moment of their joining that something irreversible had happened. He'd not considered that it had been the moment of the ultimate creation. "This was meant to happen. Don't be afraid, Branna. You'll be such a wonderful mother." He kissed her face lightly all over. Her eyes, her temples, and softly on her mouth. "Please, don't be scared. You can do this. You can let yourself be happy. Come home, darlin'. Come home to your family. I swear on my life that I'll love you, forever."

Her chin trembled."I can't believe you came for me. I never in a million years thought you would get on a plane and come after me. You really do love me, don't you?"

Michael's heart was flayed open. He cupped her face and held her close to him, meeting those bewitching blue eyes. "You're everything. You're the beating heart in my chest."

Tears were pooling in his eyes, and he took a shuddering breath as he looked at her abdomen. He put his hands over them, as if to assure them that he wasn't going anywhere. "Twins." He kissed her forehead, leaning their heads together. "I hope they're just like you," he whispered. "Tell me you're coming home with me. Tell me you'll marry me and help me raise our children in our little cottage." He paused,

"Although, if you're going to make them two at a time, we might need a bigger house in a couple of years," he jested.

She looked up at him and his smile would light up the world. There was no trace of doubt. "I will, Michael. Take me home. I want to go home."

* * *

AIDAN WAS STANDING at the edge of the deck, looking out on a beautiful stretch of beach, when he saw his brother walking with Branna. They would stop every few feet so that Michael could kiss her. It made Aidan's chest ache. Relief flooded him. "It looks like he talked some sense into her." Aidan's body roused to the sound, a sweet, high southern drawl. Damn.

"Yes, thank God. She's got a lot of people waiting for her back home. My father said if we had to tie the little hellcat to a boat and row her home, that we'd better not come home without her."

Anna laughed and it was ethereal. A sweet, musical tinkling that shot straight through him. He looked at her, and she actually hurt his eyes. The day was sunny and cool, her long golden hair was flowing wildly around her face from the wind. Light blue sweater over light, smooth skin. Green eyes. Ice green eyes with long, coppery lashes. "I think I like your daddy's style," she said with a playful grin.

He heard Michael call out. Michael was waving as he walked up the steps with Branna. "Twins! For Christ's sake, it's twins!" He was laughing. God, he was so happy. Aidan let out a whoop and ran down the beach walk. He picked Branna up and swung her around. He gave her a kiss on the forehead. Then he pulled his brother in for a hug.

Branna ran up to Anna and threw her arms around her. "I'm such an idiot."

Anna looked at the two brothers. "I'm going to have to agree with you on that one."

Branna watched her gaze. "Did you meet Aidan?" She had that tone and one brow raised.

Anna gave her a sideways glance, "Don't start. That ocean is wide, my friend. Worry about your own love life. Have you come to your senses O'Mara, or do I need to help them hog tie you?"

Michael approached, "She's assured me that she will come along peacefully, but I'll remember the offer."

Anna smiled at him. "I'm glad to hear it. I'm going to go in and give y'all some privacy."

Aidan said, "I'll head over to John's place. You two take your time, um, getting reacquainted." He noticed Anna behind them grinning, she wiggled her eyebrows at him and he barked out a laugh. They turned in unison to look at her. She smiled innocently and kissed Branna on the cheek, walking back to her house.

Michael closed the sliding door and then shut blinds. "That is quite a view. I didn't realize I was marrying such a well propertied woman."

Branna smiled mischievously. She started unbuttoning her blouse. "Yes, well I have a few more assets I'd like to disclose." She opened her blouse to reveal two full breasts spilling out of her bra.

Michael's eyes widened. "Holy shit. When did this happen?"

She grinned, "Pretty soon after the puking started."

He grew serious. "I should have been there to take care of you."

She gave him a wry grin. "There will be at least another month of it, don't worry. Then the fun starts." He looked at her curiously. "Apparently second trimester I'll have a heightened sexual appetite."

She started to whip his shirt off hastily and he winced. She looked at the abrasions and bruising on his arm and it finally occurred to her that he'd been favoring one arm. She gave him an alarmed look. "You're hurt!"

He silenced her with a kiss. "I'm ok, it was just a little swim."

She pushed him back. "Oh, God. At work? Where else are you hurt?" She started appraising him when she noticed the stitched patch at his crown. "Jesus, you hit your head? Was it on the rocks? Oh my God, I dreamt of you. There was blood in the water."

He kissed her again. He kissed her until she stopped resisting and he felt the tension leave her body. "I'm all right. Are you going to put me out of my misery and fuck me, Hellcat, or do I need a doctor's note?"

Her jaw dropped. She cupped him through his jeans and he hissed. “That may just be the hottest thing you’ve ever said to me, Michael O’Brien. And the dirtiest,” she whispered.

He kissed her hard. “Abstinence makes me testy.”

She threw his shirt and went for his fly. “I want to feel you,” she said, her voice changing to a desperate whisper. Tears were welling in her eyes, again. “I couldn’t quit thinking about you. I slept in this strange bed and tried to feel you, but I couldn’t. I’m so stupid, Michael.”

He caught her mouth with his. “Yes, you are.” She giggled through her tears. “Never again, mo chroí. I couldn’t breathe without you. Promise me, you’ll never leave me again,” he said. He was pulling her hair down while he kissed her in slow sweeps of his mouth. Then he got on his knees. She ran her fingers through his hair as he slid her pants off.

“I promise. Never again,” she answered. He shed her undergarments off, kissing and nibbling her as he went, reacquainting himself with her body. He picked her up and she wrapped her legs around his waist. He buried his face in her hair and she felt all the tension leave his body.

“I missed you, Branna. I missed you so much I thought I’d die from it. Say it again.”

She smoothed her hands over his big shoulders, as if to soothe him. “I love you, Michael.” He walked her into the bedroom and shut the door. Aidan didn’t get a call until many hours later.

* * *

Brigid ran into the pub from the outdoor stoop. She’d gone out when she’d seen an incoming call from Michael. She burst through the pub door. “He found her! They’re coming home!” Everyone cheered. Brigid yelled on the phone with one ear plugged, “Okay, I’ll check my texts. I love you, Michael. Get your ass home!” She hung up and walked over to her family. “He said he has a picture to send.” The phone beeped. She opened the photo text and looked carefully.

Sorcha squealed, "It's her ultrasound!" Everyone was poking their heads in to see.

Sean took the phone and focused on it. "Um, Sorcha love. Does something look familiarly off about this?" She looked closer, her jaw dropped.

Brigid snatched the phone back. "What? What's wrong?"

Sean was smiling from ear to ear. "Well, unless a lot has changed in twenty-nine years, that looks like two heads."

Brigid looked again. She put her hand over her mouth and burst into tears. "Michael is having twins."

* * *

AIDAN STOOD on the deck of the house and watched the sun set over the ocean. It was so beautiful. He sipped his tea, wondering about the offer Denario had made. Aidan was a Captain as well, having commissioned after he finished his degree on active duty. He'd known some British Officers that had done an exchange in the states, but no one in his regiment. If they requested him, though, he could probably make it happen. He'd never considered coming to America even for holiday. A twelve-week exchange was tempting, given the location. The training was good, really good. A chance to train with some hard core military men. He had some time to decide. He had a lot to think about.

Branna walked out and it jarred him from his private thoughts. "Am I disturbing you?" she said mildly. "No, lass. Please, come out and join me. It's so lovely I can barely bring myself to go inside." Branna came up next to him. "There's something about the sea, isn't there? It's downright medicinal. I love the sound, the smell, the vastness. I never want to be parted from it. That's part of why I love Ireland so much."

Aidan nodded, "Aye, I'm afraid my flat in Belfast is lacking such a view. I like the city, the buzz of activity. Growing up in a small town, sometimes the anonymity is nice. You're right, though. I start craving the sea, then I have to go home. I remember needing it so badly during my one deployment to Iraq. All the sand and dust and heat. I'd go to the river's edge and pretend I was home. Try to block out the rest and just look at the water."

Branna laughed, "My father did the same thing."

Aidan looked at her, wanting to say something, but not sure if he should. "Do you ever wish you'd had a different sort of man?" Branna looked at him puzzled. "Christ, I don't know what I'm saying. I guess I think if you could have chosen to have him be a dentist or an accountant or something, knowing…" He shook himself. "Forget it. It's a stupid question. I shouldn't have asked it."

He felt Branna's hand on his arm. "I know exactly what you mean, Aidan. I have asked myself that same question. It's complicated because if I say no, then I seal his fate. Right? If I had the power to change his course, then logically I should. In the end, I ask myself one question. Is it what he would have wanted? If he knew that someday he'd be killed, would he change his life? I can tell you with certainty that he wouldn't have. I respect him for that. I was so proud of him." She smiled sadly. "The life he gave me was so wonderful while we had it. I lived so many places, met so many people." She squeezed his arm. "Our family life in the military was what some people only dream of. Travel, excitement, adventure, a deeper understanding of the world, surrounded by the very best America has to offer. Men and women of deep faith, strong family values, courageous hearts, and an unwavering sense of duty. No, Aidan. I wouldn't have changed him. He was a wonderful husband and father. He gave us so much. I miss him everyday, but this was what he was meant to do. He was a warrior. I would never take that away from him. I loved him for what he was."

She hesitated, "I think if he had it to do over again, he would have still married and had a child. Even knowing the suffering that followed his death, he wouldn't have traded it for a life free of entanglements. It's not natural to go through life without love. Not when you're the type of man he was. I know what I'm talking about. I tried it. I tried to live my life like that. I thought if I didn't love anyone, it would be easier. It wasn't."

Aidan stared out at the sea, silent but for his breathing. "It's a scary responsibility. I've seen the damage it does. Not just in you, Branna."

He paused, swallowing. "I've seen things. Things I can't…" He shook himself, releasing whatever thought he had been on the cusp of revealing. "Holding another's happiness and future in your hands, I always thought it was selfish to dance with danger for a living and drag a wife and kids into it. It's like you are toying with their whole world," he said.

She put her arm around him. "And what do you think now?" He shook his head. "I don't know. I just don't know if I could ever do it. I'm not speaking ill of your da. Mine was Garda. He risked his life some days as well. Christ, I just don't know."

Branna had said everything she could to him. The rest was his struggle, but she had to know. "Wasn't there ever anyone? Anyone you thought of as the keeping kind?"

He sighed. "Once, while I was at university. She didn't understand. She was a Catholic as well. She didn't understand my need to enlist, thought I was taking up with the British. My bigger picture was irrelevant. She ended it. Once I was in the Army there was another woman, for about three months or so. I started caring for her, beyond the initial infatuation. It didn't work, though. She couldn't take the thought of separations. Even when I would train in England she'd get frustrated. She was honest about it. I wasn't what she wanted long term. I was a pleasant distraction for her. I guess deep down it was me that wasn't the keeping kind."

He looked out over the water. "In hindsight I don't think I was in love with her anymore than she was with me. It was nice, though, to have someone for more than a few nights. Now I just try to stay clear of it. It's not fair to them or me, and I'm not a one night stand type of guy."

Branna stood up straighter. "They didn't deserve you, Aidan. You're strong and brave and smart. You're also as disgustingly gorgeous as the rest of the O'Brien men," she teased. "You are perfect just how you are. Just promise me something." He looked at her, compelling her to continue. "You don't have to go looking for it. Just don't run from it if it finds you. Deal?"

Just then Michael came out to join them. "Are you charming my girl out here, brother?" Aidan took Branna's head within his palm and kissed her on the top of it.

"She's just trying to teach an old dog a new trick." He smiled down at his sister-to-be. "You don't worry about me, girl. You just take care of those little ones and make my brother happy."

* * *

THE NEXT MORNING Branna was making the boys breakfast. Aidan was back out on the deck, but he came in when he smelled bacon. "Is that rashers I smell?"

Branna answered. "This is bacon, my dear. Nothing like it. It is crispy, piggy heaven." She fiddled with the skillet, the strips sizzling and smelling up the entire house.

Aidan was thumbing through a local magazine when he spoke, "This magazine says Alanna Falk. I thought your friend's name was Anna?"

Branna snorted. "That is an old, ongoing battle between her parents. Her father wanted her name to be Alainna after his Scottish grandmother and her mother wanted Annabelle. He thought Annabelle sounded too redneck. Felicity is kind of a cross between a southern prima donna and a hippie, and she liked arguing with her husband. So it was a win, win. They named her Alanna Isabelle Falk as a compromise. Then he deployed while she was still really small. Her mom started calling her Anna anyway, told everyone else to do the same. By the time he came home, it was kind of set. He still calls her Alanna. I think it's a Gaelic name though, it means..."

Aidan finished her sentence, "Beautiful. The spelling's a little anglicized, but it means beautiful."

She smiled, "Exactly. I always thought it suited her."

"Sounds like her mother is a piece of work," Michael commented.

Branna got a little more serious after that. "Yes, she actually is and not necessarily in a good way. She left them all when Anna was twelve and Erik was thirteen. She wanted her freedom, apparently. They actually had to stay with grandparents when their father deployed."

Branna shook off that memory and turned to Aidan. "So, what did you think of her, Aidan? She's very pretty, don't you think?"

He shot her a look. He knew that tone. Brigid tried fixing him up countless times over the years. "Oh, he likes her. He won't admit it, but I can tell," said Michael. Aidan put his arms over his chest. "Oh really? How is that?"

Michael had his feet up, sipping a cup of coffee. "You pretend not to watch her, but meanwhile you track her every move."

Aidan threw the magazine at him in a whirl of rippling pages. "You don't know what the hell you're talking about. Besides, we leave tomorrow. It hardly matters." Branna was listening silently. "Didn't we already cover this?" he said with a chiding smile. "Don't start scheming, hen. I know that look. It's a long trip over that ocean and I'm a self-imposed bachelor. End of story."

She grinned. That was the same crap she got from Anna. "Whatever you say, Aidan." A knock came that interrupted them. Branna ran to the door and opened it, surprised not as much by Anna, but who was standing next to her. She dove out the door and wrapped her arms around her unexpected visitor. "Sgt. Major Falk, oh my God! I never expected to see you!" He hugged her back, "How's my girl?"

Michael exchanged glances with Aidan. Anna's father, the legendary Sgt. Major that Denario had warned them about. They walked in and he seemed to appraise them both. Michael walked over to him. The guy was as tall as him with a Scandinavian look to him. Lean and kind of mean looking, but when he looked at Branna his face was tender, fatherly.

"Hello sir, Michael O'Brien. This is my brother Aidan, Captain Aidan O'Brien."

Falk looked at Aidan. "Call me Hans. So, how does an Irishman end up in the Royal Army?" he said bluntly. Aidan stepped forward. "Having parents on both sides of the border. Royal Irish Regiment, 2nd Battalion. Pleased to meet you, Sgt. Major."

Falk's brows went up. "One parent Northern Irish and one from the Republic. Must make family reunions interesting. Infantry, huh? Good for you, son." Aidan was slightly fascinated by this man. He cut an impressive figure. He looked like a Viking berserker, but he had a mellow southern drawl. Not redneck sounding, but like old southern gentry. He'd met a few southern boys in his tours in Iraq and Afghanistan. He knew the difference.

Sgt. Major Falk turned to Branna. "I'm so glad I didn't miss you. Word has it you are headed back over the pond for good."

She smiled, "Yes, sir. No more running."

His eyes were sad. "You are your father's daughter, aren't you?"

She stood up a little straighter. "I am, and I won't forget it."

He seemed to get a little nervous. "I actually came to catch you before you left. Could I have a few minutes?" She looked at Anna who gave a slight shrug and a look that said she had no idea what her father was going to say. She brought everyone in, and she and Anna started bringing everyone coffee and tea and breakfast.

"Anna told me that you just picked up Sgt. Major. That is so wonderful. You deserve it. My father would have been so proud of you," Branna said. She smiled as she set the cups down in front of them and returned to the kitchen.

Anna's father came into the kitchen behind her, holding an envelope. "I have something for you, sweetheart. I was supposed to wait a year, and we are close enough that I think it is okay to give it to you." Branna looked at his hand, confused. "It's from your mother," he said quietly. Branna's heart lurched. "I'm sorry I had to keep it. She was adamant that I wait a year," he said.

Branna swallowed hard before she spoke, "Why a year?"

He sighed and looked down at her. "She said that maybe once a year had gone by, you wouldn't be so angry with her." Branna stiffened. "She loved you, Branna. I know you think she left you, but please take some time. Get your mind right and read it with an open heart."

She turned to him, meeting his eyes. "She wouldn't fight for me or for herself. Daddy is still fighting for me. He comes to me. Did you know that? He comes to me in my dreams. He knew about the babies before I did. He's always taken care of me. She left me an orphan because she didn't think I was enough of a reason to stick around. With all due respect, you can't know how that feels."

He closed in on her and hugged her. "Actually, I sort of do understand."

Branna winced inwardly. "I'm sorry, I shouldn't have said that. I know you lost her, too."

He smiled sadly. "She loved you. You don't know how much, but I do." He kissed her forehead and stepped back. He continued, "She was depressed, clinically depressed. I convinced her toward the end to go on antidepressants, see a therapist. It helped her get some clarity. She cried in my arms," his voice was on the edge of breaking. "She broke down one night. 'What have I done? How could I have done this to myself? My poor Branna, what have I done?' She regretted it, Branna. She died punishing herself for what she'd done to you. She couldn't undo it, the cancer was too advanced. She kept saying that Brian would be ashamed of her."

Branna was pale, starting to tremble. "She didn't tell me. Why didn't she tell me?"

He shook his head. "You were so angry, Branna. You were so hurt and with good reason. She understood, so did I. She told me to wait a year, so I did. Maybe that letter will give you some answers."

Aidan and Michael were watching the scene unfold in the kitchen. Michael knew to stay back. This was private, between Branna and this man who'd tried to save her father and couldn't. Who'd then tried to save her mother and couldn't. He needed to do something for their daughter. Michael couldn't intrude no matter how much he needed to hold her. The strong, steely Marine was strained with the effort of keeping himself composed. The emotional disclosure was taking a toll on them both.

Aidan watched in stony silence as the tall Marine in the kitchen spoke with Branna. He also watched as her best friend Anna put her face in her hands as she wept in silence. He watched her discretely go out the screen door and walk on to the deck. He knew he shouldn't follow her, but he was an idiot. So, he was going to anyway. He hated seeing women cry.

He got up and walked outside. She was leaning over the rail of the deck shaking as she released her grief and tears. She sensed him, somehow. She turned to look at him, wiping her eyes. "I'm ok. I just needed a minute," she croaked. She looked out at the water for a few silent moments, reining in her emotions. "I wonder when that girl is going to quit ripping my heart out," she managed.

He came beside her. Not touching her, but standing next to her, offering unspoken comfort. They both looked out at the water in silent companionship. "She's lucky to have you, Anna. I promise we'll take care of her," he finally offered. A shudder went through her, relief at the thought. She nodded silently.

As Branna took the envelope from her father's friend, he noticed something on the fridge. There was a rune written on the back of a receipt.

"What is this?"

Branna took it in her fingers and looked at it. "When I dream of daddy, I dream of that symbol."

He looked at her. "It's a Viking rune. It means ancestral homeland. It's sounds like he's trying to tell you something."

Branna could see the hair standing up on his arms. His piercing green gaze going from the scrap of paper to her. "I think you might be right, Sgt. Major."

He pulled her to him gently and hugged her. "I think it's about time you started calling me Hans, sweetheart. You are like a daughter to me. You know that, don't you?"

She hugged him back fiercely. "Yes, I do. You were there for her right up until the end, Hans. I'll always love you for that and I know daddy would be grateful. I just wish she would have fought for us." She put her head in his chest and cried.

* * *

THAT EVENING the O'Brien brothers were treated to a Coastal Carolina style pub night. Branna had offered to be their designated driver. They sat in the bar located out the back gate of the base. It wasn't overly crowded since tourist season was over, but there were several military types and a lot of locals. "I'm not feeling the craic, brother." Aidan jibed. "Me neither, brother. They need some lessons." Michael agreed.

"Would you two shut your gobs. This isn't Doolin, embrace a new culture! Besides, it's open mic night. You might find this humorous at the very least. We always get at least one character from the nearby trailer park that thinks he's the next Roy Orbison." Branna was sipping her club soda as she chastised her two escorts.

The first two acts were awful, like bad karaoke. Michael and Aidan were making their little silly remarks in between sips of what they considered to be substandard Guinness. Suddenly a buzz started going through the place and the MC had retrieved the mic from the last drunk towny. He addressed the crowd. "Ok, you've waited long enough. Who's ready for our local sweetheart?" Aidan and Michael perked up. The men in the place were stirring and were buzzing with enthusiasm.

The cat calling started when the MC handed off the microphone. Aidan's heart stopped when he saw Anna walk on stage holding a violin. Behind her were two men, one with an acoustic guitar and one with a steel guitar. An irrational stab of jealousy went through him as he saw her communicating with her guitar players. Aidan and Michael both bristled as they listened to the male appraisal around them. They didn't discuss their women in pubs like they were pieces of meat, and if they'd heard someone commenting about Brigid or Jenny in this manner, they'd have sorted them out quickly.

"Did I mention Anna was a musician in her spare time?" Branna said, breaking the tension.

Michael smiled at her, "No, you didn't." Branna was playing it cool, but Michael could read her like a book. She knew exactly what she was doing, teasing Aidan with this southern beauty. He looked over at his brother and was stupefied by his expression. It wasn't just simple male appreciation; it was something a little edgier. He knew that look, he'd worn it himself not too long ago. Perhaps Branna wasn't just wishful thinking.

Branna beamed as her best friend took the stage. Anna was a looker, and every eye was on her lithe body and stunning mane of coppery blonde hair. She wore loose fit, well-worn jeans, equestrian boots, and a simple, emerald green sweater. Her work and school schedule had never left much time for hobbies or men, but this occasional artistic outlet was her indulgence. She and Branna used to love to play together, but life had gotten in the way for Anna as much as for Branna. She was glad to see her friend taking a little time for her music, even if it was open mic night at a local bar.

Her eyes were fixed ahead, green to the point of glowing under the lighting as they played off the sweater color. She had two thin braids at her temples that were pulled together at the back of her head and the rest of her hair was hanging loose down her back. Branna looked over at Michael who was looking at his brother with curiosity. Aidan was stoic as ever, not revealing much. His eyes never wavered from her friend, however.

Branna snapped to attention when Anna and her two accompanists started playing. Alison Krauss's version of *Crazy Faith*. She was amazing. The entire room was captivated. She went through the first couple of verses and chorus with the dueling guitars.The man on acoustic did back up vocals and she watched as Aidan's hands fisted infinitesimally. Then her short fiddle part came and she lost herself, hair swinging, bow jutting, eyes closed. Then she finished with the beautiful song.

The crowd cheered to a crazy level and Anna demurely nodded then smiled in their direction as she exited the stage. Branna turned to Michael and Aidan expectantly. "Well, it wasn't Gaelic, but isn't she fabulous?"

Michael answered first, "Yes, she's wonderful. Don't you think so Aidan?"

Aidan looked at them as if he'd just woken from a far off place in his head. "Yes, she is. Will she be joining us, then?"

Branna shook her head. "I'm afraid not. She has to work tomorrow. She's probably leaving as we speak." Aidan just nodded. They left the bar after the next number. No one was going to upstage Anna and they had a long day tomorrow.

* * *

THE NEXT MORNING Branna hugged her old friends goodbye. "I want to stop by the cemetery before we head to the airport. Thank you both. Thank you for everything." Anna was tearing up but smiling.

Her father was quiet and thoughtful, satisfied that his task was complete. Then he spoke. "You take care of her, Michael. Her father would have liked you. He would have also told you that if you break her heart, he'll stick a knife in yours. So. I'm obliged to do the same."

Aidan gave a grunt of approval behind them. He remembered having a similar talk with Finn when he started getting serious with Brigid. "You don't have to worry about her, sir. I'll make her happy. We all will." Michael answered, steadily meeting the man's gaze.

The Sgt. Major turned to Aidan. "Be careful, son."

Aidan nodded, "You as well, Sgt. Major."

Anna went to walk away, but turned. "Goodbye, Aidan."

Aidan's eyes were intense. She was hooked arm and arm with her father. Both golden haired, same bright green eyes, fair skin. "Slán go fóill, Alainna." Michael's eyes shot to his.

"What does that mean in English?" Anna asked, tilting her head a little.

He shot a quick look at Michael. "It just means goodbye," he answered. She smiled and nodded and walked away, her father looking curiously between them.

They were in the car when Branna broke the silence from the back seat. "What did he really say?"

Aidan said, "Goodbye. I just said goodbye." She looked at Michael through the rearview. "He's withholding, spill it."

Michael grinned. "He actually said goodbye for now, Alanna."

She looked over at Aidan who was staring ahead, not meeting her eyes. "Did he, now?" she asked.

CHAPTER 29

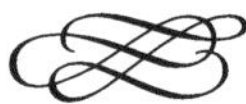

COASTAL CAROLINA STATE VETERANS CEMETERY

Branna approached the single gravesite, breathing deeply as she tried to get her bearings. She hadn't been here since her mother died. As with most veteran cemeteries, her parents shared a stone and a burial plot, one name on the front and the other on the back.

Major Brian O'Mara USMC February 10, 1964-December 12, 2004

Meghan O'Mara March 23, 1967-November 24, 2011

She knelt down on her father's grave. "Hello daddy. I know it's been a while." She was strangely composed, wanting to get out what she'd come to say. "I'm leaving. I don't know when I'll be back here. I'll take you with me, though. You know that, don't you? You've been watching over me."

She put her trembling hand on his tombstone. "I just wanted you to know that you're going to be a grandpa." The tears started coming. "You always told me that they'd let our family tree get too sparse. That's over, now. I'm going to get married and have a whole house full of children."

Michael was behind her, barely keeping it together. Aidan had his hand on his shoulder. He was silent but for his breathing. She continued, "I wanted to tell you it's okay to go now. I'm taken care of. You can go find mommy now." She was quietly sobbing. "I'm glad you were there for me. I needed you, but now mommy needs you. It's ok to go." She choked on her tears, "I love you, daddy. I promise I'll be strong."

Michael picked her up and she shook and cried in his arms for a time. He rubbed her back, offering soothing words.

She pulled herself away, wiped her face, and looked up at him. "One down, one to go." He pulled her to him, kissing her face, their tears mixing. Hers in grief, his in the sorrow that comes from being helpless. She took a deep, cleansing breath and went to the other side.

Aidan was watching his brother and Branna and he wasn't sure he could take much more. He remembered what Patrick had said to him, the day they'd brought the piano to the cottage. *It's the loving that'll break his heart, because he can't take it from her. The pain, aye? He can't take it from her.* The thought of putting some child through this, having a wife that mourned your passing so deeply that she let herself whither and die from grief. Never.

Branna spoke softly, "Hello, mommy. It's me. I know I haven't visited." She cleared her throat, "I'm sorry. I just needed time. I guess you knew that, didn't you?"

She patted her pocket, "I have your letter. I haven't read it yet. I want to wait. I want to be home and happy and pick the right time." Her jaw began to tremble, "I just wanted to tell you," Branna's voice broke on a sob, "that I forgive you, mommy. I'm so sorry I couldn't help you. I didn't understand. I think I do, now. I know what it's like to love someone like you loved daddy."

She put her head on the ground and cried inconsolably. "I wish you were here. I wish you could tell me everything about marriage and babies. I wish it was you here to hold my hand, to hold my children."

Sobs racked her small body and Michael went toward her, but Aidan stopped him. "Let her finish, brother. She needs to do this." Aidan wrapped his brother in a bear hug from behind, his face pressed to Michael's ear. He could feel Michael's silent grief, hear his stifled tears, but he gave his brother the strength to stay put.

She sat up and wiped her eyes and nose. Her voice was weak and shaking, but she found the strength to keep going. "I want you to know that I have someone, now. I have a whole family waiting for me. Sorcha and Sean, they'll do a good job. I'm not an orphan anymore." Michael put his head down and shuddered, Aidan put his forehead on his shoulder. Branna's words slicing through them both. "I have a sister and I have lots of brothers." She looked up at Aidan. He smiled sadly and nodded. "They'll all watch over me and your grand babies. I'm ok, mommy. Find daddy and be happy. Forgive yourself. I just want you to be together and be happy. I love you, so much."

She got up and walked into Michael's arms. They just held each other in silence for a few minutes. Her body shook with grief as he cradled her small body. Finally, she settled. Michael leaned back to look at her. "I wanted to say something to your da if that's okay?"

She just smiled at him, face swollen from crying. "I think he'd like that."

She backed up to give him space and felt Aidan's arms come around her. "I love you, a dheirfiúr mo chroí" he whispered.

She leaned her face into his. "I love you, too."

Michael tried to collect his thoughts. He knew what he wanted to say. He just needed a minute. He knelt down to Brian O'Mara's grave and spoke. "I just wanted to tell you that I'll take care of her. I'll love her until my last breath. She'll not feel such sorrow again. I vow it. Go with God, Brian O'Mara. You've earned your rest." Michael took out a bottle of whiskey. He drank, then he poured a dram on the ground of his future father in law's grave. "Ar dheis Dé go raibh a anam." *May his soul be on God's right hand side.*

CHAPTER 30

KELLY COTTAGE, DOOLIN, IRELAND

The flight was long from North Carolina, but Michael, Branna, and Aidan were together. Branna had burst into tears at the Dublin Airport when she'd found the arrivals area full of O'Brien's. Even little Cora had come, wrapping her chubby arms around Branna's neck.

Michael and Branna retreated to their cottage. "It's good to have you home, hen. This place was so empty without you stomping about with that cup of coffee and your grand plans."

She could hear the smile in his voice, but she could hear the hurt, too. "I never thought I would see it again. I love you, Michael."

He went over to the beat up recliner and plopped into it. "Aye, well I've grown rather fond of this old chair. You weren't getting it back." She laughed a little and joined him, sitting on his lap. "Were you really going to leave it, and your other things, your wee cabinet and desk?"

She just shook her head. "I didn't think that far ahead. I was in a panic, Michael. Plain and simple. Honestly, the only thing in this cottage that couldn't be replaced was you. Leaving you damn near killed me." The tears were threatening and her throat was tight.

"Don't worry, darlin. We'll never be parted again." Then he kissed her and didn't stop kissing her until morning.

* * *

THE PUB WAS FILLED with family and friends. It was the off-season, so faces were familiar. Brendan and his family, Jack and his wife, Ned and Diane, Jenny, Robby, all of the O'Brien's were in attendance. Fiona was there with Michael and Branna's blessing. The engagement party was casual and perfect. Everyone was either drunk, singing, or both. Branna felt a tap on her shoulder.

It was Fiona. Branna smiled hesitantly and Michael stiffened a bit, but they were cordial. "I wanted to give you something. I won't be at the wedding, but I have something for you. It's something I've been working on at the shop."

Branna looked puzzled. "At the ancestry shop?" She figured it was the O'Mara crest or maybe a collage of both.

"Thank you Fiona, may I open it now?" Fiona nodded nervously. She opened it. It appeared to be a family tree, dating back to when her father's family lived in Clare. She smiled. "This is wonderful. My father would have loved this."

Fiona looked a little impatient. "Aye, I suppose. It wasn't his bloodlines that interested me, though. It was your mother's side."

Branna's eyes shot up to hers. "My mother? She never dug into her family. Her close family was all dead. She just said she didn't know of any family that she had left."

Fiona motioned to the paper. "Well, she doesn't have much. Not in the US anyway, but," Fiona took a deep breath. "I found them. I found your family here." Branna looked up. Fiona was excited. "I checked and re-checked. I thought it was a mistake. I found the damnedest thing, Yank."

Branna shook her head and started to really look at the paper. "I don't understand. She never said she had family over here. I knew she was Irish. Her name was Meghan Gallagher."

Fiona continued, "Yes, but her mother's maiden name was..."

Someone interrupted her from behind. "Kelly. Your grandmother's maiden name was Kelly."

Michael, Branna, and Fiona turned in unison to look into the calm face of Ned Kelly. "Your mother was a distant cousin. She found me a few months before she died."

Branna's hand shot up to her mouth. It took a hard stare and a few moments for her to absorb what Ned had said. "This isn't possible. That is too much of a coincidence. It's a common name, even in America."

Ned smiled sweetly. "Well, lass. Some coincidences get a little nudge."

Branna thought about how she'd come across the listing on Burren Way. A random e-mail had come with the listing attached. She'd thought it was spam from some real estate website she'd visited. "The e-mail," she said softly. "Oh my God, Ned, did you send me the listing?"

He shrugged, "I don't know a whole lot about computers, but I can send an email. I'll admit I had the price a bit high. I was waiting to drop it. That's when I sent the follow-up e-mail telling you the price had dropped. I used a different account than when you bought the house. "

She remembered his odd behavior that first day they had met. He didn't make eye contact when he talked about not having her email. "You said you lost my e-mail." She said with a cheeky grin.

He shrugged and blushed. "I don't make a habit of lying lass, I just couldn't explain. I needed to get you here. I told Jack I didn't have your contact information because I didn't want him stopping you from coming. I must admit I felt rather like James Bond sneaking about, pulling you into our web. Bloody hard thing to do, keeping everyone in the dark. Diane nearly boxed my ears when I finally told her."

She shook her head. "How did you know about me? Did you speak with my mother?"

His face grew sad. "Yes, my dear. During the months leading up to her death, she'd call me from time to time. She started digging into her family ancestry. She wanted to see if perhaps she had some sort of family still alive. She was so sad that you might have no kin left in the world. When I got her first letter, I called her and we started talking regularly. She eventually told me she was terminal. She also told me all about her strong, beautiful daughter."

He continued, "She said she'd left you a letter, but that I should wait to approach you. I admit I jumped the gun a little. The cottage was empty and you had no one. I knew what your business was, the other properties. I just said a prayer and sent it one night, hoping you'd take the bait. I prayed every night that you would come home to your family."

Branna's eyes pooled with tears. "Cousins?"

He shrugged, "Yes, distant. You're my blood, though, and I am yours, so is Diane and my son in Kerry. That's all the particulars we need, wouldn't you agree?"

Branna threw her arms around him and burst into tears. "There, there young Branna. It'll all be grand, just as I said it would be." Branna was so taken aback with emotion. She'd always felt something. She'd never been able to put her finger on it, but she'd always felt a sort of kinship with Ned. *Oh thank you, mommy.*

Michael stood there, mouth agape. He looked at Fiona whose arms were crossed over her waist, watching silently. She was smiling wider than he'd seen her smile in a long time. "You didn't know that Ned already knew?"

She shrugged, "I suspected once I put the pieces together. She's right, too much of a coincidence. Once I found the connection, I knew that he must have found a way to get her here."

Branna turned to Fiona and tackled her with a hug. "Good God, Yank. You trying to kill me?"

Branna looked at her, tears of joy in her eyes. "You didn't know what you'd find when you started. You did this for me."

She blushed, "It's no big thing. You were kind to me. You gave me a chance when I didn't deserve it. We'll call it a debt repaid. Don't go getting all gushy about it."

Michael put a hand on her shoulder and gave a brief squeeze. "You're doing okay, aren't you?"

She just nodded. "Well, now that Ned's ruined my surprise, do you want to tell her about her American kin?" Branna looked back at him, eyes wide with anticipation.

"It's a branch of the family in Maine. Again, very distant family, but they are blood."

Branna was shocked. "I have family. I have lots of family! I have O'Brien's and Kelly's and two more on the way!" She jumped on Michael and he picked her off her feet. "Let's have a dozen kids!"

Ned Kelly laughed loudly. "Now you're talking like an Irish lass!"

Michael kissed her nose. "What do you say we get these two out first, hen? You're going to need a breather after passing two fat headed O'Brien boys."

She straightened up. "And how do you know they're boys?"

He just laughed, "I told you…"

She interrupted. "I know, I know, Halley's Comet. Don't discount my O'Mara blood." She smiled, "And the Kelly blood."

Michael and Branna went home from the pub reeling with the news about Ned Kelly. Michael was laughing to himself. "What's so funny?" Branna asked.

"Well, I asked Ned why he didn't just tell you then, give you the cottage. He said that if he'd done that, just denied me outright, the whole town would've turned against you. He thought once everyone got to know you it would go differently. If you tried to leave, not take the deal he offered, he was going to tell you."

She smiled, "So why is that funny?"

He had a crooked grin on his face. "That wasn't the funny part. The funny part was when he said, *Once I met her in person and heard the little lass tore into you at Gus's, I knew what I had to do. You'd either run from her or fall in love with her, and I have to admit I was hoping for the latter.*"

THE NEXT WEEK Branna was working in the second bedroom, once Michael's room. She hung some local art. Two small cribs were on either wall, with a small bureau in between. Michael had contracted a heating and cooling person to run some baseboard heating in the house. A wood burner in a babies room was a no go.

They bought the house from Ned. Michael insisted that he dump his entire savings into it in addition to her paying the balance. Ned had cut the price even further as a wedding gift, wanting them to have a nice nest egg for their new family.

Branna was wandering around the living room, day dreaming about having children running under her feet. She looked at the Moses baskets that Alex and James had sent her from Italy. They also sent her a top of the line double stroller and some Italian designer maternity clothes. They were unable to come to the wedding and had made up for it by overspending on their "little Yank".

Sorcha and Sean had purchased the cribs and the siblings had pitched in for two car seats. Even little Sean, who at six foot and fifteen years old was turning out to be not so little, had made a set of wooden toys in wood shop. Everyone was so excited for Michael and for her. She felt like she had been gifted a whole new family. In light of this, she'd started talking to God on a regular basis. She'd started attending mass for the first time since her mother was diagnosed. She thought about her mother and decided it was time.

She took her mother's letter out of the desk and sat in her father's recliner. Michael set a cup of tea next to her. "I'm going to go for a walk, give you some privacy. I won't go far." He kissed her mouth softly. "I love you, mo ghrá. Be strong." When he left, she opened the sealed envelope.

My Dear Branna,

If you are reading this, I have been gone a year. It is strange to think of a year going by without me, but more importantly to think of a year that I will miss of my sweet baby girl's life. I know you are upset with me, upset probably doesn't even cover the depth of your feelings of betrayal. I know that I don't deserve your forgiveness. What I did was selfish and cowardly. I want you to understand that it wasn't love that killed me, but my own inability see past my pain. To my shame, I reflect back on the last three years and pray to

God that your father didn't bear witness to that cowardice. He always told me how strong I was. It was a lie that I believed until I'd been tested.

You are like your father in so many ways. I love that about you and am sad to realize that I will not live to see you continue into womanhood. You will be a fierce and amazing woman. I won't see you marry, see you have your own children. If you don't believe anything else, know that I went to the hereafter regretting cheating us out of that time together. I orphaned my beloved daughter because I was weak. I made you witness my slow, suffering decline when I should have shown you strength. I should have rewarded your unwavering love and trust by mustering the will to live. My failure was unforgivable. Still, I ask for forgiveness nonetheless.

One thing I was able to do before I died was make sure that you weren't left with no family. I know genealogy was daddy's thing, but I ended up being pretty good at it, once I set my mind to the task. You are not alone, Branna. I found distant relatives in both the US and Ireland. I have contacted my closest kin, but have asked them to wait until your received this letter before contacting you.

My life was so very beautiful. I loved being your mother and your father's wife. He was always so strong. You got both his strength and his passionate nature. If I go to heaven, I know that the angels' voices will sound as you did when your daddy played for you, and taught you to sing. Be well my angel. I want you to love and live and maybe someday forgive. You were a gift from God, and I left you too soon.

Finally, I would like you to tell Hans something. Tell him that I'm sorry. I hurt him not only by my death, but because I wouldn't let him love me. If I had been able to pull myself out of the hole I had dug for myself, I would have seen that happiness and love could be found again. I want him to know that even though I didn't show him, I did love him, too. I should have been a mother to his children, so in need of a strong woman in their lives. There is someone out there for him, someone less broken, who will give him the second chance that I denied him.

Thank you, Branna. I love you, my dear girl. God willing, I will wait alongside your father and, someday we will see you again.

Love, Mommy

. . .

Branna was still sitting in the chair when Michael came back home. He could tell that she'd been crying, but she seemed calm now, looking into the fire. He sat down on the coffee table and faced her. "Are you okay?"

She smiled dreamily at him. "Yes, I am. I really am." She handed the letter to Michael.

"You don't have to show it to me," he said gently.

She shrugged, "I want you to see it. Maybe in some small way, you can know my mother. She was a wonderful woman." She smiled sweetly and smoothed her hand over his face. "I love you, Michael, and I'm okay. I'm not afraid anymore."

CHAPTER 31

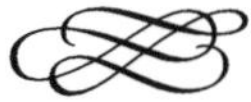

The wedding was planned quickly and was simple but elegant. Branna was already starting to show a bit, so she wore a plain white silk gown with an empire waist. It dipped in the back and her hair flowed long and silky down her shoulders and back. She carried white calla lilies and Belle's of Ireland in her bouquet. Michael wore a black tuxedo and Aidan wore his military dress uniform. Brigid wore a simple, emerald green maternity dress. It was intimate, and their friends, family, and neighbors surrounded them. It was a local gathering to celebrate love. It was the sort of wedding Michael had always wanted with a bride he'd never dared to hope for.

Sean went to the area of the church where the bride was getting ready. He knocked and Sorcha came to the door. As he walked in and saw his beautiful women, he fought the emotion welling up in his chest. "Hello, Sean. Is everyone ready?" He knelt down next to Branna and took her hand. "Call me Da." Branna's voice quivered, "Okay, Da it is."

He took out a small, aged box. "I was wondering if you would like to wear my mother's ring on your other hand. They're sapphires set in Irish gold. Sorcha and Brigid both wore it on their wedding day. It was my mother's, and it is Sorcha's engagement ring. We'd both like you to wear it." She put her hand out and he slid it on her finger. "I love you, mo iníon. When I see my son's face and the happiness you bring him, I thank God for bringing you to us."

Branna threw her arms around his neck. "Thank you for letting me be a part of this family. I don't ever want to be that lonely again." Brigid and Sorcha looked on with tears lining their faces.

The whole town piled in the church along with several Kelly's that had driven from different parts of County Kerry and County Clare to meet Branna. Father Peter was beaming as he delivered the mass and nuptials. When Ned Kelly walked Branna down the aisle to give her away, Michael thought he would pass out from joy. She was exquisite. "Take care of her, lad. Her da is watching and so am I," Ned said. Michael took her hand and turned to the altar. It was a perfect day. It even rained a bit for luck.

The party was going strong at the hall where Branna had first danced with Michael at Patrick and Caitlyn's wedding. The family and friends rotated musicians so as to let everyone enjoy the night. All of the sudden someone shouted "O'Brien Set!" Branna's heart started racing. This was it. She lined up with the other O'Brien women and stared across at her husband. He was radiant. "You ready for me, O'Brien?" she said with a mischievous grin.

He gave a husky chuckle. "Do your worst, hellcat." As they danced the old family mating song, Branna felt the ties to these strong, proud people tighten within her. Michael pulled her close, swinging her around. His eyes were intense. "I've dreamed of this, Branna. I've dreamed of this since the night I saw you dancing in the rain. You are mine now, mo chroi. My mate, and I am yours, forever."

* * *

As Michael walked over the threshold with Branna in his arms, he thought his heart was going to burst. He carried her into their little bedroom and there was already a fire made. "Look's like someone has been here," she remarked.

He nodded, "Caitlyn came to start the fire and put a bottle of sparkling juice in the fridge. We're finally alone, though." He started shedding his tuxedo pieces one by one, stopping periodically for a slow, sweet kiss.

When he was completely undressed she exhaled. "I don't think I will ever get tired of seeing you naked, Michael O'Brien."

He came toward her. "Your turn." He slipped the zipper down as he whispered to her. "You are the most beautiful thing I've ever seen. I can't believe you're officially mine, Branna O'Brien."

She beamed at this. "Branna O'Brien, I'm an O'Brien." She marveled.

He was busily disrobing her, but stopped when he saw that she was wearing a strapless lace bra, lace panties, and silky white thigh high stockings. The breath shot out of him. "I couldn't wear anything restricting. Not with the tummy I'm sprouting," she said shyly.

He closed his eyes and slid his hands down her waist and hips. "Shhhh, you're so beautiful. And that little tummy is perfect. That tummy is us."

They spent hours enjoying their wedding night. In the bed, in the tub, across the piano bench, against door. Then they fell, limp and exhausted into their marriage bed. Michael spooned her, gently biting the tendon between her neck and shoulder. He could taste the sweat on her skin and her skin smelled like the unique combination they made together, unique to lovers. She always smelled sweetly of that fragrance when they made love. "I'll love you my whole life," he whispered as she lay sated in his arms.

CHAPTER 32

Everyone was gathered at Sorcha and Sean's house. Brigid was sitting on the living room sofa nodding off from exhaustion with Cora passed out beside her. Aidan was carrying around Colin, the newest addition of the O'Brien clan in a swaddled blanket. He'd come in for the weekend again. "Do you need me to take him, brother?" Finn asked.

Aidan just looked at the baby boy and shook his head. "We'll do. You rub your wife's neck and fetch her a bit to eat."

Sorcha came by and Aidan kissed her head. She rubbed his face, "It is good to have you visiting again, mo chroí. Make sure you sleep before you drive back."

The room was buzzing, family everywhere. Michael and Branna walked in the front door and everyone jumped to attention. Even Brigid sharpened up. Sean spoke first. "Well, out with it."

Branna's smile was pure mischief. "We decided to let it be a surprise."

Everyone moaned, "What? No!"

Michael looked at her laughing, "You have no shame, woman. Put them out of their misery."

Everyone gasped, "You do know! Spill it, sister!" cried Brigid.

"Well, they are fraternal as we suspected," she paused for dramatic effect. "And we are having one boy and one girl!"

Brigid leapt off the sofa and grabbed her twin brother. "Just like us! Oh Michael, just like us."

Michael kissed his sister's tear stained face. "Aye, and if she's half as much trouble as you were then wee Brian is in for a time of it!" Everyone laughed, the room bursting with joy.

Sean smiled at Branna, "After your father. I think he would have loved that, my dear girl."

She was teary as she hugged her new father. "I think so, too. It was Michael's idea."

Aidan asked, "Have you chosen a girl's name, then?"

Michael started to shake his head no when Branna interrupted him. "I was thinking of one, actually."

Michael was surprised. "You never mentioned that. What were you thinking, love?"

She lifted her shoulders. "I was thinking Halley. Like…"

He finished her sentence with a knowing smile. "The comet. Like Halley's Comet."

Brigid and Sorcha gave each other a high five. "We're gaining on you lads," Brigid crowed.

Michael pulled Branna close and kissed her softly. "Halley is perfect."

Tadgh came in just as they were settling down. "Did you hear the news?" Caitlyn said.

He looked at her mockingly. "I'm the Godfather. I was in the waiting room." He came in and greeted everyone.

Sean gave him a nod. "How did it go?" Tadgh exhaled and put his palms on the countertop, across from his uncle. "It's going forward next month."

Sean slapped the counter. "Ha! Good for you, lad." He came around and took Tadgh in his arms. "Your father would be overjoyed, boy. You're like my own son. I know you'll make us both proud."

Tadgh closed his eyes, letting himself absorb the fatherly approval. Then they pulled apart, and everyone was gaping at them.

Branna spoke up first. "Are you holding out on me, Tadgh? What's going on?" He walked over and picked her up off her feet for a big hug.

"I did it. You were right about everything. So, I did it," he said.

She gasped. Everyone else looked at him questioningly. "What the bloody hell am I missing?" Liam said.

"He's joining the Garda." Michael answered for him. "I'm right, aren't I? You called them and told them you wanted back in the training."

Tadgh nodded, "Ma is fit to be tied. I told her she was going to have to suck it up. I can't live my life for someone else."

Brigid clapped her hands together, "About feckin' time, brother!"

Sorcha scolded her, "Brigid, language!"

She wiggled her eyebrows. "Come on, Ma. You know you were thinking it, too."

Branna squeezed Tadgh's hand. "I'm proud of you."

He patted her tummy softly. "I'm proud of you, too. Look at you all gorgeous and happy. Remind me again why…"

Michael put him in a headlock before he could finish. "Don't say it!"

Tadgh was laughing. "I'm only joking."

Michael rustled his hair. "So when do we get to shave off all of this pretty hair? I think Aidan and I could do a fine job!"

Aidan nodded his approval, "Yes, indeed. I'll get my clippers."

* * *

BRANNA LOOKED around the room at the big, beautiful family she'd married into. Sean was sneaking a kiss from Sorcha. Aidan was by the window, whispering and rocking baby Colin. Liam, Seany, and Tadgh were trying to make Finn eat a blueberry in the kitchen. Brigid and Michael were sitting on the couch with their feet intertwined like two small children. Caitlyn was by the door texting Patrick at the academy. Cora was passed out cold next to Brigid. Life was so good that she didn't want to miss a minute of it.

She walked over to Aidan and took a peek at the baby. "You're so good with children, Aidan."

He gave her a thoughtful look. "We've got the easy part. As soon as the little fiend gets hungry, I can't do much. I can't imagine having two at once."

He looked to her small baby bump. Branna put her hand over the twins. "Can I tell you a secret?" Aidan nodded. "I'm a little scared. I don't like hospitals." He gave her an admonishing look. "Don't worry, no home births. It's too risky with twins. I'm just a little scared, not of the pain. I'm afraid I won't be a good enough mother." She gave a self deprecating smile. "Don't tell Michael. My false confidence is keeping him sane."

Aidan laughed at that. "I would imagine he is shitting bricks as well. I think it would be worse if you weren't scared. It means you take it seriously. You'll both be wonderful parents. If anything, I think we're worried about you trying to birth two O'Brien babies at once. Promise me you'll take care of yourself."

She gave him a dry look. "Your brother is a tyrant. He feeds and waters me like a heifer bound for the fair. He has no care for how fat I get."

Aidan put one arm around her. "Just indulge him. It makes him feel useful." He gave her a sideways look. "I have a secret, too. No one knows. You think you can handle a secret, wee Branna?"

Branna's eyes lit up. "Ooooh, I love secrets. Hit me big guy." After he told her, she almost squealed out loud. She walked away grinning ear to ear.

Michael looked up at Branna and she was glowing with happiness. He disentangled himself from Cora and Brigid and walked over to her. He took her by the waist and put his mouth in her hair. He whispered softly next to her ear, "Take me home, mo chroí. I want to make a fire and love you all night, and then sleep all day." She sighed against him, "We better enjoy it now, I suppose. Pretty soon it will be twins with nightly feedings and these won't belong to you anymore." She looked down at her breasts as she said it.

"Oh, I think you'll have to squeeze me into your feeding schedule," he said with a husky burr. They did go home and Michael did love her for hours. He spooned behind her afterward, covering her small body with his. "I'm scared for you. You're such a wee thing. But then I start thinking about you sitting in the leather chair, nursing my son or daughter. I never thought I'd be this happy."

She squeezed his arm as he kissed her temple. "I'll be fine and so will they."

CHAPTER 33

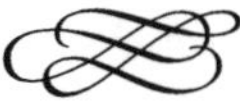

FOUR AND A HALF MONTHS LATER

Branna was walking on the cliffs edge, staring down at the beautiful cliffs and the stirring sea. She noticed a woman walking with two children. There was something familiar about all three. She heard a loud cry and turned behind her. A raven was squawking at her. As she turned back, she realized who the woman was. She approached Branna with the children, one boy and one girl, both with black hair and blue eyes, a circle of green at the iris.

"Mommy?" Branna whispered. Her mother looked at her, love burning in her eyes. "Wake up, my sweet girl. You have to wake up. They need you. They are coming." Branna shot bolt upright in bed, feeling the shock of the dream mixed with searing pain. "Michael!" She looked next to her, then doubled over in pain. She whipped the covers back and gasped. Bloody fluid.

"No,no, no! Not yet!" Michael was at work. She jumped on her phone and dialed Mary first.

"Branna, I am sending an ambulance. You are early, as you know. This could go fast. Calm down. Remember, we said this could happen. I just don't want to take any chances. You need to go to Galway." When they hung up, she called Sorcha and Sean.

Sean was trying not to sound frantic as he called Michael. Michael, on the other hand, went apeshit. "I'll pick you up on the dock, Michael. Your mother is trying to beat the ambulance there. She is in good hands; you know that. Your mother has delivered twins many times."

* * *

"SORCHA, I'm scared. I wasn't expecting this much blood." Sorcha was trying to stay calm. It was more blood than normal, but she wasn't fully hemorrhaging as far as she could tell. She didn't have the gray pallor of someone who was bleeding internally.

"Mary is meeting us at the hospital. Lass, you are thirty-two weeks, this can happen with twins. You said they were already at around 5 lbs. each. You can do this." Sorcha spoke softly, smoothing her hair back in that motherly way she had.

The paramedics knocked and Sorcha yelled for them to come in. "We're taking you to Galway per your doctor. When did the pain start?" Branna was breathing heavy.

Sorcha answered their questions. "They're about fifteen minutes apart. I think her water broke and she has quite a bit of blood in the fluid. We need to roll, lads."

* * *

MICHAEL AND SEAN walked into the ER just as the medical team was pulling Branna through the bay doors. "Michael! Oh, thank God!"

Sorcha went to Sean, and Michael ran to Branna's side. They wheeled back to meet Mary and the OB-GYN they had on stand-by. Mary spoke in her efficient, no-nonsense way. "Branna, this is Doctor Gregory. He will be here in case we need to do a c-section. We talked about that, remember?"

The nurses were busy hooking up the fetal monitors and the ultrasound. "I'm going to examine you, okay? This might be uncomfortable." After she had checked her, she spoke again. "Sorcha brought the sheet so that I could see how much blood was on it.

There is more blood than we would expect for a regular bloody show."

Branna moaned, Michael holding her hands and kissing her head. "What's wrong? What's wrong with my babies? Oh, God!"

Branna was starting to get hysterical. Michael knew the panic was settling in, she didn't like hospitals on a good day. Mary gave him a look, the unspoken message. They had planned for a panic attack. "Branna, darling I am going to get on the bed with you, okay?" Mary put the railing down and the other doctor pulled her to sitting position. Michael slid in behind her and Mary put the rail back up. Then she lifted the top of the bed to meet Michael's back as he eased them both into position. Branna was between his legs and his arms were around her. "Shhh, that's my girl. Let's calm down and have a listen." He kissed her damp hair, laying his hands protectively over the sides of her belly.

Branna's cheek was pressed to him as he kissed her temple. "I'm so scared for them." Her voice was weak and shaking. Just then the heartbeats started to come across the speaker.

"Listen, love. Listen to them," Michael soothed.

The doctors were talking. Mary said, "Branna, dear. Both the babies are okay. Your water did break though and you are starting to dilate."

Branna shook her head from side to side. "It's too soon!"

Mary patted her hand. "It's sooner than we wanted, but we talked about this. It can happen with multiple babies. They are strong." She said to Michael, "Do you think you can leave her and let Sorcha or Sean stay with her?"

Branna stiffened, another contraction coming. "Get my da. He's good with her," Michael mouthed to Mary.

Branna sharpened up. "Where are you going, why are you leaving the room to talk?"

Just then Sean came in. "How's my little girl doing?"

Branna looked at him and her face crumpled. "Oh, Da. I'm so scared."

Michael traded places with him. He stretched his long legs, crossed at the ankles and cradled her like a child against him. Branna put her face in her father-in-law's chest and cried. He rocked her and started singing to her. Michael watched them and his own tears started welling. "Thank you, Da," he whispered. His father just gave him a soft smile as he hummed to his new daughter.

Mary, Dr. Gregory and Michael went out of the room to talk. Sorcha joined them. Michael spoke anxiously, "What aren't you telling her?"

Mary sighed, "Dr. Gregory will explain."

The doctor addressed Michael, "The babies both have a heartbeat, but one is struggling a bit under the stress. We are going to do an ultrasound, but my suspicion is that only one of the amniotic sacs has ruptured. The labor has started, the amount of blood present suggests a small placental rupture, perhaps a detaching placenta on the same side. Simply put, one of them is in danger if we don't act. The other is fine, but the labor has started."

Michael began pacing. "What does this mean? She can't just deliver one can she?" The doctor nodded. "Right, one of them has to come out so they both will. Trying to stop her labor doesn't help the already compromised fetus. Time is not our friend. Do you understand? They've been doing great, according to Mary. We feel that they are developed enough to do this."

Sorcha asked, "Caesarean, then?" The doctor just nodded. "It's the fastest and safest route. We don't want a full placental detachment. Right now the separation is partial and the bleeding is not life threatening. If we do this quickly, before her labor progresses, she could come out of this and fully heal. We don't want to risk the babies or the mother or future fertility trying to push it. We need to act during this window we've been given. We are very lucky she woke up when she did."

Michael paled. Risk the mother? Future fertility? His breathing started getting labored. "Michael, you need to pull it together. She can't see that panic. Do you hear me?" Sorcha's tone was militant.

He straightened. "You're right. Christ, you're right."

The ultrasound screen was showing both babies and Michael was trying to keep Branna calm while they explained everything. She grabbed Michael by the collar, "I don't care what it takes. You do what you have to, do you hear me? If they put me under, you do what you have to in order to protect our children!" Michael looked at Mary.

She knew what he was thinking. Save the mother at all costs. Mary had assured him, earlier, that it wouldn't come to that.

Dr. Gregory broke the tension. "Ok, our suspicions are correct. One sac is intact. The female fetus is in that one. The male fetus is the one that has decided to break out of jail early." Branna sobbed, "Oh, Brian. Please baby, hang in there."

The doctor took her hand. "The bleeding has eased since we have had you here, but I don't want to wait. Their lungs look good. Do we have your permission? Are you ready to meet these two troublemakers?"

Branna barked out a laugh that was half a sob. "You bet your ass, Doc. Does Michael get to be there? Can he stay with me?"

The doctor nodded, "As long as we don't have to put you under, he gets to stay." Michael slid out from behind her and they laid her backward. "We need to prep her. Go with the nurse and she will get you outfitted for the OR"

Sean and Sorcha were in the waiting room when Brigid, Patrick, Caitlyn, Seany, and Liam came in the building. Liam was on break from school. Sorcha looked at him then at Seany. "He threatened to start hitchhiking if I left him."

Sean Jr. straightened his back. "I'm no child, Ma. I'm nearly sixteen, and old enough to be here with my family. That's my niece and nephew in there. I'll not go."

She looked at her husband who's eyebrows were up and a look of grudging respect on his face. "You O'Brien men are as stubborn as a herd of oxen." Seany sat next to Brigid as if the matter was settled.

After they filled the rest of the group in, Patrick spoke. "So, as long as they work fast, everyone should be okay?" he asked. "Tadgh has been ringing every two minutes. I need to give him word. He's freaking out, ready to leave his training."

Sean stood up, "I'll call him. Stay with everyone and I'll go outside. Did anyone call Ned and Diane?"

Brigid answered, "Yes, da. They're on their way as well."

As if on cue Finn walked in with Ned. "Who's with the babies?" Brigid asked.

"Diane asked me to drive Ned. She doesn't drive much at night. She's staying with Cora and Colin."

Finn went to Brigid and kissed her with an edge that bordered on desperation. He could sympathize with Michael on a level that none of his brothers could. "How are they? Jesus, please tell me everyone's okay. Aidan has been calling every ten minutes."

Brigid took a deep breath and took out her phone. "They are all okay, Finn. Come and sit over here. We will put him on speaker and I'll explain it to both of you."

* * *

MICHAEL WAS on the verge of his own panic attack. He walked into the operating room and Branna was strapped down with a mask over her face and tubes sticking out of her. She looked like she was being readied for crucifixion. "Holy God." He stopped in his tracks.

Mary approached him. "She's not restrained, this is normal. Breathe, Michael. She needs a cool head. Come and talk to her."

He approached her. He expected her to be frantic, terrified. Whatever he expected, it wasn't what he saw. She was cool as a cucumber. She smiled and the anesthesiologist took her mask off. "You look like you are walking the last mile on death row, O'Brien. Did you change your mind about fatherhood?" He coughed out a laugh. She smiled warmly at him. "Come here, mo chroí." He was amazed as he walked to her. "Give us a kiss, there's a fine lad." She was trying to sound Irish again, which always lifted his mood.

He put his hand on her head that was covered with some sort of paper shower cap and kissed her. He put his forehead to hers. "I'm okay, Michael. I can do this. This is supposed to happen. My mother, she came to me in my sleep. She woke me so that I would know I was bleeding. She's taking care of me and the babies. We are all going to be okay."

Michael looked at her, the hair standing up on his neck. "You've got some powerful people watching your back, darlin. I don't doubt it. Now, the entire family is ready to storm the doors. Even Seany is here. Tadgh was threatening to go AWOL. You ready to show them what you're made of?"

She smiled. "Absolutely, big daddy."

* * *

MICHAEL WAS bone weary as he walked into the waiting room wearing his scrubs. Nearly the entire clan of O'Briens, one Murphy and one Kelly shot to their feet. "Everyone is fine. Branna, Halley, and Brian. They're all perfect." Everyone cheered.

Brigid tackled her brother. "I love you, brother. I need to call Aidan and Tadgh. Tell us everything."

Michael stood for a moment, hands on his hips. His voice broke. "Christ, she was amazing. She was awake the whole time. That fat headed son of mine is already 6 lbs. Halley is a little smaller at 5lbs. 2 oz. They're small, but breathing on their own. Oh, God. They're beautiful." He lost control, putting his hand over his eyes.

It was Finn who got to him first, putting him in a big manly bear hug. "I told you, brother. There is nothing like it in the world. Our women, they are fierce aren't they?"

Sean grunted behind him in agreement. "The fiercest."

Michael wiped his eyes, looked at the family. "I can't thank you enough for getting here so quickly. Da, you got me here in time. You helped take care of her. If Brian O'Mara is watching, he's well pleased."

Sean hugged him. "She's our girl, now and forever."

Michael took a hearty breath, calming himself. "They're cleaning them up, they've stitched her up. I can see them in recovery in five minutes. They'll keep them for five days, Halley longer if she doesn't put on weight. Everyone is grand, though. You should see the head of hair on them both. Black as night."

Sorcha thought to herself that if Michael's grin was any wider, his face was going to break. "How is Branna, is all well with her? Is the bleeding stopped?"

Michael answered her reassuringly, "Yes, no issues. Obviously she'll have to be watched now and when she conceives again, but no permanent damage."

Sean Jr. shouted at that. "Again? What gets into you men when you get older? How the bloody hell do you keep letting them do this? Scaring the devil out of everyone. You're all insane!"

The entire group burst into laughter. His father took his face in his hands, kissing his head. "You have a wise and valid point, lad. We're all nutters for putting our women through this. Think about this, though. If we had stopped having babes after the first one or two times, we wouldn't have gotten you, aye?"

Seany smiled, "Yes, I suppose you did save the best for last." Which was followed by another burst of laughter.

* * *

Michael walked into the hospital room and his breath caught in his throat. Branna had her hair knotted on top of her head. She was pale and tired, but she was radiant as she looked up from their son. He could tell by the blue blanket that it was Brian in her arms. He approached quietly, thinking he was sleeping but then he saw the child suckling at her breast and he broke down. Tears coming, breath stuttering, he met her eyes. She smiled through her own tears. "This son of yours didn't need any lessons or invitation. He's hungry."

Michael leaned over them and thought his heart would burst. "That's the most beautiful sight I've ever seen. Look at him, mo chroí. His little hand is already resting up there like he can't bear to be parted from you. He loves you, so."

She looked down at him, a tear dripping down the tip of her nose. "I suppose he does, doesn't he? Did you call Anna for me?" she asked.

"Yes, there was a lot of screeching, as you'd expect. She told me to tell you not to be such an over achiever." He laughed when he said it. Then he looked at the bassinets.

"Where's the lassie? Is she okay?" Panic was in his voice.

Branna hastened to reassure him. "She's taking her turn under the lamp. It's for jaundice. She isn't latching as well, either. She's going to be our stubborn little stinker."

Michael grunted. "Aye, that's that O'Mara blood. Gotta force them to drink, make them eat. Her first request better not be for one of those bars or some sort of rabbit food. She's Irish. Meat, potatoes, cheese. No feckin protein bars, ever."

Branna was quietly giggling, trying not to disturb the baby, but Brian popped off the breast and started wiggling his limbs. "See, he agrees with me," Michael said, satisfied with the male solidarity.

Just then, the nurse came in with Halley. "Are you ready to try again, mum?"

Michael realized Branna had one too many babies to hold. "All right, lad. Time to come to your da. Let these women sort it out and I'll give you some pointers. I'd bet my eye teeth that twin of yours is ticklish." He leaned in and kissed Branna, then Halley. "I love you, mo chroí. Forever."

EPILOGUE

The large family was gathered at the home of Sorcha and Sean; even Aidan was there for the weekend. They were laughing and toasting to the babies coming home. Halley stayed another few days, but had rapidly started gaining weight when her brother left. "She doesn't want him getting all fat headed about getting to go home before her." Brigid jibed. "You know how those O'Brien boys get."

Everyone laughed in agreement. The twins were dressed adorably. Halley was dressed in lilac and Brian in green. Finn held Brian who was busy gnawing on his fingertip. Aidan walked around with Halley, singing to her softly. They instinctively knew that the happy couple needed a break.

Tadgh, Patrick and Liam were absent for this particular celebration. "I thought they got liberty at this point?" Michael asked. Sean answered. "Aye, usually. They've pulled every spare man for the marathon. They want a strong presence there after the Boston bombing. They're doing a tribute and they need eyes everywhere."

Branna shivered, "I know people who ran that race. None of them were hurt, but still. I am so tired of this. I am so tired of the carnage." Sorcha hugged her. Branna smiled. "You know first hand, don't you?

What people do, the terrible things they do in the name of religion and politics. It amazes me sometimes to think about what your youth must have been like."

Sorcha gave her another squeeze and looked at her husband. "Aye, but sometimes you get a prince to come in and sweep you away. Then life gets sweeter with every passing year." Sean's eyes burned with emotion, then he hugged his wife fiercely. "I love you, mo chuisle, mo chroí."

Aidan cleared his throat. "I have an announcement. I wish everyone could be here, but this is the last chance I might get this many of us together at once." Branna smiled at him. She knew what was coming. She watched the big, beautiful O'Brien warrior hold her daughter so gently, and a pang of tenderness hit her. Captain O'Brien was going to have an interesting summer.

Everyone was looking at him but Michael. "You know something, hen. I can tell." She grinned knowingly. "I promised to keep quiet until he decided." Michael was baffled. He had no idea what was coming.

"While Michael and I were in North Carolina, a friend of mine, Captain Denario, made me an offer to do an exchange. He convinced his command to request me for the next tour. I'll be leaving for Camp Lejeune, North Carolina at the middle of May. I'll be gone for twelve weeks."

Everyone was stunned. "I suppose that's a step up from Afghanistan or Iraq." Sean commented.

Aidan just gave a small grin at that. "Yes, certainly. There's a catch, though. When I get back, they will transfer me back to 1st Battalion. Most of these men in the North are reserves and since I've been promoted, it's time to move."

Sean gave him a look of understanding. "Back to England then, to Shropshire?" Aidan nodded.

"Will you be in the officer's barracks with the Marines?" Sean asked.

Branna interrupted. "Actually, he will be staying in my house on the beach. I cleared the rental schedule."

Michael was shaking his head. "Schemes upon schemes." She just gave him a cheeky grin.

Aidan sighed, "Branna, we talked about this. You are going to lose income during peak tourist season. My housing funds won't come anywhere near covering that holiday rent."

"You are not going to be stuck in the BOQ in a one room efficiency when I have a perfectly good beach house for you to enjoy. You know I'll have my way on this, Aidan. Just submit," she said.

Sorcha clapped her hands together. "Well, then. I thought you were going to tell me you were headed off to war again. I can do twelve weeks in my sleep if I know you are playing around on the beach." She kissed him on the cheek.

"I won't be playing. I'll be training. This is a good opportunity. This training is top notch. Field medical training, transition teams, side by side with some of the best in the US military. I can bring that knowledge back to my men. It's amazing that I managed to get this rolling."

Brigid gave a snort of disgust. "Right, and then you'll come home every night and drink a feckin' beer on the beach. I think I dislike you right now, brother."

Sean Jr. joined in, "Aye, and looking at American girls in their little bikinis!" Seany never failed to get everyone laughing. Aidan raised his brows with a grin and gave his little brother a fist bump with his free hand.

Michael leaned into Branna and whispered. "I don't suppose your eagerness to house him has anything to do with that southern belle next door?"

She smiled, "I no more considered it than Aidan did."

Michael laughed, loudly. "You are sly. Answer without admitting a thing. You should be KGB." She just wiggled her brows at him. Michael kept his voice quiet. "He is so incredibly in over his head. Does she know he's coming?"

She leaned in and whispered. "Now where's the fun in that?" Michael burst out laughing again and the whole room looked at him, everyone but Aidan. He was looking at Branna, eyes narrowed.

"Pack your swim trunks, brother. It gets downright steamy in the summertime," Branna said to Aidan with a sweet southern drawl.

Michael elbowed her discretely. "You've been reading those romance novels again, hellcat." Michael asked her, "Aidan's held out this long. What makes you think this girl will change his mind?"

Branna looked at him, her face more serious. "I don't know if she will or someone else will catch his eye but he's lonely, Michael. Surely you see it? He'd never admit it. That stoic, stubborn man would go to his grave not complaining. Maybe the change of scenery is just what he needs. God knows it worked for me."

Michael leaned in and kissed her. "That it did." He looked at his brother cradling baby Halley in his arms. "Aye, I suppose I do see it." As the family started getting back to the food and drink, Branna watched her brother-in-law with the baby. He touched her face, kissed her nose and whispered to her as he rocked her in the crook of his arm. She said a small prayer that whatever lie ahead, Aidan would have a woman and children of his own someday.

AUTHOR NOTES AND ACKNOWLEDGEMENTS

First, I would like to thank my beta readers Stacey, Michele, Sara and Brandy. These are the friends that supported me, reading my rough drafts, finding my typos, boosting my ego. You know who you are and I love you. Starting this process was a scary thing, but there were a few of you that were willing to gut it out with me. Such is the spirit of the military family.

I would also like to thank my dear friend and old college roommate Christine Stevens, a talented graphic artist and all around awesome lady from Stevens Design. She helped me put together a digital cover, when I was up to my ears in fonts and formats.

This book came to me slowly after a trip to Ireland. We visited Ireland while we were stationed in the Middle East. The cool rain, coastal wind, and the sweeping, green landscape, was a well needed respite from the heat, sand, and civil unrest of our current home. I'd like to thank the people of Doolin, County Clare, Ireland. You don't know me. I passed through your little town like any other tourist, but the people and music and coastal waters of your small village captured my imagination like nothing else in my life has ever done. And Bridhe really does make the best breakfast you've ever tasted, homemade marmalade and all.

The music that is strewn throughout this book came from several sources. I had a playlist, gorgeous songs to pull me along this path on which I'd set myself. One of my favorites is an album called *The Music of Dingle,* where you will find some songs that were used in the book. *The O'Brien Set* was actually inspired by a song on this album performed by Sean Leahy and Jeremy Spencer called *The Foxhunter/The Silver Slipper/Pilleadh Wellingtons.* I could so vividly see the O'Brien men swinging their women around the dance floor to this traditional musical arrangement. *The Lighthouse Tale* was written by Adam McKenzie and Chris Thile. *Dearthairin O mo Chroi* is actually an old civil war lament, but my favorite version is by Pauline Scanlon. *School Days Over* is an old folk song written by an Englishman named Ewan Macoll, but Mary Black did an amazing version of the song which is how I heard it first. The West coast of Ireland is full of beautiful music, and to see a full list of my musical inspiration, please check out my website.

I hope you enjoyed this book as much as I loved writing it. The story of the O'Brien family isn't over. I will continue to tell their stories as long as they keep coming to me. Not only will you get to read Aidan's story, the self proclaimed bachelor and soldier in the RIR, but you will have to follow up with Tadgh, because they are both too amazing to be alone. You might even get a journey back to the beginning, during The Troubles in Northern Ireland to learn about Sean's rocky journey into the arms of his beloved Sorcha. So stay tuned, and thank you for reading.

Made in the USA
Columbia, SC
08 June 2022

61509171R00259